Also by Omar Tyree

Diary of a Groupie
Leslie
Just Say No!
For the Love of Money
Sweet St. Louis
Single Mom
A Do Right Man
Flyy Girl

And the Urban Griot series
Cold Blooded
College Boy
One Crazy A** Night
The Underground

OMAR TYREE

BOSS LADY

Simon & Schuster
New York • London • Toronto • Sydney

SIMON & SCHUSTER
Rockefeller Center
1230 Avenue of the Americas
New York, NY 10020

SIMON & SCHUSTER and colophon are registered trademarks
of Simon & Schuster, Inc.

For information regarding special discounts for bulk purchases,
please contact Simon & Schuster Special Sales at
1-800-456-6798 or business@simonandschuster.com.

Designed by Davina Mock

Manufactured in the United States of America

10 9 8 7 6 5 4 3 2 1

Library of Congress Cataloging-in-Publication Data

Tyree, Omar.
    Boss Lady : a novel / Omar Tyree.
        p. cm.
    1. African American motion picture producers and directors—Fiction.
2. African American motion picture actors and actresses—Fiction. 3. Hollywood (Los Angeles, Calif.)—Fiction. 4. African American screenwriters—
Fiction. 5. Motion picture industry—Fiction. 6. African American
women—Fiction. 7. Young women—Fiction. I. Title.

PS3570.Y59B67 2005
813'.54—dc22
                                                      2005042582
ISBN-13: 978-0-7432-2868-8
ISBN-10:   0-7432-2868-5

Dedicated
to all the old and new flyy girls
who can relate
and to those
who only dream about it

Black America, 2003

It's high stakes now when she rolls
the highway tolls have been taxed by Jones's inflation
a proud Black Nation no longer exists
and although the boot straps of evidence still persists
the honest effort is no longer relevant
only eight figures pay the new cost of rent
forcing fast, luxurious cars to keep pace in haste and ignore the dents
until the green, silver, platinum, and gold is all spent
causing superstar Negroes to holla, "Damn!
Where all my money went?"
while in need of cool-headed, financial consultation
and less heated, overemotional stimulation.

Contents

BOSS
LADY

Vanessa

Hi. *My name is Vanessa Tracy Smith. I'm Tracy Ellison's oldest second cousin on her mother's side. Many of you first read of me in Tracy's sequel book,* For the Love of Money. *But some of you are a little confused now. That's okay. I'll explain everything.*

My big cousin Tracy became famous ten years ago after publishing the story of her life in a book called Flyy Girl, *as told to author Omar Tyree. She finished undergraduate school at Hampton University in Virginia, and continued school to receive a master's degree in English. Mission accomplished, she moved back home to Philadelphia, passed all of her teaching certificate exams, and found a job as a junior high school English teacher. However, my cousin could never be satisfied as a schoolteacher. Not the flyy girl. So after thinking it over, she decided to quit her job as a schoolteacher and move to Hollywood, California, to chase her dreams as a poet and screenwriter. She had already written two volumes of unpublished poetry.*

Out in Hollywood, Tracy took a few courses in screenwriting at UCLA, made friends in the television industry, and worked herself from an assistant writer position for a science fiction show on cable, into a proven staff writer and a freelancer for some of the major networks. But my cousin didn't stop there. In perfect flyy girl mode, she attempted to create her own sitcom, Georgia Peaches, *about a southern girl trying to break into the music and entertainment industry. Failing at that, she penned her first feature-length screenplay entitled* Led Astray, *about an African-American woman who exacts revenge on several Hollywood players who betray her.*

While continuing to make new friends in high places, my cousin not only found a producer and a studio to develop and green-light her first film, but she walked away with the starring role and an associate producer credit.

1

Led Astray went on to triple its budget in ticket sales at the box office, my cousin became an instant star, and she was able to sign on the dotted line for a lucrative, three-film deal worth millions of dollars.

Pretty unbelievable, isn't it? I would say. But that's when I come in.

I had been told about my big cousin Tracy ever since I was a toddler. But what I heard of her was rarely a good thing. My mother would beat me over the head with negatives about my cousin as if it was a punishment.

"Girl, you think you're so damn cute. You act just like your cousin Tracy. The world don't revolve around you!"

Granted, I barely even knew who Tracy was at the time. It wasn't as if she visited me, my mother, and my sisters while we relocated like nomads to different run-down apartments and houses in North Philadelphia, with my mother chasing her crazy ideas of love. All I knew was that Tracy was my mother's first cousin, and that she was raised in a stable home in the better parts of Germantown. However, I had seen pictures of her, and if my mother believed that naming me Tracy and berating me with how similar I was to my namesake would somehow stop me from trying to emulate my cousin, she was wrong.

All of my mother's name-dropping only made me think of Tracy night and day, whether she visited us in North Philly or not. My cousin soon became the focus point of my constant daydreams of a better life. Then her first book came out.

You would think my mother would have known about the book as much as she seemed to despise Tracy. But my mother was never much of a reader. So she didn't know about the book that had her name, my aunt Marie, my grandmother Marsha, and my great aunts Patti, Joy, and Tanya in it until I had first started to read Flyy Girl at age eleven. It had been out for a few years by this time, and it had not been published nationally yet. It was still kind of underground.

I hid the book from my mother and read it day and night for three days straight until she finally caught me with it in my room. I was all the way at the end and had gotten a little careless with it.

She asked me, "What's that you readin'?"

I didn't even notice my mother when she walked into my room. I was just so into that book. It had me hypnotized. It was that good. But

I got so nervous from being busted that I fumbled the book out of my hands and dropped it on the floor.

I mumbled, "Ummm . . ."

I was terrified and didn't know what to say. My mother could read the surprise all over my face. I was sure she knew about the book. I tried to pick it up and hide it from her, like a fool.

"Gimme the damn book, girl," she told me.

"Mom, it's just a book," I whined.

"Vanessa, if you don't give me that damn book, I will break your damn hands!"

I was still hesitant until my mother reached out and snatched it from me.

"Gimme this damn book, girl!"

My little sisters looked at me as if I was nuts.

"All that over a book."

They didn't get books like I did. I had a lot more to dream about, I guess.

Anyway, my mother read the title out loud.

" 'Flyy Girl. Inside the big city there's a mad obsession for gold, sex, and money.' " She looked at me and asked, "What are you doin' readin' this? And who gave this to you? Is this some kind of X-rated sex book?"

My two younger sisters began to eye me in alarm with hushed silence and wide eyes.

I was confused as I don't know what. Didn't my mother know about Tracy's book? I had given her the benefit of the doubt, but maybe she didn't know. Then she studied the artwork on the cover, with the gold earrings that read Tracy in script, and she just froze.

"What in the world . . ."

My mother was as shocked as I was. I was shocked that she didn't know about it, and she was shocked that she was just finding out.

Then I got slick and tried to downplay it.

"It's just a book about some girl growing up in Philly, Mom."

My mother ignored me and began to flip through the pages after reading the back cover summaries.

"Where did you get this book?"

I didn't want to tell. Tracy's book was quite mature for an eleven-year-old girl to read. It was detailed with graphic sex and hard lan-

guage. So my friends had all been hiding it from their mothers. We all realized that it was hard-boiled and secretive material.

"You better tell me, girl," my mother warned me.

"Friends," I answered.

"What friends?"

"Just friends, Mom."

She was headed for the third degree, and it was beginning to look like a very long night.

"I want names, girl."

By that time, my sisters were no longer silent.

"Uuueww, Va-nes-sa."

"Shut up!" I screamed at them.

I was irritated by the whole thing.

My mother said, "No, you shut up, Vanessa. And you tell me what I wanna know. Right now! I want names!"

To make a long story short, my mother got me to tell on my circle of friends, who had all realized before she did that the book was about our cousin.

So my mother got to calling around to all of our family members, and they all confirmed it, which gave me an even lower level of respect for her. I mean, how could she not know?

Anyway, that drove an even bigger wedge between my cousin Tracy and I ever meeting and getting to know each other. My mother was convinced that I would run around and try to be flyy in the same fast ways that Tracy had. But I was already my own person. I could see where letting guys have their way with a girl had led my mother into having three girls from three different daddies. So I was in no way ready to allow a book to influence me to do something that real life had already shown me an ugly reflection of. My girls and I all knew better than to live how Tracy had; we all read the book as a tale of what we shouldn't do, as opposed to how many of our parents felt about it. They were not giving us much credit for our intelligence.

A few years later, Flyy Girl was picked up by a major publisher, and it was in bookstores everywhere. My mother had given up on trying to keep me away from it, along with thousands of other teenaged girls' mothers. And a powerful thing was beginning to happen; girls who wouldn't be caught dead reading a book were all of a sudden swearing by my cousin's book. I was so proud of her that I didn't know what to do with myself.

I realized that Tracy had attended Hampton University, and I wanted to go to a black college, too. Tracy wrote poetry, and I wanted to write poetry, too. Tracy had lived her life the way she wanted to, and I wanted to live and learn from her mistakes and not make them. And when I finally got a chance to hang out with my cousin after years of dreaming about her, I wanted to make sure I kept my cool. I didn't want to come off as a geek or anything. I had read what she thought about Girls High and Central being "nerd schools," and my high school, Engineering & Science, was in the same vein as those. But I was also certain that Tracy would feel differently about education as an adult, and she would be proud that I attended E&S and had maintained good grades. Even her brother Jason had graduated from E&S. I just wanted to make sure that my cousin would be nothing but proud of me when I finally met her.

We finally met and hung out in the spring of my sophomore year, and Tracy was very open with me about everything. She complained about how much her life had changed since breaking into Hollywood, but at my school, we were still sweating her for her book. I don't think she understood how much of an impact her book had had on urban American girls. Tracy was more concerned about her present and future, like most go-getters are. They don't live in the yesterday, they live in the now and the tomorrow. So I accepted my cousin's complaints and allowed her to say her piece about fame and fortune, and the ups and downs of wealth and popularity. She even had a frank discussion with me about boys, just when I had one who could have broken me. Talk about your perfect timing.

Nevertheless, my mother wasn't having it. She bitched about me hanging out with Tracy as if the world was coming to an end. She gave my cousin no respect at all, as if she was still a teenager looking for a hot boyfriend. Tracy deserved much more respect than that. She worked damned hard for hers, and no man had gotten in her way.

So when my wildest dream was realized—Tracy asking me if I wanted to spend a summer in California with her—I was blown away. I mean, like, wow! I had waited my whole life for that. Not that I would have died if it didn't happen, but I surely wasn't going to turn it *down once it did. That's when the shit hit the fan. My mother went into overdrive and started nagging me about everything. She was getting on my last damn nerve!*

Honestly, I saw nothing left that I could gain from my mother. She couldn't pay my way to college. She couldn't help me with my ideas and aspirations. And she didn't have anything left to teach me. I could even get better jobs than she could once I finished high school, because my mother never applied herself enough to master anything. But there she was trying to deny me the opportunity of a lifetime instead of supporting me. It wasn't as if I would just up and leave the family. It was only for a summer.

Tracy's invitation to Hollywood was the end of the end for my mother and me. The beginning of our problems had started a long time ago, and we were both ready to explode. So when I started reading up on Hollywood to prepare myself for Tracy's world, my mother went right ahead and pressed my last button.

She snatched my Entertainment Weekly *magazine right out of my hands and shouted, "Do your fucking homework!"*

I mean, that wasn't even called for. I was just sitting on the living room sofa, minding my own business, when she walked in from work and said that to me. It was nearly nine o'clock at night, and my homework had been finished before seven. My mother knew that. I always completed my schoolwork early. She was just trying to pick a fight with me, like a jealous hater. She wouldn't even allow me to work after school. My job was to look after my younger sisters every day. And I was just tired of it; tired of everything.

I stood up and said, "Mom, I've already finished my homework. Now can I have my magazine back, please?"

I knew she wasn't going to give it to me. I was already preparing myself to fight her. I had backed down from my mother before because I had nowhere else to go. But once Tracy offered me somewhere else to go . . . Well, that was it for my mother's bullshit.

She responded to my request by smacking me upside the head with the magazine and shouting, "You're not going to any damn California. So you don't even need to be reading this shit."

Isn't that pitiful of a grown woman? I couldn't believe she was acting like that. So I grabbed the magazine to stop her from hitting me with it, only for her to smack me in the face with her free hand. I used to cry when my mother treated me like that before, but not anymore. I mean, how much can a daughter take just because someone's your mother? It's not as if I was running the streets and getting into trouble like Tracy had done. I was an obedient, intelligent, and dutiful virgin like Tracy's girlfriend, Raheema, and I was being ignored and disrespected in the same way that she had been.

I had no more tears left to cry over my mother. She was wrong. So I backed away from her and let her have it with a straight right hand to her mouth. My mother's head popped back like a rag doll and it shocked both of us. I felt for sure that my life was going to end right there, but when my mother tried to attack me, I held her away from me with both hands and was actually stronger than she was. I couldn't believe it! I'm not a strong girl at all, or at least not physically, but it was just in me at that moment to fight her for my life and for my own dreams.

I'm not telling every girl to do what I did, but that's just how it went down for me. And if someone wants to blame my cousin Tracy for that . . . Well, I can't stop them. But I look at it as if it was fate. As crazy as it may sound, it was like my whole life had been preparing me for a meeting with my cousin, and my mother had started it all when I was a kid. It was like she knew all along that I would leave her for Tracy, and my mother was already preparing herself to hate my cousin for it.

So after my mother threw my high yellow behind out, I ended up at my great-aunt Patti's house in Germantown, where she called Tracy in California. Tracy was back out in Hollywood to shoot her next film, a thriller called Road Kill. I explained to her what happened with my mom, she listened to me, and the next thing I knew, arrangements were being made for me to join her for the summer in California. But since Tracy didn't really have time to spare while she finished filming her new movie, she planned to fly her brother Jason out to California for the summer as well, just to keep an eye out on me.

What to Do with Jason?

I was prepared to fly out to California on Monday, June 19, 2000, with my cousin Jason, who was supposed to watch over me while Tracy finished filming her movie, Road Kill. Or at least that was the plan. But I could tell immediately that it wouldn't work out that way. And it wasn't that I was against Jason looking after me. It was no big deal to me. I was just happy I was getting a chance to go to California and expand my horizons. My cousin Jason felt the same way. He was really into expanding his horizons—or I should say, his opportunities. He was feeling himself a little too strongly on our plane ride from Philly.

Jason sat next to me wearing Cool Water cologne, with a fresh haircut, Rocawear clothes, and brown leather Timberland shoes.

He said, "I can't wait to get out to L.A. I hear it's a whole different world out there."

My cousin had bright stars shining in his eyes already. I just smiled at him. I was trying to keep my cool and stay focused. I had never been on an airplane before.

He asked me, "Aren't you excited?"

I looked into my cousin's eager face and imagined what he was thinking about. Girls! His breath even smelled good. He had a pocket full of peppermint chewing gum just for talking that talk.

"You want some gum?" he asked me.

I hadn't even gotten a chance to open my mouth. Jason was that overzealous about our trip, and for some reason, I didn't see that as a good thing. I felt like I should have been the one who was extra-excited. Not that Jason couldn't be, but just not as much as I was. He was supposed to be the more mature one.

I nodded to him and held out my hand for a stick of gum.

I answered, "Yeah, I'm excited. Of course I am. But why are you so excited?" I asked him. I still had my hunch.

Jason smiled it off. He said, "I'm just planning on having a good time out there, that's all."

I was betting that he was. I turned away and looked out the window.

"So, you leaving a boyfriend behind or something?" he asked me. My cousin caught me off guard with that.

"Why?" I asked him.

He shrugged his shoulders and said, "I don't know. Girls are always leaving guys behind."

"Who are you leaving behind?" I asked him back. Jason looked good enough to leave a few girls behind. He was tall, dark, and handsome with not a blemish on his smooth brown face. And I'm sure he knew it.

He laughed and turned away.

"I don't have no ties," he mumbled.

I smiled in Jason's direction and told him, "That's what they all say."

He just grinned and chuckled at it.

As our plane raced down the runway, lifted up into the air, and started rattling around, I was as nervous as I don't know what. Jason saw me clenching the armrest and began to tease me.

"We may not make it, Vanessa. Maybe we both should have stayed home."

I couldn't believe he said that. He was joking at the wrong damn time. Even some of the other passengers shot looks at him. But Jason didn't care. It was all a joke to him.

I told him, "Don't say that, man."

I was dead serious. I had too much to live for to go down in an airplane crash. Especially on my first plane ride. All I could think about was the R&B singer Aaliyah Haughton, who had died in a plane crash. She had so much going for her.

Jason nudged my arm and said, "Stop sweatin' it, girl. Be brave like you was when you clocked your mom."

Now that was low. I was beginning not to like Jason, and we had a six-hour plane ride before we landed in L.A.

I started to say something, not anything nasty, but just to ask him why he would say something to me like that. I mean, I wasn't a bad girl. My mom was just . . . she just went too far that day. But I didn't want to be reminded of that all of the time. Everybody makes mistakes. Then again, fighting my mother didn't even seem like a mistake to me.

I told Jason, "I just did what I had to do."

I wasn't planning on saying that. It just rolled out of my mouth. But I really meant it. I didn't want anybody to hold me back anymore. I didn't care who it was.

Jason looked at me and nodded.

He said, "I heard that. You not goin' for it."

I didn't want to talk about it anymore so I let it be. But Jason seemed majorly insensitive to me. I tried my best to ignore him for the rest of the plane ride. When he fell asleep, I looked at it as my good fortune. However, I wasn't able to sleep at all. I kept thinking that if that plane went down, I would at least want to be prepared instead of having to wake up and find out. I even pictured myself jumping over people to wrestle the last parachute out of the closet if I had to. I was that nervous about it.

We arrived in L.A. safe and sound, and Jason was after the girls just as I had expected he would be.

"Hey Vanessa, you see that Asian girl I was talking to on the plane?"

"Who?" I was still trying to pop my ears with both hands pressed against my eardrums.

"That Asian girl. Was she good-looking to you?" he asked me.

He was pressed to holler at someone before we even got off the airplane.

I just shook my head and blew it off. I didn't care about anything he had to say. But Jason wouldn't let me be.

"Here she go right here," he whispered to me.

I had to at least take a look at the girl. My cousin was practically forcing me to, and I didn't want him to make more of a scene if I didn't look.

Sure enough, I looked, and the girl wasn't bad. She wore a pink Bebe tank top, blue Giraldi jeans, and pink loop earrings to match her shirt. I can't even front, the girl had it popping. She even had a little bit of height and some curves on her. More curves than I had. She looked like a magazine ad on a hip, fashion page. She had her own style about her. I was even ready to warn her not to talk to my lame cousin because I knew he was ready to put something on her. She looked approachable to a black guy. I could see it in her face. She had that "I know you're feeling me" look about her. I was almost certain that other black guys had tried to talk to her before.

My cousin wasted no time. He strolled right over to her as soon as she walked out of the bridge behind us.

"So hey, Ma', where you goin' from here?"

I couldn't believe it. He sounded like a hip thug. And my cousin was not at all the thug type. He was more like an irritating comedian pretty boy. But there he was trying to use gutter street slang on this girl. He had his head dipped to the side and everything.

I was so embarrassed. Why couldn't he just say, "Hi, I'd like to talk to you for a minute?" But no, he had to take it all the way to the street corner. Then people wonder why black people get stereotyped so much. To make it worse, the girl responded to it.

She answered, "I have to hook up with my family. But once I do that and settle in, you know, it's whatever."

Jason asked her, "It's whatever?" He seemed as surprised as I was. Maybe he was still joking around, but she was taking him seriously.

She smiled and said, "Well, it's not just anything, but, I mean, what do you have in mind?"

The girl was game, but she still had a lot of innocence about her. Trust me, I had been around enough hard-core girls to know the difference, and this girl was not giving me those vibes. She was more on the multicultural, MTV side of things. So I sized both of them up. They were both playing the role. She wanted to go for a stereotypical black guy and my cousin was willing to give her one.

Jason said, "Sasha Kim, right?"

She nodded to him and was pleased that he remembered her name. And of course he did. Jason was a smart kid like I was, an Engineering & Science graduate. But she didn't know that.

She said, "Jason . . ."

"Ellison," he filled in for her.

She dropped her head a second and said, "Thanks, but I was gonna remember it."

Jason said, "I don't think I told you my last name."

She said, "You told me now."

I smiled. It was a good answer on her part. Otherwise, she would have looked silly. So I gave her a few cool points.

Anyway, they traded contact information and all that, right down to email addresses. No kidding. Jason asked the girl for her email address.

I asked him, "What made you ask for her email address?"

Jason looked at me and said, "You don't know? She's Asian. They probably got like five computers in their house. But if she was black, I would have asked her what her favorite television show is."

"Oh my God," I told him. "So black girls watch too much television? Is that it?"

Jason answered, "Yup."

I couldn't help but smile at it. The boy was crazy.

I asked him, "And what if she was white or Hispanic?"

"Then I would ask them what they think about Britney Spears or Jennifer Lopez," he answered. "Oh, my game is tight out here, cousin. Don't sleep. I'm pullin' out my A-game for these California girls. I'm just serving them notice. I mean, it's not like I'm gonna be out here long. So I'm going for broke, ya' heard."

"And what if you end up out here for longer than you think?"

"What do you mean? Like if I stayed out here?"

I know I planned on staying longer.

"Yeah. Then what?" I asked him.

He answered, "Well, like she said, it's whatever then."

We met up with Tracy's agent, Susan Raskin, at the baggage claim. She was a small, dark-haired white girl holding up a sign with "Jason & Vanessa" printed in large letters. We walked over in her direction.

She noticed us and said, "Hey, how are you guys doing? How was the flight?"

Jason grinned at me and said, "My little cousin thought she wasn't gonna make it."

I smirked. "Yeah, he kept talking about the plane going down," I told her.

"Oh no, that's the worst," Susan said.

Jason spotted our luggage and immediately went to grab it. I tried to help him with it, but he kindly asked me to step aside.

"I got this."

So I backed up and allowed him to be the man.

"So, what's the plan?" he asked Susan once he gathered our luggage.

She said, "Well, first I'll take you back to the house to drop off your things. Then we can get a bite to eat if you'd like. I know the airplane food is not always the best. And after that, I'll take you to the set to see if you can talk to Tracy while she takes a break between scenes."

Jason said, "I know she didn't tell you that I gave her a lot of the ideas for this movie, did she?"

Susan smiled while we followed her through the airport terminal toward the parking lots.

"As a matter of fact, she did," she answered him.

Jason looked surprised. "Get out of here. My sister actually gave me my props?"

"She sure did. And plenty of them."

Jason smiled wide and said, "Well, I deserve some of the writing credit and a piece of the pie then."

I grinned and shook my head again. That boy just didn't quit. It was like he had no conscience about his joking.

"Sounds like you need the right agent," Susan joked back to him.

"Oh, I'm serious, too," he told her. "I got a lot of ideas."

We found Susan's black BMW in the parking lot and loaded her empty trunk with our things.

Jason rudely jumped into the front seat of the Beamer ahead of me, but I didn't mind. I liked watching things from a backseat view anyway. From the backseat you were not usually forced to talk as much. I wanted to check out my surroundings and talk later. And that's what I did.

* * *

We arrived at my cousin Tracy's house, which was up on a hill in an area called Marina Del Rey that overlooked a nearby shopping center.

Jason climbed out of the car and commented on the scenery.

"Man, I feel like the big dog up here. This hill makes you feel like you're special."

Susan grinned at him. But I had to agree with Jason for a change. Overlooking the landscape and the general population of Los Angeles did make you feel important. It was like we were sitting up on a mountaintop.

"Yeah, that's a major selling point for this area," Susan told us.

Jason said, "I bet it is."

Susan took out a key and led us to the double wooden doors that opened Tracy's half-empty, high-ceiling, three-bedroom home.

Jason walked in and hollered, "HEY, Hey, hey!" like an echo.

Susan started laughing. "That's exactly what Tracy did when she first moved in."

I walked in silently and looked around. I was simply glad to be there. I only saw houses like hers on TV and in the movies. I mean, I knew they existed, I just hadn't been in one.

"You ever been in a crib like this?" Jason asked me on cue.

"Only in my dreams," I answered him.

"Well, you're not dreaming anymore, cousin. Wake up and smell the money," he told me.

Susan said, "Tracy told me to show you guys around and to your rooms."

To our rooms? I loved even the sound of that. It reminded me of the minor trips I had taken with my family down South to amusement parks and such, where we would stay in low-budget hotel rooms. But those hotels had nothing on the tall flight of stairs that Susan began to lead us up. Tracy's second floor must have been thirty feet high, or at least it seemed that high to me. It was very impressive. I liked it a whole lot.

"Tracy told me that Vanessa gets the guest room, and Jason, you can have either the computer room or downstairs on the foldout sofa in the living room," Susan told us with a grin.

Jason took one look inside the small computer room that had a computer station, file cabinets, a black leather office chair, and a futon that was pressed up against the wall, and he headed straight back down the stairs.

"Aw'ight," he mumbled to us on his way down.

The living room area had a deep, dark brown, leather sofa with a giant-sized, floor-model color television set that sat directly in front of it. The guest room, where I was to stay, had no TV at all. But I wasn't concerned about a lack of a television in my room. The peace and quiet there was a real godsend. I rarely had any peace and quiet in my house in North Philly. My two younger sisters were constantly getting into something, so I had learned to tune out the extra noise around me.

I stretched out on the burgundy comforter on the queen-sized bed in the guest room and was content with that. I didn't even feel like getting back up to go meet with Tracy on the movie set. I didn't even have to eat, really. I was already full with satisfaction.

Susan stuck her head into the room and said, "All right, well, we better get a move on if we want to get something to eat and still meet up with Tracy on the set. She has a pretty tight schedule to keep."

I understood my cousin's tight schedule and everything, but we had just gotten off a six-hour flight from Philly, and my body was beat. I hadn't gotten a chance to sleep much that week, while anticipating the trip. And once I felt the comfort of Tracy's guest room, my mind and body were ready to shut down for the night.

"How far is the set from here?" I asked Susan. I was stalling. I didn't want to leave.

She took a look at me relaxing on the bed and read my mind.

"You're experiencing jet lag, hunh?"

"Who?"

She smiled and shook her head. "Never mind. I'll just tell Tracy that you guys are a little worn out from the plane ride today. I kind of figured you would be."

"Yeah, I need a relaxation break for a minute," I told her.

It was only four o'clock in L.A., but it was seven o'clock for Jason and me. And my body felt as if it was ten o'clock already. I guess that's what Susan meant by jet lag. I wouldn't know. Not only had I never flown on an airplane before, I had never traveled out of my time zone. The South had the same time zone as Philly, only it was much hotter.

Susan nodded her head and made a call on her cell phone. That was the last thing I remember before I crashed.

When I woke up, Jason was standing in the doorway laughing at me with a slice of pizza to his mouth.

"Guess what time it is?" he asked me.

"What?"

"Eight o'clock."

I grimaced and said, "God. I've been asleep for four hours."

Jason shook his head and answered, "It seems like two days in one to me. And that just means it's more time for me to get into things."

I smiled in my cousin's direction and closed my eyes again. He was still on track to do what he planned to do.

We met with Tracy on the set of her new movie the next day. She was all made up in her gear as the character "Alexis," wearing dark lace, black leather, and plenty of makeup. There she was, my cousin, the nationally known book writer, screenwriter, and actress. I was so proud!

Jason and I were chilling in the trailer with her before her next action scene, just eating it all up. Susan had left us there alone while she handled her business.

"You really need to wear all that makeup?" Jason asked his sister. I was thinking the same thing, but I wasn't going to ask. I was content with just being around her and on an actual movie set.

Tracy answered, "It's for the hot lights of the camera. You don't understand."

"So, I would have to wear that much makeup, too?" he asked her.

"Why, you want a scene in this movie, Jason?" she asked him back.

"I'm just asking."

Tracy told him, "Well, before you start criticizing something you know nothing about, understand that everything has a purpose here. I'm not just wearing this makeup for the hell of it. Okay?"

She was all business.

Jason was silenced for a hot second before he responded, "Whatever."

I guess he felt that he had to say something. His big sister knew exactly how to handle him. I sat back and took mental notes for myself.

"So, how are you doing, Vanessa?" she asked me.

"Oh, I'm fine." I didn't have much to say. I just wanted to take everything in. It was all a daydream for me. I still couldn't believe I was there.

Tracy studied me for a second and asked me, "Have you called your mother yet?"

I wasn't sure how to answer that. I hadn't looked forward to talking to my mother about my trip to California. I figured it would have been rubbing it in her face, because she was so dead-set on me not going. I didn't even feel comfortable with calling my sisters about it. I'm sure they would have felt left out. Nevertheless, Tracy had a point, they were still my family.

"I'll be calling them soon," I told her.

She watched for my reaction and nodded. She was really studying me. I guess she was still trying to figure me out.

"So what are your plans?" she asked me next.

"My plans?"

"For the summer? For your life? For school?"

She was dead on me.

I stumbled and said, "I . . . I mean . . ."

"Well, you need to think about it," she told me. "And Jason, when we get this car for you, for while you're out here with Vanessa, I want you to act like you got some damn sense. Because you just can't act any way you want to out here. L.A. has a different way of doing things, and you can find your smart ass in hot water before you know what hit you."

Jason began to smirk. His sister was putting us both in check. But it was her right to do so as our guardian for while we were out there in her care. I couldn't blame her. She had to let us know who was the boss, I guess. And we got the point. Quickly!

However, once Jason and I were out on our own in L.A., my cousin went right back to his plans of becoming a summer gigolo from back East, while hollering at as many California girls as he could. He was making crazy U-turns inside the Lexus they had rented for him and everything.

"What are you doing?" I asked him from the passenger seat. I could see my life passing in front of me as cars peeled out in our direction.

"I got this, girl, stop sweatin' me."

"No, you need to stop sweating them," I responded, referring to all the girls he insisted on talking to. I just didn't understand guys on that level. How many girls could you actually concentrate on at one time and keep your focus with anything? It just seemed to me that the more girls he talked to, the less he would get out of them. Unless he was just looking for whichever one would give him sex the fastest.

"Hey, Ma', you need a ride somewhere?" he swung next to the curb and asked a caramel girl in long, brown braids.

She looked inside the car and directly at me.

Jason read her eyes and said, *"Oh, don't worry about her. She just my little cousin."*

Before the girl could clear her mind, I said, *"Oh, so now I'm your little cousin. I wasn't that before you tried to get some,"* I said loud enough to instigate a scene. I was getting fed up with Jason.

He looked into my face to read my game plan.

He said, *"Vanessa, stop trippin', all right."*

"No, you need to stop tripping," I responded to him. *"I mean, that's just downright bold. You gon' say that right in front of my face."*

The girl read my insanity inside of the car and got to stepping. But it looked as if she was ready to talk to him before I started my scene.

Once it was over with, Jason was pissed.

He asked me, *"Why you do that?"*

"Do what, Jason, protect my peace of mind? I mean, why you gotta talk to every girl you see out here? I mean, at least do it when I'm not around. You can even drop me off at the house first."

Jason looked into my determined face and began to smile. I guess he finally realized how foul he was being. But then he said, *"That's a good idea. I should leave you home from now on."*

I don't think that's what Tracy had in mind for us out in L.A. while she finished her movie. The next thing I knew, Jason was on several solo missions daily, and he actually started to pull several girls over to the house.

I asked him real civilly, while he had company over the house one day. I said, *"Jason, do you think it's smart to invite more than one girl over to your sister's house? I mean, I'm not trying to cramp your style or anything, but what if you start to have girls camping out in the neigh-*

borhood and ringing the doorbell and everything. I mean, have you thought about that at all?

"I mean, I can understand you talking to enough girls to choose the right one or whatever, but please don't invite every one of them over here," I told him. "I mean, that just doesn't make any sense."

"Look, I'll handle mine, Vanessa. Okay. I'll handle mine," he snapped at me.

He was really showing off. So I shut the guest room door tightly and minded my own business, while my dick-happy cousin entertained himself all over Tracy's house. When I walked out of the room to get some water that night, I caught Jason dead in the act on Tracy's leather sofa.

"Wait a minute, wait a minute," the girl pleaded to him. I made eye contact with her as soon as I headed down the stairs toward the kitchen. This girl had her big ass out while my cousin did her from behind.

Jason yelled, "Oh my God, Vanessa! Why you sneaking down the stairs?"

I wasn't sneaking down the stairs. I was getting a glass of water, and I had a right to. He shouldn't have been all out in the open with the girl. But I was so shocked by it that I couldn't even say anything. I just turned around and headed back up the stairs to the room. And man, at that point, I was about ready to dime on his trifling ass. I didn't want to make my cousin my enemy, but he was ruining my stay in California. I began to feel that I would have been much better off out there by myself.

As fate would have it, Tracy had been taking note of everything, and she had her own ways of checking up on us.

Jason and I had both been given cell phones, and in the middle of the night, I received an unexpected phone call from Tracy's girlfriend, Kendra, who lived nearby. We had met her a few times and she was pretty cool.

"Is everything all right?" she asked me over the line.

"Hunh?" I answered in a daze. I don't even know what time it was.

"Is Jason around?" she asked me.

I said, "Umm . . . I don't know."

"Okay, well, I'm on my way over there," Kendra told me.

I didn't think anything else about it. I mumbled, "All right," and hung up the phone to get back to sleep. Tracy had given her friend the spare key to check up on us, so I figured Kendra would let herself in that night. And that's all I remembered.

The next afternoon, Tracy was back home for a minute, and I overheard her in a heated conversation downstairs with her brother.

"So what time did you get back here last night?" she asked him.

"It wasn't after one," I heard Jason tell her. He sounded defensive.

"So what time was it then? Was it twelve forty-five, or what?"

"Yeah, around there," he told her. "But I mean, I'm almost grown now anyway, Tracy. I'm just out here to help you out. I'm not trying to be on no curfew."

"Yeah, almost grown," she reminded him. "So what if something happens to Vanessa while you're out here running the streets? I didn't get you that car for you to leave your cousin behind."

Jason said, "That girl ain't gon' get in no trouble. She quiet as a mouse. She just happy to be here. But I'm trying to enjoy myself while I'm out here."

"How, by fucking every little girl who lets you?" Tracy asked him.

I had to hold my breath. Big cousin could get downright raw when she had to.

She said, "You didn't learn anything from my Flyy Girl book, did you?"

Jason started laughing.

He said, "I mean, I still gotta live my own life, Tracy. And I saw who you fell for—the players."

"So, what are you trying to do, emulate the guys in my book? Because they didn't all end up in good places. Nor were they college graduates like you're about to be.

"And I don't see anything funny about it, Jason," she told him. "That's just plain disrespectful. I mean, you're out here acting like you never had a girl before. And diseases are everywhere, I think you should realize that."

He said, "Man, I'm always protected."

"Yeah, I just wish somebody was protected from you," she snapped at him.

"Aw, don't even try to hate on me like that, Tracy. You went for the same game when you were young," Jason commented. "And you still sweatin' that Victor dude now. I heard you went past his store when you were home. And the dude's married now."

I was surprised that he said that to her. Jason had nerve of his own. I just awaited the verdict.

Tracy asked him, "So, that's how you validate what you're doing? You're just going to rationalize things based on what I did in my life?"

"Naw, I'm just doing me," he told her.

She said, "Well, you know what? I think you need to go do you back home then. Because I don't want any drama coming to my house. And you know damn well that Mom wouldn't let you bring it to hers. So you need to just stop frontin', Jason, and act like you got some damn sense! You're only doing this because you think you can get away with it."

I opened my mouth in shock. Tracy was ready to send him back home without even giving him a second chance. Things were getting intense.

Jason said, "Well, send me back home then. That girl don't need no babysitter no way. But if she mess around and get pregnant because no-body's around to look after her, then that's on you."

I couldn't believe he was trying to put me back in it. That was foul. I wasn't even thinking about boys like that.

Tracy said, "Look, you let me worry about that. But right now, I'm more worried about you. Because you're the one acting all immature out here. You're the loose cannon, not Vanessa."

"Oh, so now I'm all immature because I like girls."

"It's not about you liking girls, Jason, it's about you acting reckless with your opportunities," she told him.

Before either of them could get another word in, the doorbell rang. I stayed glued to my spot in the room to hear what else would happen.

Tracy answered the doorbell and asked, "Yes, can I help you?"

"Ah . . . is Jason in?"

It sounded like a startled girl. Maybe Jason expected Tracy not to be home again, while he invited over whoever he wanted to invite.

"And who exactly are you?" I heard Tracy ask.

"Sasha."

It was the Asian girl from the airport. Once I heard that, I decided to step out of the room and walk downstairs. I was curious to see how Sasha would respond to Jason getting busted.

When I spotted her at the door, I noticed that she was not alone. She had a Hispanic girl with her. They were both gorgeous, wearing bright soda-can colors, with long ponytails.

"Oh my God, aren't you Tracy Ellison Grant from Led Astray? *I love that movie! I watched it like five times," the Hispanic girl shouted into my cousin's face.*

Sasha put two and two together and said, "So, Jason Ellison is your little brother?"

It was only obvious. Tracy didn't even have to answer that. We all looked like family.

Jason started smiling in the background.

He said, "Hey, what's up?"

Tracy cut straight through to the chase, still concerned about her brother's player behavior.

"So, what did he tell you, that he lived here?" she asked the girls.

Sasha said, "Well, he said he was staying at his sister's house for the summer. But I didn't know who his sister was."

"And he didn't tell you?" Tracy asked her.

"No," Sasha answered.

"But he did invite you over to the house."

The girls paused and looked at each other.

"Well, yeah," Sasha answered.

Tracy took note and nodded her head.

"So, what are you two, fashion models or something?" she asked them.

They sure looked like it to me, from head to toe.

"We're trying to be," the Hispanic girl answered. "Oh, my name is Jasmine Flores," she said with her hand extended.

Tracy shook her hand and calmed down. By that time, I was right downstairs with them. Tracy spotted me and introduced me to the girls.

"This is my cousin Vanessa. She's staying the summer with me, too. You guys all look around the same age," my cousin stated.

"You were on the airplane from Philly with us, right?" Sasha asked me.

I nodded. "Yeah. Are you from Philly, too?" I asked her.

She shook her head. "No, I'm from Delaware. I just fly out of Philly. And I have family all over."

Jason finally took the opportunity to get himself out of hot water. He said, "Aw'ight, well, I'm glad everybody met and everything, but let's talk out front," and he walked out the front door to lead the girls away.

Tracy told him, "We will finish our conversation as soon as you get back, Jason."

"Yeah, aw'ight, I got you."

"Nice meeting you," Jasmine told my cousin.

"Yeah, what a pleasant surprise," Sasha added with a smile.

Tracy nodded her head to them and said, "Okay. You two just be careful."

"Oh, we will," Jasmine promised her.

Tracy shut the front door and turned to look at me. "Do you believe that? So he's using my house as a roundabout way of getting him some. These girls know you have to have money to live up here."

I just smiled at her. She was right. Jason was using her house to score.

She asked, "So, did you hear what we were talking about before they rang the doorbell?"

I came right out with it. "Yeah, I heard you." There was no sense in me lying about it. I wanted to look after myself anyway.

"And what do you think about everything that was said?"

"Well, all I know is that I'm the oldest in my household at home, and I act like it. But Jason was the youngest in his household . . ."

Tracy nodded and said, "And he acts like it," just like I knew she would.

She said, "So, you actually think you can take care of yourself out here?"

I answered, "Once I get to know my way around."

"And what about you getting pregnant?" she asked me. I guess she felt she had to.

I said, "Well, I'm not out here looking for boys like Jason's obviously *looking for girls. But if it'll make you feel safer, you can put me on birth control, and you can have every boy I talk to disease tested before I kiss him."*

What the hell, I was going for broke. Tracy would have done the same. So I was taking a page out of her book of boldness.

She began to laugh. She said, "All right, we'll see if you stick to that. I can give them the condoms, too, and watch you to make sure they're doing it right?"

I wasn't expecting her to go that far with it. Her even bolder response made me embarrassed. I had to bury my face in my hands for a minute.

"If you're gonna talk the talk, then get ready to walk the walk," she warned me. "Because I never got pregnant, nor had any diseases. But what do we do with Jason?" she asked me.

I shrugged my shoulders. I said, "I don't know. Doesn't he have to start back at Temple in August? He's not even planning on being here long."

I was hinting big time. I didn't care if Jason went back home tomorrow. That would make more peace and quiet for me. I didn't need a lot of company. I could handle being alone.

Tracy nodded her head in deep thought about it. She said, "I have to think this over. Then I'll let you know."

Personal Assistant

Jason was pressed to find out what his sister and I had talked about after he left. He was sure we had had some girl talk. And he was right.

"So what she say?" he asked me.

Tracy was on her way back to her movie set in North Hollywood. They had finished all of their scenes out in the Nevada desert a week before we had arrived.

"What do you think she said?" I asked him back.

Jason said, "Look, I don't have time for no guessing games. Just tell me what she said."

So I told him. "She said she'd think about having me look after myself out here. And by the way, I caught that little comment of yours about me getting pregnant, and I didn't appreciate it."

Jason looked me in the eyes and said, "I'm just stating the facts. I mean, you can be all mousy if you want, but as soon as the right guy get up in you, it's a wrap. And the quiet ones are the worse ones for that."

He said, "Tracy knows it. That's why she had me out here with you in the first place."

I said, "Well, thanks for your vote of confidence in me, cousin," and I walked away from his ass to leave him standing there.

Jason had nothing to say for a change.

Over the next few days, Tracy invited me out to the movie set in a chauffeured limo to serve as one of her "personal assistants." She didn't work me too hard though. She mainly had me watching the process of her other assistants. They were mostly young white girls. It seemed like everyone out there but Tracy was white. I don't know if that was a good thing or a bad thing.

25

"You need any more water?"

"You want me to get that?"

"Is that cold enough for you?"

"You need to make a phone call?"

I was unnerved by it all. I mean, I had seen the catering to the stars process on TV and in the movies, but to see it up close was really something. I don't know if I had what it took to work for someone like that. Or least not by my own free will.

"Have you made amends with your mother yet?" Tracy asked me. I guess she was trying to see when she could expect to send me back home.

"No," I answered. I had talked to my sisters, but my mother refused to have any words for me.

"So, she's not even accepting your phone calls now?" my cousin assumed.

"That's what it looks like."

I felt like I was in the middle of a bridge. Tracy had invited me out to her world, but she still was not inviting me all the way in. She was leaving the door wide open for me to return. I couldn't blame her though. Like she said, she hadn't had any children, so it was hard for her to accept me barging in on her life. Nevertheless, she had invited me there.

Tracy finally broke down and asked me, "Vanessa, what would you do in my position?"

I guess we were reading each other correctly. We were both in deep thought about our dilemma.

I answered, "I'd give my little cousin a chance to prove herself."

What else could I say? I believed in myself and I wasn't planning on turning back.

I said, "I realize that everybody may not get an opportunity to really do something in life, but I feel like you're able to give me that opportunity."

"Give you the opportunity to do what, Vanessa? To act?"

I shook my head and said, "No, but just to be in the middle of things, where I can make up my mind on which way to go and where I really want to be. And it's not in Philly right now."

"What's wrong with Philly? They have the neo-soul movement popping right now. The new Sixers . . ."

I cut her off and said, "But you're not there because you realized that you had to make things happen elsewhere. Sometimes it's just better to leave home."

I had Tracy stumped for a second.

She finally said, "We'll see." She wasn't going to make it easy for me.

By the time August rolled around, I was on solo missions of my own, finding my way around L.A., and Tracy was nearly done filming her second movie. Her next project was already lined up, writing For the Love of Money, the sequel to Flyy Girl.

She began to talk about the process of interviews with author Omar Tyree, who was supposed to fly out to L.A. to ask her a thousand questions about the next phase of her life. After Tracy's adolescence and teen years had been published to huge success, she and Omar planned to team up for more of the same.

I still had not been able to rectify the situation at home with my mother, so it looked more and more like I would either be staying out in L.A. with Tracy, or returning to Philly to stay with my aunt Pattie.

So, for the rest of my days in L.A., I worked hard on being the best personal assistant to Tracy that I could be. I took mental notes on what she liked and didn't like, where and what she liked to eat, who she wanted to talk to and who not. I cleaned and organized the house. I collected her news and magazine articles and filed them alphabetically in folders. I met her business associates, publicist, hairdressers—you name it. And I listened to and tried to understand her every complaint and suggestion. I basically forced myself to map out my cousin's entire psychological profile, all so she would allow me to stay with her for as long as I wanted. I had to allow her a chance to see that I would be more of an asset to her than a hindrance.

In the meantime, Jason had worn out his welcome with more than a few California girls, who began to realize that his slash-and-burn attitude was counterproductive to a meaningful relationship with them. The reality was that if he was so set on only a temporary stay in L.A., then what was the point of getting too close to him? And once they began to figure him out, Jason felt less opportunistic about his chances.

"Aw, man, I'm about to get up out of here," he complained. "Y'all jinxed me. Ever since that day we had that argument, these girls've been acting funny on me."

I smiled and said, "You had it coming. You were just a little too cocky."

He said, "Aw'ight, well, you're about to get your wish then. I'm about to start getting ready for school now. But what about you? You gon' go to school out here?" he asked me.

I said, "I want to."

Jason nodded. "Good luck then."

It was the only time he said anything of encouragement to anyone outside of himself since he had been out there in L.A. Too bad it was only because he was leaving. But I'd take it however I could get it.

"Thanks," I told him.

As soon as Jason took that plane ride back home to Philly and left me all alone with Tracy in L.A., I became more nervous about what her verdict would be with me.

I attended a wrap party with her for Road Kill in Santa Monica with the intention of being as perfect as I could. Most of her new Hollywood friends were there, and I wanted to make a great impression.

"So you're the infamous Vanessa Tracy Smith?" her lawyer friend Yolanda Felix asked me with a glass of wine in her hand. I had heard about her, but I had not met her until then. From what I had heard about her, Yolanda Felix was a hell of a character. She had the golden-brown, Hollywood skin, the long dark hair, the fancy clothes, the slim physique, the expensive jewelry, and the twinkle of a high-class and viperous woman. I figured I needed to be as forward with her as I could to keep her from intimidating me. She was definitely the intimidating type.

I said, "And you're the infamous Yolanda Felix?" just to throw her comment about me back in her face.

There was no mistaking who she was. Some people will always stand out in a crowd. I knew that from high school, and Hollywood was only the tenth degree of the same process.

"So what did you hear about me?" Yolanda asked me.

I kept my guard up with her. I had too much to lose if I didn't. She was the kind of in-your-face sister who would figure you were weak if you let your guard down with her.

I asked her, "What did you hear about me?"

She smiled. She said, "You're Tracy's cousin all right. So how long will it take before you're in movies?"

Her question threw me for a loop. I wasn't thinking about movies for myself. I just wanted to be behind the scenes.

I said, "I think you're more of the movie type than I am."

"Not from what I've heard," she insisted.

I became nervous for a minute. I started to wonder what she had heard. She was breaking me down.

I said, "You must have heard the wrong things then," and lost my eye contact with her.

"Are you sure?" Yolanda pressed me.

I was wondering if Tracy had told her about my scuffle with my mother. I doubted it, but I wasn't certain. That's what pressure makes you do. Yolanda was running me through a test to see how much guts I had.

"Hey guys, what are you two talking about?" Susan Raskin popped up to rescue me. I took a breath and relaxed.

I answered, "Movies," and caught Tracy's nod to me from across the room. There were too many people smothering my cousin as the star of the movie for her to just break away, so she sent her agent Susan over to me just in time.

Yolanda asked her, "What do you think about her chances?" referring to me in starring movie roles.

Susan took a good look at me in my lime green satin dress and said, "As long as she prepares herself accordingly, Vanessa has the chops to do whatever she wants to."

It was a good answer. Susan was helping to encourage me while keeping me on my p's and q's about proper preparation. It was one thing to lift a person up, it was something else to tell them the truth while you're at it.

I was learning what to expect rather quickly there. The wrap party was like a Hollywood crash course. A couple of older guys even tried to come on to me, rich white men.

"So, ah, I hear you're the star's cousin out of Philly."

"Yeah," I answered a blond-haired white man with poise. He looked around forty, but he was probably older than that. I was aware that people in Hollywood spent millions of dollars to maintain their youth.

He slipped out a business card without telling me his name and tried to slide it inside my small purse.

"If you need anything you just let me know, okay?"

I moved my purse away from his reach and told him, "I can't take that. I'm underage."

I was embarrassed again, and wondering who was watching us. It was simply too many people in the room to think that no one would see it. I'm sure he knew it as well.

So he performed a quick trick with his hand and hid the card inside of his palm.

In passing, he told me, "There's no such thing as underage in Hollywood, my dear."

That was it. Mr. Man moved on to the next conversation.

I was tempted to fade into the corners of the room and keep out of sight at that point. But a lime green, satin dress made that hard to do.

"How are you? I love this color," an older white woman said, while rubbing my dress material in her fingers. She didn't even ask if she could touch it first.

I looked into her aged face and said "Thank you." I don't know how old the woman was, but she had so many lines in her face that I realized instantly why so many older white men chased after girls who could pass for their daughters.

I must admit, I was ready to leave that place early. It wasn't my kind of party. They had no hip-hop or R&B music, few people my age, and few people of color.

"Are you having fun yet?" Tracy's friend Kendra asked me. She was being sarcastic. I'm quite sure she could read the look of bewilderment on my face. I had no idea what I was getting into out in Hollywood.

I took a deep breath and responded, "This is really different."

"Tell me about it," Kendra said. She blended in a lot better with the crowd in her black business suit. But she was one of the brownest faces in the room.

She said, "By the fourth party, you'll get good and used to it. But that still doesn't mean you have to like it. I only come to these things because Tracy asks me to, to keep her grounded in reality. So when she sees me, she relaxes. We have a little system going."

I told her, "I see. Are there any black parties out in Hollywood?" I asked.

I was just curious to know where the black stars did their thing.

Kendra said, "Oh, there's definitely black parties. We just don't have as many because we don't wrap as many movies as they do. You know what I mean?"

I nodded to her. Hollywood was white America's biggest invention, and I would not soon forget that.

By the end of the wrap party I was worn out, and it was only eleven o'clock. However, spending a few hours with those people was quite enough.

I leaned back into the black leather seats of our stretch limo, alone with my cousin, and Tracy went right at me.

"You see how this game works?" she asked me.

Did I ever. I just nodded to her. One Hollywood party like that was all it took.

"And you think you can handle this on a regular basis?"

I wasn't so sure anymore, but I was still willing to try.

"I mean, won't it be different at a black party?" I asked her. I had never been surrounded by that many white people before. Or at least not in an intimate setting.

Tracy answered, "A little bit. But at the white parties, at least you stand out. I've been to black parties where everybody's waiting for Denzel Washington to show up. And he won't show until the party's nearly over. So what fun is that?"

"What about the younger stars?" I asked her.

"What younger stars? The television people? Nobody gets excited over them," she told me. "They're all trying to get into movies."

I was confused a minute. Was my cousin telling me that we really didn't have any stars in black Hollywood? Because I would have been excited to meet a few.

She read my confusion and said, "Understand this, Vanessa, if you understand nothing else about fame and stardom. There are really only two levels in this game: stars who are in projects, and actors and actresses who are trying to get into projects. And you're only a star when you're attached to something. That's how fickle this business is."

"But what if you leave Hollywood and do movies back in the cities?" I asked her. I was thinking about her shooting a Flyy Girl movie back home in Philadelphia. Everyone talked about that at home. It would be an urban hit. No question about it. All Tracy had to do was find the right people to put in it.

My cousin smiled at me and said, "I can see exactly where you're going with that. And I've been discussing the Flyy Girl project, believe me. But first I have to prove that we have a big enough urban audience to green-light a Flyy Girl film."

I said, "But we would see that movie two and three times if it came out. Everybody says that. All you have to do is shoot it and advertise it."

"I wish it were that easy," my cousin told me. "But to do it right, it would still take more than independent money."

"How much would it cost?" I asked her. I was sure that with the huge budgets that I read about in Hollywood movies, that they had the money out there to shoot Flyy Girl. What was so hard about getting it?

"It would cost us about twenty million dollars," Tracy answered.

I thought about it and said, "Will Smith gets that all by himself."

"Yeah, but not for black movies. He doesn't even do black movies anymore. He's, like, the science fiction king."

She was right. I just laughed at it. Will Smith was like the only black person in the past five movies that I saw him in.

"So what kind of budgets do they give for black movies?" I asked my cousin.

"Generally between eight and sixteen million, and those are for proven all-star casts. And usually, you're dealing with comedies, not dramas. And Flyy Girl is definitely a drama in an age group where we don't really have stars."

"What about if you use all rappers and singers?" I joked. They were stars.

Tracy said, "That's exactly my point. We would be shooting in the dark. We don't know if we can invest twenty million dollars in unproven talent. That's what rappers and singers are when you put them in movies. It's not automatic. They really have to make it work."

I said, "Well." I didn't want the conversation to end. There just had to be a way to make Flyy Girl happen.

Tracy grinned and said, "Let's save this argument for another day."

But I had no idea how many days I had left.

I said, "Tracy, I know this is a big decision for both of us, but I really want to be here. I mean, I dreamed all my life of being in this position, and I don't want to just come out here and lose it. I mean, I could help you in whatever you would need me to help you with. I'm learning how to be a good assistant. I'm learning how the Hollywood game works. And remember, I'm only sixteen now. So if you keep me around the right people, I'm real confident that in a few more years, with more experience under my belt, I'll be a real asset to you. I mean, I promise you that."

We were cruising through Hollywood, dressed to impress and sitting in the plush leather seats of a black stretch limo. You think I wanted to give that up so easy? No way!

Tracy just leaned back in her seat and stared at me. Then she smiled.

She said, "I had already made up my mind that I would let you stay here, Vanessa. I just needed to make sure that you really wanted to. Because this is not a passive decision. Hollywood is not about just being there, it's about working it. Plain and simple. So if you wanna stay out here and help me, then get yourself prepared to work."

I said, "I can do that. That's what I want to do."

Tracy nodded her head and said, "Aw'ight then, little cousin. If you really want it, you just remember that you asked for it."

The Boss Lady

Let's Make It Happen!

By the spring of 2003, I was a second-semester freshman studying media relations at UCLA. I was still hanging in there and learning the ropes of the Hollywood game, and freelancing as the personal assistant of my celebrity cousin, Tracy Ellison Grant. However, her shine in the film world was no longer as bright as it was in the book industry. I was involved in the majority of the interview and fact-checking process when Tracy wrote her sequel book, *For the Love of Money*, with author Omar Tyree, and the book set the market on fire as soon as it was published. *For the Love of Money* hit the *New York Time*'s bestsellers list in a week and went on to win an NAACP Image Award for Outstanding Literature. But *Road Kill*, my cousin's second feature film, tanked at the box office. It pulled in a mere twelve million dollars after the production company spent close to thirty million to produce it. Tracy followed that up with an ignored film called *Jump-start*, about a con woman who finds a change of heart when she adopts a younger cousin, who loses her single mom to a drug overdose.

The films were not that bad, actually. The reviews were even balanced. Some critics liked them, other critics did not. No one hated the projects or lambasted Tracy's performances in them. I just don't think that many people cared. You had to give the people what they wanted, and at the time, I guess no one wanted to see a black woman vigilante in an action flick, or a black woman play a change-of-heart wheeler-dealer. Or maybe no one wanted to see Tracy play those roles.

Tracy and I talked about it from different angles.

"J. Lo and Halle Berry are getting press more for their lifestyles than their film careers, if you really look at it," I assessed to my cousin.

"And that role that Halle won the Oscar for, I mean, I hate to say it, but that was some raw stuff she did in that movie."

Tracy grinned and agreed with me.

"You got that right. She outdid me with that one."

We were eating strawberry ice cream with our feet up on the coffee table in the living room while we watched *Entertainment Tonight* on the floor-model television set. And we finally had enough furniture in the house to stop visitors from joking about echoes.

Tracy said, "J. Lo has won a couple of weekends at the box office though."

"She just came out on the right weekends," I commented. I wasn't trying to hate on her, I was just stating the facts.

I said, "In the long run, *Led Astray* will make you just as much money or more than J. Lo's and Halle Berry's films. It was just well done. And it's racking up the rentals now at Blockbuster."

"What about *Road Kill* and *Jump-start*?" my cousin asked me with a smirk.

I smiled at her with ice cream on my tongue.

"You can't win them all," I answered.

We laughed about it and kept talking.

I said, "But I know one movie of yours that would blow everybody out of the box."

Tracy looked at me, took a deep breath, and sighed.

"Here we go with that again."

"I mean, you know it's true," I argued. I was talking about none other than *Flyy Girl*, the movie. Or even *For the Love of Money* for that matter. After they had read and fallen in love with the book, Tracy must have gotten at least ten emails a day, *every day*, from inner-city girls begging to have *Flyy Girl* made into a movie.

Tracy asked me, "And who could open the movie in my role?"

"Meagan Good is real hot right now after *Biker Boyz*," I answered. "She could do it. Or Beyoncé's little sister, Solange Knowles."

I had already done my homework on it. I had a whole list of black girls who were moving up the ranks in the entertainment world, who were still teenagers or could still pass for one.

Tracy grinned, realizing I was prepared to defend my argument.

She said, "Meagan is okay. I don't know about Solange, though. I mean, I hear she wants to get into the entertainment business, but you know how it is with the lesser-known family members. It just doesn't seem to work. It seems like the Wayans and Baldwin brothers are about the only ones who can get away with that."

"Well, let's go talk to Meagan's people then. We don't have to use Solange. She looks closer to you though."

I was just ready to do it. We were all out there in Hollywood already. What was the big holdup?

Tracy said, "Susan and I have already discussed the project with several producers, and none of them seem to get it. It's just too many unknowns involved for them to want to finance it. *Biker Boyz* was jam-packed with known stars, and it still tanked."

"But it did wonders for Meagan and Derek Luke," I noted.

"Yeah, but neither one of them can open a movie, Vanessa," my cousin argued. "What did Derek Luke do for *Antwone Fisher*, even with Denzel Washington co-starring and directing it? Nothing," she answered for herself.

"It was up for an award at least," I argued. I said, "And I think it depends on who they're trying to open a movie for. If you asked urban teenagers, they'll go see them in the right film every day of the week, just like they did for John Singleton's movies. But if you're counting on these stuck-up–behind Hollywood people to see it . . ."

My cousin cut me off and said, "You sound just like a college student. I used to be the same way when I was at Hampton. You get up in college and all of a sudden you think you can just up and change the world."

She was halfway laughing at me.

I said, "Well, isn't that why we go to college in the first place, to be the next wave of movers and shakers? *You* did it. I mean, you're out here in Hollywood now, and a lot of girls look up to you. They may not have agreed with all of the things you did, but they love the fact that you represented the urban reality so well, and that you survived it. And they just want to see that representation on the big screen."

"And you think I don't? Some things just take more time, Vanessa," she argued.

My cousin had a point of course, but I was already on a roll. I said, "What about when Spike Lee was doing all his New York movies? I mean, if we need to leave starstruck Hollywood and go back to the streets to get it done, then that's what we need to do."

I had put in overtime doing research on black films, while renting and watching them all. I had gotten gung-ho about the entire filming process.

Tracy said, "That was a different time back then, Vanessa. Independent films were a lot easier to be picked up for distribution back then. But now we have a lot of those same films going straight to DVD instead. Is that what you want to happen to *Flyy Girl*? I know I want a theatrical release myself, and not some underground rental sleeper. What's the point in waiting all of this time to do that?"

She stopped me in my tracks with that one. I wanted to see *Flyy Girl* on the big screen, too, in a breakout blockbuster weekend, with teenaged girls lined up all across the country. I just felt that urban American girls deserved our own breakout film. We needed our own *Boyz n the Hood* and our own *American Graffiti*. *Flyy Girl* was it.

Before I could get out another word on the subject, Tracy's cell phone went off. She looked down at the number before she stood up to answer it.

"Hey," she answered while walking toward the kitchen. That's all I needed to know. It was her "friend." That's all she called him, and she had been "friends" with him for over a year. But she never let him stay over at the house. She even used me as her excuse to keep him at bay. I would have liked to have lived on UCLA's campus, but Tracy had gotten used to having me around the house with her.

"We were just sitting here talking about movies," she told him as she strolled into the kitchen.

I smiled, realizing her game plan. She didn't feel like having her friend over for company that night. That's why she said "we." Otherwise, she would have said that she was just sitting there watching television, as if I wasn't in the room with her. I knew all of my cousin's M.O.s by then. She was an interesting case, thirtysomething and as free as she wanted to be, and with all of her own money to pay the bills.

I was still a virgin myself, and I was not even looking out for guys. They were all case studies to me. Maybe I read too much into things, but their conversations never added up.

"Are you doing any homework tonight?" a guy at school would ask me.

"Yes, I am," I would answer.

"You need any help with it?"

"You have media relations courses?" I would ask.

"No. I'm studying business."

"So, how can you help me with my homework?"

That's when they would start to stumble.

"I mean, I'm just saying if you would need any help with any-thing."

"Well, why would you want to help me?"

"I mean . . . why not?"

Then I would ask them, "Don't you have homework of your own to do?"

"Yeah, but it's not that much?"

"So, you would spend that extra time just to help me?"

"Yeah."

"But what do you get out of that?" I would ask them.

That's when they would look confused.

"What do I get out of it?"

Then I would break it all down. "Time is money, right? So why would you want to spend your money on me just to help me to do my homework?"

That's when they would forget how to add.

"I'm saying, I'm not even thinking like that. I'm just trying to help you with whatever you need help with."

See what I mean? That explanation doesn't add up. Nobody does something for nothing. If they did, then why would they make a choice about whom they would do something for? I had been an ex-cellent student my entire life. I didn't need the extra help. But I knew plenty of girls who didn't look like me who did, and they didn't get of-fered help for anything, unless they had a "friend" of their own. Sometimes not even then would they get help.

Like I said, maybe I was reading too much into things, but my understanding of the situation was not helping me to become comfortable with dating.

My cousin, on the other hand, had all the experience in the world in the men department. So when she walked back out of the kitchen with a can of Sprite in her hand, and was already off the cell phone with her friend, I was curious as to what happened with him.

"You hung up on him already? Is he coming over? I need to go upstairs now?"

Tracy shook her head and said, "You're moving too fast, girl. You need to pump the brakes."

"I'm saying, you walk out one minute talking and you walk back in the next and it's over with," I told her.

"He was just saying hi, which is still too much information for you," my cousin told me. She retook her seat on the sofa.

I asked her, "Do you ever think about getting married and having kids now?"

Tracy looked at me and tried to decipher where my sudden question had come from.

"Is that a requirement in being a woman?" she asked me back. "You're in college now? You tell me?"

I said, "No, but it is a part of life, and people expect it, especially when you look good."

"Well, I expected you to have a real boyfriend by now, but that hasn't happened either."

She was right, I had none.

I grinned and said, "I have plenty of time for that."

"So you're not in a rush then?" she asked me.

"Not at all."

"Well, why should I be?"

It was a set-up question.

I said, "Because . . ."

I didn't want to be too bold about it, but my cousin was asking me for it?

"What, I'm getting old and running out of time?" she assumed.

I grinned at her and ate my last spoonful of strawberry ice cream.

"They're your words, not mine," I told her.

"Yeah, but they are your thoughts."

"I mean, people want to know," I leveled with her. Readers were even asking her the husband-and-kids question through emails on her website.

"People also want to know when they can win the lottery," my cousin joked.

"Whatever."

We continued to watch *Entertainment Tonight* on the television in silence for a minute. They were doing a report on the success and the wealth of the Olsen twins, who were syndicated with reruns of *Full House* on cable. Since *Full House*, Mary-Kate and Ashley Olsen had grown into teenagers, and they had made a fortune on straight-to-video movies as well as a gang of products that young American girls were going crazy for.

"They don't have to work another day in their lives if they don't want to," Tracy commented with a sip of her Sprite.

That only got me started again.

I said, "You'd be in the same position if you made a whole line of Flyy Girl products."

Tracy stopped and stared at me.

"Would you let it go?" she asked me. "It'll happen when it's supposed to happen."

"And when is that?"

I just couldn't control my mouth about it. I didn't even mean to say that.

Tracy shook her head for the last time and didn't say another word to me that night.

When we walked up to bed and went our separate ways to our rooms, I decided to keep my comments to myself. I don't know. It just seemed to me that my cousin had gotten soft and a little bit lazy. She was not the kind of woman to take no for an answer before, but there she was, living in a fully furnished Hollywood crib, with the black Mercedes parked out front, while telling me no about a project that she *knew* would work and would benefit her more than anyone.

My cousin was the official Flyy Girl. No one could ever deny that.

Her book had come before all of the other urban-girl books and be-fore the urban-girl clothing lines. There were no Baby Phat or J. Lo lines before *Flyy Girl*. Tracy could have racked up with Flyy Girl everything.

I thought about the Flyy Girl franchise all night long. I just couldn't get the idea off of my mind. I mean, you have to understand, that with me waking up and going to bed near my cousin every night, it was like living with chocolate on your lips that you were never al-lowed to taste. So you walk around pushing your lips away from your tongue to keep from accidentally licking the chocolate off. You know what I mean? It was driving me crazy.

I had a million ideas about how to blow up Flyy Girl Ltd. as an urban-ladies clothing line. But Tracy always managed to cut me off and ignore me. One time, in the heat of the discussion, she even told me that maybe I should think about my own career and stop sweating hers. I ignored her at the time. People always say things in heated arguments they don't mean to say. Then again, a heated argument is also when the truth comes out. And maybe that was the truth. *Flyy Girl* the franchise was dead, and I needed to think about something else worth my time and effort.

I figured maybe I could start my own flyy girl following. But I couldn't call it that. My cousin wouldn't allow me to. She still pro-tected the name. So maybe I would call my club The Urban Ladies. Or better yet, The Urban Miss. That title had more pizzazz to it. I wanted to create something that symbolized the fact that urban American girls had it going on. Black girls, Puerto Ricans, Asians, mixed girls, and everybody in between who just wanted to fit in with the urban scene.

I mean, we rarely got a chance to shine in our own light. We were always the trifling girlfriend, the unknown girl waiting at the bus stop, the invisible secretary with no lines, or more commonly, the swimsuit-clad, dance-video chick. Hip-hop videos were what urban girls were becoming the most known for. And that was a crying shame, because they were pushing nothing but sex. Make it shake and bounce, swing it to the left, swing it to the right, drop it like it's hot, stick it out the back window, pull it in, push it out, wiggle it all around, slide it down the pole, rub it up against the wall, now stop, and do it all in slow motion for me. Thank you very much. Here's your paycheck and free CDs, and make sure you come out tonight to the after-party.

Need I say more? We needed better imagery than that. And I was becoming more pressed by the minute to make it happen.

Tracy woke me up that morning after I had gotten about three hours of sleep. It was a little after eight o'clock in the morning, and I hadn't gone to bed until after five from thinking so much about my ideas.

I strained to look up into my cousin's face. When I focused on her, she looked like she had seen a ghost that morning. She had that deadly still look in her eyes.

I asked her, "What's wrong?"

"Susan's uncle died in his sleep last night."

I just stared at her for a minute.

"Edward Weisner?" I asked her to make sure.

Tracy nodded. "Yup," she said. "So I need you to drive over there with me."

I had classes to go to, but I wasn't about to say it. My classes were not until later that day anyway. But I was still tired as hell.

I mumbled, "Okay. Let me get up and get myself together."

We hit the middle of L.A.'s rush-hour traffic while trying to make it to West Hollywood Hills, where Susan's uncle had lived with his wife, maids, and caretakers. I didn't know exactly where it was, but I couldn't seem to stay awake for the ride. We were not getting anywhere fast with L.A. traffic jammed up anyway. Los Angeles was a real headache to get around.

Tracy didn't have much to say for the first part of the drive. She was keeping her calm. What else could you do when a family member of a friend dies? My cousin had to keep her poise for when we arrived at the house.

Out of the blue, she said, "He liked *Flyy Girl*, too. Once he got a chance to read it, he called it a naturalist's book, unapologetic and without political agendas. He said it flowed exactly the way it was supposed to. So the people who got it, got it, and the people who didn't, shame on them."

I opened my eyes for a minute to see what Tracy looked like when she told me that. She had a slight smile on her face.

At that point, I didn't want to rub anything in on her. I had already stated my piece and had started thinking about my own ideas. So I decided just to listen for a change.

She said, "He told me that every movie you do should be a dream movie. He said to write every film like it's your last . . . because the inspiration of your people is at stake."

Man, I was just *itching* to say something about *Flyy Girl* then, but I didn't. I was going to see if Tracy would put together the ironies for herself.

"You have to *believe* that you can make a difference," she commented.

She seemed energized by the memories. She was remembering all the important things that Susan's uncle had told her.

"What are you gonna do with your opportunity?" she asked rhetorically. "You have to live your life with passion, because to live life without passion is like not living life at all.

"And those who create for the love of the *art* are *consistently* getting better, but those who create for the love of money . . . those guys are forever getting worse."

I finally smiled and said, "That's where you got the title of your sequel book from."

Tracy looked at me as if I should have known that already.

She said, "You heard me say that before. You have read the book, right?"

I grinned. I did know it already, but her saying it was a fresh reminder.

I said, "Of course I read it. I was there when you two were putting it together. I just hadn't heard you talk about the things that Edward Weisner told you lately, that's all."

She nodded and said, "He made a lot of good points. He was the one who inspired me to do such a good job with writing *Led Astray*."

"And what about now?" I asked her. It was my sly way of continuing to bug her about writing a great script for *Flyy Girl*.

Tracy didn't look me in my eyes when she said it, but I know she felt me.

She said, "I know what you're getting at, Vanessa. And we'll just have to wait and see."

We arrived at the Weisner house, which was in the side of the mountain behind the hills of Hollywood. No way in the world would I live on a mountainside like that, especially with earthquakes reported in the California region. I was nervous about just being there.

There were plenty of cars parked in the driveway and in front of the garage, so we had to stop and park on the street.

"How many times have you been out here?" I asked Tracy.

"Only a few times. It's not like this was a hangout or anything," she answered as we walked to the front door.

After we rang the bell, an older Mexican woman answered the door.

"Oh, Tracy, how are you doing?" she said and hugged my cousin.

"How are you, Mrs. Sanchez?"

"Maria," she fussed at my cousin. Then she looked at me.

"And who is this?"

Tracy had never taken me over there with her. It was my first time. She answered, "This is my cousin Vanessa from back home in Philly."

I slid out my hand to shake Maria's, only for her to wrap me into a hug.

"A cousin of yours is a cousin of mine," she said to Tracy.

I was still too tired to recall everyone I met there that day. The majority of the visitors were family members, old associates, Hollywood powers, Maria's family, and Tracy and me. That let me know how close Tracy had gotten to Susan and her powerful Hollywood family. But there was no crying and mourning in the house. They all seemed to use the gathering as a meaningful get-together that was overdue. They were even drinking wine in there. Tracy was shocked herself.

She asked Susan on the low, "How come it doesn't look like . . . anybody's sad in here?"

Susan smiled it off. She said, "My uncle Eddie has been telling us all for years that he doesn't want a bunch of crying and carrying on when he dies. Nor does he want us fighting over his fortune. He just wants us to come together with wine and talk about him to everyone who will listen."

Tracy grinned and said, "That sounds just like him. Let me go and get a glass of wine then."

I know it was wrong, but all I could think about while I was there was how many millions of dollars we could borrow from the Weisner family to make our movie. It wasn't as if we wouldn't get it back. *Flyy Girl* was as sure a hit in my book as a Tom Cruise movie.

"So, what's going on in your mind, Vanessa?" Susan asked me with her glass of wine in hand. She said, "I can see that your wheels are turning? You're always thinking about something."

Susan knew me real well. But it wasn't hard to figure me out. I mean, I didn't talk a lot around people I didn't really know, but I was always thinking.

I told Susan, "Nothing in particular. I'm just a little tired from being up all last night."

"You had a big assignment for school that was due?" she asked me.

"No, I was up thinking about other things."

"Oh, it's those naughty boys," she assumed with a smirk. "They've been known to keep many a girl up late at night."

On second thought, maybe she didn't know me well. Not to say that I wouldn't want a man eventually, they just were not on my mind at the present. But I was never scared of boys like Raheema was in her day. I was just two steps ahead of them, and they still had not quite caught up with me yet.

To humor Susan, I said, "I wish I did have a boy to keep me up late. But they don't seem to like girls with a plan. I guess they look at it as too much competition."

Susan looked at me and started laughing.

She said, "Have you been reading my diary? You are so on with that."

I didn't know whether to smile or frown at her. Weren't we all there because her loved and respected uncle had died? I just couldn't get into the celebration-of-a-loss thing. I understood the theory, I just felt a little hesitant about practicing it.

Tracy arrived just in time to save me from my conflicted thoughts and feelings about Susan.

"So, I guess you'll be having visitors here for the next couple of days?" my cousin stated. We were all watching new visitors walk through the door.

Susan looked at her and said, "Try the next couple of *weeks*. My uncle Eddie knows a boatload of people. So the only thing that will stop this boat ride is my aunt Jillian getting a little worn out from it all."

I looked over at the frail, gray-haired, and still attractive widow, who was meeting and greeting a gang of folks inside the house, and I wondered how much energy she would have left for herself when it was all said and done.

Susan then joked to Tracy, "I was just talking to Vanessa about her recent man problems. She says she was up all last night."

Tracy looked at me and took a sip of her wine.

"She may have been up all last night, but she wasn't thinking about any guys. She was thinking about something else," she commented.

I was itching for Tracy to say what it was in front of Susan and the Hollywood powers-that-be who were inside that room. But I had to wait it out. It would have sounded like a setup if I broke down and said it myself.

"So, what were you thinking about?" Susan asked me.

I looked at Tracy, and she gave me a look of concern. I knew she wouldn't want me badgering Susan about a *Flyy Girl* movie as much as I bothered her about it, especially at a mourning for her uncle.

So I backed down from it. I said, "I was just thinking about what I need to do to carve out my own particular niche in life while living under the roof of a famous cousin, that's all."

Susan stared at me. She said, "Hmm, now that is a dilemma. However, sometimes it's better to get behind a wheel that's already rolling instead of trying to push a brand-new one. And then once you understand the laws of momentum, you'll be able to roll your own wheel with much less muscle. You know what I mean?"

She was telling me to stay behind Team Tracy and not think about Team Vanessa yet.

I said, "Well, what if the wheel doesn't want to move in the direction that you would like to help and move it in?"

Tracy looked away as if she wasn't in it.

Susan looked at my cousin briefly and then back to me.

"I can't imagine Tracy not wanting to try new things. She's always been the adventurous one. So, what direction are you trying to push her in? You have me curious now."

Tracy finally spoke up about it. "She wants me to get involved with a complicated film project that we've already talked about, and I told her that we'll all have to wait it out for the best time to do it."

Susan looked at me and asked, "Is it something you've written? I wouldn't mind taking a look at it. My uncle Eddie taught us all to always make new opportunities available."

Susan was really reaching out to me. I appreciated that.

I answered, "No, it's something that Tracy's written that all the urban girls I know are already waiting on."

"You can't speak for everyone else," Tracy told me. "A lot of people get overzealous about the ideas, but then they become lukewarm to the reality. I've seen that happen many times in the film world now.

"People said they loved *Road Kill* and *Jump-start* as ideas, just like I did," she told me. "But they didn't show up to give us love once the movies hit the theaters. So don't believe everything you read about or hear from these so-called fans."

"So what project is she talking about that you've written already?" Susan asked. She was still in the dark.

Tracy finally coughed it up. "*Flyy Girl.*"

Susan's mouth dropped open before she let out a big, "Oh." She said, "Yeah, the problem with that is the lack of known stars in that age category."

I said, "I see movies with white teenagers every month, who don't have big names either."

Susan said, "Yeah, but many of those guys are coming from the ranks of television. And they may not be known stars to you, but they do have a television audience to build on."

"So do our rappers and singers," I countered. "They have a built-in audience, too."

"Yeah, but they don't have acting credentials," Tracy butted in.

"Nor did you, but you came out and blew *Led Astray* out of the water," I snapped at her. I was getting fed up with all the talk about the actors and actresses making the movie. What about the story making unknown actors and actresses into stars? Doesn't anyone believe in the power of the story anymore?

I said, "Nick Cannon was an unknown from television, but look what *Drumline* did for him? So I know it can be done."

Tracy gave me a look, and I realized I was in there doing exactly what I told myself not to do, causing a public ruckus over the *Flyy Girl* project. There were a few people there who began to eye us curiously. So I went ahead and apologized.

"I'm sorry. I didn't mean to get all worked up about it. I guess I just need to stop thinking about it."

"But why would you do that?" Susan asked me. "You're supposed to work toward the ideas that you want to happen, Vanessa. That's one of the first rules of making a project work, figuring out exactly *how* to make it work."

"Yeah, well, she's been driving me crazy about it," Tracy stated. "*Flyy Girl* this, *Flyy Girl* that," she mocked me.

Susan grinned and finished off her glass of wine.

"Sounds like something we need to sink our teeth into," she mumbled over the rim of her glass. "But let's talk about this a little later."

"I agree," Tracy added.

I nodded. "Okay."

Then we all went back to mingling and chatting with Edward Weisner's crowd of family members, close friends, and Hollywood associates.

The Game Plan

Tracy was pissed at me on the drive back home.

"I don't believe you marched right up in there and did that."

I said, "I wasn't trying to, but you heard her asking me about it and digging for it."

"Well, you should have just been polite and declined to talk about it."

"Why? Are you afraid of doing this movie or something?"

I just wasn't getting her angle.

Tracy shook her head and looked away from me. I didn't sweat her though. I needed to get back to class at UCLA anyway, and it was right up there in Hollywood. I had all of my school things with me already.

She said, "Now you're gonna have me do all this work . . ."

It sounded as if I was finally breaking her down.

But by then I was getting tired of the conversation myself.

I said, "If you really don't want to do it, then there's nothing I can do about it. I'm just trying to get you to see the bigger picture. It may be a lot of hard work for *all* of us, because I'll definitely be included in that. But in the long run, I know we'll have a movie that will be watched forever, and even redone a couple of times.

"As you already know, they're redoing a lot of classic movies and television shows now," I commented.

Tracy smirked and continued to drive.

She mumbled, "What the hell have I gotten myself into with you?"

I didn't say a word. There was no need to. Slowly but surely, I was getting Tracy to see the picture . . . and on the big screen.

* * *

After Jason had stopped chasing the women of California and returned to school at Temple, I ended up making fast friends with Sasha Kim and Jasmine Flores. It was a coincidence that Sasha liked Jason and ended up meeting me. She never got too serious about Jason—she was only trying him out as a friend first. But once she realized that my excitable cousin was only out to score and break camp back East, she and Jasmine decided to stay in touch with Tracy and me. Of course, Tracy had less time for them than I had. They were all closer to my age anyway. I then included a couple of other girls who filled out our model/actress/go-girl clique. So I had plenty of pals to run my ideas past.

They all stopped by the house that week, and we all got to talking about ideas for an urban girl's club, fashion line, and social activities group. We had soda, chips, pretzels, juice, cake, and the television set on MTV inside the living room.

"So, what do we do, create, like, memberships, like the Girl Scouts or something?"

That was my friend Tonya. She graduated from high school with me at Dominguez. Then she attended USC, which was closer to the 'hood of South Central L.A., Inglewood, Compton, Carson, and Long Beach. Tonya was taller than all of us, medium brown, short-cut hair, played all kinds of sports, and she loved to talk before she thought. So we all laughed at her Girl Scout comment.

Jasmine said, "Oh my God, don't compare us to the fuckin' Girl Scouts. That's kid shit."

"Wait a minute, I was a Girl Scout for a year," Sasha told us.

"And were you a kid?" Jasmine asked her.

"Of course I was."

"Well, okay then. And I see you never told me that."

"It never came up."

I broke up the tangent chatter and redirected our conversation.

"Anyway, I think the best thing for us to do is to start a website at UrbanMiss.com, give out email addresses, and open up chat lines. That would be the fastest and easiest way for us to attract members and grow."

"Oh, and I could get my brother to set up the website. That's all that boy's into now."

That was Petula. She went to UCLA and studied media relations with me. She was dark brown, with braided hair, and from Nigeria. She had a very large and educated family.

"Yeah, and then we'd have a bunch of computer geeks all calling themselves whatever," Madison Davenport commented. We called her "Maddy" for short, and the name fit, because she always seemed to be mad about something.

Maddy was the roughneck of the crew, medium brown, curved in all the right places like a video girl, and was always doubting whatever we tried to do. She had a job at a Virgin Records store in Torrance, and she was always up-to-date on the new music.

"Yeah, if we just did the website thing, then how would we get to choose who we want to join?" Alexandria asked us.

She was one of Sasha's friends, as light as me, with long brown hair and hazel eyes that changed to different colors. She was the most exotic-looking of the bunch and she usually got the most attention from guys. Alexandria was also the most exclusive. Everybody had to pass her cool points test to get in with her.

Sasha said, "Well, we still have to give them the email addresses. It's not like they can just create them on their own."

"But why are we calling ourselves Urban Miss anyway? I mean, what's up with the Flyy Girls?" Jasmine asked the group.

"Yeah?" Tonya agreed.

Then they all looked at me.

I shook my head and turned the idea down.

I said, "I already tried talking to my cousin about that. I talk to her about it all the time. But she's just not feeling it yet. I guess she's trying to build up more Hollywood muscle before she goes all out with it or something."

I had talked about the *Flyy Girl* film situation with my friends before. And none of them understood it. *Flyy Girl* was a surefire hit to every one of us.

Sasha said, "Well, if we make a big deal out of it and build the hype on the street level, it should make more Hollywood types take notice. Don't you think?"

Maddy said, "If they can have some damn *Cheetah Girls* then I know we can have a *Flyy Girl*."

"I know," Jasmine agreed.

Petula said, "I like the *Cheetah Girls*. We needed something like that."

"We need *Flyy Girl*, too," Maddy insisted. "I mean, you ever notice how they always wanna do that safe-and-sound shit but never the real?"

"Because safe and sound sells more," Sasha stated. "PG always outsells R."

I spoke up on that myself. "No, it doesn't. Especially not in our community. If you look at the majority of the classic black films, or even Asian and Latino films for that matter, the majority of them are dramas that really meant something to the people, and that's why we still watch them. Like, *Cooley High* has always been a classic to watch in Philadelphia. And now we have Spike Lee movies, John Singleton movies, the Hughes Brothers. And they were all dealing with mature content.

"So that PG shit doesn't work for us," I told them.

"But it works for Hollywood. And they don't care about any classics. They care about making their money right now," Alexandria argued.

"Well, that's why we can't make *Flyy Girl* then. We have conflicting interests," I responded. Our argument about the movie went back and forth.

"But you don't think *Flyy Girl* would make any money. I think it would," Petula spoke out. "Because American girls are very materialistic, and they like looking back in time at other fashion statements. I mean, *Flyy Girl* is all about the eighties, right?"

"I thought we were supposed to be talking about starting an urban girl's club," Tonya asked us. "How did we all of a sudden start talking about *Flyy Girl* again?"

Jasmine said, "Because I think Flyy Girls is a better name for us than some Urban Miss. I mean, what if they're not even from an urban area? It just alienates people. But anybody can be a flyy girl. You can be a flyy girl and live on a farm."

Maddy said, "No, you can't. You can be a damn *cowgirl* if you live on a farm, but not a flyy girl."

Alexandria agreed with her. She said, "I know. You just make it seem like any girl can be flyy."

Jasmine said, "Being flyy is just a state of mind to me."

I told her, "My cousin Tracy said that, in her day, you had to be flyy in attitude, your clothes, your man, everything. You just didn't throw that word around on anybody, you really had to *be* flyy."

"That's what I'm talking about," Alexandria agreed. "And you tell your cousin that if she need me for the movie, I'm right here."

Jasmine said, "Here we go. Just because you have rainbows for eyes does not mean that you fit the part. Because you're way more stuck up than she is."

Alexandria looked appalled by it. She said, "Stuck up? Why, because I don't get all excited about everything like you do?"

"I don't get excited about everything."

"You don't? Oh, you could have fooled me. 'There's Tyrese! There's Tyrese!'" Alexandria mocked her from a past visit to the Beverly Hills Galleria where we spotted the singer/actor shopping with his boys.

Jasmine smiled and said, "Well, I happen to like Tyrese."

Petula said, "I have a younger brother who looks just like him. But he's too young for you. Onan is only sixteen."

"She'll take him, as long as he's jet black," Maddy joked. "She loves herself a dark-skinned black man."

"Shut up!" Jasmine told her.

"So, how are we gonna do this, Vanessa?" Tonya asked me again, concerning the membership.

We were getting way off the subject.

I said, "Again, I think setting up a website is the best way. And we can post all of our ideas, discussions, and events, and have all of our members respond to them."

All of a sudden, Tonya shouted, "Wait a minute, wait a minute, they're about to show Fifty Cents' crib!"

Maddy said, "You like him? He is not cute."

"His money is though," Tonya responded with a laugh.

"Yeah, and he just got that yesterday," Maddy told her.

Tracy walked in the door on us in the heat of everything.

"Hi everybody," she said in passing. She headed straight past us and right up to her room.

My friends were all in silent shock.

"Should we ask her about using the name?" Sasha asked us all.

"I'll ask her," Jasmine dared.

I said, "No, if anything, I'll be the one to ask her."

"Well, ask her then," Maddy instigated.

"Not right now," I told them. "I mean, you can tell that she's busy right now."

Sure enough, Tracy headed back down the stairs with a bag of her things and headed straight for the front door.

"Be good, Vanessa. Bye everybody," she told us on her way back out.

Maddy said, "I bet she has a hot date out there waiting for her. You can see his headlights still on."

We all chuckled at it.

Tonya said, "A girl's gotta do what a girl's gotta do."

Jasmine said, "Well, she's not a girl anymore. She a real woman now."

Petula smiled. She said, "We are all girls at heart, we just have to make women's decisions when we get older. But even an old woman can be a girl. My grandmother in Nigeria taught me that. She said a girl's heart keeps a woman young, and so does a boy's heart in an old man."

It all made sense to us, so no one argued about it. Because we were all girls at heart.

As much as I hated to admit it, I was growing out of my eagerness to continue sweating my cousin about turning her book into a breakout film. It was really wearing me out, and like she said, I had my own life aspirations to figure out. I couldn't live my life through her. So I was not pressed about asking her if we could use FlyyGirls.com for our new website name and membership emails. It looked like another long, uphill battle. I still liked my own idea of UrbanMiss.com anyway. However, I did recognize that an already popular name would maximize our efforts to attract members. But Tracy just wasn't ready to go there.

I considered her procrastination a waste. I mean, you get all that power and name recognition and then you sit there and do nothing with it just because someone else says it won't work. I couldn't believe that. My cousin had me losing respect for her. We all looked up to the flyy girl who would just get up and go for it, not the one who wouldn't even try. We knew plenty of people who wouldn't try. What good was that? So I was steadily thinking about finding ways to make things happen for myself.

I was in my room just about ready for bed after reading another chapter of *The 48 Laws of Power,* when Tracy walked in on me.

"Okay, you got me," she said out of the blue.

I was confused. "I got you?"

I didn't have any idea what she was talking about.

She said, "I'm gonna start writing a screenplay for *Flyy Girl,* and you're gonna help me to set everything up for a casting call. You've been asking me for this workload, Vanessa, so don't start whining when I give it to you."

I sat up in bed and got excited. I said, "Oh, bring it on then."

"That's exactly what I'm about to do," she told me.

I said, "So what made you change your mind all of a sudden?"

"It wasn't all of a sudden. I've been thinking about it," she told me. She grinned and said, "Probably not as much as you have, but I have been thinking. And it's only a matter of time before I have to start putting this thing together anyway. It's either now or later. It's not gonna go away. And since I haven't decided on my next project with the studios, I figure I may as well get my own fire burning again."

I asked her, "So the production companies are totally against *Flyy Girl* as your next movie?"

Tracy said, "After *Jump-start,* they are not feeling the black woman's issues right now."

I said, "But that's a totally different kind of movie from *Flyy Girl.*"

"Nevertheless, it was a multiple black women vehicle that didn't work."

I went hard on my cousin and said, "Well, who asked for that movie? I mean, I felt like you did it to connect to me, but no one really wants to hear a sob story about a relative taking in a sibling unless it has some major drama in it. The sibling would have to be in some type of big trouble or create big trouble."

To my surprise, Tracy began to laugh at my frank comments.

She said, "Yeah, like you're creating trouble for me right now. But you know what, Vanessa, I think I needed you. After these last two films bombed, it took a lot out of me. Now I'm turning back into the public school teacher who complains about people not getting how hard I work."

"They don't care," I told her. "That's just the way people are. They want what they want and that's it."

Tracy took a look at the book I was reading. She asked me, "What are you doing with that?"

It was her book.

I smiled and said, "I was reading it."

"How far did you get in it?" she asked me.

"Well, I wasn't reading it straight through. I was kind of jumping around to the different chapters that I was interested in."

"What are your favorite chapters so far?"

"Umm . . ." I had to remember them. I said, "Well, I just got finished reading Law Twenty-nine, to plan all the way to the end. That was pretty good. And the one before that one, to move with boldness, was good, too."

My cousin continued to smile at me. She said, "A lot of those laws are dealing with natural personality traits. I've always been bold. But are you trying to be a leader by reading that, or are you just reading to be reading?"

I smiled back at her. I said, "Actually, I'm already like a leader." I decided to keep it at that. Tracy would tell me what she thought about it anyway. So I waited for her to do so.

She nodded and said, "Law number one, never outshine the master, or you'll find yourself out on your ass. Anyway, I have a lot of things I want to go over with you," she told me.

She said, "I know this girl Charmaine Dearborn who asked me about starting an urban girl's fashion line a while ago, and at the time I just wasn't thinking about it. I was too busy making movies.

"Well, I'm gonna put you in contact with her to start coming up with ideas for Flyy Girl minitees and ponytail hats," she said. "I want bright, summer colors like orange, lime green, hot pink, sky blue, and a rust color. I don't want any yellows. Yellow is weak, so we'll use rust instead. And you and your girls will be the first ones to wear them."

As my cousin continued to talk, I felt like I needed a pen or something to jot it all down.

I said, "Wait a minute. Let me get something to write this down with."

Tracy told me, "You'll write it down later. I just wanna get some of these ideas out while I'm thinking about them."

I was conflicted. I still wanted to write them down, for both of us. But at the same time, Tracy was on a roll and I didn't want to break her flow.

I said "Okay" and planned to use my memory instead.

She stood inside the room at the foot of the bed and told me, "I'm gonna get my lawyers to copyright Flyy Girl Ltd., and we'll design the logo off of my *For the Love of Money* book jacket pose, where I'm all glammed out and holding the purse at my side."

I stopped her and asked, "You want an image as a logo instead of just the words. That's old school. Nobody does that anymore."

My cousin told me, "Exactly. I am old school. I'm from the eighties, and I'm about to bring it back. Now, you have to understand that if we do this movie right, then we'll have to talk to Jordache, Sergio Valente, Gloria Vanderbilt, Coca-Cola, Gucci, Lee Jeans, Laura Biagotti, Members Only, Izod, Le Tigre, Aigner, Guess. And if you think for one minute that I'll have any of these old designers in my movie without having my Flyy Girl Ltd. out first, with a logo that young girls *and* old can lock in their minds on *sight*, then you gots to be crazy."

She said, "I don't even need words in Japan, just my logo. I don't need words in Germany, just my logo. I don't need words in Brazil, just my logo. And then when I show up, looking flyy as usual, they know it's me without any spelling or language barriers."

I started smiling. My cousin was just running off at the mouth. It was like she was back from the grave, man. The dark cloud had passed her by.

She said, "So what we do is this: I finish writing this screenplay, and instead of us calling up Hollywood actresses, who may or may not have the drawing power to pull this movie off at the box office, hell, we roll up our sleeves and go on the road to find our own flyy girls for a multitude of purposes; extras, co-stars, models, assistants, you name it.

"And we can take it from city to city, starting with Philadelphia," she told me.

I said, "That's how J. Lo got her start, while casting for the role of the Mexican singer Selena."

"That's also how your favorite film icon, Spike Lee, discovered a lot of people," Tracy told me.

"He's not my favorite," I told her. "I just talk about him a lot because he deserves respect for starting it all."

"Actually, Melvin Van Peebles started independent black films fifteen years before Spike Lee."

"Yeah, and it was someone else doing black films fifteen years before him," I argued with a grin. I was sure happy to see Tracy back, though. She hadn't been her spunky self in my opinion for *months*.

She said, "Anyway, getting back to what I was saying. I can hire cameramen and photographers and start up the clothing line with a hot buzz and limited sales in the cities where we host the flyy girl casting calls. That'll help me to break even with our travel and setup expenses while we build the hype. And by the time we're done, any production company that would not take advantage of the momentum we build would be insane."

I sat there and had to remember all of that with no pen. But it was going to be easy. It was a simple game plan. Still, knowing my cousin and the way the world worked, I assumed her simple plan would change twenty times before everything was all said and done.

Tracy said, "So I'll talk to you again sometime tomorrow afternoon when you get back from school, and we'll jot everything on paper then, after I've called my lawyers and let them know everything I'm planning."

Then she walked out the door and left me dumbfounded and gleeful. I immediately jumped up and grabbed my pen and a notepad to start writing down everything I could remember. I knew one thing was for sure, I would be up all night working on ideas of my own to add to hers. And with my cousin knowing me, I could imagine that she already knew that.

Like Lightning

T racy told me the truth. I had been asking her for the workload, and she was finally giving it to me. But I didn't mind it at all. It was exciting. We were finally starting the Flyy Girl franchise, something my cousin should have thought of doing years ago.

"Have you received any baby-tee sample designs from Charmaine yet?" she asked me, weeks after we had revved up the process and served notice to everyone involved. I had plenty of notes and a cordless telephone on the dining room table, which served as a makeshift office while Tracy looked into renting office space in L.A. She wasn't sure if she wanted to rent a high-end office or just keep it simple, with offices in L.A., Philly, and New York. She was really thinking a mile a minute now.

Tonya, Jasmine, and Petula were all at the dining room table with me, sorting out our lists of things to do. My friends were all fully involved in the process. I had made sure of it. Besides, we were all jumping at the opportunity to be the first girls to model Flyy Girl Ltd.

Tonya answered Tracy's question before I could.

"She said she should have something to us by the end of the week."

"And what about contacting Freedom Theater in Philly about holding our first auditions there in June?"

Jasmine spoke up on that one.

"They haven't called us back yet. I left them three messages already."

"Did you tell them that we're paying them for it?"

Jasmine looked confused.

"Was I supposed to?"

"No, but that would have made them call you right back," Tracy joked.

We all laughed at it.

"Money talks," Petula added.

"How far along are you on the screenplay?" I asked my cousin. "Can we read some of it yet?"

Tracy said, "Even when I'm finished with it, I won't let you read it. I have to do at least three rewrites before I'll be satisfied. But we will have at least the first two drafts by the time we head to Philly in June. Once we finish the first couple of casting calls, I'll assess what's working and what's not, and I'll do another rewrite."

Jasmine asked her, "Is that your normal process?"

"Well, I try to do as many rewrites that are needed to get the job done. But no process is mistake-proof," my cousin answered. She said, "Sometimes you can even overwrite by trying to analyze too much. And for book adaptations, you're always trying to streamline material. But I won't have a problem with the screenplay for *Flyy Girl* because I know just where to start."

"Where is that?" Tonya asked her.

Tracy smiled at her. "You'll see once the casting calls begin."

It was late afternoon, and more of my girls were on their way over. They were all getting used to Tracy as our boss lady, so to speak. She was calling the shots, and we were all her loyal servants.

"Vanessa, I have a meeting with Susan, then I want to check out a few more office spaces, so you hold down the fort until I get back," she told me. In the next second, she was out the door again.

"So, how does it feel?" Petula asked me as soon as my cousin had left us.

"How does what feel?"

"You know, being related to her?"

I thought about it and began to smile. I said, "It's like, you're proud on one hand, but then on the other hand, you're always thinking about how you fit in. You know?"

Jasmine shook her head and said, "Yeah, you're on some competition thing, Vanessa. Just be happy for your cousin and do what you need to do for her vision. I mean, I can be a team player. I can do that."

"Nobody said anything about that, Jasmine," I argued.

"Yeah, but I can hear it in you. That's what you're really saying.

'Where am I on her level?'" Jasmine said to me. "I guess that's just the Philadelphian in you. People from the East Coast are always like that."

"You don't think about that?" Tonya asked her. "I know I do. It's just natural."

"Aw, that's because you're into sports, Tonya. You don't count," Jasmine told her.

"I'm competitive with my brothers and sisters," Petula said. "But Tracy Ellison Grant is on a whole other level."

"Yeah, but she has doubts and confidence lapses like the rest of us," I told them. "It took me nearly a year of bugging her just to get her to this point."

"That's true," Tonya agreed.

"So what? She still has the name to do it. Everybody deserves a break every now and then," Jasmine stated.

I wanted to get her point so we could move on. It sounded like a meaningless argument to me. We were all helping out with the process of hyping the Flyy Girl brand, film, and clothing line, re-gardless of how we felt individually, and that was that.

So I asked Jasmine, "What's your point? You think I ride my cousin too much? I'm just trying to get her to use what she's got to move forward, and now she's finally doing it."

"Yeah, and you're making sure that we all know that *you* deserve the credit for it, too."

"Well, it's her cousin," Tonya stated. "None of us live with Tracy like Vanessa does. She has to think about it every day. She has no choice."

"She really doesn't," Petula agreed.

Jasmine finally gave up on her petty argument.

I said, "Well, at least I'm not just sitting here sponging off my cousin, which a lot of people in my position would do. I'm sitting here spending my extra time trying to help her."

"We all are," Tonya reminded me. "And none of us are getting paid for it."

There was a minute of silence after Tonya's comment regarding money. Then Jasmine smiled.

"Yet," she told us.

Petula grunted, "Unh hunh, we see where your mind is, Jasmine. That's a shame."

"Naw, man, I don't even think like that, I'm just saying."

"Oh, we'll be paid eventually, in some form or another," I promised them. "You never know what this kind of exposure can do for your career. And we all look good in our own ways. So all we have to do is work it."

As soon as I finished my statement, the phone rang.

"Hello," I answered.

"Yes, this is Freedom Theater in Philadelphia calling back in reference to using the stage for a casting call for a film."

"Yes," I answered. "It's for the Philadelphia-based novel *Flyy Girl.*"

"Oh, yes, that book is very popular with a lot of our young performers," I was told.

"Yeah, well now we're finally writing a screenplay for it."

"Okay, that's good. So for what days would you be needing the stage, and for how long each day?"

"Wait one second, let me gather my notes," I told her.

Things were moving like lightning, they really were. We had Freedom Theater set up for our opening casting call in Philadelphia. Tracy was nearly finished with the first draft of her script. Susan was starting to get the buzz going with P.R. contacts. Yolanda Felix was locking down all the legal work. And Tracy had rented office space in Inglewood all by mid-May.

We had office space in a two-story building that was low key, but also allowed us a chance to mingle with the people in the community. We had our first samples of the colorful FLYY GIRL baby-tee shirts, with my cousin's logo pose from her sequel book going down the sides, and a one-liner that read Flyy Girl across the left breast. And boy did they work! We could barely walk in and out of the building without people stopping to ask us about the shirts and our matching ponytail hats. They couldn't even get them yet. They were only rough samples.

Tracy didn't even like the shirts at first. She said, "You can't even see the logo unless you're standing sideways. And then your arms are in the way."

I kind of agreed with her on that. We needed a logo that people could see immediately. Otherwise, what was the point? But Charmaine had a different view.

She said, "I consider a flyy girl one who moves and gets things done. So I wanted to design a sample that highlighted movement. And unless you walk with your arms stuck at your sides, people will eventually see the logo. But since it's not in your face, it makes them more curious to know exactly what it is. You want to get people curious enough to ask about it, want to touch it, and see it up close, especially with a sample.

"Good design also saves you from wasting all kinds of money to market your line," she said. "The best marketing for your new line is the human body. But if you do what everyone else does, then why should anyone buy your line over an already established one, outside of the fact that you're new? So I want to always think outside the box on how we can make a line work off the thought and creativity that went into the design itself, before we put any marketing money into it."

Once she explained her philosophy, her ideas made all the sense in the world. Charmaine Dearborn was a very controlled woman, too. I saw immediately that there was a lot we could all learn from her. She was a full-sized, deep-brown sister who kept her temper intact and explained everything that she did with poise. So whenever anyone got too excited around her, they made themselves look irrational.

My cousin's emotion-filled energy had little or no effect on Charmaine, which made her the perfect check and balance for business. It also allowed Tracy an opportunity to relax around her, because she realized that the sister knew what she was doing. And before we all knew it, we had a box of sample shirts and hats ready for our kickoff casting call in Philadelphia in June.

The Quiet
Before the Storm

We were two days out from our trip to Philly in June. I had been home over the Christmas break in 2002, and my mother was still peeved at me about everything that had gone on between us years ago. However, she understood that I was a college student now and was out of her house. I was doing quite well, too, so she left me alone. But now she had to deal with my two younger sisters on her own, which was a lot more hectic than when she had to deal with me, or when she still had me around the house to deal with my sisters for her. So I gave my mother and sisters a long-distance phone call from the living room sofa, just to touch base with them and to test their temperatures before I arrived back home.

I dialed the numbers to our North Philadelphia house and waited for an answer. It was after seven o'clock West Coast time, so I knew everyone would be home after ten in Philly.

"Hello," my mother answered. It startled me. I guess I expected to hear Veronica or Tiffany answer the phone. They were both teenagers now—seventeen and fourteen.

"Hi, Mom," I answered back. I never knew what to expect from my mother, so I waited again.

She screamed, "Vanessa! Thank God you called, girl! Now talk some sense into your sister. I caught her dating a much too older man. The boy's nearly thirty years old."

"Twenty-seven," I heard Veronica state in the background.

"Like I said, he's damn near *thirty*," my mother argued. "And that's way too old for you."

Things were changing fast. My mother never allowed me to talk back to her like that without smacking me upside the head afterward. She was slipping. Was I the cause of that, or was it only a matter of time? But my sisters were a lot more hardheaded than I ever was.

My mother wasted no time in giving Veronica the phone to talk to me. They had me on the spot. I wasn't expecting that at all.

"Hi," my sister answered dryly.

I had been around my cousin Tracy long enough to know exactly how to handle the situation. So I used a little reverse psychology and went straight for the jugular with my sister.

I said, "I know Mom is right there breathing down your neck, so I'm gonna do everything in code language, where all you need to do is answer the questions. Okay?"

My sister grunted, "Hmmph. All right." She had no other choice.

I asked her, "Do you like this guy?"

"Yeah."

"Does he like you?"

"Of course."

Veronica had much more body than I had. For guys who were into young girls with the junk in the trunk, she was a prime catch.

"Does he have other women?" I asked her.

She paused on that one.

"No."

"Is that what he told you?"

"No, he don't have to tell me."

"Oh, you just know that for a fact, hunh? So is he ugly?"

"Unt unh, I'on even go out like that."

"So he looks good?"

"*I* think so."

"And no one else does?"

She paused again.

"They know what time it is."

"And he uses protection every time?"

There was another slight delay.

"I'm saying, what are you trying to ask me?"

"I'm asking you if he uses protection."

"No, that's not really what you wanna know. You try'na be smart, Vanessa, but I ain't no dummy."

"Who are you talking to like that?" my mother yelled at her. "That's your older sister on the phone."

Veronica said, "Yeah, and she still thinks she's smarter than everybody. I can see what she try'na do. I don't care if she went to some Engineering and Science and UCLA. I ain't no damn dummy. Gon' ask me if he uses protection."

"What?" my mother asked her.

"That's what she asked me," Veronica explained.

My mother said, "Give me that damn phone. Vanessa, what did you ask her?"

I said real calmly, "Mom, she's getting us off the subject. You shouldn't be thinking about what I asked her, but what the answer is. So yes, I did ask her about protection, because I want to cut to the chase and see how serious she's already gotten with this guy. Now, if she hasn't gotten that serious with him, then she would have answered that she's not into that."

My mother paused. I could immediately see her dilemma. If she agreed with me, then she was admitting that I could handle the situation better than she could. Nevertheless, she had given me the phone to talk to Veronica because she knew I *could* handle it. She couldn't back out now and let my sister create a smoke screen. That would put my mother in another bad situation. Veronica was nowhere near as angelic as I had been.

My mother finally said, "Well, answer the question, Veronica. Does he use protection or not?"

"Mom, I don't believe you're taking her side on this."

"This is not about taking damn sides, girl. Just answer the damn question. Yes or no."

"Well, what if we're not doing anything? Have you thought of that?" Veronica asked.

I said, "Mom, does he have a car?"

"Yeah, that's where I caught her, climbing out the car with him," she told me. "She tried to be slick by climbing out the car around the corner, but she didn't see me walking out the corner store."

"And they haven't done anything in the car?" I asked her.

My mother relayed my question to Veronica.

"You didn't do anything in that car with this man?"

"Is that what Vanessa told you to ask me?" I heard my sister ask. She was working a reverse psychology game of her own. I had to give it to her.

My mother said, "You got one more time to say some smart shit to me before I ram your head through that damn wall. You hear me?"

I didn't hear my sister respond to that, so I guess she did hear.

"Can I talk to her again, Mom?" I asked.

"Yeah. Here, Veronica," I heard my mother say.

"What she want?" my sister responded.

"Girl, if you don't get on this damn phone . . ."

"Yeah," Veronica answered with snap. "Ow!" she yelled into my ear. "I'm talking to her, Mom."

"Well, I don't like your attitude. Now straighten it up," my mother told her.

I didn't want to waste any more time with my concerns, so I moved to wrap things up.

I said, "I apologize to you, Veronica. And you're right, you're no dummy. But I'm just trying to get you to ask yourself more questions about the relationship you're in and why you feel you need to be there."

"Why do you feel you need to be where you are?" she asked me.

I asked her, "You don't want me here?"

"You can be wherever you need to be. I don't have any control over your life."

"I didn't ask you that."

"Well, I'm telling you."

I said, "Are you acting like this toward me because Mom put me on the phone like she did, or are you mad at me for some other reason?"

She gave me no immediate response. I began to wonder how much my sisters regretted me leaving the way I did. We never really talked about it. They just asked me general questions about moving to California and about the weather and everything. But we never got into any deep conversations about me leaving. I just figured they both understood my mental abuse. But maybe they didn't, and maybe I didn't understand theirs.

Finally, my sister said, "Look, you got your life, and I got mine. That's all there is to it."

"But you're still my sister," I told her. "I still care about you. And you should still care about me."

No response again.

"You done talking?" she asked me

What else could I say? A lot of things actually, but I didn't feel like it. I would rather do it face-to-face. So I decided to wait until I arrived back in Philly to talk to my sister again.

"Do you mind if I take you out to eat somewhere when I get back home?" I asked her.

If she said no to that, then I would be convinced that something was definitely wrong with her, because my sister loved to eat.

I said, "We can go to that Jamaican restaurant you like on South Street again."

She said, "Aw'ight. Whatever."

"Whatever? Do you want to go or not?" I reiterated.

"I said, yes," she told me.

It wasn't the truth, but I would settle for it. I guess I had a lot of catching up to do with my sister. She was seventeen and not a kid any-more. We needed to have more mature conversations, and that's how I planned to regard her from then on, as mature.

My mother got back on the line and said, "We've been hearing all over the radio about this casting call thing for *Flyy Girl*. I wouldn't be surprised if a thousand kids showed up down there.

"So when do you fly in?" my mother asked me.

I guess my mother was finally loosening up, right as my sister was becoming sour to me.

I said, "In two days?"

"Where are you staying?"

"At the Marriott downtown."

"The new one on Market Street?"

"Yeah."

"Oh, that's nice. Tracy's paying for it?"

It was a rhetorical question. My mother surely knew that I wouldn't be paying to stay at the Marriott for a week.

I answered the question anyway.

"Yeah, but I'll still come up to the house."

"I know you will. Look, you wanna talk to Tiffany before you go?"

I really didn't. Veronica had already killed my energy for the night. But I had to talk to my baby sister. It wouldn't have been right not to. Then I would have another sister upset with me.

"Yeah, I'll talk to her."

My mom screamed, *"Tiffany!* Vanessa's on the phone for you!"

I had to wait for Tiffany to receive the phone, which drained more energy out of me.

"Hey Vanessa," she answered. At least she was upbeat. She said, "Tell Tracy I want to be an extra in her movie."

I smiled and said, "Join the crowd. We all want to be extras."

Talking to my family back home in Philly really made me think about how far I had come in life, and how easily I could be back in North Philly, ripe for pregnancy by some penis-minded, wannabe street hustler, pimp, or thug. Of course, there were a lot more honest men to date and life paths to take, but after talking to Veronica, she reminded me of just how simple it was for a girl to lose her way while looking for love in the wrong places at the wrong times. You gotta have your own drive in life. That's just all there is to it. Nobody can make things happen for you. You have to make things happen for yourself.

"What are you thinking about now?" my cousin Tracy asked me.

"Whoa, you scared me," I told her.

She startled me. I didn't hear her walk up to the sofa from behind me.

"Yeah, because you're down here daydreaming. Who were you talking to on the phone, your mother and sisters?"

I nodded. "Veronica got herself an older guy and, of course, my mom is all over her about it. She had me talk to her."

Tracy looked at me and chuckled. Then she took a seat next to me on the sofa.

"So, she had you talk to Veronica about guys? Hell, that's like me talking to a high school about wrestling. I know nothing about it."

I smiled. "Well, I do know something about boys," I told her.

"Well, what did you tell Veronica? Let me hear it so I can tell you what will happen and how to prepare for it."

"I mean, I just asked her a few questions and told her to think about why she's really involved with this guy."

"Did she snap at you?"

I smiled even wider. "Of course she did. But I got past that. We're gonna have a sit-down over Jamaican food on South Street when I get back home to see her."

Tracy nodded again. "That's good, that's good," she repeated.

Then I began to study her. She had something on her mind. She was only waiting for the right angle to break it to me. I knew my cousin good by then.

"What are you thinking about?" I asked her back.

She sighed deeply and said, "We're about to do it. We're about to get started with producing this *Flyy Girl* movie, and already my little friend is starting to act up."

I looked into her face and asked her, "He doesn't want you to do it? I mean, he knows you have a career in films, right. What about when you're shooting your other movies?"

Tracy nodded. She said, "He knows that I'm on set for months at a time. I thought he was cool with it. Now he's starting to say things like, 'I don't know if I can keep him in storage for one woman that long.' Ain't that some shit? Makes me not want to deal with him. I don't know what ovens he's gonna try and bake himself in."

I grinned. She had a nice way of putting it. Then I thought about my part in her troubles. Was my obsession with the *Flyy Girl* project breaking her up with her man?

I said, "I'm sorry. I didn't know that was gonna happen. I didn't even think about it."

Tracy blew me off. "Girl, you have nothing to do with that. I'm always gonna be doing something. So any man who can't handle that can't handle me. I'm not the housewife type—*yet.*"

I smiled, and didn't want to continue on the subject. What was the use? Guys will be guys, and when a girl has plans of her own that don't involve them, they can either support their woman in what she wants to do, or act like spoiled little boys. And there was nothing I or Tracy could do to change that.

I asked her, "How far are you on writing the screenplay?"

I wanted to stay excited about things. It's so easy to lose your excitement because of complications. I didn't want that to happen.

But Tracy stopped all of my excitement when she asked me, "You think all of this is easy, don't you?"

I didn't know what to say. She caught me off guard with that. She was dead serious, too.

I answered, "No . . . but it can be done."

"Obviously it can be done, but you have no idea what the process is like, even with a small film," she told me. "I mean, I literally got lucky with *Led Astray*, Vanessa. It was a luck-of-the-draw movie. But after my last two films flopped, now I know, it's not an easy thing to be here."

I said, "You just have to make sure you pick the right movies."

"It's not just picking the right movies, Vanessa. It's a lot more complicated than that. There's a whole lot of other work involved. You really have to work this machine. And that's what it is, a *machine*.

"Every day you have to put more fuel in it just for it to turn on, let alone to work well," she told me. "This is a real tedious lifestyle."

"But people get it done every day," I argued. I just couldn't see giving up the dream. I had traveled too far, and my cousin was already *in*. I had read and memorized her poem about it in her sequel book *For the Love of Money*. It was called "Prisoners of Fame." So I quoted it to her:

"I have a vault filled with gold / and thousands of Benjamins / that belong to my tribe. / And when I get horny at night / if I wanted a man / to even lick the crack of my ass / he would pay me to do it. / And I wake up every morning and step on / every little nobody / who wouldn't give me the time of day / yesterday / but now them same motherfuckers beg / to see me for tomorrow. / And I have never worn a damn / red-and-white Santa Claus suit / so why is every day Christmas? / Then I become the Grinch / who stole it / whenever I say no.

"Would you like to join my tribe? / It's fun! / But once you join us / and the vault door closes / you can't get back out / unless you fall out / and end up strung out / and begging / to get back in."

Tracy smiled hard at me, then joked, "Where did you get that from?"

I played along with her. "Oh, I don't know. I can't even remember. I guess I must have read it somewhere."

She said, "And did you ever read this one:

"The machine has no emotions / no face / no warm blood / no family / no friends / no loyalty / no memory / and no future.

"The machine only knows the now / this year / this month / this week / this day / this hour / this minute / this second / and counting.

"The machine is only programmed / to laugh / to smile / to lie / to market / promote / and sell / to consume / the hopes / of humanity.

"While the line of seduction / moves the humans / rapidly forward / into the mouth / of the machines / like next / next / next / next / next . . .

"Swallowed alive / and never to return / to their innocence."

I could only smile at my big cousin. I mean, what could I say? Tracy was Tracy. There was no replacing her. She was an original human, and I was impressed by her creative vision as usual. Her poetry was just so . . . so . . . *relative*. I mean, you just get it, and you ask no questions.

I said, "It reminds me of *The Matrix*."

"And the Matrix has been around for a million years. Even the Egyptians talked about sacrificing the individual soul for the dream of the masses," my cousin told me. "So how do we maintain our sanity in the midst of it all? Well, you're about to find out, little cousin."

She smiled at me real wide and repeated herself, "Yup, you're about to find out."

Philadelphia

We all arrived at Los Angeles International Airport on Saturday morning, June 14, 2003—me, Tracy, Sasha, Madison, Jasmine, and Alexandria—to fly to Philadelphia. Petula and Tonya were staying put in L.A., but they met us at the airport to say their good-byes and to help with our luggage. Petula was taking summer college courses and Tonya was still involved in summer sport activities, which kept them both from being able to spend weeks at a time on the road with us.

"You guys let us know how everything goes," Petula told us.

Jasmine said, "Oh, of course."

"You think her big mouth wouldn't?" Maddy joked about it.

"Whatever."

"IDs, girls," Tracy told us at the curbside luggage booth.

We all scrambled to pull out our IDs and hand them over to the skycap. He was an older black man with plenty of gray hair. He looked over our IDs, matched them up with our faces, and prepared our tickets. Then he smiled with straight, white teeth and said, "Philadelphia, hunh? Must be a model convention going on there or something. 'Cause every last one of you look fine."

"Well, thank you," Tracy told him. She gave him twenty dollars for handling our bags. I thought he looked a little too old to be grabbing luggage the way he did, but he was obviously stronger than I thought. He grabbed those bags and tossed them on the luggage belt like nobody's business.

He slid the twenty dollars into the wad of cash he'd taken from his dark blue uniform pants pocket and said, "Thank you. And you ladies have a good trip."

"Oh, we will," Jasmine told him.

That next second, some unknown white man on a motorbike stopped right in front of us and whipped a camera from his neck to snap about eight fast pictures of Tracy helping us with our airplane tickets. It happened so fast, it took all of us by surprise before we could respond to it.

After the man sped off, Alexandria frowned and said, "What was that about?"

"Paparazzi," Sasha explained.

Maddy grinned and shook her head. "Now you know you've made it big when that shit happens."

Jasmine said, "If you ask me, I think those people need to get a life."

Maddy looked at her and smirked.

She said, "Jasmine, you seem like the type to do that shit yourself, as crazy as you are about stars."

Tracy smiled it off and kept us moving. "Let's go, we're running late."

We hurried over to the security lines and started stripping down to the basics to pass through their carry-on belts and metal detectors. What can I say? I was excited about the entire experience. I was taking notes on everything.

We moved through the airport in a hurry and made it to our gate as travelers continued to notice my cousin.

"Isn't that Tracy Ellison Grant?" someone asked.

Tracy heard them like we all did. She turned to smile and wave to them, but she had no time to stop for any autographs.

As we moved through the gate, down the bridge, and toward our waiting flight, Tracy told me, "I have to get my attitude right before talking to a lot of people."

She said, "I don't have to do that as much in L.A. But in Philly . . ." She shook her head and didn't even have to say it. I was from Philly. I already knew.

Philadelphians forced you to speak to them. Either that or be called out and talked about in nonappreciative ways. Tracy couldn't afford any negativity while trying to produce a Philadelphia story that had become legendary in less than ten years. She knew what she was up against before we arrived anywhere near Philly.

We moved through the jam-packed airplane and took our seats on the left side, right below the exit rows in the middle. Tracy had a left window seat next to my aisle seat.

I looked at her and was confused. I could understand me and my girls flying coach, but I expected Tracy to fly first class. We all expected that.

I said, "You didn't get a first-class seat for you?"

She grinned at me. "I have my reasons." That's all she had to say about it. So I sat down beside her and didn't sweat it.

"Excuse me, aren't you an actress?" a white-haired older woman asked my cousin from the seats in front of us. She popped her head up just enough to peek over the headrest.

Tracy smiled and answered, "Not today I'm not. Today I'm just another traveler."

The woman smiled and nodded. She said, "Oh. Okay. But you are an actress when you're working."

"Yes," Tracy told her. "I am."

I had gotten used to people responding to my cousin by then, and I was always impressed with how she handled herself, even when she ignored them or got upset with certain people. After you've been around a person long enough to really feel them out, you know how they're going to react sometimes before they do.

My girls continued to talk about each other all the way up until the flight hit the runway.

"You just keep bragging about how you handle everything like a pro. But we'll see how you handle yourself once we get to Philly," Sasha was saying to Alexandria. "We'll see."

"I don't know what you expect to happen. I am always in control of my game," Alexandria stated.

Tracy overheard her and began to smile. I wondered what my cousin thought about Alexandria. She was definitely the closest to Tracy in looks. Yet Tracy never really responded much to her.

"You think they bicker too much?" I asked her about my friends.

Tracy shook her head. "I think it's cute," she told me. "I'd rather hear them doing that than being all friendly with each other. Bickering is real. And it keeps my writing skills sharp."

I thought about that for a minute.

I said, "But don't you think we do a little too much of that in our movies?"

I was using the term *we* in reference to black women. It seemed that we were always running off at the mouth in our films.

My cousin surprised me when she answered, "Yes, and that's why I always have to remind myself to keep the nonsense to a minimum. So in a sense, it's good to hear it so I can always judge when it starts to wear on me. But you have to have it there, or your girl movie is not going to be authentic."

She looked me in the eyes and said, "We're women, Vanessa. Bickering is what we do."

I just smiled at her and dropped my head. She was telling the truth, and I was embarrassed by it. I bickered with someone every day of my life, and I barely realized it.

Tracy said, "And since you've been asking about it so much." She reached down into her carry-on bag, pulled out a fresh script of *Flyy Girl*, and set it on my lap. My heart nearly jumped in my throat.

She said, "Keep your composure, and don't talk to me about it until you're done." Then she gave me a notebook and a pen. "This is for your notes."

Sasha looked over at me from her aisle seat beside me and asked, "Is that it?"

Maddy, Jasmine, and Alexandria were all sitting beside her in the middle section.

"One at a time," Tracy told them. "So don't bother her while she's reading it. Sasha, you can read it next. But no talking about it. You all read it, take your notes, and then you talk to me."

The boss lady had spoken, so we all nodded our heads and agreed to her terms. Then I jumped into reading the first draft of the *Flyy Girl* screenplay. I took a deep breath and turned to the opening scene.

My cousin was taking the excitement of her book by the horns. Her opening scene was a Germantown playground party, with a DJ and turntables on the basketball courts. She had red Kangol hats, box haircuts, dyed hairstyles, Gucci pocketbooks and shoes, Gloria Vanderbilt jeans, Adidas sweat suits, hip-hop dancing, thugs slap-boxing, hustlers tossing dice up against the walls, flyy girls profiling, and plenty of camera movement to capture the full sounds and sights of Philadelphia during the 1980s.

Nearby, on the playground football field, we zoom in on a wide-eyed cheerleader (TRACY ELLISON) standing with her teammates on the sidelines of an ongoing game. The attractive teenaged girl eagerly watches the team's star running back (STEVE) score on a long touchdown run as the fans of the home team cheer him on.

At the end of the football game, we leave the playground crowd and focus on the cheerleader and the star running back on a one-on-one walk to her house, where she talks him into giving her his jersey, straight off his back. We immediately see TRACY's manipulative powers over unsuspecting boys.

From there, we meet the obedient next-door neighbor (RAHEEMA) right before her wayward older sister (MERCEDES) drives up and hops out of the passenger side of her boyfriend's Mustang 5.0. MERCEDES's glamorous appearance and original flyy girl attitude impresses TRACY, while it repulses her younger sister RAHEEMA, showing us the connection, goals, and polarity of the three Germantown-raised girls. Then we meet their mothers, BETH in MERCEDES and RAHEEMA's home, and PATTI in TRACY's home.

As I rapidly read the screenplay, I could see and feel all of it. It was extremely visual and sensible. Every scene had a purpose. Nothing was wasted. I could feel my heart racing as I read it. Tracy had started with the beef of the book, and she had tied in every important component, while killing all of the drag time that would not translate well on-screen. It was just a splendid job, right down to all of the Philadelphia slang; cuz, trippin', straight up, chumpees, jawns, thorough, decent, all that, bangin', chicken head, gettin' new, et cetera. She had detailed *everything*!

I finished reading the screenplay before our airplane landed, but I didn't have many constructive criticisms to offer my cousin. I even teared up at the end with VICTOR's letter from jail. Tracy had somehow managed to wrap up the screenplay in one hundred twenty-four pages from a four-hundred-fifteen-page book, and she had maintained all the beef. What more could I ask for?

"What do you think?" she asked me with a grin. I believe she already knew how tight her screenplay was. I decided to humor her any-way after wiping the small tears from my eyes.

I asked her, "What happened to your poetry?"

She shook her head. "I told the story I needed to tell on-screen. They can get the rest of it from the book." She smiled and said, "And I'll make royalties off of both."

Sasha asked me, "Can I read it now?"

I gave her the screenplay with the notepad and pencil that I didn't bother to use.

I told Tracy, "I didn't really see anything to comment on. I think you did a good job."

"What about finding typos or spelling errors?" she asked me.

I said, "You know what? I really wasn't even focusing on that. Maybe I can read it again and be more technical. But on the first read, I was thinking more about how you would do it, and now I know."

I said, "But by killing the poetry, you also killed the line where Ra-heema says that you'll be rich and famous one day if you keep writing. I mean, I think that's important, especially looking at where you are now. You *are* rich and famous from writing. Raheema was right."

She said, "Yeah, but in listening to girls talk about the book over the years, and getting the emails and everything, I really didn't see where too many readers got the poetry. And for the ones who did get it, if they care enough about it, then they'll tell me about it after they see it missing from the movie. And then I can sell them my books of poetry online or something."

"Good idea," I told her with a nod. "Well, I have nothing else to say then. I'm just looking forward to going through the process of casting, producing, and shooting the film."

"And marketing and selling it," Tracy added. "It's not over with after shooting it. The machine wants to eat everything," she joked.

Sasha looked over at us both and said, "Can I read it now without you two giving away the ending?"

"My bad," I told her.

Sasha then looked past me to Tracy.

She said, "And Tracy, I *did* get the poetry, but that's just me. Be-cause I write poetry, too."

My cousin had already made her decision.

She said, "That's great, Sasha. But like I said, you'll just have to get more of those details from the book. It's there."

Sasha said, "Yeah, but the poetry made you much more than just a regular girl growing up in the 'hood. It gave you depth, especially in your sequel book."

"However, the sequel book would not stand up to the first book on the big screen," Tracy argued. "It's too cerebral. Look at the mess John Singleton made of Maya Angelou's poetry in *Poetic Justice*. Some things are just better done in book form."

Sasha nodded and finally agreed with her. "Yeah, that's true. I've already fallen asleep on the first two of those *Harry Potter* movies. They were just a little too drawn out for me. So I'm not planning on seeing the third one."

"I know that's right," Maddy commented. "I didn't even see the second one."

Tracy said, "All right, no more talk. It's your turn to read it, then you write down what you think, and we'll discuss it later."

So Sasha got to reading as we continued on our long plane ride to Philly.

When we arrived at the Philadelphia International Airport, we had a limo driver waiting there to pick us up. He helped us gather our luggage, and we made our way over to the black stretch limousine. Tracy, however, was still busy saying hi to more fans who recognized her at the airport.

When we finally climbed into the limo, Jasmine said, "Oh my God, I'm loving this. This is how life is supposed to be." Then she joked and said, "Tracy, can you adopt me? You can carry me around like luggage and I'll just sit on the floor or in a corner and stay out of your way. I promise."

We all laughed at her crazy behind as we drove off from the airport.

"Now, I'm not even gonna comment on that," Maddy told us.

Tracy ignored it and got us all situated.

She said, "Now, I hate to give you girls a curfew, because I know you think you're grown and everything, but while I have you out here with me, I don't want to be looking for any of you. So I want you to all stay together, no matter what. And when I call Vanessa's cell phone, somebody better answer it."

We were all older than eighteen, but Tracy had a point. We were on her time, doing a job for her that we all wanted to do. So we had to agree to her rules.

Sasha was the oldest at twenty-one, and she spoke up first.

"You're the boss. I'm just happy to be working with you. But I do want to visit my family in Delaware."

"And you'll probably take Jasmine with you, right?" my cousin asked her.

"If she wants to come, yeah."

"Oh course I want to come," Jasmine told her. "You've been talking about Delaware ever since I first met you."

I looked at Alexandria to see if she would go, but she shook her head and declined.

"I'll probably just get some rest tomorrow. I'm feeling jet lag," she told us.

Tracy ran with that and spoke to Sasha and Jasmine. "Well, you two just let me know when you're going and when you're getting back," she told them. "And keep that cell phone working."

Sasha nodded to her. She said, "We'll probably go tomorrow morning and get back by the afternoon."

"Wait a minute, how early tomorrow morning?" Jasmine asked Sasha.

We all laughed again. Jasmine was not a morning person.

Tracy looked at Alexandria for about the first time and spoke to her individually.

She said, "Well, this is it, girl. Can you handle Philadelphia?"

Alexandria looked my cousin straight in her eyes and said, "Who, me?"

"Do you see me looking at anyone else?" Tracy asked her.

Alexandria laughed it off and looked a little unsure of herself.

She said, "Yeah, I'm ready."

"Okay," my cousin responded. "I'll say no more."

Then she got on her cell phone and started making calls regarding our arrival at the hotel. Tracy had a New York–based casting agent and camera crew that would be joining us at the hotel, and we all planned to set up for the casting calls that would go on that week at Freedom Theater.

We arrived at the Marriott Hotel in downtown Philadelphia at 7:32 PM, and Tracy's New York team was already waiting there for us.

"Hey, Tracy, are you ready for all of this?" an ebony brown sister in short dreadlocks asked my cousin. She was wearing the rust-colored Flyy Girl Ltd. shirt with blue jeans and brown leather sandals. By then, Charmaine had come up with various different styles of shirts, but they all had the same summer color schemes with rust as the wild card.

"Hey, Robin. I'm as ready as I'm gonna get with this monster," Tracy told her.

"Well, I love these Flyy Girl shirts and hats you're working," Robin stated. She spun around to show it off. She said, "You're gonna make a *killing* with this line. I wish I had thought of it first."

Tracy laughed and began to introduce us.

"This is my cousin Vanessa Tracy Smith, who's been living with me in L.A. since her last few years in high school. And if it wasn't for her bothering me about this damn thing, I definitely wouldn't be here right now."

"So, you're the one who finally pushed her into doing it?" Robin asked me with a handshake and a smile. Robin Antoinette was the casting director who would be running the show with Tracy that week, to select all of the possible stars and extras.

"I figured it was gonna happen sooner or later, I was just pushing for sooner," I spoke up and told her. I wanted to back down from taking too much of the credit though. It could be a real headache for me if things didn't work out in the end. But there I was in the middle of things.

Tracy introduced Robin to my crew, and Robin introduced us to hers. They were mostly personal assistants and film students who were still in film school from New York.

Tracy said, "Okay, first thing first. Let's get all the girls up to their rooms, let them sort out their outfits for the week, and then while they run along to South Street to play, we can go over our game plan and run it down to the girls for tomorrow."

"Sounds like you got it all covered," Robin stated.

"Well, let's jump to it then," Tracy told her.

We all received the keys to our hotel rooms, dragged our luggage up on the elevators, picked out our Flyy Girl Ltd. shirts for the week, and got ready to go out to South Street to enjoy the sights and sounds of Philadelphia.

"Philadelphia, here I come," Jasmine yelled into the night air as soon as we walked out of the hotel that evening.

"Yeah, so everybody get ready to cover your ears," Maddy joked.

We giggled like the girls we were and started walking toward the weekend excitement on South Street.

Wow!

First thing Monday morning, Tracy had me accompany her to the radio station at Power 99 FM. But she had my girls report straight to Freedom Theater for instructions from Robin Antoinette and her casting crew. I was decked out in my Flyy Girl Ltd. baby-tee, the lime green one, with the matching hat and matching lime green pants. Tracy wore the rust-colored tee with black jeans and no hat.

"So you're finally doing the *Flyy Girl* movie?" Golden Boy was asking Tracy at the station. We were inside the live recording booth with the Power 99 morning team, minus Wendy Williams, who had moved on to her own syndicated show in New York.

Tracy answered, "First we need to find the right people to put in the movie."

"You got a cameo spot for me?" the comedian Dee Lee asked her. "I can play a drug dealer with a sense of humor. Only I don't sell no drugs, I sell jokes all day. And my jokes are so hot on the street, that they're addictive. Hell, you can do a whole movie off of that. Let me write that down for my own first movie."

"Sounds like a plan to me," my cousin humored him.

I had never seen the Power 99 morning show team in person, but Dee Lee was as light as I was with tight curly hair, and Golden Boy looked just like his name. He had golden brown skin and brown eyes. There were also two young women on the show since replacing Wendy Williams, but I didn't know who they were.

"So you're having a casting call today at nine o'clock?" they asked Tracy.

"At the Freedom Theater on Broad Street," my cousin filled in.

"And just any old body can come and try out for the movie?" Dee Lee asked.

"Anyone can come, but we're seeing agency actors and actresses first, and then it's first-come first-serve with everyone else."

Dee Lee nodded. "So if you're not represented by an agency, then you could be standing there in line for like two hours."

Tracy answered, "Do you want to be in a movie or not? I mean, you gotta do what you gotta do. I have to be there all day long. And when you're actually shooting a movie, you're there on the set for months. So you might as well get used to waiting now."

"I heard that," they all responded.

"I see you're also starting a Flyy Girl clothing line," one of the young women on the show commented. They had already commented on it when we first walked in, but now they were bringing it up on the air.

Tracy smiled and pointed to me. I had a few of the Flyy Girl Ltd. shirts in a large carry bag.

She said, "Yes, I am, and we brought you guys a few samples to sport for us."

"Oh, thank you, thank you. Freebies are always nice," the women hosts responded with smiles as I handed them the shirts.

Tracy said, "We'll have shirts and hats for sale at the casting calls, but we only have a limited supply, so get it while it's hot. That's why it's called Flyy Girl Ltd. We're not into the one-size-fits-all bag. We're going after the tailor-made audience who like one-of-a-kind apparel."

"So you're still on your hustle," Dee Lee stated. "Oh, I know you're from Philly now, girl."

"You know that's right," Tracy responded with a chuckle. She said, "But a lot of my hustle now is coming straight from my little cousin right here, Vanessa. And she's straight out of North Philly."

Dee Lee said, "Oh, that's my neck of the woods. What street?" he asked me.

I was nearly ready to faint. I was in there just to assist my cousin, not to be put on the spot like that.

I stepped up to the big black microphone with my heart racing and said, "Twenty-second and Girard."

Dee Lee started smiling wider. He joked and said, "I probably passed you standing at the bus stop in the cold a hundred times and didn't even offer you a warm ride."

He had us all laughing in there.

I said, "That's all right. I wouldn't have known who you were anyway. I just know your name and your voice," I told him.

He joked again and said, "Yeah, I could have been some light-skinned maniac. Your momma wouldn't let you jump in the car with me."

"Probably not," I told him.

"So, outside of *Flyy Girl*, are you working on anything else right now, something you can give us the scoop on before you film it?" they asked her.

"Well, to tell you the truth, my last couple of Hollywood films were not all that much to talk about," Tracy told them.

Dee Lee jumped all over that. He said, "Well now, I wasn't gonna say nothin' about it, but since you brought it up. What the hell were you thinking? What were you trying to be, *Sheena of the Urban Jungle*? I saw that *Road Kill* movie at the dollar screen and couldn't believe it. I mean now, *Led Astray* was good. That was good. But *Road Kill* . . ."

"I kind of liked that movie," one of the female hosts spoke up. "We don't have to always be the damsel in distress. We can kick butt, too."

Dee Lee said, "You know what, I really think we need to leave that kicking butt to the Asians, or *The Matrix* movies."

To make a long story short, we did our thing on Power 99's morning show, and got out of there to make it down to Freedom Theater.

"What do you think?" Tracy asked me after the show.

I was still thinking about her giving me so much credit for what she was doing. I mean, I was flattered by it, but it was really not expected.

I said, "I didn't know you were gonna put me on the spot like that?"

"Why not? I'm only telling them the truth. You did push me into this."

"Yeah, but . . ." I didn't know what else to say, so I thought of a way where I could make her think twice about it.

I said, "So, since it was my idea, what percentage of the profits do I get?"

I felt for sure that my cousin would change her tune after I said something like that. But she surprised me again when she said, "Name your price."

I looked at her and was stunned, but Tracy didn't appear to be joking.

"Are you serious?"

"Name your price," she repeated.

I took a deep breath and thought of a fair number for a minor producer.

"Ten percent."

"Of what?" she asked me next.

I was stunned again.

"Of what?" I thought it was obvious. I said, "Of the movie."

"And what about the clothing line?"

I thought about it and said, "Yeah, that too."

A lot of it was my idea. I mean, Tracy had finally decided to run with things, but . . .

"And the television rights?" she asked me.

I wasn't even thinking about all of that. She was far ahead of me.

She said, "If you're gonna play the role of power, then you have to understand what you're getting into. You have to think about everything. Now, I'm gonna hook you up, Vanessa, but only because you're my little cousin, and I want you to do well. But in real-life business, you get everything that you need to get on paper before you press any GO buttons. You hear me? So I'm glad we're having this conversation. Because I really believe that you have what it takes to be a real power broker. Even Susan noticed that in you."

She said, "You're a lot like me in some ways, Vanessa, but you're totally different in others. Like, you're not really a show-off like I was at your age, but you definitely want to be in control. And you're much more pushier than I was. I would beg and scheme for a lot of the things that I wanted, but *you* . . . you just make your own way. Even how you gathered your group of girlfriends. You're younger than most of them, but you can't tell, because you always know what you're doing.

"So yeah, I give you a lot of the credit for this," my cousin told me. "Because you deserve it, and I see something in you that I want to work with. So this is really more about me developing you than it is me. Now don't get me wrong. I'm gonna get mine. You can best believe that. But at the same time, you're family, and I want to build you into someone powerful. Then you can continue to help me in whatever it is that I need to do, just like Susan and her family do. Black people don't do that enough. And that was one of my main reasons for finally deciding to do this. I want to get *you* ready."

I was speechless. I sat there feeling all clammy and good inside. But I was scared, too. I mean, it was one thing for my cousin to do what she was doing with me as her sidekick, but once she made it known that she was watching me, that seemed to change everything. Because now I *knew* that she was watching.

As we drove toward Freedom Theater, right past my old neighborhood on Girard Avenue in North Philadelphia, I was in a dream world. Could I really handle the power that Tracy was trying to prepare me for? I didn't know. But it was too late to back down. The next level of the game had already begun.

Tracy chuckled to herself in the silence of the limo as we got closer to Freedom Theater. She said, "Don't get scared now, Vanessa. Be who you were meant to be." She said, "Your whole generation is a step up from mine. We used to think about making it on a minor level with a family, a husband, and kids. But you guys . . ."

She shook her head and said, "You guys are thinking about running girl companies. Every last one of you."

I said, "I don't know about all of that." Tracy was starting to exaggerate.

She said, "We'll see. And if you start with something as big as *Flyy Girl*, then where do you go from there?"

When I thought about her question, it scared me even more. What was I about to get myself into? *Flyy Girl* was big! I still don't think my cousin understood how big it was, or it could be. I mean, I could be satisfied with running Flyy Girl for life, with Tracy's blessings of course. I could see Flyy Girl scholarships, fashion shows, reading centers, even a doggone sorority organization or something. I would never have to leave the Flyy Girl brand. And we could have everything we needed in house.

I finally spoke up with a smile on my face. I said, "Like you told me, law number one is to remember never to outshine the master."

I was no damn fool. I was still a young nobody next to a giant, who just happened to be my cousin. Without her power, her hard work, and her hustle, I wouldn't be worth a phone call. So I had to play my cards like I had some sense.

Tracy smiled at me real easy from her side of the limo and said, "Good answer." And that was all she needed to say.

We arrived at Freedom Theater on Broad Street, and I was amazed by the crowd.

I opened my mouth and said "Oh my God!" It looked like a concert line out in front of the building. People flowed all the way down the block and wrapped around the corner. We couldn't even see the end of the line. More people were hopping out of cars, off of buses, and crossing Broad Street to join the line. And it was only just after nine o'clock in the morning, which meant that a lot of the people at the front of the line were out there at eight o'clock or earlier.

Tracy looked over at me and smiled again.

"Now you see what I'm talking about?" she asked me. "This is what you got me into. And we don't even have a green-light for this film yet."

I thought fast and said, "Well then, we need to take a picture of this line and show it to your producers."

Tracy looked at me and said, "Another good idea. Girl, you are just bubbling with them." She said, "I'm gonna get a cameraman out here immediately."

I couldn't believe it. She had me afraid to speak anything else. I was only getting myself deeper in trouble with every idea that I came up with.

When the driver opened the limo door for us to climb out, I became nervous as hell. All eyes were on us. I wasn't used to that. I was used to all eyes being on Tracy in Hollywood. They didn't pay much attention to me once they realized I was only the little cousin. But in my home city of Philadelphia, on a casting call that I had instigated for *Flyy Girl*, I felt a thousand eyes on me, and I was ready to puke. I was preparing to step out of a limo with my cousin, while wearing original Flyy Girl Ltd. clothing that I had helped to come up with, and it was a totally different feeling for me.

Oh my God! a little voice inside my head continued to scream. *Just walk straight in behind her*, I told myself. *Just walk in behind her.*

But as soon as my feet hit the pavement among murmurs of "There she goes" from the people in the line who recognized my cousin, someone yelled out, "Vanessa! Hey, Vanessa! I knew I'd see you down here."

I looked back nervously and spotted my girl Danielle Watkins from my Engineering & Science High School days.

She said, "Oh, now that's flyy," in reference to my lime green Flyy Girl Ltd. shirt, hat, and matching pants.

"We'll have them for sale inside," I told her.

"Let's go, Vanessa," Tracy told me. "We got work to do."

Before I could leave, Danielle whispered, "Get me in there, girl. Get me in."

As they say, I was stuck between a rock and a hard place.

I squirmed in response to my old girl and said, "I can't. But I'll see you inside."

I felt ready to hurl with each step I took toward the entrance. It got worse when we stepped inside.

Robin grabbed Tracy by the hand and pulled her behind the stage. She said, "Girl, this is the craziest casting call I have ever been involved with in my life, and we haven't even started yet.

"We have about two hundred agency talents here already, and a thousand people who are just walking in off the street. So I let my agency people in to sit them down in the front audience seats. Then I started letting some of the first walk-ups in and directed them to the back rows. But I can already see that this here is gonna be a mess."

Robin was excited with big eyes and everything.

Tracy responded as if she had ice water in her veins. "Well, we'll just move them in and move them out. I know what I need to look for. Do they have their script sheets?"

"Yeah, but we ran out of them real fast," Robin answered.

"So we'll just have our assistants collect them and redistribute them."

"Exactly," Robin agreed.

Tracy then addressed the Freedom Theater staff.

"We don't know if it was a good idea to go on the radio and advertise this," an older black woman told Tracy. She said, "We didn't expect a crowd as large as this. People have literally been here waiting since seven o'clock this morning."

Tracy had run advertisements on Power 99 Radio for a week before we had arrived.

"We'll try to make things move as swiftly as possible," she said. "In the meantime, you have thousands of new supporters and talent to sell on Freedom Theater."

That was part of the deal with us using the Freedom Theater. They would get to collect information from potential supporters and solicit new talent from the crowd.

Tracy had no time to waste, so she moved on toward the front of the stage where the auditions would take place. I hurried behind her, and caught Jasmine rushing past with paperwork in her hands.

She spotted me with wide eyes of her own. And despite it being nine o'clock in the morning, or six o'clock L.A. time, Jasmine was wide awake.

"Do you see all of these people in here this early? Is this an East Coast thing or what?" she asked me.

I hadn't seen the people in the audience yet. I was still moving toward it.

"Wait till you see it," Jasmine told me.

I took another deep breath and walked out to the front of the stage, behind my cousin's lead. I don't know how many people Freedom Theater could hold, but there was no room left in that place. The entire audience was packed to capacity.

I spotted Sasha, Maddy, Alexandria, and the other assistants and camera crew from New York, all working their positions and wearing the Flyy Girl gear.

My girls spotted me and shook their heads in my direction. None of us could have imagined that kind of enthusiasm for the *Flyy Girl* movie. Then again, we could, but actually seeing it made it more unbelievable than the dreams we had all shared.

There were four tables set up in the middle of the stage, with a camera pointed toward the audience at dead center. All of the casting crew were sitting at the tables with Tracy to judge the talent, while everyone in the audience watched. So if you were afraid to perform in front of a crowd, then you were definitely in the wrong place.

As I moved closer toward a chair that actually had my name on it, I heard Tracy giving instructions to one of the cameramen.

She said, "I want you to take the small, handheld camera outside with someone to interview the crowd about what *Flyy Girl* means to them. But don't put them on camera until you know they've read the book and they have something worthwhile to say."

The cameraman, a young guy in his mid-twenties with uncombed hair, nodded to her.

"Okay, we can do that."

"Good. Because that crowd outside is phenomenal, and we want to make sure we document their responses to all of this. Plus, it makes their wait a lot less painful. So make sure you guys move all the way to the back. Don't spend too much time at the front, and make sure you turn the camera on while you're walking past the line. If they want to scream out at the camera while you're moving, let them. But don't stop unless you find someone who can really work it for us. You know what I mean? We want people who are camera ready, and not the nonsense."

The young cameraman took it all in stride and said "I got you" before he gathered his camera and a couple of staff members. It must have been about forty of us in there, all doing our part.

Tracy then grabbed a microphone and addressed the buzzing crowd in the audience.

"Hello everyone. In case you didn't know, my name is Tracy Ellison Grant—better known as the original *Flyy Girl*."

As soon as she said that, the crowd at the back of the auditorium got extremely loud with their cheering.

"Yeaaah! Yeaaah!"

The agency people in the front rows, on the other hand, were all cool, calm, and collected, concentrating on the task at hand—to impress my cousin with their acting skills.

Tracy went on and said, "We're gonna try and make this process as simple as possible. And for those of you who are used to a more private or secluded room to audition in, I apologize in advance, but this will be a movie with plenty of extras, so you all need to get used to the crowd."

"I know that's right!" someone yelled above the cheering from the back rows.

Tracy said, "But once we begin this process, we're going to need complete silence from each and every one of you, as if you just paid a thousand dollars on Broadway."

They all laughed with her. My big cousin was working it like I only wish I had the courage to do. It was easy to talk behind closed doors about all of my grand ideas, but Tracy was the one who could really work it out in the open.

She said, "And if you like the Flyy Girl Ltd. clothing line all our assistants are wearing today, well, I just want you to know, you can all buy it on your way out."

They all laughed again, but Tracy was dead serious about her hustle.

"So, without further ado, let's get it started."

We had acting agency people who had traveled from New York, New Jersey, Delaware, Baltimore, Washington, D.C., Virginia, Atlanta, and as far south as Florida. And of course, Philadelphians were definitely in the house. Many of the actors and actresses were pretty people, and some of them were not. But one thing was for sure, just because you were signed to an acting agency didn't mean that you were a lock, because some of those agency people were quick to overact, or totally misread the scene and their lines. I was actually wondering how many of those people had read the book, and if so, how many of them understood what they were even reading. Some of them were that bad.

As soon as we finished with one load of people, in came the next hundred. There were more than a few performers that I actually liked for a callback though. Tracy spotted some of the same performers that I had taken notes on. So did some of the other casting crew. But we all had to keep the show rolling nonstop, so we made our notes and kept the lines moving onstage, offstage, in the door, and out the door.

"What does that line look like outside now?" Tracy asked Maddy after noon.

Maddy shook her head. She said, "It looks like it didn't even move. You just see the same people moving closer to the front, and people you haven't seen before in the back."

Robin said, "You know it's no way we're gonna see the rest of this line today. So we may as well cut it in half and give the rest of the people numbers for tomorrow. It's a good thing we gave ourselves a week to do this."

Tracy nodded. She said, "I knew what I was getting into. People have been waiting for years for a *Flyy Girl* movie."

Sasha walked over to report on the clothing sales with a money box in hand.

She smiled and said, "We're sold out of our line for today. They had me taking orders for tomorrow."

Tracy looked at me and grinned.

"We'll have Charmaine FedEx us a few more boxes for the end of the week. If we sell out of everything, not only will we break even, we'll make a slight profit."

"And everybody will spread the word on the new line," Sasha commented.

Tracy said, "All right, well, let's keep this machine moving." She winked at me and hollered, "Next," to the crowd of patiently waiting hopefuls.

We were all ready for a lunch break and couldn't take one. So we had to order in and keep right ahead, eating while we worked.

By seven o'clock that night we had cut the line in half for the next day, just as Robin had said, but we still had another hundred to two hundred people to see.

"You think we've seen enough by now?" Tracy asked me specifi-cally. I had taken notes on at least five people I liked to fill every role of the movie, including girls for Tracy's lead, who had the same hazel eyes and everything. We had watched girls there who were prettier than all of us. Nevertheless, the process was the process, and the love-at-first-sight phenomenon, the casting crew had explained, was very risky when dealing with unknowns. That was the general reason why you called people back, to make sure you were getting what you thought you were getting.

I answered, "You never know. The next one may be the one."

"Please," Tracy commented. "But you're right. That's why we have to make time to see every last person." So we got right back to work until we had seen them all—we finally finished at nine o'clock.

"You mean to tell me we have to get back up tomorrow and do this all over again?" Maddy asked. We were all helping to clean up the facility.

"Yup," my cousin answered. "But you knew that already. Other-wise, we wouldn't have booked the hotel rooms for a week."

That was all she needed to say to shut Maddy's mouth. We were all there to take care of the business of *Flyy Girl*, and that was it.

"So, you're actually gonna do it, hunh? You're gonna make a movie out of our lives?" someone asked Tracy from behind.

I turned and spotted Mercedes. I figured it was her. I knew her voice from her phone calls to L.A., but I had never actually met her before. She had cut her hair into a short bob, but you could tell that it could grow long. It was straight and soft with no perm needed. And she still had a look of distinction in her face, although it was a little rough around the edges. Her hardened eyes proved that she had lived a serious life, yet she had remained attractive in her brown skin.

Tracy asked her, "How long have you been here?"

"For about the last hour. I heard it was crazy crowded in here though. I didn't want to come in the middle of all of that."

Tracy nodded. "Yeah, it was."

Mercedes said, "I like the shirts and hats. Who designed them?"

"My girl Charmaine from L.A."

All of my girls were watching and listening in silence. I think they already knew who it was. They were putting the pieces together from Mercedes's grand entrance, her life story comments, her jaded personality, and her physical appearance. We were all sizing her up against my cousin's book. Mercedes was the high-stakes girl we had all read about, and she was standing right there in front of us. She wasted no time in getting my cousin's attention either.

"Can I talk to you for a minute, Tracy?"

It sounded so obvious that it was surreal. I could just imagine Mercedes asking Tracy for money to do a film that revealed painful parts of her own life. And they were indeed painful. But after Tracy had agreed to write Mercedes a check for the down payment on her house in Yeadon, how dare she extort her for more money?

I didn't have any proof of this as they spoke in private, but I was surely planning to ask Tracy about it afterward.

"Is that who I think it is?" Alexandria whispered to me.

"In the flesh," I told her.

"It is?" Jasmine whispered to Alexandria. Sasha and Maddy were standing close by her as we all prepared to take the limo back to our hotel.

Alexandria nodded her head to them. "Yup."

Tracy broke away from her private conversation with Mercedes and said, "Okay, we'll talk later then."

"Aw'ight," Mercedes mumbled as she headed off.

We were all itching to ask Tracy what had been said, but none of us dared to start that conversation.

Everyone helped to wrap up the camera equipment and lug everything back to the vans. Then we took the limo for the ride back down Broad Street toward downtown. Robin rode in the limo with us, and she was the only one with enough guts to ask Tracy the big question out in the open.

"So, that was the infamous Mercedes?"

We all looked on in curiosity for an answer to the obvious.

"Her character speaks volumes, doesn't it?" Tracy answered with a question. She seemed to be staring into the multicolored nightlights of the limo.

"What did she ask you?" Jasmine asked before I could. However, I had planned to do so in private.

Tracy didn't even look at Jasmine.

She said, "Some things are better left alone."

"That's what she said about the movie? So, she doesn't want you to do it?"

Jasmine was asking the very questions racing through my head.

Tracy told her sternly, "I'm talking about *you*, Jasmine. Now let it be."

That was answer enough for us. Whatever Mercedes had said, it had definitely gotten under Tracy's skin.

So we rode the rest of the way down Broad Street in a whisper.

The Marriott

When Tracy called me to her hotel suite that night, I knew she was pissed before I entered the room. So I prepared myself for a solid ear drumming. I was aware that she may need someone she could trust to vent to, and I was the one. But when she let me into her room, she was already on the cell phone letting her steam roll all out.

"Look, I've been away before and it hasn't caused you this much of a problem. So why are you acting like this now?"

She shut the door behind me and paid me no mind. So I quietly walked in and took a seat in the comfortable black leather chair behind her executive desk. There was a beautiful skyline view of downtown Philadelphia from her room. And I must say, it was very nice to be there.

I looked around the floor trying to preoccupy myself while my cousin argued over the phone. She had boxes of bios, photos, and attached notes to the talent she liked. On top of the desk, she had a box of tapes from the cameraman's casting footage that she was still watching on the room's nineteen-inch color television set. So I went ahead and watched some of the tape.

"So it's over, just like that?" she asked into the phone.

I wasn't really trying to listen, but how could I not? Tracy was right there in the same room with me, and I was shocked by her conversation. I realized by then that she was talking to her friend out in L.A., but I didn't believe that he would be that serious about breaking up with her that soon. He had to have planned it all along.

"Now you know that's out of the question. Dalvin, what kind of ultimatum is that? You know how much this project means to me."

Tracy paced the room in front of me while they spoke.

Was she giving up her man for the *Flyy Girl* movie? I felt bad again. But what kind of man gives up a woman just because she has the drive to accomplish the things she wants to do? I don't think I would have liked a man like that for myself. I know I wanted to do a lot of things in life, and no man was going to stop me from doing them.

"Okay, well, let's just discuss this when I get back to L.A."

Now she sounded like she was trying to compromise.

"Well, there's really nothing to talk about right now, because I'm going to be here for a week. And you know that already. I just can't up and leave. How would that look?"

She made sense to me, but her friend made no sense at all. I didn't even have to hear his argument. It sounded like your typical male ego tripping. He wanted his woman home, barefoot, and naked.

The next minute, Tracy looked at the phone and then over at me without ever saying good-bye.

"He hung up?" I asked her. The question just slipped out of my mouth.

She said, "Of course he did. And he's being a complete asshole about this."

I didn't want to add to anything so I held my tongue. It sounded like she had the right assessment to me. I didn't want to break up my cousin's relationship, but her friend was not my friend, and Tracy was not married to the man. Therefore, I had no loyalty to him.

She shook her head and said, "Anyway . . . I'll deal with him later." Then she took another minute to gather her thoughts.

"I can't believe that damn Mercedes today," she commented. "That's why I didn't want to get any of my friends and family involved in this thing yet. I wanted these first few days to be just us looking at talent. *Period.*"

She took a deep breath and said, "In the process of making every film, there are a million different challenges to overcome. You try to predict most of those challenges, but you still end up improvising due to things you can't control."

She was speaking from experience. I had already been around the process with her last two films. They may not have done well at the box office but they both got done. So I was perfectly poised in my role of assistance and support.

I asked my cousin, "Do you mind if I ask you what Mercedes said?" I was still curious.

Tracy slowly nodded to me. She said, "Well, you know she never liked me writing about her asking for a down payment check for her house in Yeadon in *For the Love of Money*. She said it was embarrassing. Now she's saying that a movie that may show her drug addiction days as a teenager may not only get her fired from her job, but may also inhibit her from getting other jobs in the future."

I joked and said, "Halle Berry's career blew up after portraying a crackhead in *Jungle Fever.*"

It was bad taste in the present situation, but it had slipped out of my mouth anyway.

My cousin looked at me and said, "This is not a fictional portrayal, Vanessa. Mercedes has some valid points."

"So, you just take out her drug and tricking scenes, and just have your characters talk about it," I suggested too quickly.

Tracy said, "And then I'd lose one of the most dramatic character arcs in the script. That scene affects everybody. You can't talk about something like that. You *have* to show it. But that's really not the point, Vanessa. Mercedes knows I can't take her scene out. She's trying to use her concerns to get more money out of me. If anything, people would see how she's changed her life around. I did a lot of crazy things, too. We all did, and we'll all share in the risk, pain, joy, understanding, et cetera in this movie."

"You won't all share the money though," I blurted out. I don't know what the hell was wrong with me that night. I was really being insensitive. Some assistant I was.

But instead of getting upset with me for telling the blunt truth, Tracy smiled.

She said, "That's always the dilemma in doing a real-life project that affects more than one person."

"They get away with it in these reality shows," I commented.

"That's not real content," Tracy responded. "Those shows are as phony as they wanna be. And those people are all sacrificing their privacies for a few thousand dollars and a magazine article."

Tracy hit the nail right on the head.

I was supposed to be in there listening, but I guess I was just too damn tired at the moment. That's when you start yawning and rambling on at the mouth—and I was doing both.

My cousin noticed it and said, "Okay, I think you're a little tired now."

After all, it was approaching midnight on the East Coast, which I was no longer used to, and I had been up since six o'clock in the morning with no time for a nap. I was wondering how Tracy could do it. I guess that's why she was the Flyy Girl and I was only the little cousin. We could all relate to some of her drive, energy, passion, and flair, but only she possessed it to use on a regular basis.

I said, "I'm sorry," and tried my best not to yawn when I said it. But it didn't work.

"Go on and go to bed, girl. You gotta get up early tomorrow morning and do it all over again anyway," she told me. "And make sure those girls of yours are in bed, too." Then she grabbed me by the arm and escorted me back to the door.

When I got off of the elevator on my floor, I spotted Maddy talking to one of the camera crew guys from New York. They were standing in the hallway outside of her room, two doors down from mine.

"Speak of the devil," the New Yorker commented to me.

He was a short and stocky Columbia University student named Shamor.

"So who was talking about me?" I joked to him.

"We both were," he answered.

Maddy only smiled in my direction.

"Good things or bad?" I asked them both.

Shamor spoke up again before Maddy could. "Only good things, of course."

"So I'm not a devil then," I told him with a grin.

He shook it off and said, "It's only a figure of speech. Don't take it personal."

I didn't plan to shoot the breeze with them. I was already tired. So as soon as I reached my door and pulled out my key, I let them know.

"Well, I'll see you guys tomorrow. We have another long and early one," I commented.

Maddy finally spoke up. "Don't we know it."

"So, we'll see you bright and early tomorrow then." Shamor sounded extra chipper for midnight. I guess it was a New York thing. They slept much later than everyone else.

As soon as I walked into my room, I heard a good amount of noise coming from my girls in the room beside me. I was still tired, but then I got curious. I heard male voices in the room with them. I debated about letting them be, but Tracy had told me to look out for my crew. So I took a deep breath, gathered an extra tank of energy, and walked over to their room to see what was up. Maddy and Shamor were out of the hallway by then.

I knocked on the door.

Jasmine looked through the peephole and said, "Oh, it's your cousin Vanessa." I could tell it was her from her voice and her quick steps to the door.

She opened the door, wearing a long, gold Los Angeles Lakers jersey as her nighty.

I looked at her Lakers jersey and said, "Good idea. We should do Flyy Girl jerseys like that."

"I'd wear that," she promised.

"Of course you would," I told her.

I walked into the room and spotted my infamous, girl-chasing cousin Jason sitting up in the sofa with one of his boys. They both had freshly braided hairstyles.

"What, did y'all just get your heads done?" I asked them. The braids looked very much intact, like they jumped straight out of the braiding chair.

Jason's small-eyed friend said, "My hair stays done." That's all I needed to hear from him to know that he was another skirt-chaser. He just had the look. However, two brown pretty boys up in my girls' room at close to midnight when we had work to do in the morning didn't sit well with my conscience. And the fact that it was my cousin allowed me to be bolder about it than I would have been had I not known them.

I said, "Well, you know we have to get up early to work this casting call again tomorrow." I was addressing my girls. Then I addressed Jason, "Have you checked in with Tracy yet? She's still up and busy. But we all need to get some rest," I told him on behalf of all of us.

Jason said, "They don't look tired to me. Let them speak for themselves."

Sasha spoke up on cue from across the room. She was the only one sitting up on her bed.

She said, "I'm pooped, man. I was a clothing-selling, order-taking machine today. It's gonna be the same thing tomorrow. But this new line is really gonna work, Vanessa. These girls were literally fighting over the last pieces of clothing that I had out on the table today. I think they took the term *Limited* to heart."

"Yeah, that's an easy sell right now," Jason's friend spoke up. "Anything with a tight fit, colorful, and a cool name like Flyy Girl will sell all day long."

Jason looked at Sasha who was still dressed in her sky blue Flyy Girl Ltd. clothes.

"So, you're ready to go to bed on me now, hunh?"

He was still sweating her comments on being tired.

Sasha said, "I've been ready for bed ever since Jasmine opened that door. I won't even lie to ya'."

I was pretty secure in knowing that Sasha wouldn't throw herself around too easily. Even Jasmine was a tight one to pull. I mean, she got excited about things easily, but she would rather have good, clean fun with a guy than go to bed with him. So a lot of guys would get burned after reading her extroverted personality the wrong way.

After being shot down by Sasha, my cousin looked back to me. He stood up from his spot on the sofa and walked toward me to pull me toward the door.

"Vanessa, let me talk to you right quick."

I asked him, "What, you have to take me out of the room to do that?"

He kept pulling me by my arm as if my comment was meaningless. So we walked outside into the hallway where my eager beaver cousin asked me, "Who is that girl with the eyes, you know who I'm talking about, in the other room? Her eyes tighter than Tracy's. She got like them rainbow rings in her eyes. Is Tracy trying to cast her?"

He was referring to Alexandria Greene. Everyone assumed that she would make the movie, at least as a camera-ready extra, but Tracy had yet to address her.

I asked him, "Have you tried to talk to her yet?" I imagined that he had.

"I mean, I said hi, but you know. She slipped into the room too fast. I didn't want to be out here knocking on her door. But why don't you just introduce me to her right quick."

I was too tired to even smile at how pressed my cousin was.

I said, "What about Sasha?" I just wanted to hear his response.

Jason frowned at me. "What about her? I mean, we just cool, man, she not like my girl. I haven't even seen her since I was out in L.A. I wouldn't talk to her like that seriously anyway."

I asked him, "Why, because she's Asian, or because she's not as easy to get in bed as you thought she'd be?"

Jason said, "For real, for real . . . *both*. I mean, I wanted to try something new, but if she ain't really wit' it . . . I mean . . . anyway, man, who's this girl? She could be the one."

I couldn't help but laugh. He was pitiful. You would think he'd be a lot more mature about girls after having such a famous sister. I don't know if that fact made Jason better or worse as a person. I began to wonder what he would be like if he *didn't* have a famous sister.

I was ready to go back into the room without even responding to him.

Jason grabbed my arm and pressed me.

"Come on now, Vanessa. All I'm asking you to do is knock on the door and say, 'This is my cousin, Jason Ellison, Tracy's little brother, in the flesh, and he just wanted to meet you and say hi to you right quick.' You know, and I'll just go from there."

I smiled and shook my head. My cousin was telling on himself.

I said, "So you do use her name to get girls."

"Who, Tracy? Naw, I'm saying, I'll say it right now. But on an everyday thing, I mean, y'all on the other side of the world from us. How I'm gon' use her name like that?"

"Jason, *Flyy Girl* is more popular in Philly than anywhere. What are you talking about?"

"I'm saying, if a girl read the book, that's on her. It's not like I bring it up. You know my game is stronger than that. I don't have to do that. I was just joking with you anyway."

"I seriously doubt that," I told him.

"So are you gonna introduce me to this girl or not? First of all, what's her name?"

He was serious. He wasn't going to let it go.

I said, "Jason, it's midnight, and we all have to get up early tomorrow. So if you want to meet her so badly, you know where you'll be able to find her tomorrow."

He said, "Yeah, I heard it was off the hinges down there today."

"It was," I told him. "How come you weren't down there?"

"Tracy told me not to come, man. She said she didn't want the distraction on the first couple of days. Those are her exact words," he told me.

It sounded about right, too, so I said no more about it.

He said, "That's why I'm trying to meet this girl tonight. I could have her meet me somewhere tomorrow when y'all get done."

I leveled with him and said, "Don't get your hopes up. She's about the hardest girl to talk to."

He nodded and said, "Yeah, that's always the case when you get with them girls who know they look good. But I look good, too. It ain't nothing but a word to me. Introduce me to her."

"She's probably in bed now anyway," I told him.

"Yeah, 'cause you keep wasting time."

He went ahead and knocked on the door while holding me there beside him.

"You are so pressed," I told him. So I had something in store for his behind.

Maddy answered the door instead of Alexandria.

"What's up?" She was in her nightclothes, a long, light blue cotton T-shirt.

I asked her, "Is Alexandria still up? I got a pressed boy out here who wants to talk to her."

Jason didn't flinch. He kept his cool about it.

Maddy said, "She's still up, but she's not dressed."

"That's what I told him," I commented to her.

"Tell her I only need a minute. I just want to introduce myself to her."

Maddy looked him over, shook her head, and grinned. I'm sure she could see for herself how pressed my cousin was.

She looked back into the room and said, "Alex, somebody wants to meet you out here."

There was silence in the room while we waited at the door.

Jason spoke up and said, "Tell her it's Tracy's handsome brother."

Maddy looked at him again and said, "You do look like her."

"Yeah, but I'm taller, darker, and I'm all man."

I had to give it to Jason, he was pretty bold with his bullshit. He was really putting himself out there.

Alexandria finally came to the door and she looked irritated.

I said, "I'm sorry about this. I tried to stop him, but he wouldn't leave me alone about it."

Jason wasted no time. He stuck out his hand to hers and said, "Look, I just wanted to meet you. I've been hearing a lot about you, and I only got a chance to say hi, so I just wanted to say a little more and see how you were planning to occupy your time while you were here up in Philly."

"What did you hear about her?" I asked him. I wanted to stop his bullshit immediately before my friend started to think that I told him something when I didn't.

Jason looked me right in my face and said, "You just told me that she was the hardest girl to talk to, and that you'd be surprised if she would talk to me. And then I said that I'm handsome, too, and that it ain't nothing but a word to me. I mean, we just stood here and had that conversation, did we not?"

He had me on the spot like I don't know what.

"I didn't say all that," I grumbled.

"I mean, I don't know your exact words, but that's how you put it. You made it sound like she didn't like guys or something. 'Cause I know it ain't nothing wrong with me."

That boy needed to be in his *own* damn movie. He was working it. He even had Alexandria smiling. At first she looked like she was ready to curse his behind out.

Then he took the whole cake. He asked her, "I mean, you do like guys, don't you? Please don't waste your prettiness hanging around all these girls all day. You need a nice, tall, handsome man on your arm sometimes."

He said all of that while he held on to her hand at the door.

I finally broke down and said, "This is my cousin, Jason, Tracy's younger brother."

He said, "I'm still older than you though, so don't let that younger brother stuff go to your head. My sister was just born before me."

Alexandria opened her mouth and asked him, "So how did you feel about her writing a book about your family?"

"I mean, it's life, man. What can I do about it? What I'ma sue her for it? She didn't say nothing bad about us. She just told the truth."

Alexandria's question didn't sound like one you would ask at midnight unless you planned to be up for a while. That meant one thing: she liked him. Because if she didn't, she wouldn't have asked him a question at all. Jason obviously had impressed her, and she was ready to go there with him, into long-form conversation.

He said, "But I don't really like to talk about that. I got my own life to live. You know what I mean? I got stories to tell of my own."

Please! I thought to myself. That boy was so full of shit.

I said, "Well, I'll let y'all go ahead and talk, because I'm going to bed now."

"Aw'ight, I'll see you tomorrow then, Vanessa."

He was even making it sound like we were the best of cousins. But I just decided to let it go. Somebody needed to break down Alexandria's high-horse–riding behind anyway.

Before I walked into my room, I told Jason, "Don't forget about your friend in Sasha and Jasmine's room."

He said, "Aw'ight, I got 'em in a minute," and went right back to talking to Alexandria.

I gave them one more look and shook my head before I used my key to get back into my room.

Day 2

This seventeen-year-old girl named Shannon Gray from Willingboro, New Jersey, was killing the lead as TRACY. Her interpretations were as natural as you could get to the real thing. So we had her perform five different scenes from the script to see how she would interpret each one of them.

In the drug house scene with a MERCEDES character to play off of, this girl actually made herself cry with real tears. We were all impressed.

Tracy asked her, "How many times have you read the book?"

She looked stunned. "Oh my God. At least twenty times."

"And you were practicing the scenes in the mirror?" Tracy asked her. It was obvious that this girl was very much prepared.

"Since I was like, thirteen," she told us.

She had the light eyes, the pretty face, long hair, and a nice body, but she lacked the imposing height of a real-life Tracy. But who said you needed to be exact on everything. This girl could really play the part. She fit.

"So this role would be a dream come true for you, hunh?"

Shannon placed both of her hands across her heart. "Very much so."

She spoke like a true academic, but she could play the role like a real home girl. Yet, she was still innocent and witty in her interpretation, and we all liked that. Many of the young actresses performed the lead character too hardened and street, which was the wrong interpretation, especially while performing in front of the real thing.

Tracy was very much aware that many urban girls read her teenaged behavior as "ghetto." But Tracy always considered herself more spoiled than anything else. She was used to getting what she wanted by any means necessary. And she had always made it clear that she never lived in the ghetto, nor could she relate to girls who did, including my mother, Patricia, her first cousin.

I understood exactly what Tracy meant. I was born and raised in the ghetto of North Philadelphia, but I never *acted* ghetto. That was not me. I've always been academic, and every 'hood in America still has girls who have their heads on straight. There are plenty of people from the ghetto who attend Catholic schools, private schools, and full academic schools, who never get caught up in their surroundings. Nevertheless, my two sisters, who grew in my same household, represented those other realities. On the whole, the black community was a lot more complicated than many of the interpretations and stereotypes gave it credit for.

Tracy explained that the neighborhoods of Germantown and Mt. Airy were unique in that they mixed kids who had been born and raised middle class with new kids who were just moving into the neighborhood from bleaker areas of Philadelphia, developing what she called a "hybrid" of middle class and lower middle class. These were kids who walked the line of having the option of doing what they needed to do to go to college, or getting caught up with the wrong crowd, where you could end up pregnant, in jail, strung out on drugs, or dead. This girl Shannon Gray from Willingboro, New Jersey, was able to capture that fine line dead-on in her performance. So Tracy scribbled four stars on her file.

When we took a lunch break and stepped away from the stage for a minute, an important discussion broke out between Tracy and Robin.

Robin said, "Tracy, I just want to warn you about getting these girls' hopes up too high for these roles. This is a very serious movie you have on your hands, and you don't want to undershoot it with too many unknowns. Now, I like this girl Shannon too, but can she open a movie? And does she have star personality? Because these performers are gonna have to help us to sell this thing."

Tracy said, "I know, but at least we can have some of these people as the base of what we need from the roles. I mean, I could have this girl Shannon coach whoever else would play the role from a Hollywood perspective, because she really understands it. But do we really want a Hollywood perspective at all?"

"Do you want Hollywood money?" Robin asked her.

"Do we?" Tracy questioned herself. "Because if we shoot this film right, it becomes a cult classic that these urban girls, who have read the book ten times each, will buy on DVD to watch over and over again. But if we do it the Hollywood way and it becomes just another vehicle for B-level stars, then it gains a little more exposure up front just to lose that cult following. Because the *Flyy Girl* readers would recognize the Hollywoodization of the story and not like it as much."

"Or, these B-level stars could become A-level by giving a great performance here that becomes their springboard for other roles," Robin argued. "So you still achieve the cult following that you want, with real up-and-coming stars who can always make reference to the film, like with Ice Cube, Laurence Fishburne, Cuba Gooding Jr., Morris Chestnut, and Nia Long in *Boyz n the Hood.* You see what I mean? Let's just make sure we mix it up."

Tracy said, "Oh, well, you know that's gonna happen. This is only the preliminary castings. There are real stars I want to go after, including Lynn Whitfield to play my mother."

Robin said, "Well, I also don't think we need to go to a bunch of different cities, looking for more unknown people. I mean, this is a Philadelphia movie, right? We're going to end up shooting it here, so I would use all of the people that we can use right here, and fly in the other performers that we'll need. Because you're giving yourself a bigger workload and spending more casting money when you don't need to."

Tracy said, "But the casting calls would spread the excitement for the film on a national level to make producers want to get in bed with us on it."

Robin said, "Tracy, we can do that with a good P.R. firm."

"What about the opportunities to sell my Flyy Girl Ltd. merchandise?"

"Oh, girl, you'll have plenty of time to do that. The Flyy Girl name will never stop being popular. You came ready-made with a brand name."

Robin had some good points. All I did was listen.

Tracy then looked at me, with the last of a turkey hoagie in my mouth.

She asked me, "Vanessa, what do you think?"

I was caught off guard by it. I nodded my head and pointed to Robin.

I mumbled "She's right" through my food.

Tracy nodded back to me. She said, "Okay, let's get back to work then. We need to narrow this talent down."

I was still munching on my food, so I stayed put a little longer.

"Those hoagies hit the spot, don't they?" someone asked me.

I looked to my right and spotted Shamor with his camera gear. He was smiling at me.

I smiled back and nodded to him. "I grew up on cheesesteaks and hoagies," I told him. "I'm from here."

He said, "I know. I was wondering if you could take me around to show me some places."

I paused for a minute. Was he asking me out? I thought he was hollering at Madison.

I said, "Yeah, we could all hang out together, if we get out of here early enough. I know I was worn out from yesterday."

I wanted to see how he would respond to a group situation.

He hesitated before he said, "Tell me about it. But ah . . ."

His look said it all. The boy was feeling me. He was trapped in his words while watching me eat. And I was so hungry that I didn't even care. I was just going to have to be a food mouth. I wasn't there to impress anybody. I was there to get a job done. But no wonder he was so eager to talk to me the night before. Maybe he was feeling me more than he was feeling my friend. Or he could have been running game on both of us. I didn't really know him, so what was I to think.

He said, "Well, we'll talk later. It's time to get back to work."

He smiled at me again and returned to his camera station.

I tried to hurry up with my food to get back to work myself. And as soon as I looked around the room from eating, I caught Maddy staring at me. I wondered immediately how long she had been watching me and if she had caught my brief conversation with Shamor. I figured that she had. But it didn't bother me. I wasn't there to meet guys. She could have him.

* * *

After a while I knew exactly what we were looking for in each *Flyy Girl* character. Not that I didn't have my own ideas already, but through the casting call, I was learning how to see through Tracy and Robin's eyes.

Of course, the lead role of TRACY had to really work the film, but the lead of VICTOR needed to be even stronger. VICTOR had to out-match TRACY's wit immediately. It was similar to the superhero and the villain in an action movie. VICTOR had to be a scene snatcher for us to believe that TRACY would fall head over heels for him. We all had to fall for him for it to work.

We had a guy from Washington, D.C., named Mark Fletcher, who really did it for me. He had smooth, dark brown skin, with dark, curly hair, and had an amazing presence about him. He knew that he was special even when he stood still. And when he performed for us, he presented an abundance of swagger, just what the role needed. There were plenty of other guys who worked magic as VICTOR as well, but Mark Fletcher was definitely my leading pick.

For the roles of MERCEDES and RAHEEMA, we were looking for girls who could play solid opposites, but also have some similarities in appearance and attitude. They were both Catholic school sisters from the same household, who felt oppressed by a tough-as-nails father, and a soft-as-a-feather mother. They just responded to their emotions differently. And to tell the truth, there were so many people we saw who could fit in either one of those roles, that I figured they would be better cast to professionals who could help sell the film for us. So I agreed totally with Robin on that one. It wasn't as if someone could ask for a potful of money for the co-starring roles. However, there was a good amount of beef on the bone in both parts that could really move a person's career forward. You would definitely have important screen time. So it was worth a shot for us to go after a few known names and faces for those roles.

For the parents—PATTI, DAVE, BETH, and KEITH—the opportunities were wide open. We could cast known names and faces, or a mix of the two. Tracy definitely had some Hollywood folks in mind for the parents. Nevertheless, we selected a few talents who fit the model that Tracy was looking for. They had to look thirty-five, have believable chemistry, and basically fit their prospective families. And even though Tracy was forced to kill their backstories for the screenplay, the *Flyy Girl* book gave all of the information that a person would need on how to portray the parents.

For the girlfriend roles of JANTEL and CARMEN, Tracy thought of using a real high-school track star, either locally or nationally, and a nationally known video girl.

"Some of these rap video girls are getting extremely popular nowadays. And they all want to act," she commented. "So we just grab one of them from BET to play CARMEN. They just have to look young enough and deliver their lines."

For the boyfriends—BRUCE, TIMMY, CASH, and CARL—the opportunities were endless. BRUCE was clean-cut and straightforward. TIMMY was criminalistic and violent. CASH was a charismatic hustler. And CARL was a college jock.

Then you had KIWANA and her COLLEGE GIRLS, all of VICTOR'S CREW, and a hundred smaller roles that needed to be filled, mostly by Philadelphians.

"This'll shape up to be a grand-scale movie with all of the extras you have in this thing," Robin stated.

Tracy smiled. She said, "But that was the eighties. It seemed like we had a larger teenaged population back then, didn't it? Nowadays, a lot of kids stay in the house more, doing whatever. But we were out and about during the eighties. I want to represent that extroverted personality of the original hip-hop generation in this film. I mean, that's what being flyy was all about in the eighties, being seen out at the parties."

Robin grinned and said, "You got that right. Kangol hats, fat shoelaces, and graffiti."

There were plenty of ways for everyday people to be seen in this *Flyy Girl* movie, that was for sure. We even looked at little boys from ages six to ten to play JASON as the kid brother. Could you imagine watching a gang of cute, brown boys who were all learning to memorize lines? It was just too much. Then I looked over at Alexandria, who had fallen for the grown-up Jason, and I knew that she was in big trouble. She was standing there watching plenty of gorgeous little boys, one of which would be selected to star as JASON in the film, while she got to talk to, and possibly date, the real thing.

I shook my head, grinned it off, and wondered about it. I didn't
sweat my cousin Jason at all, but I could see now how a girl could fall
for him. I never said that he was bad-looking. He was just . . . *ill*, my
cousin.

That second day at Freedom Theater wasn't as bad as the first. We
got out of there by seven o'clock instead of nine.

On our limo ride back to our hotel rooms at the Marriott, Robin
asked Tracy, "So, who do you have on your short list to direct this
film? You know, Chuck Stone from those 'Whassup?' Budweiser com-
mercials is from the Philadelphia area. He's getting serious looks from
Hollywood right now, and he's still inexpensive. And I hear the video
director Benny Boom is starting to look at scripts now, too. He's from
the Philadelphia area as well."

Tracy said, "We don't necessarily have to have a director from
Philadelphia. I mean, they're still going to be getting most of the information from me. I wrote the script and I'll be a part of the whole
process. We just need good camerawork."

It was already understood that Tracy would be a co-producer on
the film. She was used to producing now, and was already setting
things in motion. So Robin began to smile real wide as other ideas ran
through her mind. I had a feeling I knew what she was going to ask
Tracy next, but I waited for it to come out of her mouth before I
jumped the gun on it.

She said, "Knowing you and your reputation, I wouldn't be surprised if you tried to direct this movie yourself. No one is going to
know what you're trying to get across more than you do. And you're
right, you're the total visionary on this film."

"That's a great idea," Jasmine butted in. "I can see you directing
this, Tracy."

Tracy gave my girl a look to shut her big mouth. Jasmine read it
and did just that.

Tracy said, "As much as I hate to say it, Robin, I wouldn't want to
turn this film into a chick flick by me getting too involved with it. I
mean, you know how people get. Too much of my involvement may
have ruined my last two films. And I still view *Flyy Girl* as more of an

eighties story than just a girl's story. It's a representation of all of us, guys and girls."

Robin said, "But you still have to figure that *we*, black women and *girls* in particular, never get a chance to tell our own stories. I mean, what are we looking at—*The Color Purple*, *Waiting to Exhale*, and *What's Love Got to Do with It*. They were all based on books, written by black women but directed by men. Even Oprah Winfrey used a male director when she produced Toni Morrison's *Beloved*. I still felt she should have used Julie Dash from *Daughters of the Dust*, but what do I know about a black woman's perspective? I'm only a black woman. And none of those films dealt with the young, urban girls of our era."

Robin was in her early thirties, like Tracy. They were both first generation hip-hoppers.

Robin said, "We need a *Flyy Girl* movie right now more than anything. This is perfect timing. And it would be great for a woman to direct it. That's all I'm saying. I mean, look at all of those black male movies we've had over the years: *Boyz n the Hood*, *Juice*, *Menace II Society*, *South Central*, *New Jack City*, *Friday* and *Next Friday*, *Straight Out of Brooklyn*, *The Inkwell*, *The Wood* . . ."

I cut Robin off and said, "We had *Love and Basketball*."

She looked at me and said, "Thank you, Vanessa. And what is that, one movie out of twenty?"

"It had a woman director, too," Maddy added. "What about if you got her to direct *Flyy Girl*?"

Tracy said, "But she was very close to that story."

"Just like you're very close to yours," Robin commented.

Tracy shook her head and said, "I'm not even gonna talk about it anymore."

For a minute, everyone sat silently. Then we all started laughing. There was no way in the world Tracy was not going to talk about her movie. It was a ridiculous comment to make. But we all understood why she had said it. It was a lot to think about.

Robin asked, "Well, what does Mr. Omar Tyree have to say about your script?"

Tracy said, "He hasn't seen it yet."

"Are you planning on showing it to him?"

"Eventually. But I didn't want too many different opinions about the screenplay on my first draft. I just wanted to write it as I saw it first. He doesn't have any screenwriting credits anyway, and I do."

"What do you think he'll say about it?" Robin questioned.

"I mean, he's trying to write more guy stuff right now for himself," Tracy answered. "It's just hard to get girl projects done. Sister Souljah's book, *The Coldest Winter Ever*, has been talked about as a vehicle for Jada Pinkett Smith for years, and that hasn't gotten done either."

"Well, this project is gonna get done," Robin insisted. "But I hear that he's hard to deal with anyway."

"Who, Omar?" Tracy asked her for clarity.

"Yeah. I mean, he didn't want to write your sequel book, *For the Love of Money*, right? And then you guys ended up winning an NAACP Image Award for it."

Tracy said, "You know what, a lot of people talk about me the same way, and have never met me. 'I heard Tracy this,' and 'I heard Tracy that.' The bottom line is that he gets his work done, just like I do. So I gotta respect that. 'Cause a lot of people will hate on you for no good reason. But as long as you keep doing what you do, you'll keep meeting new people who want to work with you. And that's all I can say about it. He's doing his thing right now and I'm doing mine."

Well said. I agreed with Tracy. I had met Omar Tyree myself, and he was a straightforward, no-nonsense guy. He came to do what we came to do, and he went on about his business. I never saw him as a public entertainer or anything. He was a writer, and that's what he continued to do.

When we made it back to the Marriott Hotel, I had my eyes glued on Alexandria. I knew my cousin Jason was trying to get at her. And it was early enough for him to get a lot more time out of her than he had the night before.

"So, what do you guys want to do tonight?" I asked the group. We were walking through the hotel lobby on our way to the elevators.

Out of nowhere, Shamor popped up with a few of the camera crew members from New York. I had forgotten all about him.

"Hey, where's everybody off to tonight? What's poppin' in the city?" he asked us. "I'm ready to shower, get dressed, and go out."

I glanced at Maddy for a second to see how she would respond to him. I hadn't had any words with her about Shamor yet, but I was sure that she was thinking things.

Sasha spoke up first.

"We want to go to the movies and hang out on Delaware Avenue near the water."

Shamor was still eager. He said, "That sounds like a plan."

"At the United Artists?" I asked Sasha. She was familiar with the Philadelphia area. It was a thirty-minute drive up I-95 North from where her family stayed in Delaware.

She said, "Yeah." Then she asked, "Do you think Tracy will let us borrow the limo?"

They were all ready for an answer.

I said, "I don't know about that. I have to ask her. The limo driver may be done with us for the night. We don't have him on standby all night."

"Dag," Jasmine pouted. "We wanted to get him to drive us down South Street."

"What, and be stuck in traffic for an hour?" I stated.

"It doesn't take that long to make it through," Sasha argued.

I said, "Just about."

Shamor spoke up and said, "Well, we can all walk then. That's more fun to me, anyway. I want to see this city out in the open."

I glanced at Maddy again, and she looked back at me. I just didn't feel comfortable between them. But maybe I was overreacting to things. They weren't a couple or anything. They were only talking out in the hallway, just like Alexandria and my cousin. However, I knew what my cousin's intentions were, and I didn't know Shamor's intentions with either one of us.

I also didn't want to single Alexandria out, but I noticed that she had nothing to say about anything. So I was tempted to ask for her opinions on things just to see what she would say about her own plans.

However, Tracy walked by us all in the lobby with a few words for me before I could address my girl.

"Hey, Vanessa, I want to talk to you in my room again before you run off tonight," she told me. She, Robin, and a few of the older casting crew members had caught up to us at the elevators. They carried boxes of camera equipment, lighting materials, tapes, and bios from the day.

I said, "Okay." I figured I would catch back up with my girls afterward, and we would decide to do whatever.

So I grabbed two boxes to help carry to Tracy's room.

"I'll be back," I told my crew.

They all watched me get onto the elevator with Tracy while they continued to decide on their plans for the night.

I rode the elevator up with my cousin, and as soon as we stepped off to go to her room, she asked me, "So what do you think about me directing?"

I hadn't thought much more about it after the discussion inside the limo. I figured everything would work itself out in time.

I said, "I don't know. What makes a good director?"

"You have to have a particular vision and execution for the film," Tracy answered.

She made it sound too simplistic for me to believe her.

I asked her, "Is that all you need to have?"

"Well, you need to know what you're doing, first of all. But you generally work your way through it, knowing what you want out of each and every character, and each and every scene."

It sounded as if Tracy was trying to convince herself. She was trying to talk herself into directing by making the process sound extra simple.

I said, "They have co-directors right, like the Hughes Brothers? You could do something like that, just to make sure that you're doing it right. Because I would hate to see you not have it done the right way because you're trying to do too much on your own. I mean, I hear Robin's point, but I also heard your point. And I think the more important part is getting the film done right, and not so much about whether a man or a woman is directing it."

Tracy looked at me and grinned. She said, "You don't think I can do it."

I didn't want to say that, but I was skeptical of whether she was ready for directing.

She said, "Remember, Vanessa, I'm not going to be starring in this movie. So I finally get a chance to watch the development of the whole process."

I didn't know what to say. How could I tell my cousin not to direct her movie without it sounding like I doubted her?

I said, "I just don't want to see you make a big mistake with this movie based on what Robin is saying." I told her, "Sometimes it's better to be the hero who lets the other heroes do their parts, like *X-Men* or something."

Tracy said, "I see. Well, just to keep a balanced perspective, I was wondering if you'd like to tag along with me for when I meet up with the real-life people who my story is based on. You already know what I'm looking for."

I didn't see a problem with it. It would be fun meeting the real characters from *Flyy Girl*. So I nodded to her and said, "Okay. I can do that. So, when do you want us to start?"

I needed to make room in my schedule for hanging out with my girls, and for meeting up with my mom and sisters.

Tracy said, "I already started contacting them. So you just keep your schedule open."

I got back to Sasha and Jasmine's room and was dressed and ready to go. Everyone was there but Alexandria.

"Did Tracy say we could get the limo?" Jasmine asked me.

I had forgotten all about it. I said, "I didn't even get to ask her. We were talking about some other stuff. But where's Alexandria?"

Maddy looked at me and said, "She had something else she wanted to do."

I looked at Sasha to see how she would respond.

Sasha read my look and said, "I'm not bothered by it at all, Vanessa. I'm no more than friends with Jason. I mean, I did like him like that at one time, but . . . you know, you grow out of it."

It sounded like denial to me, but Sasha wasn't the kind to sulk. She was always getting offers.

She said, "So let's go out and have a good time, man. The next movie starts at ten-ten."

Jasmine said, "But how do we get there with no limo? Isn't that too far to walk?"

She had a point. Delaware Avenue was at least a ten-block hike.

Maddy frowned at her and answered, "We take a damn cab."

I asked, "So are we waiting for Shamor and them, too?"

Maddy answered, "I guess so."

She made it sound as if it was a problem. I didn't get into that. I just planned to have a good time.

When we met up with Shamor and his camera guys and walked out from the hotel, headed for Delaware Avenue, all I could think about was Alexandria and Jason. I wondered what Tracy would think about the two of them together. And I wondered if she would get mad at me for my girl doing her own thing. Then again, Alexandria was older than me. She was twenty. So whatever she was up to with my cousin was on her.

"What are you over here thinking about?" Shamor asked me.

He brought my attention back to our outing as we attempted to wave down a few cabs.

I said, "Oh, I'm just daydreaming. Don't mind me."

"Well, what do you daydream about when you're daydreaming?"

Shamor was obviously trying really hard to converse with me, and the more he tried, the more I avoided it. I even jumped in a separate cab from him and Maddy to send him a clear message—talk to my girl, not to me.

Jasmine even picked up on it as she rode in the cab beside me.

She smiled at me and whispered, "It looks like somebody's feeling you around here."

I smiled back at her and said, "I know."

And all night long I tried to avoid Mr. Cameraman, who made my night a lot more draining than I had planned.

Sisters

Y ou said you was gon' take me out to eat on South Street when you came back home, and you just calling me now? You been home since this weekend."

My sister Veronica was chewing me out over the hotel phone.

I told her, "Yeah, but I'm not home on pleasure. We've been running around nonstop since we got here."

"Yeah, well, my girlfriend Tara said that she saw you down South Street last night with a bunch of models or actresses or something."

I was stuck. I should have just taken my sister out Sunday night and gotten it over with before we got too busy with the casting calls. It was now Wednesday, June 18, and we were starting our workday at noon instead of at nine in the morning, like we did on the first two days. We were getting a little more downtime, so I finally called my sister. However, she was right. I should have called my family earlier. Procrastination kills.

I said, "Well, what about if we go out to eat tonight?"

"What if I'm busy tonight?" my sister responded to me.

"Busy doing what?"

"Whatever I'm doing."

I paused a minute. I needed to clear my head before I said anything irrational to her. Veronica liked twisting your words into weapons.

I said, "You want to come down to the casting call? It'll be much less crowded today."

I decided to change the subject to try and brighten the mood.

Veronica said, "I'll let you talk to Tiffany about that. I don't care about this movie like she does."

My sister was really beginning to disturb me. It seemed like she was giving me a hard time just for the hell of it, but I knew there had to be a reason.

124

I said, "Well, what do you care about, Veronica? You're always saying you don't care about something."

"I don't care" was Veronica's favorite phrase, ever since we were kids: *I don't care about this, I don't care about that, I don't care about whatever.*

She said, "Whatever, Vanessa. I'm getting dressed right now. You can call me back later."

"Well, let me talk to Tiffany, then," I told her.

"*Tiffany!* Your sister's on the phone!" Veronica hollered through the house.

I held the phone away from my ear and shook my head. I could understand if Veronica was mad about her predicament in life, but attitude problems only made the situation worse. She had to learn how to be more proactive and less negative.

I said, "You hurt yourself more than you hurt others when you make bad decisions, Veronica. I just want you to know that."

I figured I'd slip a few words of wisdom out to my sister while she still held the phone in her hand.

She snapped, "What? What are you talking about?"

"I'm talking about your attitude."

"I don't have an attitude."

"Are you sure?"

My sister got mad and let me have it again.

"Look, Vanessa, I don't have time for your mental games this morning. Now I told you, you're not as smart as you *think* you are. So go play them mind games on somebody the fuck else!" and she slammed the phone on my ear before I could talk to Tiffany.

I took a breath and called the house right back. I was assuming that Veronica would let the phone ring and allow Tiffany to answer it. But it didn't work out that way.

"Hello," Veronica answered again.

I paused. Did I really want to continue a dispute with her, or simply move on from it.

I said, "Let me talk to Tiffany." It was time to move on. I decided it was too early in the day for me to waste too much of my energy on obvious immaturity.

"*Tiffany!*" Veronica yelled into my ear again.

I took a deeper breath and maintained my poise until my baby sister was on the phone.

"Hello," Tiffany answered.

I immediately asked her, "What is her problem?" referring to Veronica. She was really frustrating me, and I couldn't even talk to her.

Tiffany answered, "PMS," without missing a beat.

I couldn't help but crack a smile. I went from a serious attitude sister to a jokester.

She said, "Anyway, what's up with the casting calls for *Flyy Girl*? Can Tracy put me in the movie as an extra or what?"

I could see Tiffany in a movie scene as clear as day. She was a medium brown, lanky, and humorous teenaged girl who could crack jokes with the best of them.

"Can you write your own lines?" I challenged her.

Tiffany went right into her own scene:

"That girl Tracy swear she the shit. But she need to wipe her ass, 'cause I can smell her from over here. *Bitch*."

I had a delayed response to it. At first it was shocking, but then I began to smile. It was a sour kind of humor that you had to think about.

I said, "This is not an R-rated movie, Tiffany."

She said, "So, let me get this straight, we can't cuss in this movie, after all the cussing she did in her book?"

It appealed to me at that moment that Tiffany had always had a foul mouth, but she got away with it because she used a humorous touch.

I said, "Actually, the screenplay doesn't have as much hard language as the book. And there's not a whole lot of speaking scenes for extras. That's why I asked you if you could come up with something."

"Oh. Well, let me play the Jantel role. You know I'm going to Simon Gratz this year. I might go out for the track team," my sister told me.

I paused. I didn't want to get her hopes up for something too big.

I said, "I think you need to focus on just a role as an extra. I'm not even going to talk about any other role with you. These people are professionals."

"And I'm not?"

I said, "I think you could be a professional one day, but you're not right now. You're not even in high school yet."

"Tennis players become professionals at my age."

"You're not a tennis player either," I told her.

"I could be," she responded. "I'm built like a tennis player. You could even call me Tiffany Williams."

I could see that my conversation with Tiffany would end up all over the place. She always had a flighty mind like that. She would jump from one illusion to the next.

I asked her, "What time are you planning on coming to the auditions? I can have someone looking out for you at the door. You can at least see what everyone else looks like."

We were narrowing down the performers we wanted to call back for quality roles and screen time.

Tiffany said, "Can you pick me up and take me down there? I'm a little weak on bus fare right now."

"If I pick you up, it'll be around eleven-thirty, and I'll have no time to wait for you to get ready. Or better yet, you could just ride your bike over?" I suggested.

She said, "Ride my bike? All the way to Freedom Theater? What do you think, I'm going out for the Tour de France sometime soon, and I need training? That's a long way."

I smiled again. I said, "If you really want to be there, you'll be there. I won't be picking you up every day when we start shooting this film."

"Yeah, but I might have money by then," she told me.

"What, you're getting a summer job?"

"No, but I play the lottery. I'm gonna win any day now. You watch."

Tiffany was full of jokes.

I joked myself and said, "Okay, you can buy yourself a role then."

Tiffany paused and mocked me.

"Ha-ha, ha-ha, ha-ha. You're not even funny. Get ready for early retirement."

"Whatever. Well, I was just calling to check up on you," I told her.

"When you coming to the house?" she asked me.

"For what? She don't want to come over here. She's a California girl now," I heard Veronica pipe in the background. I wondered how much of the conversation she had listened to, or if she had just walked back into the room.

"PMS," Tiffany whispered to me again. "I hope I never get it bad like that."

Tiffany had me locked on a smile. I was glad she was there to talk to. She had lessened the pain of talking to Veronica.

I said, "If I come back home, it sounds like Veronica'll be there camped out to beat me up."

Tiffany said, "Please. Only one sister in this house had heart enough to put her hands up to Mom. But I'ma do it too soon . . . when I wake up."

That joke wasn't funny. I didn't know how I felt about that. Hitting my mother was like a permanent black eye to my character. Anyone could bring it up at any time. And they did.

However, I was curious.

I asked, "Do you and Veronica talk about that a lot?"

"Umm . . . what do you consider a lot?"

"More than five times since it happened."

I was just throwing out a number.

Tiffany said, "Oh, well, we always talk about it then. We talk about it five times a week. We make sure we mumble it under our breaths though. 'That's why Vanessa bust you in the mouth.' "

I had to force myelf not to laugh. Tiffany must have fallen on her head too many times as a baby, because she had obviously lost a lot of her marbles.

I said, "Don't let that slip out on you. But I have to start getting myself ready now. It's almost eleven o'clock."

"So, you're not gonna pick me up then?"

She was pressing me.

I said, "I'm gonna be with a group of people and I won't be driving."

"Yeah, Veronica said you was hanging out with the Oxygen Foundation now."

"Oxygen Foundation?"

I didn't know what she was talking about.

She said, "Yeah, your crew got their noses all up in the air, sucking up the oxygen. Won't you tell them to save some for us."

That was about enough for me. Tiffany could run her mouth for hours, and all about nothing. So I cut her short and said, "Okay, I will."

When my girls and I were all dressed and ready to go, wearing our third set of Flyy Girl Ltd. clothes for the week, I found myself itching to ask Alexandria how her night had gone and what all she had done. She had never been one to talk too much about her personal life. Nevertheless, I couldn't think straight without knowing something.

"Did everybody sleep good last night?" I hinted. We were standing at the elevators, ready to catch one down.

"Like a baby," Jasmine responded. She responded to everything.

One down, three to go, I told myself.

"What about you, Sasha? The bedbugs bite you hard last night?"

"Oh, I was up watching HBO. They always have those good original movies at night."

"So, we came from the movies, and then you went right back to watching more movies?" I asked her.

"Yeah, I was just up," she told me with a chuckle.

"You stayed up, too, Maddy?" I moved down the line and asked.

Maddy answered "No," real curt. She seemed like she had an attitude with me, and I knew exactly why, but I didn't want to comment on it out in the open with everyone.

Before I could get to Alexandria, the elevator doors opened. Four people were already riding it down from the higher floors. I knew I couldn't get Alexandria to talk in that environment, so I waited for us to reach the bottom. When we finally did, Robin, Shamor, and the rest of the New York camera crew were all waiting for us.

"Hey, it's time to go, girls. Let's go, let's go, let's go."

Robin practically pushed us through the hotel lobby toward the limo that was parked outside at the front entrance. Tracy was already waiting inside. I didn't want to get into a conversation about Alexandria being out with Jason in front of Tracy. I still had to figure everything out first.

"So, what did y'all do last night?" Tracy asked us.

"We went to the movies, South Street, Delaware Avenue," Sasha answered.

"Any guys try to get those digits?" Tracy joked to us.

"That's always," Jasmine answered.

Tracy looked at Alexandria and said, "What about you, Alexandria? You find anything you like in Philly?"

My heart jumped into my throat. I just didn't know what to think about a Jason/Alexandria connection. But what could I do about it? If they liked each other, they liked each other. Then again, Jason had forced me to introduce them.

After Tracy's question to her, Alexandria cracked a smile. I sat there and watched her every move.

She said, "Maybe. You never know."

Maddy grinned and looked away.

"What are you grinning about, Madison? You meet somebody here, too?" Tracy asked her.

I looked away after that. It seemed that the same guy had somehow intertwined himself with Maddy and me without my even trying to be involved in it.

Maddy answered, "Not exactly," and everybody got real quiet.

Then my cousin looked at me.

"What about you, Vanessa? Any old fling get your eyes open?"

I didn't feel like having that kind of conversation. But since she was asking me, I decided to play devil's advocate.

I said, "What if they did? And what if I had company over last night? How would you respond to that?"

I knew that a good discussion would throw things off of me, so I was willing to give it a try.

Robin looked over at Tracy in the limo with a raised brow.

It was weird. We had all read about how wild Tracy was as a teenager, but there we were, walking on eggshells with her about our own personal lives.

She asked me, "What would you expect me to say? I'm not your mother."

Jasmine spoke up again. I guess she just couldn't help herself.

She said, "Yeah, but you did bring us out here. And I think we all feel like we don't want to let you down. Especially Vanessa. She has to live with you."

For once, Jasmine's big mouth actually made some sense.

Tracy nodded to us. She said, "You guys have all read about me in my books. I've made mistakes, so you already know that I'm far from perfect."

Sasha said, "Yeah, but that was a long time ago. And we all understand that . . . and you know, you've made some great accomplishments. So even though we know what you've been through, we also see where you are now."

Maddy said, "In fact, since we know you're not perfect, we can't really front like you don't know what time it is. You know what I mean? It's like, you already know the ropes."

"And that's all the more reason for you guys to open up to me," Tracy argued. "I know what it's like trying to make the right decisions as a girl. And I don't even have kids yet, so please don't treat me like a parent."

We all laughed a little. Her joke loosened up the tension in the back of the limo.

"I see what they're all saying though, Tracy," Robin stated. "I mean, you do understand that you're not just a regular person anymore. Whether you like it or not, these girls look up to you now, and I'm not just talking about the girls in this car. You literally have *thousands* of urban American girls who have read your book and who swear by you. That's why making this movie is so important, so the girls who still haven't read it can be affected by your story now."

"And you guys all think my story is that important?" Tracy asked us all.

"Yeah," we all responded to her.

Robin said, "Tracy, you have *theee* coming-of-age book. No other book comes close to it."

"Sister Souljah's," Maddy commented.

Robin said, "Yeah, but everybody's daddy is not a drug dealer. I'm sorry, but I did not relate to that one."

"A lot of people do though," Maddy argued.

"Generation gap," Robin commented. "*Flyy Girl* has less of a generation gap, and I believe that more black *women*, in general, will relate to it. So this film can reach a much wider audience. Hell, even white girls can relate to running too fast after the wrong boys."

"Asians, too," Sasha spoke up with a proud grin.

"And Latinas," Jasmine told her.

"I can't see why we can't do both movies," Maddy suggested. "We have a lot of different perspectives in the black community."

Robin said, "Oh, believe me, if *The Coldest Winter Ever* or *Flyy Girl* gets made, and either one of them is successful at the box office, you can plan on seeing many more of them. That's just how Hollywood works."

"They didn't make a lot more movies after *Set It Off*," Alexandria finally spoke up. She had been quiet for most of the ride.

Robin smiled and said, "Yeah, you're right. But they didn't need to make more movies like that one. That movie had the wrong messages everywhere you looked."

"But it was about sisterhood," Alexandria commented.

"That movie was about *foolishness,*" Robin argued strongly.

Alexandria smiled it off. She said, "Sisters can be foolish, too. That's all a part of real life. Everyone can't play the good-girl roles."

"Yeah, but it seems like the bad girls get all the attention," I commented myself. I had been quiet, too, just listening to everyone.

Tracy nodded to me. She said, "That reminds me." She held her index finger up and kept her thoughts to herself for the moment.

But when we arrived at Freedom Theater for that third day of casting, she pulled me aside and said, "I want you to go out with me to dinner tonight. Raheema's coming into town this afternoon, and I'm going out to eat with her and Mercedes, and I want you to be there to vibe with us."

I was speechless. It was an honor.

I said, "Okay. But what about my girls?"

I didn't want to just abandon them in Philadelphia.

Tracy answered, "I'll have Robin hang out with them tonight."

So what else could I say?

"Okay."

* * *

I was sitting at a four-chair table with Tracy and Raheema at the Zanzibar Blue restaurant and jazz club on Broad Street downtown. And I was nervous. I had met Raheema a little earlier at the casting call when she stopped by, but to have her and her sister Mercedes at the same table was different. It was as if I could feel the tension before Mercedes even arrived.

"Excuse me, aren't you Tracy Ellison Grant, the actress and book author?" a long-blond-haired white woman stepped up and asked.

Tracy looked up and nodded to her. "Yes, I am."

The blond woman flashed a million-dollar smile on cue. She looked like a tall, lean, top-flight model.

She said, "I love your work. Let me give you my card."

She reached into her purse and pulled out a card to hand to Tracy.

She said, "I'm Ellen Carter, runway model and aspiring actress myself. So if you need a blonde in any of your upcoming films to beat up or tell off, then I'm your girl."

It was a great line. She got a laugh out of us.

Tracy took her card and said, "I'll think of something."

As soon as the woman left us, Raheema grinned and commented, "I guess she feels that you can't get along with a white woman in your films."

Tracy shrugged. "Maybe I can't. I haven't gotten along with them so far."

I tried to relax and just enjoy their company. But then Raheema looked dead at me.

"So, how do you get along with your sisters?" she asked me out of the blue. Her hair was cut shorter than Mercedes's, with the same fine texture, and her complexion was as light as mine. She wore a dark blue pants and shirt set that blended in with the dark ambience of the restaurant. Her personality was extremely calm and professional. She carried herself like the college professor that she was, and she was in her early thirties, like Tracy.

I said, "Actually, I was supposed to take my sister out to eat, too."

"Who, Veronica?" Tracy asked me.

"Yup."

"And she didn't want to hear about you being busy, did she?" Tracy assumed.

I didn't want to put all the blame on my sister.

I answered, "I should have taken her out to eat Sunday. I did promise it to her."

Tracy said, "You'll do it tomorrow. We'll have even more down-time then."

I said, "And now Tiffany keeps asking me about the casting call and being an extra in the movie."

"Oh, don't worry about that," Tracy told me. "If we shoot it in Philadelphia, she'll be in the movie. And most likely, we'll be shooting this movie in Philadelphia."

Raheema smiled. She asked, "How many of the roles have you locked in already?"

"None," Tracy answered. "Nothing is set in stone until this film has been green-lighted with a giant paycheck."

"When do you find that out?"

"Really, there's no time line on it. I've written the screenplay, we're casting people, we're scouting locations, we're identifying food caterers, we're thinking about directors. . . . The more we can account for in a prospectus budget, the easier it becomes for producers to back us on it."

Raheema nodded. "I see. So in other words, you're getting the party started so the producers can decide if they would like to dance to the music or not."

"Exactly."

I became more concerned with watching the entrance of the restaurant for when Mercedes would make her grand entrance. I understood how much of a stir Mercedes was capable of making, so I guess I was expecting a display of fireworks from her.

"Excuse me, do you mind if I ask you for an autograph. You can sign it on the back of my card."

I looked up and spotted a dark brown man in a dark sports jacket and a burgundy tie. He placed his business card on the table next to Tracy, face up. But she picked it up and gave it right back to him unsigned.

She looked into his handsome dark face and said, "Maybe when I'm done eating."

He nodded and said, "I'ma hold you to that. By the way, my name is Rick Bailey. I'm an attorney."

She said, "Yes, I saw that."

"So I'll speak to you later then?" he pressed her.

"We'll see."

When he walked away, Tracy looked irritated. She told Raheema, "It looks like I'm gonna have to tell these people at the restaurant to put some security guards around us or something to stop people from fucking up our dinner."

"You mean security guards around *you*. The rest of us are just fine," Raheema stated. Then she looked down at her gold-plated watch. "It looks just like old times," she commented of Mercedes's tardiness.

Tracy only grinned at her while taking a sip of the chicken broth appetizer she had ordered.

It was nearing ten o'clock, and the dinner meeting had been set for nine. But we hadn't arrived until quarter after nine ourselves.

Of course, as soon as I stopped watching the entranceway, Mercedes slid inside the door and made her way over to the table to surprise us.

"Nobody was here at nine, so I made a quick stop at the bookstore," she explained to us as she took the empty seat directly across from me. She carried a Borders purchase bag in her left hand with a black leather purse in her right. Opposite Raheema's dark blue, Mercedes wore blinding yellow that stood out in the dark.

Tracy smiled at her. "No big deal," she commented. "We're all here now."

"This is your cousin, Vanessa?" Mercedes asked in reference to me.

"Yeah."

Mercedes reached her hand across the table to me. I took it in mine and shook it lightly.

"So now I finally get to place your face," she stated. We had talked briefly over the phone on several occasions. Mercedes then shook Raheema's and Tracy's hands as if we were all at a serious business meeting. I guess she was thinking all business.

"I was at the casting call the other day when you stopped by, too," I told her.

"Yeah, I was just in the neighborhood that night and remembered that Tracy was at Freedom Theater."

I didn't believe her, but I wondered how badly I was judging her based on the books that Tracy had published. I realized that Mercedes was right, I was judging her behavior almost solely on the material that I had read about her. So what would everyone else do?

"You need to order," Raheema told her. "We got tired of waiting for you."

Mercedes picked up the menu that was set out on the table in front of her. She said, "It's a simple order for me. If all else fails, order chicken."

And that's what she ordered when the waitress came back to serve us.

"So now we have two books and a movie about us in the works," Mercedes commented.

"You don't feel good about it?" Raheema asked her. "I look like a crybaby and a wimp in the first one, and a survivor in the second."

Mercedes grunted, "Hmmph. Well, I don't look good in either one of them." Then she looked at me.

"What would you do in my position, Vanessa?"

She had me on the spot. I was only there to observe. Why was she calling me out?

I said, "The only thing I can think about doing is making sure that my life has changed so I can use whatever as a stepping-stone."

It was the best answer I could come up with to play both sides of the coin. The truth was the truth, but every person deserved their right to privacy. Then again, Mercedes's right to privacy would kill a major part of *our* movie. And I call it "our movie" because Tracy's story had become very meaningful to everyone, and Mercedes happened to be a major part of that story. Therefore, the overall power of the book overruled Mercedes's own concern for privacy. She was still able to live and be employed. She just had to make the best out of her life. Hell, if she chose, she could have used her downfalls as a teenaged drug addict to speak at drug centers across the country about how to turn your life around after being addicted and decimated by recreational drugs. However, I didn't dare say that to her in public. I would offer that advice to Mercedes in private, and hope that she wouldn't chew my head off for it.

She stared at me and grinned. "Use it as a stepping-stone, hunh? To do what?"

"You don't have to answer that," Tracy told me. She was already becoming irritated with Mercedes, but I figured I could handle myself, so I answered her question anyway.

I said, "You could speak about it and make your story just as important as Tracy's and Raheema's. I mean, it is, really. Without you, there would be no Tracy or Raheema. Somebody had to start things in motion, and that somebody just happens to be you."

"Start things in motion?"

Mercedes eyed me across the table with a grill. I don't believe my attempted logic was making the situation any better.

Raheema said, "She's right, both of us were drastically affected by you."

"Oh, so now everything is my fault?" Mercedes asked us.

"Yeah, it's your fault," Tracy told her. "Without you, none of us would be famous."

Mercedes said, "I have nothing to do with what you did, Tracy. Are you gonna give me credit for writing your poetry, too?"

It was a complicated question.

Tracy said, "I give you the credit for creating the stimulus of my thought process, but it was up to me to decide how to transform that into something that can be used for all of us."

Great answer! I was proud of my cousin.

Raheema said, "We all have that choice to challenge ourselves and make something positive out of the chaos that may be around us. And the truth is, your situation brought both of our families back together in a stronger way, Mercedes. Tracy was on her way to being kicked out of her house, and I had no way of healing my own pain without you coming back home like you did. So you have to stop looking at it as if you were going through everything by yourself. We were there with you all of the time, and we still are. You're our big sister no matter what."

Wow! I felt like crying and calling my own two sisters. *You're our big sister no matter what?* That statement from Raheema meant a lot to me. I was a big sister myself. And Mercedes couldn't argue with it.

"Hmmph," she grunted again. "Some big sister I am. I should be proud of both of you. But all I'm thinking about is myself."

No one responded to that.

Mercedes took a deep breath and said, "Okay. So you guys wanna make this movie. I just have to deal with it then. I can't stop you from telling the truth."

"Nobody's gonna chastise you about the role you play in it once they see the entire film. You have the most redeeming role in the movie, hands down," Tracy commented. "It has to be there. And it's gonna outshine both of us."

Mercedes let it all sink in. She nodded her head at the table and said, "Okay." Then she smiled. "So, who's gonna play me?" she asked.

Tracy smiled right back at her. She answered, "We don't know yet. We'll keep working on it. But whoever it is, they'll have to act their asses off."

"I know that's right," Raheema agreed with a chuckle.

"Yeah, because the real thing is a serious character," Tracy added.

Mercedes looked at them both and said, "Look here, don't patronize me. I know good bullshit when I hear it. Now, I'll let y'all do this movie without interfering, but I still won't like it until it's all over and done with."

I sat there and listened and made note of everything. I still didn't feel that Mercedes understood the importance of her story within Tracy's and Raheema's stories. It would never be all over and done with. Once we made a movie based on the book, based on real life, all of their stories would become an urban bible, whether they liked it or not.

The Good, the Bad, and the Ugly

"That was beautiful the way you two explained your love to Mercedes tonight," I told my cousin.

Tracy just looked at me and shook her head with a frown. She said, "That conversation is hardly over with. Mercedes is gonna need money, or *think* she needs money, long before this film is in the can. And she is most definitely going to ask me for it."

We were on our way back to the hotel, and since Zanzibar Blue on Broad Street was literally three blocks away from the Marriott on Market Street, we decided to walk.

I smiled and asked, "So, you think she's going to continue to bring up money, hunh?"

Tracy gave me a look and didn't bother to repeat herself. I got the point. She knew Mercedes well. And Tracy never did autograph a business card for Mr. Bailey. But I knew that wasn't going to happen. My cousin already had her hands full, and a new man was not on her menu.

When we arrived back at the hotel, I began to think about Jason and Alexandria again.

"So, did Robin take my girls out, do you know?" I asked Tracy. I was just about to call them on the cell phone.

"As far as I know, they went out somewhere," she told me.

I decided to knock on their doors and check their rooms before I called them.

"So, what are you gonna do for the rest of the night, order some movies?" my cousin asked me. It was after eleven o'clock.

"Probably not," I answered. "All I seem to do is fall asleep when I order hotel movies. I guess it's too much of a relaxed environment for me."

Tracy smiled at me. She said, "Well, I may have someone else for you to meet tomorrow. My girl Kiwana is coming down to the casting, and I've already made a couple of phone calls to get in contact with Bruce."

I looked into her eyes to make sure.

I said, "You're gonna contact Bruce from your high school days?"

"Why, is there something wrong with that?"

"I mean, what are you gonna ask him?"

"You just let me do the talking, girl," she huffed at me. "You don't worry about that, just listen and keep an open mind."

"So, how many of your old friends are you planning to meet up with?"

She told me, "Plenty of them. I have a few more phone calls to make right now to track them all down. Why, are you afraid to meet them?" she asked me. "They're all regular people. And you better get used to meeting all kinds of people if you want to be in the film business, Vanessa. You won't have any time for being shy."

Once she got started, who would ever think that I actually had to push my cousin into producing her life story for film? She was really taking the bull by the horns.

I said, "I'm not afraid to talk to them, I just have to prepare myself for it."

We had made it up to my floor on the elevator.

Tracy said, "Prepare for what? You listen, respond, and take your mental notes. What's there to prepare for?"

I was at a loss for words when the elevator doors opened.

"Uhhh . . . okay," I told her.

Tracy held the doors open. She said, "If you must, then put a few of your thoughts down in reference to Bruce, Victor, Carl, Kiwana . . . I mean, you've read enough about all of them to have plenty of questions and comments. So prepare away, and I'll talk to you in the morning."

I was certainly excited at being an insider on all of the meetings between Tracy and her old friends, I was just a little nervous about it, that's all. Who wouldn't be? These people were practically icons as far as I was concerned.

Anyway, as soon as I approached my hotel room, I remembered that I wanted to check up on my girls. I walked to Sasha and Jasmine's room and heard nothing, so there was no sense in even knocking on their door. They were not in. Jasmine even slept with the television on loud. I felt sorry for Sasha. Then again, Sasha had a way of tuning things out and zoning into her own little world. So I guess the two of them were a perfect tandem of friends.

I moved on to Maddy and Alexandria's room. They were nowhere near as loud as Sasha and Jasmine. I didn't expect to hear much out of their room. Most likely, they were all out with Robin anyway. But then I caught a feeling. I leaned my ear up against the door to listen in on the room like a spy. And I thought I heard something. I readjusted my ear to the door to listen again.

Real faintly, I thought I heard soft moaning. I tried to concentrate on bed noises and movement inside the room, but I couldn't hear any. So I went back to concentrating on the moaning.

"*Mmm . . . mmm . . . ooh . . .*"

I leaned back away from the door and was shocked. There *was* moaning going on inside the room. But I had to give it to them, they were being real discreet about it.

I thought about knocking on the door to bust things up, but what right did I have to do that? Then I got curious and listened again.

"*Oooh, Jason . . . oooh, yeah.*"

Alexandria's moaning was getting louder, and the bed was beginning to squeak. I guess I had caught them at the perfect time. Even Jason began to moan.

"*Ahh, ahhh, ahhh, oooh, ooh, oooh.*"

"*Yeaaah, yeah, yeaahh.*"

"*Oooh, ooh, oooooh . . .*"

That was enough for me. I had heard all I needed to hear. Alexandria and Jason were surely getting into things, full throttle. So I walked back to my room and took out my cell phone to call Maddy.

"Hello," Maddy answered with plenty of noise in the background.

I cut straight through to the chase. I asked her, "Is Alexandria with you?" I knew the answer already, I just wanted to make sure.

Maddy answered, "No, she got sick on us."

"She got sick? What do you mean by that?" I asked her.

"What do you think I mean?" Maddy snapped at me. "She said she didn't feel good."

I guess Maddy and I were not on the best of terms with Shamor between us. I wasn't even feeling the boy like that.

"What time was it when she said that?" I asked.

"As soon as we got back to the room. Look, why don't you call her and ask her yourself? Better yet, why don't you go knock on the door?"

Once Maddy asked me that, I realized that I had made a mistake. I wasn't supposed to call and drop the bomb on Alexandria. I was supposed to beat around the bush and let my girls tell me what I wanted to know on their own. But it was too late for that. But at least I called Maddy instead of Jasmine. And there was no way I was going to call Sasha about it. Because if Alexandria was sick, there was a good possibility that my cousin Jason was involved in her sickness. Sasha would have known that, but I believe Maddy did as well.

I asked her, "When are you guys planning on getting back?"

"Why?" she asked me back. Then she said, "Look, I don't have time to sit here talking to you, I'm trying to enjoy myself. So you figure things out on your own." And she hung up on me.

I then thought about calling Alexandria and Jason on the hotel phone. That girl had some nerve to do my cousin right there in the hotel room that Tracy had provided for her. Miss High and Almighty turned out to be quite raunchy. And she had only known him for a few days.

I couldn't believe it. In fact, I snuck back out in the hallway with my cell phone in hand to call her hypocritical behind. I stood right by the door and listened again, and they were still both at it. I guess they were on their next round of moaning or whatever, and they were both making more noise.

"Ooh, yeah. Ooh, girl. Yeah . . ."

"Yes, baby, yes. Ooh, Jason. Ooh, baby . . ."

I froze like an iceberg. My heart was racing like I don't know what. I just couldn't believe it. Alexandria was giving it to my cousin when she had just met the damn boy. I thought again about calling her to bust their damn groove, but the idea seemed silly and useless at that point. They were already doing the do. So I just walked back to my room and left them alone.

When I closed and locked my door, I was seriously conflicted. What was Alexandria's real purpose with Jason? Did she really like him, or did she have ulterior motives? And what about Jason? Was Alexandria really the bomb for him, or just another notch on his ho' belt?

I thought again about her question to Jason concerning Tracy's book, his family life being public knowledge, and about the whole movie production. I thought that maybe Alexandria Greene had slipped right by me as an undercover groupie. I don't know. Maybe I was just underestimating my cousin's pimp skills simply because he was my cousin. I mean, Jason did have the look, the height, the gift of bullshit, and confidence for days. But he was just . . . my damn *cousin*! How could Alexandria fall for him?

"They both got some nerve," I mumbled to myself as I paced inside my room. "They're gonna do it right here in the hotel room that Tracy paid for, and where anybody can come back to the rooms and bust them. Stupid!" I expressed to myself.

My room phone rang and startled me. I had no idea who it could be.

"Hello," I answered.

"I got good news, Vanessa."

It was Tracy. My heart started beating fast again, as if *I* was the one who had done something slimy.

"What?" I asked her.

"I finally talked to Bruce tonight, and he said that he can make it to dinner with us tomorrow night."

I said, "I thought we were gonna go out with Kiwana."

I didn't really want to be around my cousin with old flings of hers. It just didn't feel right. It felt like I would be in the way or something, whether she still had feelings for them or not. I would rather just hang out with her and her old girlfriends.

She said, "No problem, we'll meet with them both, and I'll introduce them to each other. They're both married now anyway," she told me.

I guess she realized what I was feeling.

I said, "Oh, okay."

Tracy paused. Then she asked me, "What's wrong?"

"Hunh?"

"What's wrong with you?"

"Nothing," I lied to her. I couldn't tell her the truth, that my friend Alexandria, Miss I'm-Too-Good-for-Anybody, was giving her brother Jason some you-know-what in her hotel room.

"Nothing's wrong, hunh?" Tracy asked me. She chuckled and said, "Well, I may not be a parent yet, but I do know when people have something on their minds. So you're telling me that you don't have anything on your mind right now?"

"I'm not saying that, but . . . you know, I may not want to talk about it."

And I didn't.

Tracy said, "Okay. That's fair enough. We all have a right to privacy. But where's, ah, Alexandria? Have you talked to her since you've been back to the room?"

"No. Why?" I answered as calmly as I could.

"She's not with the girls. And I talked to Robin. She said that they told her Alexandria was sick."

"Oh yeah? What, she had a headache or something?" I asked.

"I don't know. But when I called the room, she didn't answer. So I may need you to go over there and check up on her."

My heart jumped in my throat again.

I answered, "I'm already in bed, but if you call her again and she still doesn't answer, I'll get up and go over there."

"Well, why don't you call her?" Tracy asked me. "She's your friend. You're not concerned about her?"

I was stuck again.

I said, "Okay, I'll call her." I couldn't keep going back and forth about it. Tracy might have gotten suspicious.

"All right. And call me back once you find out where she is and how she's doing."

"Okay."

I was just about to hang up when Tracy said, "Vanessa."

"Yeah."

"Has she met somebody here?"

Oh my God! I thought to myself. *Why me?*

"Why do you ask me that?"

Tracy said, "I just have a feeling about that girl."

Interesting. I wondered what her feeling was.

"A feeling about what?" I asked my cousin.

She said, "I don't know, I just . . . that girl just seems sneaky to me."

That's probably why Tracy never paid Alexandria much attention. And now she was creeping with Jason. Was it my fault? All I did was introduce them after Jason had begged me to.

"I'll go ahead and call her," I said, just to get off of the subject with my cousin.

"How well do you know that girl?" she asked me.

All of a sudden I became defensive.

"I mean, you act like she did something to you."

Tracy thought it over and paused.

"Yeah, you're right. I have no reason to jump to conclusions about her. But I just don't like how quiet she is sometimes, like she knows something."

"I'm quiet, too," I reminded my cousin. As soon as I said it, I remembered why I was staying in L.A. with Tracy in the first place, for defending myself against my abusive mother. But no one else saw it that way. They all thought I was crazy.

Tracy didn't bring it up to rub it in my face, but I know she was thinking about it.

She said, "You go ahead and call her then."

When I hung up the phone, I took a deep breath and prayed that Jason and Alexandria were finished doing what they were doing so she could answer the phone and lie to me, or whatever she planned to do.

So I picked up the phone and dialed, assuming that she probably wouldn't answer it. It rang once. It rang twice. It rang three times, and then I went ahead and hung up the line.

I waited a few more minutes, itching to either call Alexandria back or make another snooping visit to her door for a listen. I was hoping that Jason would be making his getaway soon.

I even got up and walked to the door to look through the peephole. The elevator was in the direction of my room, so Jason would have to walk past me to leave. So I wanted to see if I could at least see or hear him walking past.

Sure enough, I could hear faint voices in the hallway, but I dared not investigate. I didn't want to catch them in the act of the escape. So when the voices stopped, and someone walked toward the elevators, I made it back over to the phone to call Alexandria again.

"Hello," she finally answered, sounding sleepy.

I guess she had to get her little act on. I acted right along with her.

"Hey, girl, where have you been? Everybody's been calling for you."

She said, "I've been in bed. They didn't tell you I was sick?"

I said, "I called you and nobody answered the phone."

"Yeah, I fell asleep for a while."

"Well, what's wrong with you?"

"I just had a headache. I mean, I'm not really used to working this many long hours."

Alexandria came from a wealthy California family. I even wondered if her family tree was linked to the first California gold rush or something. She sure acted like it sometimes.

I said, "Ain't it the truth. Tracy said I was asking for it. Now she's giving me all the work I need, *and* some."

"Yeah, and you included us in this mess," Alexandria commented.

I said, "So what happened with you and my cousin Jason? Y'all got to talking that night and I have no idea how long you two were up."

It was the moment of truth.

She answered, "Not long after you went in. Your cousin is funny though."

"You think so, hunh? Well, did you give him your phone number to stay in touch?"

She hesitated. She said, "Why, you wanted me to?"

"No, I didn't say that. I was just asking."

"Oh," she responded. And that was it on the subject. She spoke no more about it.

"So, how come you didn't go back out with everybody else?" she asked me.

Because I wanted to catch you in the act of banging my cousin, I thought to myself evilly.

But instead I told her, "I was too tired to go back out."

"I hear you," she commented. "This trip is wearing me out."

Yeah, I bet it is, I thought to myself.

I said, "All right, well, let me call everybody back and tell them that you're okay."

"Who was asking about me?"

I wanted to be careful with my answer at first, but then I figured, what the hell. Alexandria had gotten herself into her own mess, so she would have to get herself out of it.

"Tracy called me about it," I told her. That was all I planned to say.

"Why?"

"Because you didn't answer your phone when she called your room earlier."

"Why was she looking for me?"

"Because you wasn't with everyone else."

"Yeah, I was sick."

"So, what is that supposed to mean?" I asked her. "We can't talk to you because you're sick? We can't wonder how you're doing? I mean, what is the matter with you? My cousin was just worried about you, and when she got no responses from her calls, she asked me to check up on you."

I said, "Actually, she wanted me to knock on your door, but I told her I was in bed already."

I wanted Alexandria to know just how close she had come to being busted. In reality she was busted, she just didn't know it yet.

"How long ago was this?" she asked me.

"About twenty minutes ago, maybe longer."

She said, "Well, I probably wouldn't have answered it. I mean, I'm just waking up now."

Yeah, whatever, I thought with a grin. She was tripping. I was getting a chance to see Alexandria's true colors. Tracy was right about her. I guess my big cousin had had enough interaction with women and girls through the popularity of her book to know all different tendencies and types.

I said, "All right, well, let me go ahead and call everybody back then and tell them that you're okay."

"All right," she told me.

"You are okay now, right?" I asked her to make sure.

"Yeah, I guess I just needed some rest, that's all."

"Well, whatever the doctor orders, you just make sure you get it," I bullshitted to her.

She said, "I know that's right."

When I hung up the phone with Alexandria, all I could do was shake my head. I felt like calling my damn cousin Jason and asking him how it was, just to let him know that they were busted. Then he would call Alexandria and let her know that I knew. Then she would call me and either get mad about it, or continue to lie like it never happened. Then I would feel even worse about her than I was already feeling. I mean, if you're going to be a ho', at least be honest about it. I guess she was trying to be a discreet ho'.

I don't know how long I sat there thinking about it, but the next thing I knew, Jasmine, Sasha, and Maddy were back. You could hear all of their noise through the walls. I jumped up out of bed in my nightclothes to return to Sasha and Jasmine's room.

I knocked on the door, just to see someone looking through the peephole.

"I'm sorry, but we won't be having any booty calls here," Jasmine joked through the door.

"Are you sure?" I asked her. "What if I was Allen Iverson?"

Jasmine damn near broke her arm to get the door open.

"Hi, A.I. Is there anything I can get or do for you?"

We all broke up laughing. Jasmine was a big Allen Iverson fan, especially while we were still in Philadelphia.

She said, "Oh my God, don't let me see him while we're here. Because I swear, I will go there in a heartbeat."

I looked at Sasha and said, "See that. That's where a girl gets into trouble."

"Whatever," Jasmine huffed at me. "So, you wouldn't let A.I. in if he was knocking on your door?"

I asked, "Why would I? I don't know him."

"Whatever," Jasmine said again. She said, "Okay, would you let Nelly in your room then?"

I smiled. I was a big Nelly fan.

Sasha said, "Now how are you gonna like Nelly and not like Allen Iverson? They could practically be cousins."

Jasmine and I looked at each other.

I said, "Okay, what are you trying to say, they all look alike? You better watch yourself, Sasha."

"Yeah, because people always say that about Asians," Jasmine joked.

"Well, you know I look good, so that must mean that all Asians look good," Sasha bragged.

"What, just because you got a black butt? You still can't dance," Jasmine teased her.

"I don't have to. All I do is move to the beat, and the guys swarm me every time. 'Can I get a dance, Ma'? Can I get a dance?' "

"Oh, like I don't get that," Jasmine commented. "That's all night long, honey. All night long."

I really wasn't there to shoot the breeze with them all night. I really wanted to make my way over to Alexandria and Maddy's room to look Alexandria in her eyes and sniff her room. I had never been there to home base before, but I could imagine things based on what I had heard about it.

I said, "Well, I haven't seen you guys all night, I just wanted to check in with you."

"Aww, now aren't you a good mother hen," Jasmine joked to me.

"Shut up," I told her. "Now let me go check on Maddy and Alex."

"Make sure you tuck them in good," Sasha added to the joke.

I looked back at her and said, "Don't even start."

I walked to Maddy and Alexandria's room and took a deep breath. I had to get my act together. I knocked on the door and waited. Maddy answered the door.

"What's up?"

Maddy seemed to be holding me up at the door, not intentionally but just standing in front of it.

I pushed her out of my way and said, "Let me come in, girl. What are you hiding, a man up in here?" I was just about to say Shamor, but I stopped myself. That wouldn't have been in good taste.

Maddy remained stoic and said, "No comment."

I walked further into the room and spotted Alexandria under the covers with her nightclothes on. I could see them from her shoulders.

"So, are you guys going to be up all night or what?"

It smelled normal in there, like an air conditioner, carpet, and hotel sheets. Alexandria looked normal, too. Her light brown hair was still intact, and her face was not flushed or sweaty. I guess I didn't have any idea what to expect out of a sexcapade.

Maddy said, "You're in the wrong room for that shit. We have to beat on the walls five times a night to stop Sasha and Jasmine from goofing the hell off. I know you can hear them in there."

"Yeah, I can hear them," I admitted.

I looked at Alexandria under the sheets. She looked totally relaxed and satisfied.

I said, "So I guess you're going to be well rested for tomorrow now."

She nodded her head and said, "Yup."

I couldn't find any way to attack her. She looked too damned poised.

I said, "Well, I guess I'll leave you guys be then. Don't let the bed-bugs bite," I joked.

"What bedbugs?" Maddy asked me.

"The ones that crawl up in your sheets at night and give you the itches," I commented. I was just talking to spark any conversation I could from them.

Maddy looked at me and frowned.

She said, "Girl, it sounds to me like you need to see the damn doctor."

All of a sudden, Alexandria started laughing loud, louder than usual for her. Even Maddy looked at her funny.

She said, "You been in here smoking something, girl? It wasn't that damn funny."

Alexandria shook her head and didn't comment.

I looked at her and said, "Have you been out of bed at all since you've been in the room tonight?" I wondered if she would walk funny or something. I was looking for anything.

She said, "Yeah, to use the bathroom, and for room service. What else am I gonna get up for?"

I looked around the room and spotted a room service tray with the remains of a nearly finished small pizza. I then looked for signs of dinner for two, but there was only one tray and not enough food on it for two. That was a long shot.

I finally said, "Okay."

Alexandria asked me, "What are you looking for?"

I wondered if she was on to me.

I said, "Nothing."

"It seems to me like you're looking for something," Maddy commented.

"I know, right," Alexandria added.

I looked over at Maddy. Was she trying to help Alexandria out?

I shook my head and said, "All right, let me get to bed. You guys are boring," I told them.

"You know that already," Maddy told me. "If you want a slumber party, go next door."

Alexandria started laughing again.

Maddy looked at her a second time and said, "You must have been smoking something. Who brought you some reefer?"

"Whatever," Alexandria told her.

I repeated, "Reefer? You use that word? I thought it was chronic."

"What does it matter, you don't smoke either one of them," Maddy commented. She was a lot more street than any of us.

I said, "And you do?"

"I did. I have. Yeah," she answered.

I asked her, "How does that stuff make you feel?"

I had never touched a blunt or a cigarette a day in my life.

Maddy said, "Damn, you sound like a square bitch."

Alexandria laughed a third time and shook her head again.

Maddy looked at her and didn't comment.

I said, "Okay, well, let me retire to my room."

"You said that three minutes ago and you haven't budged yet," Maddy stated.

I joked and said, "I have to warm up to it."

"Well, warm your ass out of here."

I shook my head and left the room. I guess Alexandria had gotten away with her creep. I wasn't planning on telling anyone. For what? So I went on about my business.

At the final casting on Thursday, we had really narrowed down our potential actresses and actors. That's when things got really tense. We had had a peaceful time up until then. But we had too many non-professional girls all vying for a role they each considered to be their life calling.

I still liked Shannon Gray, but she was no longer the clear leader. We had a girl from Baltimore, one from Chicago, and one from St. Louis, who had flown in and were getting the job done. Ironically, no girl from Philly was strong enough in the lead. Philadelphians were locking down most of the minor, one-line roles, but that just wasn't good enough for some of them.

There was a crew of girls who had auditioned from South Philly, and two of them were still left for the lead. However, when Tracy told them what I thought she would—that they just were not convincing enough—they caused a ruckus.

"Wait a minute, so you're telling me that you're going to have a girl from somewhere else play this role? I mean, you don't have any-body from Philly playing any of the leads."

I guess they had been checking the bios and asking around to see where people were from.

Tracy said, "You don't have to be from Philadelphia to play a Philadelphian, but you do have to be convincing in this movie."

"And I'm not convincing?" the South Philly girl questioned.

She was a little too hard-edged for me. She didn't have enough of the innocence that we really needed in the role of TRACY. She wasn't jaded enough to play MERCEDES. She didn't have enough body for CARMEN. She didn't look as athletic as we felt JANTEL should look. And playing the roles of RAHEEMA or KIWANA was out of the question for this girl. But I surely felt she could have played a TRACY HATER in the movie. She was convincing enough in that role.

Tracy maintained her poise with the girl.

She said, "You're convincing in some things, but not enough in others."

"Well, isn't that what practice is for?" the second girl from South Philly jumped in and stated. They were both in the same boat.

Robin spoke up and said, "You can practice all you want on your own time, but talent is talent, and as of right now, you don't have enough of that to play a lead in this movie."

Whoa! Robin was a lot more forward than Tracy had been, but that's why she was the casting director.

"Well, that's fucked up!" the first girl stated. "And I do have talent. We both have talent. But what are y'all looking for?"

Robin spoke up again and said, "We're looking for girls who are professionals; actors and actresses who do not curse out the casting director and the producers, actors and actresses who are on time, actors and actresses who come prepared for the role, and talented people who *know* that it takes hard work and dedication, and not self-righteous *attitude* to get the job done."

Robin had told them what time it was *quick*. However, my cousin Tracy went soft on them.

She said, "We'll keep your names and contact information. I believe that you are talented, and I'll be willing to work with you."

The girls thanked Tracy and cut their eyes at Robin as they left.

Robin pulled Tracy to the back of the stage and spoke to her in lowered tones, but I could still hear them.

She said, "Tracy, like I told you before, you are going to create a mess by giving these girls so much false hope. Now if they don't make the cut, they don't make the cut."

Tracy said, "Look, we can't come to Philly and piss everybody off because it will spoil their support for the film."

Robin argued, "Tracy, do you actually believe that these people won't go and see this movie once it comes out? Now they're all going to come back and enjoy their roles as extras, I promise you that. But for right now, we have to focus on these leads. And as we already know, the leads we're choosing may only be temporary, if we really want this film to work."

She said, "It happens all the time. You start with a working cast as a model, then you upgrade the film with real stars to sell it, and the people who can stick through and fight their way in, God bless their souls. But you need to know this by now, Tracy. They are not you, and they can relate to your story all they want, but the reality is the reality. A star is a star is a star, and excuse my broken English here, but everybody ain't gon' be one."

Even though we had less people at the final casting audition on Thursday, it was definitely the hardest day of the week for all of us. The tension was fatal in there. Everyone wanted what they wanted, and the results left us all exhausted and still incomplete. We still had several people we all liked in several of the roles, so Tracy decided to leave it up to the next stage, which was finding out if any star attachments would pay off.

Before we were able to pack up for the day, an older black man came out of nowhere and took to the stage. He appeared drunken and homeless, while staggering and singing.

"I can see the rainbow / I can see the clouds / I can see the pot of gold / waiting for me now . . ."

Tracy looked at Robin. Robin looked at Tracy. Then Tracy looked at me.

"Who the hell is he?" my cousin asked me.

Shamor, my girls, and the rest of the camera crew all began to laugh, but no one had any idea who the man was or where he had come from. He just walked up onto the stage. So I shrugged my shoulders, and Tracy went ahead and called for security.

"I don't know who this man is, but he's not with the casting," she told the Freedom Theater staff. So they approached the man to escort him out, and he got extra loud with them, but he didn't try to fight them or anything.

"I was told there was auditions going on in here. I only wanted to audition. I'm a star. I just need my opportunity. I just wanted to sing for y'all. And I write my own songs myself."

He was busy talking while they led him out the door.

"I'm telling you, I'm a star. You gon' need me."

Everyone continued to laugh at him. However, in the back room, while we packed everything up, Robin continued to have her concerns about all of Tracy's walk-ins. She said, "That crazy man is a perfect example of what I'm talking about. You are making this process a lot harder on yourself and everyone else. And you're gonna end up having chaos on the set if you don't get a firm grip on things from the beginning."

Tracy ignored her gloom and decided to look on the bright side.

"Well, at least we sold out all of our shirts and hats. The marketing ideas will be working in our favor now."

Robin had to admit the truth of that.

"Yeah, that was a stroke of genius. But getting this film deal with major distribution and a studio behind it, with a bunch of nobodies, is gonna be something else."

Tracy looked at Robin and let out a deep breath.

"Okay, if you want to start sending the script around to the stars and their agents, now is the time to do it. I never said that I wouldn't contact who I need to talk to. I know how movies are made. But I also know how great ideas are ruined by a lack of execution from people who you may *think* are great, and are not."

Robin said, "I'm only going to send it out to people I feel will fit the bill, Tracy. It's not like I'll be scavenging. Lynn Whitfield can be contacted. Meagan Good can be contacted. They were in *Eve's Bayou* together in the same roles as mother and daughter, so they already know each other. These video girls can be contacted. And young track stars are everywhere. Outside of that, we can fill in who we need, and use all of the fantastic extras from Philadelphia that you want in this film."

It sounded good to me. In the meantime, Tracy could continue to push the new clothing line.

Tracy saw Robin's simplified point and agreed to it.

"Well, that's a wrap then. We start the next phase of the process," she commented. "So tomorrow and Saturday, we film the locations I want to use around the city, and we all sit back and enjoy the rest of our stay in Philadelphia. I haven't even been up to my parents' house this week," she mentioned.

I hadn't been home to North Philly to see my family, or to take my sister Veronica out to dinner. Nor had Tiffany showed up at any of the casting calls.

"You ready to go clubbing tonight, Vanessa?" Jasmine snuck by and asked me.

Tracy overheard it. She answered, "Not tonight. Vanessa and I have a few more dinners to go to. We're over here to work. So you guys can hang out with the casting crew again."

What could I say? Tracy was the boss, and I had been the one to push her into it.

So I shrugged my shoulders and told Jasmine, "She's the boss." But Jasmine knew that already.

Shamor and Maddy overheard the brief conversation as well. I guess that gave them more time to get together or whatever without me in their way that night. And I was perfectly fine with that.

Tracy wanted to meet Bruce and Kiwana at Zanzibar Blue again. It was within walking distance with great food and great ambience, she told me. So I left it alone.

But when we arrived at Zanzibar Blue for the second night in a row, Kiwana had brought her newborn baby with her. She and Bruce were there at the front entrance talking to each other with a detachable car seat in Kiwana's hands.

It was amazing to me that most of Tracy's friends still lived in Pennsylvania. Tracy said that Bruce had joined the air force and had returned home, and Kiwana commuted back and forth to New York for Broadway.

Bruce was tall, clean-shaven, with a thick mustache, and a tapered military haircut. He looked like he was still in the military. Even his dark blue suit looked spotlessly clean.

Kiwana, on the other hand, was all loose. She wore a long silk or rayon multicolored dress with an orange top and brown leather sandals. Her hair was loose and flyaway, and her face was so smooth that she looked like an all-fruit eater. Maybe I was stereotyping both of them, but that's what I thought as soon as I saw them there waiting for us.

Tracy said, "I see you two have met already. And Kiwana, you've brought another surprise for me," she said in reference to the new child.

We both looked into the car seat to eye the gorgeous, hairless little girl Kiwana had brought with her. The baby looked right up at both of us with light-colored eyes that reminded me of Alexandria.

"Awww, look at her," Tracy crooned. She then held out her index finger for Kiwana's daughter to hold on to.

I just stood there and smiled.

"Yeah, we've been standing here chatting. They said our table should be ready in a minute," Kiwana told us.

I didn't even know you could bring babies to a fine restaurant like Zanzibar's, especially at night while their jazz sets were playing. But what did I know?

Bruce stepped back and looked my cousin over.

He said, "Well, don't you still look good. I'm about to turn into a teenager all over again."

Tracy grinned and said, "Thank you. You still look handsome yourself. I wouldn't mind going back to our teen years for a minute."

Kiwana gave them both a look and said, "Okay, let's cut it out. We get the point."

Tracy finally got around to introducing me.

"This is my cousin and personal assistant, Vanessa."

"Hi," I told them both.

Bruce looked me over and said, "Good looks must run in the family."

I smiled and said, "Thank you."

"Don't mention it. Just don't break the hearts of the good guys like your big cousin did."

Tracy smirked. "Here we go," she responded to him.

"What, did I say something that wasn't right?"

"Yes, you did. But I want to leave that alone and have a good time tonight," Tracy told him.

"Amen to that," Kiwana agreed.

We walked on in and they showed us to our table, where I noticed that Kiwana was already looking at her watch.

She said, "I won't be able to stay too long, Tracy. Treasure's only four months old, and I'm breast-feeding her."

Tracy said, "Treasure?"

Kiwana smiled at her daughter and said, "That's what she is."

Then she pulled out wallet-sized family pictures of her white husband and her two mixed daughters to pass around the table. Tracy looked at the pictures and nodded.

"Beautiful," she commented while handing them back.

She said, "So, let me get this right out in the open for the both of you. How is the married-with-kids life?"

Tracy told me that Bruce had four sons.

Kiwana answered the question first. "It's wonderful."

Of course she would say that in front of her newborn baby.

Bruce smiled and grunted before he answered. He said, "You sound like a happy wife. 'Wonderful,'" he repeated to her.

"You don't agree?" Kiwana asked him.

Bruce was more thoughtful about it. He said, "It's ah . . . interesting."

"What's so interesting about it?" Tracy asked.

He said, "Well, you're supposed to pick one person to share the rest of your life with . . . I mean, that's just heavy material right there."

"That's why you have to pick the right person," Kiwana told him.

Bruce looked her in the eyes and said, "And you believe that there's only one person you could have picked?"

"I didn't pick. The pieces just fell where they were supposed to," she answered.

"The pieces just fell where they were supposed to," Bruce repeated her again. "So, hypothetically speaking, there is no other man on God's green earth who could have been, not a perfect, because no one is perfect, but a solid mate for you?"

I must admit, I liked Bruce immediately. He had this sarcastic way of thinking and speaking that left me with a lot of intrigue. I didn't like Kiwana's "Wonderful" answer any more than he did. It sounded too simple, as if she was reading her response from a children's book. And I knew that marriage had to be a lot more complicated than that. I had been around too many grown-ups in L.A., married and unmarried, to believe in simplicity. Every situation had its strengths and struggles.

Kiwana answered, "I don't even think about other mates. I have no reason to."

"Does your husband think about it?" he asked her.

Kiwana looked at Bruce as if she was appalled that he had even asked the question.

"No, he does not," she told him.

Tracy had opened up a hot can of beans before we had even received our appetizers.

"Are you sure?" Bruce asked.

I had to hide my face behind my menu to stop from smiling. I could tell that Kiwana was irritated by it. But I'm sorry, I agreed with Bruce. Maybe I just hadn't been around enough happy-faced marriages to believe in what Kiwana was saying. I would rather hear the real deal and not the Hallmark card. I was still confused as to why she would bring a child to an adult meeting at night inside a jazz restaurant.

Kiwana finally told him, "Look, just because you're not happy with who you married does not mean that the roof is falling in on my house like it is on yours. Okay?"

Now she had my attention. Her spice was real, but her sugar . . . I just needed to have it with the spice to make sure that Kiwana was balanced in the world. Because every time my cousin Tracy had written or talked about her, it was as if Kiwana was a holy angel who could do no wrong, even after she decided to marry a white man. I mean, to each her own, but . . .

Anyway, Tracy finally decided to cool them off.

"You think we could have been a happy couple, Bruce?" she asked.

I was beginning to like this dinner. I was sitting right in the middle of things. I had the best seat in the house again.

Bruce answered, "Honestly, I would have to say no to that twice. No, we wouldn't have made a good couple out of high school because you were far too materialistic for me to be able to keep up with. And no again after college, because you had then grown to be too headstrong."

"So, in other words, you like meek, do-what-I-tell-you-to-do women?" Kiwana jumped in and asked him.

He answered, "No, I actually like strong-willed women, but I also understand that it would be a bad decision on my part to marry one, because I'm not able to transform into the docile husband I needed to be to make that union last."

"Okay, so that means that you can't have two strong-willed people in a successful marriage? Is that what you're saying?" Kiwana questioned.

Bruce said, "Somebody has to take the lead and there can't be a lot of confusion about it."

Tracy said, "Don't they have copilots on a plane?"

He *was* a member of the United States Air Force.

"On a *commercial* plane," Bruce answered. "And they're not working the same equipment at the same time. But we don't have commercial marriages," he commented. "Marriages are extremely personal."

"So what is your beef with your marriage? You don't love your wife anymore?" Tracy asked him.

"It's not that I don't love her anymore, it's just that there are so many infinite possibilities out there."

Kiwana began to smile as she sized him up.

"Greedy," she told him to his face.

"Well, what if you had one pair of shoes for the rest of your life?" he asked her.

She said, "We're not talking about shoes here." Her baby began to cry before she picked her up out of the car seat to hold in her arms.

I was openly chuckling to myself at that point. I felt the two of them together was hilarious. You had an optimistic dreamer in Kiwana and a scientific mathematician in Bruce. However, Bruce dreamed about experiencing other situations, whereas Kiwana applied the math of one to her situation.

"Are you thinking about divorcing your wife?" Tracy asked Bruce.

"I don't believe in divorce. I plan to finish what I started," he answered.

Kiwana shook her head with disgust.

"Marriage is not another military objective to be dealt with, it's a sacred and beautiful bond that has been around for hundreds of thousands of years."

Bruce looked at her and nodded. He said, "Hundreds of thousands of years, hunh? That sounds like a mighty long time."

Judging from Tracy's minimal participation, I figured she was enjoying their conversation as well. They were really going at it. It was a battle of the minds. But then the baby started really acting up and having a fit.

"Okay, okay, Mommy has you. Mommy has you," Kiwana tried to console her daughter while rocking her in her arms.

Bruce looked at me. I was certain that he was thinking the same thing I was thinking, *Why did she even bring the baby?* So I just smiled at him, knowingly.

We finally began to order our entrées. Kiwana, however, was looking at her watch again while Treasure continued to act up.

She said, "Yeah, I'm really gonna have to go, Tracy. I knew this was a little too late for me. I'm sure you understand." She set her pouting daughter back in the car seat and gathered her things to leave.

Bruce said, "Nice meeting you."

"Likewise," Kiwana told him.

It was the cordial thing to say, but I don't believe she really meant it. She then hustled away with her baby in her arms and left us at the table.

As soon as she walked out the door, Bruce smiled and mumbled, "Why would she bring her baby here with her? If the older daughter's at home or somewhere else, then why couldn't she have left Treasure there as well?"

"Like she said, she's still breast-feeding her," Tracy explained.

"So you feed her right before you leave, and you feed her as soon as you get back home. I know the breast-feeding game. My wife breast-fed two of our boys."

"Well, maybe her daughter needs to be breast-fed more often," Tracy suggested.

Bruce smiled and said, "Well, that's one spoiled baby then. And she needs to check that before it gets out of hand."

Tracy looked at him and said, "Excuse me? I don't believe you just said that. You don't know her like that. That was totally uncalled for. Say something like that to her face."

"She left too soon," Bruce commented. "But you see how the baby was acting up. She's already spoiled. And she got her way again, didn't she?"

I started smiling again. Bruce didn't seem to hold his candor at all. He was telling the truth, and nothing but the truth.

Tracy looked at me, and I didn't have anything to say about it. I wasn't loyal to Kiwana like she was. It was not that I didn't like her or anything, I just didn't idolize her because I didn't feel I knew her well enough to do so. I knew Tracy, and Bruce was showing more of himself than Kiwana was. Hell, we only got to talk to her for ten minutes. I did feel that talking about Kiwana behind her back was bad taste, but people always talk about each other when they're not around. I was sure Kiwana would say a few things about Bruce had he left before she did. So I respected Bruce's honesty in the situation.

Tracy asked him, "So, is that how you treat your wife, with blatant disrespect? I see why you don't like marriage. I wouldn't like being married to you either," she told him.

He said, "I know you wouldn't. Like I said earlier, I could never handle you back then, and I can't handle you now. But I'm mature enough now to understand that reality. The world is all about imbalances and trying to figure out an even playing field for all of us."

Tracy waved her hand with the whole conversation. "All right, whatever. So anyway, what is your take on the movie we're trying to put together?"

That's what we were all there to discuss before we got off on a marriage and kids tangent.

Bruce asked, "Will they even do a film like *Flyy Girl*? I mean, it's not really a comedy. And since it's not dealing with me . . ."

"You're in it," Tracy cut him off and told him.

He said, "Yeah, but the title is *Flyy Girl*, and I'm assuming that it has to be sold that way."

"Not necessarily," my cousin stated. "We could use different trailers where we have more of a masculine presence. Hollywood does it all the time, they cut up the parts that fit your marketing angle."

Bruce said, "Well, if I'm not mistaken, inner-city girls are the main supporters of the book, are they not?"

"Yeah, but they write me about the guys in the book all the time."

Bruce smiled and said, "Yeah, and I know just who they're writing about, Mr. V.H. How is, ah . . . *Qadeer* doing now anyway?" he asked my cousin.

Tracy smirked and chuckled at it. She said, "You're still a smart-ass, I see."

"And you're still in love with the man," he told her. He said, "Now if you really want to push this movie and make it work, you find a young heartthrob for the girls to go crazy over, and you make it work from that angle. Kind of like what Terry McMillan did for Taye Diggs in her movie."

"So, you don't believe this movie has any other value to it than that?" my cousin asked him.

Bruce stared into her eyes and remained poised. He was in total control of himself.

He said, "Tracy, in this country, the entertainment industry is all about three things: sex, drugs, and violence. And in the movie industry, they also like special effects. That's why we have such a craze for this comic-book mentality in the movies right now. I've been to theaters all around the world, where the stories still mean something. Then I come back home to the theaters in America, and it's all the same things: sex, violence, drugs, and special effects. Now what does your film have?"

"Sex, violence, drugs, and music," I told him. It just jumped out of my mouth. I was following Bruce's entire train of thought. And we did have those things.

I said, "*Flyy Girl* is loaded with drama, but it also has a heart to it. It's just like *Spider-Man* to me. It's packed with action, it'll have plenty of hype, it has a lot more than a kiss, and people will definitely want to see it again."

"Black people," Bruce commented, "and not white folks. And that's the major difference between *Flyy Girl* and *Spider-Man*. Or even *Harry Potter* for that matter. I didn't see one black face in that movie, but we were all in the theaters watching it."

"Why wouldn't they watch it?" I asked him referring to white Americans. "They're into hip-hop. Majorly."

Bruce looked at me and nodded. Then he smiled.

He said, "I can see you're one of the many *Flyy Girl* fanatics this book has created, including my wife. She would love to see this book made into a movie. But my point is this: If the idea is so sure-shot, then how come it hasn't been produced already?"

Tracy said, "It took *Spider-Man*, what, forty years to make? And how many years for *X-Men*? I've been seeing those comics for years. So all we have to do is prove that we have an audience for it and make it happen."

Bruce gave up his argument and shrugged his shoulders.

"Well, if you have it all mapped out, then what do you need my comments for? Make the movie. I'll go see it, if just to see how the people react to my character," he responded with a grin. "Who you got in mind to play me?" he asked.

Tracy lightened her mood by saying, "Any old cornball would do. Your character's not that hard to portray. All the young actor has to do is walk around with his nose being pulled open."

Bruce chuckled at that. He said, "Yeah, that's about right. But make sure he still has the flyy gear on. I was always a sharp dresser. Just like you were."

Tracy agreed and nodded to him. "I'll see what I can do. But we may have to dress him in awkward clothes to nail the point home that he was a sucker for love."

I chuckled at that myself. Tracy was giving the candor right back to him.

Bruce said, "Or, you could just have a good actor to nail the point home that this guy was really infatuated with the glitter, but under that glitter was some real gold that he was happy to experience for a minute, no matter what he had to pay for it."

I looked at Tracy and wondered how she would respond to that. He was actually paying her a compliment.

She said, "Is that really how you feel about me?"

"It's the truth, Tracy. You're a special woman," he told her. "And every time you make another move in your progress, you prove it. So I expect for you to make this film, and I expect for it to be good, too. And after that, you'll be thinking about doing a sequel, and then a television series, and then you'll become an even bigger urban-girl icon than you already are."

He opened up his palms and said, "That's just who you are. And the thing that makes me know is that you don't even really think about it. It's just there for you. And you can turn it on or turn it off"—he snapped his fingers—"just like that."

Tracy was speechless. She only nodded to him.

"Well, I thank you," she told him.

He said, "Don't mention it. Now, where's this food? I'm ready to eat."

As soon as he said that, our server arrived with our entrées.

"Now that's what I'm talking about right there."

I grinned. Bruce was not a big beefcake of a man, but I could tell that he had an appetite. He had ordered a large steak dinner to prove it, and I was quite certain that he would put it down. He struck me as just being real with it, and I still liked him in a fatherly kind of way. Just give me the facts, and let me deal with the conclusions.

So I went ahead and asked him what I was thinking.

"Why did you seem so hard on Kiwana?" I wanted to hear more of his honesty. Tracy looked at him for an answer herself.

Bruce chewed up his first bite of steak dinner and mumbled, "Good question." Then he looked at Tracy with his answer.

He said, "She may be your friend on one hand, but I've been around enough fence-jumpers in my life to know one when I see one. There are certain types of black people who will carry the pompoms for you on one end, and then shoot you in the back on the other. I'm here to tell you that many people in our community, after they see the film, will not like it no matter what. I mean, these people have this delusionary idea that everything we do is supposed to be perfect. And it ain't. It never has been, and it never will be."

He said, "So yeah, I can join the military on one end, but I did so to put myself in a mental and professional position to be able to do many of the things in our community that need to be done, and at the same time be respected for the time that I served in uniform for this country, where nobody can tell me what I can't say or do. You feel me? It's called paying your dues. And there are times when you just have to stand up and support the cause for black folks past your individual desires or shortcomings.

"That's what I mean by marriage being interesting," he continued. "I had plenty of white girls that I could have married. White girls are easier for me. I'm not gonna lie about it. But at the end of the day, easy is not what I want to stand for."

He looked at me again and said, "So I learned to call a spade a spade. And if people get offended by it, then they should stand up and defend themselves."

Tracy said, "Well, I'll defend my friend since she's not here right now. Because I know she's not a fence-jumper—"

But before my cousin could get started, Bruce cut her off. "Of course you would defend her. You have that inner-city loyalty about you. You're loyal to all of your friends. I just wonder if she defends you the same way you defend her. I know Raheema would. Even Mercedes, in her twisted kind of way. But this Kiwana girl?"

He stopped and shook his head. "She's a fence-jumper, that's why she brought her baby with her tonight. She wanted the distraction, and she planned to leave early all along. And I don't believe she's sincere about her support for you either."

"I don't think you know her," Tracy insisted. "And she has a right to take her kids wherever the hell she wants to."

Bruce chomped down another bite of his steak before he responded. Tracy had ordered fish; I had chicken.

He held his fork in the air and said, "You just do me this one favor. You ask her to help out in this movie of yours, and I'd be curious to see what she says about that."

"If she has the time, she will," Tracy assumed for her.

Bruce nodded and smiled.

He said, "Just ask her for me, that's all. Just ask her."

As Tracy and I walked back to the hotel after dinner, a man stopped his car and rolled down his window to holler in our direction.

"Hey, Tracy Ellison Grant. You're very sexy, baby. And I love your work."

Tracy smiled at him, said "Thank you," and kept on walking.

I really felt she needed a bodyguard sometimes, in case someone tried to take things too far, but Tracy liked doing things on her own without the extra hassle of too many people around her.

So she ignored the whole scene on the street and asked me, "So, how do we do it, Vanessa?"

I looked at her in confusion. I didn't know what she was talking about.

"How do we do what?"

"How do we live without having men in our lives? Well, a younger man for you, but you get the point," she said.

I smiled at her. I said, "You do have a man." I was assuming that she would work things out with her friend in L.A.

My cousin looked me in the eyes and said, "Look here, if you're a woman in your thirties, like I am now, people expect you to have a husband and kids, so my little 'friend' doesn't mean anything. And maybe that was the message Kiwana was trying to send me by bringing her baby out with her tonight."

"Is that what you think?" I asked her.

She said, "I don't know. But I have to find peace with myself about this whole attitude that society has that says I have to be married with kids to be happy. I mean, I look at that as the biggest lie in the world. Bruce was right about that. A family doesn't necessarily make you happy by itself. That family has to work out for you."

She said, "My mother wasn't happy. Raheema's mother wasn't happy. Your mother's not happy. But you find a way to keep doing what you do and you make things work for you however you have to. You know what I mean?"

I understood her, but my approach was a lot simpler than that. I had yet to live through the relationship drama that Tracy and other women had lived through.

I said, "Well, I'm not saying that I'm not interested in guys, or that I won't be, but right now I'm busy."

"Exactly," my cousin agreed. "I used to be busy chasing an excitable daddy, but I don't have the time or the energy to do that anymore. I can talk to my daddy every day now and create my own excitement. And when I need a man for company, I can get one. Hot dates are a dime a dozen, just make sure you have your own car and your own money in your pocket."

I smiled and chuckled. I always considered Tracy a player anyway. A lot of people read the book wrong, but the guys she went out with rarely chose her. She had always chosen them and made it seem like it was their choice.

I said, "What if you don't own your car or have your own money?"

"In that case, you're in the dark ages where a woman wore an apron but no shoes, and waited at the front door for her man to come home with the money."

She said, "Now, I may have dreamed about that love, marriage, and kids thing when I was your age, but do you really think I can sit home and wait for somebody while they have a regular day at the office or whatever? I'm just not that girl, Vanessa."

I asked her, "Has someone mentioned marriage and kids to you since you've been home?"

I imagined that someone had. That was a big part of returning home. People always wanted to know what new things were going on in your life.

"Oh, that's been every day this week," Tracy told me. "My mother, Raheema, Kiwana, emails. Carmen and Jantel are married now. Kendra back in L.A. Even Susan is thinking about getting married on me."

"What about Yolanda Felix and Mercedes?" I asked her. They were the two single women who were without kids, husbands, or fiancés.

Tracy looked at me and said, "Do I really want to be compared to them?"

She had a point. Mercedes and Yolanda did not seem to be content women at all. So I nodded and kept right on smiling as we reached the hotel.

Loose Ends

When we walked back into the hotel, Tracy asked me, "What do you think about what Bruce had to say tonight?"

"I thought he was just telling the truth. He could have said it nicer, but it was still the truth."

"Yeah, his truth," Tracy responded. "He needs to learn how to loosen up a bit and stop labeling people."

"So, what does Kiwana think about the movie?" I asked her. I was curious myself. Bruce had pushed the issue.

Tracy said, "Of course she's supportive."

"She told you that?" I asked my cousin. I needed her exact wording. I wanted to see what I could read from Kiwana's exact words.

"She doesn't have to say it. I know she supports it."

That changed everything for me. I needed more proof of Kiwana's loyalty. Bruce had turned me into a skeptic.

"Are you gonna ask her like he told you to?"

Tracy eyed me with conviction. She said, "Yes, I'll call the girl and get it out of her. Okay? Is everybody happy now?"

I smiled. She was overreacting.

I said, "If you're gonna act like that, it makes it seem like Kiwana doesn't have your full confidence."

"She does have my confidence."

"Well, then, it shouldn't be such a big deal to you."

"All right, let me call her right now. I know she's up with the baby and everything."

I walked to the elevators with Tracy and waited. She then took out her cell phone and dialed Kiwana's home number while we waited for the elevators to arrive.

She waited for the phone to be answered. "Hey, how are you? I'm sorry to call this late, but is Kiwana still up with the baby . . . Oh, okay . . . Yeah, she can call me back. It's not urgent or anything, I was just calling to make sure she made it back in . . . I'm fine. And how are you?"

When Tracy disconnected the call, she said, "I don't believe I called them at this time of night." It was close to midnight.

I said, "Well, I'm tired. I don't think I got enough rest last night."

"What were you up doing?" Tracy asked me.

We were still waiting for the elevators.

I answered, "Just thinking about a lot of things. I still need to take my sister Veronica out to eat. And I still haven't gone home to see my mother."

"You and me both," Tracy stated. "But I'm surprised I haven't seen Jason hanging around here this week. Has he tried to call Sasha and Jasmine?"

"They haven't talked about it," I told her.

As far as Jason was concerned, my plan was to give my cousin short answers and nothing more.

She said, "I told him to stay away during the beginning of the week, but I didn't think he'd actually listen to me."

I had no comment. I didn't want to talk about Jason. He was out of my hands.

But as soon as the elevator doors opened and guests walked off for us to walk on, Jason and his boy rounded the corner of the lobby with Maddy and Alexandria. They were on their way to the elevators as well.

Tracy looked and said, "Speak of the devil."

"And the devil appears," I added nervously.

The charade was all over with. They would tell on me as quickly as they could, and I would finally be able to wipe my hands of the whole mess. It wasn't of my doing anyway. All I did was introduce them.

Jason and Alexandria looked hesitant for just a second, before they loosened up to speak. They couldn't run away now. They were busted.

Tracy asked, "And where are you all going at this hour?"

Jason thought fast. "We're just walking them back to the elevators," he answered.

"From where?"

"From just hanging out."

"And where are Sasha and Jasmine?"

Jason shrugged his shoulders. "Doing their own thing, I guess."

It was only a matter of time before they brought me into it. I was only counting the seconds as to when.

"Well, how do you know Alexandria and Madison?" Tracy asked her brother.

"We met them through Sasha and Jasmine." Jason lied.

Damn he was quick with his tongue. And I guess he was leaving me out of it, or trying to.

Tracy said, "Oh, so you just dropped one set of girls and moved on to the next, hunh? Why, nothing was poppin'? Or has it already popped and now you're moving on to the next party?"

Jason answered, "We're all just hangin' out, Tracy. It's not even that deep."

He was the only one doing the talking.

Tracy looked them all over and sized them up.

She said, "I thought you were sick, Alexandria."

Alexandria said, "Yeah, but that was yesterday."

"Oh, so you're all better now."

"Yeah, I'm okay."

"And are you kicking it with my brother now?" Tracy asked her bluntly.

Oh my God! I panicked. My cousin was that *raw* when she wanted to be.

Alexandria looked at me for a hot second, and that was all that Tracy needed to put two and two together.

"Oh, so Vanessa introduced you to him?"

Alexandria was answering by not answering. She wasn't quick on the tongue like Jason was.

Jason said, "She's not kicking it with me, and what difference does it make who introduced us. We're all just hanging out, Tracy."

"And where were you about to go? Were you just walking them to the elevator?" Tracy asked her brother.

He said, "Yeah, most people walk a girl to the door."

The elevator door was still open. Maddy tried to walk right on and leave us.

Tracy said, "Get off that elevator, girl. We're not finished talking yet."

Maddy said, "I thought you told us you were gonna be cool about things."

Jason said, "I know, man. What's up with this third-degree shit?"

His pretty-boy friend was standing there smiling with not a word.

Tracy stopped cold in her tracks. She nodded her head and said, "Okay, okay, I get it. So go on back to what you were doing. Go on up to the girls' rooms in the elevator, and I'll act like I never saw you."

Jason insisted, "We weren't going up to their rooms."

"Well, why walk into the hotel at all then? These girls are safe as soon as they walk into the building. You can't get in at this hour without a key."

"We didn't have no key to get in," Jason's friend spoke up.

"Did I ask you?" Tracy snapped at him.

"Naw, but . . ."

"Okay, then," she cut him off.

He smiled, looked away, and shook his head.

Jason said, "What's the big deal anyway? Nobody's kids out here."

"That's what I'm saying," Maddy agreed.

Tracy said, "Well, get back on the elevator and do what you were doing then."

Jason stuck to his story. "We weren't doing anything."

Finally, Alexandria shook her head and said, "I'm going up to bed."

"Good answer," my cousin told her. "And that's where you and your friend need to be going," she told her brother.

Jason shook his head at her.

He said, "You trippin', man. You playing yourself."

"No, you're playing yourself. Out here creeping. You didn't show up at one of the castings this week, but then you pop up at the hotel. What is that?"

"You told me not to come to the castings until Wednesday. You said I would be a distraction."

"You would."

"Well, that's why I didn't come."

Alexandria and Maddy stepped inside the elevator to ride it up to their room.

Tracy said, "Go on up. You, too, Vanessa."

I jumped on the elevator with my girls. Tracy remained in the lobby with her brother and his friend to discuss whatever. And when the doors closed, we rode the elevator up to our floor.

Alexandria asked me, "What is wrong with her?"

I played the innocent role. "What? What is wrong with who?"

"With Tracy?" Maddy answered.

I asked them, "Were they about to come up with you guys?"

"Of course they were," Maddy answered.

"So why didn't you say that?"

"Because we can see that your cousin's not having it," Maddy answered again.

"I thought she said she was going to be cool with us," Alexandria brought up.

"Well, I don't know if that extended to hanging out with Jason," I commented.

"Why not? Doesn't she trust her brother? I mean, what is he gonna do to us? And you're the one who introduced me to him."

Alexandria had a valid point.

I said, "I know, but that doesn't make it right."

"Well, what's wrong about it?" Maddy questioned. "Boys meet girls every day. And we're not even boys and girls anymore. We're young adults."

"Yeah, but we're still under my cousin's supervision while we're out here. And we all have to respect that," I told my girls.

That was all that needed to be said.

We arrived at our floor and walked to our separate rooms. Before I walked away from them, Maddy asked me, "Vanessa, do you like guys at all? I never see you with one. You don't even talk about guys. You're not gay, are you?"

Alexandria looked and started laughing.

I answered, "What do I have to do, sleep with a guy to prove to you that I'm not gay. I'm just doing me right now. Can't a girl do that without worrying about a guy twenty-four/seven?"

Maddy said, "That's all well and good, but you never even seem to talk about guys. I mean, that's just abnormal for a straight girl."

"Well, maybe I'm just different then."

"Whatever," Alexandria mumbled under her breath. I guess Tracy and I had busted her back-to-back groove with Jason. Then again, maybe they had gotten busy before, and I had only caught them on one of the occasions.

Maddy seemed ready to get her grove on as well. I had already busted her up with Shamor, so she had moved on to the next guy, Jason's friend. And they were both right about me, I wasn't even thinking about boys. I was thinking about shooting a very important film, and there would be plenty of guys to build a relationship with in the process of making the movie. Besides, I wanted a guy who understood my life goals and passion.

I walked into my room, thinking about my own other half, and Mark Fletcher from Washington, D.C., who was up for the role of "Victor," popped into my head. I wondered what he would be like in real life. But I didn't know much about Washington, D.C. All I knew was that they partied to go-go music. Then I started thinking about the real-life Bruce, and I couldn't get him off my mind. I wondered what he would think about my interest in another Victor type? It all seemed hypocritical. Were most girls hypocrites, asking for good guys while choosing the bad ones?

Before I could answer that question, there was an urgent knock on my door. I walked over to answer it and found my cousin Tracy at the door. I figured she would want to talk to me again that night, but I assumed she would call me up to her suite to do it. I didn't imagine her knocking on my door.

I invited her inside and prepared myself for whatever she had to throw at me.

"So, how heavily are they involved?" she asked.

I figured there was no sense in beating around the bush about it. I wanted to wipe my hands from the situation and let my cousin deal with Alexandria and her brother on her own, if that's what she wanted to do.

I said, "Ask Alexandria, because I don't want to be a part of this."

"Well, you did introduce them, right?"

"Yeah, because Jason begged me to and he wouldn't leave me alone about it."

"But I thought he hadn't been over here at all," Tracy said.

I looked my cousin in the face and said, "I didn't want you to think that I couldn't control my girls, but they are their own people. I can't tell them who not to talk to. That wouldn't be right anyway. I wouldn't want them telling me anything like that. I mean, they can give me their advice and their opinions, but that doesn't mean I have to listen to it."

"So when did they all meet?"

"Monday night."

Tracy just stared at me. Then she shook her head.

She said, "Now I'm wondering if she was really sick last night, or if she just wanted to be alone with my brother. I always had a funny feeling about that girl."

I said, "Why are you acting like that? Why can't Alexandria and Jason have something? I mean, why do you have us all feeling this way? We're human like you are. And we want guys in our lives like you did at one time."

"Oh, so what are you saying?"

"I'm just saying that we all feel a tremendous amount of pressure to please you and to measure up to your standards, when we all know that you were not perfect to begin with."

"Nobody asked for you to be perfect," my cousin told me, "but I still want you guys to sidestep a lot of the mistakes I made. And if you understand the book at all, then that should be obvious."

"But everybody deserves an opportunity to make their own mistakes, Tracy. That's life."

Tracy raised her fingers to her temples and took a deep breath to calm her nerves.

She said, "You guys have no idea how this book has affected my life. The sequel book was much easier for me to take because I was a mature woman by then. But they don't talk about the sequel, they talk about the first book, where I was wild and reckless. Now I'm just trying to make sure that I'm not standing idle while someone else is wild and reckless, because they may not end up where I am today."

I listened to my cousin and began to smile at her.

I said, "I know you're gonna hate me for saying this, but that sounds just like some parents. They haven't all written books about their lives like you have, but many of them have that same idea, that they don't want to let their daughters make bad decisions. Nevertheless, we have to learn how to make decisions on our own regardless, or we'll never be able to become women.

"I mean, what are we gonna do, call home whenever we have snap decisions to make with the opposite sex?" I asked her. "Sometimes you just have to go with your gut, and sometimes your gut may lead you astray. But that's life. You can't stop that. And I'm wondering now how much of your life lessons I've already internalized that makes me adverse to guys. I mean, maybe it's not just about me being busy. Maybe I'm busy on purpose, to keep away from having to make decisions about guys. You know?"

"Hmm," Tracy grunted. "You think that's the case?"

I said, "I don't know. But you may be in the same boat yourself. I mean, maybe, since you've spent so much time explaining and defending your younger years, you're not willing now to give up control of your life to really commit to a love relationship. Maybe now you keep a mental distance from guys on purpose, to stay in control, almost as a reaction to your lack of control as a teenager. I don't know."

Tracy took a seat in the chair at the small desk in my room. I seemed to have silenced her with my ideas.

She nodded her head and said, "You may be right. I mean, it makes sense. But how do you stop that behavior? I can't just let go. I have too much riding on my shoulders now."

I listened to her question and thought about my own goals in life.

I said, "That's the dilemma for all women who have things they want to do in life. How do we do what we want to do, and have a husband, and raise kids? I mean, you're gonna have to make sacrifices, and either you do or you don't, but those decisions are always gonna be there."

I said, "Look at Kiwana. She had to bring her baby to dinner with us tonight for whatever reason, but Bruce didn't. He's the man. He was ready to talk to us all night long while his wife is at home with his kids. Is that fair? It may not be, but that's what it is."

All of a sudden, my cousin began to smile at me. She said, "You were always a thinker, weren't you?"

I said, "I can't help it. But all of my thinking may mess me up with guys. It makes things too complicated for me. I mean, I look at exactly what it is, a guy gets to go inside of you. And I don't know how I really feel about that. Do I even want a guy inside of me? Why can't I go inside of him? You know?"

My cousin started laughing at me.

She said, "You'll change your mind once you feel it. You'll want a guy inside of you. Trust me."

I said, "Okay, what if I called Shamor, the camera guy from New York, over here to break me in tonight? Would that be right or wrong? I know he likes me, but I haven't given him the time of day. I even messed him up with Maddy, because I think she liked him at first. But he was too obviously trying to holler at me."

"For real?" she asked me.

I said, "Yeah. He says something to me every chance he gets. But you've made it easier for me to avoid him with these dinners we've been going to. But what if I did do him? Would I be stoned to death for it? And am I supposed to marry him just because I want him inside of me?"

Tracy shook her head. She said, "Now this is what I have the biggest problem with. There should be more meaning behind a young man and a young woman forming a union. I mean, what is the reason for it?"

"What was the reason for you?" I asked her. She had formed several unions in her youth.

She said, "I just wanted the possession. But in possessing a guy, they end up possessing you. So now I try to stay unattached, like you said."

I said, "I know. And that's why I don't want to possess them. It's a trap. You become owned by a man. And marriage sets you up for ownership. But do men want to be owned? Heck no. They call it the ball and chain."

Tracy said, "Everybody's owned by something, Vanessa. There's just no way around that. Your job, your contracts, your house, car, credit card payments, your God. Everything. Nothing comes without some form of ownership."

I said, "You're right. And right now we're all feeling owned by you. You're the boss lady, and I pushed you into this. Now we're all ready to complain about it, just like in a marriage. So I really got what Bruce was saying tonight. Marriage is interesting. That's the most intelligent way to describe it. Because it's not simple for anyone, no matter what Kiwana says."

My cousin stood up from the chair as if she was ready to leave. She said, "So you think I should just leave Jason and Alexandria alone? What about the other two? Is Maddy feeling his friend now? What happened with Shamor?"

I shrugged my shoulders. I said, "I don't know about them. And I guess she just blew Shamor off, like he blew her off. But with Jason and Alex, if they really want to be together, and we're still going back to L.A. this Sunday, then they'll have to figure out what they're going to do. So I wouldn't even sweat it until they start trying to travel.

"Like they said," I told my cousin, "they're just hanging out right now. Jason was hanging out with Sasha and Jasmine, too, and nothing happened there. So . . ."

My cousin nodded. She said, "I get your point. I'll just let her know that she should make her decisions based on something real and I'll move on from there."

She walked toward my door as I followed her to relock it. Then she turned to ask me before she left, "By the way, what do you feel about going with me to visit Vic— I mean, Qadeer Muhammad's store in Germantown tomorrow morning?"

I smiled. I said, "I still have to do something with my sisters and see my mom and everything."

She said, "We'll have plenty of hours for that tomorrow. We'll be on the road all day. So we'll drive up to his store early, then I'll drop you back off at your mother's house after that."

I said, "So, what's the strategy for him this time?" She still had never been able to master the man. I was nervous about meeting him myself. But I definitely wanted to. And I noticed that Tracy was be-

coming accustomed to my opinions on things. She was growing attached to me. I never would have thought that could happen.

She said, "There is no strategy. I just want you to be around him
for a minute to tell me what you think of him. You're becoming, like,
my second pair of eyes and ears to see and hear things more clearly. So
get ready for it. He's the real deal."

I smiled as she opened the door to leave.

I said, "I know he is." And I was already thinking about Mark
Fletcher in the film role. But I kept that information to myself.

Talk about being nervous, I thought about meeting Tracy's very own
Victor "Qadeer Muhammad" Hinson, and I couldn't even eat my
breakfast that morning. How could one man have so much of an impact over women? It was unexplainable. I had never heard his voice
and had never seen his face. Nevertheless, his aura seemed to be
smothering us. It was just as much Victor's movie as it was Tracy's.
Bruce was right again.

Jasmine and Sasha knocked on my door and were ready to go by
9:30 AM. Alexandria and Maddy moved a lot slower and quieter, but
they were ready to go as well.

I opened the door for my girls, and they were already pumped
with energy. They just bum-rushed my room.

"We're getting the full Philadelphia tour today, hunh?" Jasmine
asked me.

Sasha grinned and shook her head. "Is it too late for Ritalin?"

"For who?" Jasmine asked her. "I know you're not talking about
me."

Sasha continued to grin and declined a response to it.

I said, "You guys are at it bright and early."

"Hey, I've been waiting to see the city, man. We've been cooped
up inside Freedom Theater every day this week. It's about time we get
to enjoy ourselves during the daylight for a change."

She said, "We talked to Petula and Tonya last night, and all we
had to talk about was the casting call and South Street, basically."

"Well, you'll get your chance to see plenty today," I promised
them. "But I won't be there with you."

They both stared at me in alarm.

"Why not?" they asked me.

"I haven't seen my family since we've been here, and now we're down to the last two days, so I have to see them. They're already pissed at me."

"Yeah, you gotta see your family, man, that's for sure," Jasmine commented.

I grinned and said, "But first, I get to meet Victor Hinson with Tracy this morning."

Sasha asked me, "Are we going to meet him, too?"

"Don't tell me you're splitting up from us again?" Jasmine whined. "Man, I feel like such a stepchild. You get to meet everybody who means anything."

"I'm the personal assistant," I bragged.

"Well, what are we?" Jasmine asked.

I answered, "Regular assistants."

Sasha laughed. She said, "You're her cousin, that's about it. That's why you get to go and we don't," she said. "If Tracy was my cousin I'd be in the same position as you."

"So you don't believe I bring anything to the table?" I asked her.

"Like what, your pencil and notepad?"

Jasmine laughed and said, "Oh, that's low."

I told them, "If it wasn't for me, none of us would even be here. I was the one who jump-started this whole film thing, and the idea for the clothing line."

Sasha nodded and said, "That's probably true."

"Oh, so you do give me credit for that?"

Jasmine said, "Wait a minute, Tracy already said that she had been trying to get the *Flyy Girl* movie produced, and that she had friends in the fashion industry, so you didn't jump-start jack. You just got her to stop sitting on the couch and make it happen. But the ideas were already there for her. And it was her idea to bring us all to Philly for this walk-in casting call."

I looked at Jasmine and joked, "What? Let me find out if Jasmine has all her facts together?"

She said, "Look, I may talk a lot, but I know what time it is. Tracy is the beast. She's really doing it. She's my new idol, man."

I had heard enough. I said, "All right, let's get a move on. They're probably all downstairs at the limos waiting for us."

We walked out into the hallway and were met by Alexandria and Maddy.

"Speak of the devil," Alexandria stated.

"That's what we said about you last night," I told her. It just slipped out of my mouth.

"What? What she do last night?" Jasmine asked. Everything slipped out of her mouth.

Alexandria huffed, "I minded my own business."

It seemed as if she had a bone to pick that morning. I could read it as soon as we met up with her in the hallway. I wondered how much she and Maddy had talked about me in their room the night before. And if they talked about me, then I was sure they had talked about my cousin. You know, it's hard keeping the peace among ladies sometimes.

I asked them, "Is everything all right this morning?"

"Does everything look all right?" Maddy asked me back.

I stopped and stared for a minute. I just knew they weren't blaming me for them getting busted.

I said, "We don't have issues this morning, do we? Because I didn't cause them."

"Whatever," Alexandria mumbled.

It was obvious that they were beefing with me.

Sasha asked, "What's this all about?"

She could feel the tension herself.

"It doesn't have anything to do with you," Maddy told her.

"Well, what does it have to do with you?" I asked Maddy. I wanted to get it all out in the open before we even started our day.

Maddy said, "All I'm saying is that we're not fucking kids. And I don't appreciate being treated that way."

I said, "Well, why beef with me about that? I said the same thing to my cousin last night. I was defending our right to make our own decisions."

"Well, what happened last night?" Jasmine still wanted to know. She was left out in the cold.

Alexandria told her, "None of your damn business, girl. You're always running your fucking mouth about something."

Before I knew it, Jasmine had mugged Alexandria into the hallway wall.

"You think you're the shit. You're not the fucking shit, you whore!" Jasmine screamed at her.

Maddy jumped on Jasmine's back and yanked her head by her ponytail.

"Owww!" Jasmine yelled.

I jumped on Maddy to try and pull her away from Jasmine. Alexandria then caught her balance and rushed at all of us.

"You fucking bitch!" she screamed at Jasmine with wild, flailing arms.

Jasmine got loose from Maddy and rushed Alexandria into the wall again with a loud thump.

Boom!

Maddy turned and faced me. She said, "Oh, I've been waiting for this."

Sasha pleaded, "What is wrong with you guys?"

But it was too late for that. Maddy was ready to attack me, and Alexandria and Jasmine were already throwing down in a full-fledged fight in the Marriott hallway.

Maddy tried to reach out and claw my face with her nails, but I backed up and slapped her arms down. Then I threw a left-hand cross to her face and knocked her backwards. That only seemed to get Maddy going stronger. She was a lot thicker than I was, so I had no ground to give.

When Maddy rushed me in the hallway a second time, I must have thrown about ten lefts and rights at her face like a Mexican boxer. I didn't even know where I hit her, but I do know that she didn't get a chance to hit me. I wasn't going for it that morning. I hadn't done anything wrong to them. They were acting like damn fools just because we had caught them with my cousin.

"Hey, hey, hey!" someone yelled out from behind me.

I turned and noticed an older white man with his wife behind him. He was attempting to break up the fight.

Maddy tried to rush at me a third time, and the older white man restrained her.

She screamed, "I'ma fuck you up now, bitch! This ain't over with! Get the fuck off of me!"

"Someone call security!" the white man yelled as he struggled with her.

Sasha was shaking her head saying, "I don't believe we did this."

I guess she was embarrassed by it. Sasha was the only one who wasn't caught up that morning.

I was too on edge to be embarrassed at the moment. But there we were, acting like uncivilized, ghetto girls in the hallway of the Marriott Hotel in downtown Philadelphia.

The next thing I knew, the hallway was filled with hotel guests who were peeking out of their rooms to find out what the hell was going on so early in the morning. Someone else had managed to pull Jasmine and Alexandria apart. Then the hotel security showed up, followed by police officers with guns, all for us.

"What's the problem here?" the officers asked us.

They were both black cops, dark brown males in their thirties. Sasha answered, "It was just a catfight that escalated into . . . *this.*"

I wasn't much for words at the moment either. I was still in defense mode I guess. Then my cell phone went off. It was Tracy calling us from the limo downstairs. She had no idea of the mess we were now involved in.

"Who are you all with?" the officers were asking. They were filing a disturbance report and everything.

I answered my cell phone and told my cousin, "You're gonna need to come in and get us."

Tracy was pissed again. After everything had been settled, she got me alone outside the hotel and asked me, "So who started this shit?"

I didn't want to dime on anyone. So I asked my cousin, "What did you say to them in their room last night?"

"I can't remember," she answered too quickly.

"Well, whatever it was, I don't think they liked it too much," I told her.

She calmed down a bit and put things together.

"So they started this shit this morning?"

I still didn't want to answer that question. I said, "All I know is that I had to finish it. But I don't know how they're going to feel about me now as their friend."

I liked having a crew of girls to support me. I can't lie about that. So I felt empty after the fight. It wasn't a win for me. I had lost my peace with my friends, if I still wanted to call them that.

Tracy shook her head. She was still trying to figure out what to do.

She said, "I guess I'll just have to put them in separate cars until they all cool off. And you're still coming with me. But now we're running an hour late."

At first, I was actually surprised that my cousin was sticking to her schedule. But then I thought about the movies she had made, and the determination on the set to finish each day of work, and I realized that nothing would stop Tracy from doing what she had to do once she decided to do it. She was used to jumping over, and piling through, unexpected roadblocks, and our fight that morning was no different from any other technical difficulty. The show had to go on.

We walked back over to the second limo and I climbed inside while Tracy had a few words with Robin.

"The chauffeur has my list of locations, and you just keep these girls apart until they get it all out of their system," she said. "Vanessa is going with me."

Robin nodded to her. "Okay. I got you covered."

Tracy hopped inside the smaller limo with me and took her seat across from mine. And as we pulled off, headed for Germantown Avenue, she began to smile and shake her head.

I had no idea what was so humorous to her, so I sat silently and didn't respond to it.

She said, "So you finished it, hunh? And busted Maddy's face all up. You're from North Philly all right. Madison didn't know who she was dealing with."

It wasn't right, but I cracked a smile with her. I didn't even see Maddy's face. I wasn't thinking about it.

I said, "So, we're still going to meet with Victor this morning?" just to change the subject. I felt awkward viewing my friends as adversaries. And I still considered Maddy and Alexandria to be my friends.

Tracy looked at me and answered, "No doubt about it. You should have known we weren't leaving Philadelphia without seeing him. That's a given," she told me.

I grinned and shook my head.

I asked her, "What is it about him that gets to you?"

Tracy shook her head back to me.

She said, "He's a dominant black man. He's the one white men are the most afraid of, and in awe of."

"What makes you say that?" I asked her. My cousin would speak in poetic riddles every once in a while. I needed more straight talk. Not that I couldn't understand her deeper meaning, I just wanted to make sure.

"Victor makes and lives by his own rules. That's what all dominant men do. They follow the rules they want to follow, and bend or break the rules that they don't."

"What about you?" I asked her. She did the same thing.

She caught on to my logic and smiled. She said, "I'm a dominant woman. And so are you. That's why you're living with me now. You refuse to be the victim. You refuse to be oppressed. You seek what you want. And you map out how to get it."

She said, "That's dominant theory in itself. And that's how you have to be."

I nodded to her. It all made sense to me. And I was growing closer to my cousin every day. So if she connected so well to me, I wondered why she was so adverse to connecting to Alexandria. What was it about my friend that turned her off?

"So what do you really think about Alexandria?" I asked her.

I still knew what I knew about Alexandria, I just wanted to hear more of my cousin's views on her.

Tracy's eyes narrowed into slits. "Like I said, I just don't trust that girl," she told me. "And if I got Mercedes around her, Mercedes would pick her ass apart. She's a pro at reading people. It's a part of her survival mechanism."

I said, "How do you think Mercedes reads you?"

"Oh, she suckers me all the time," Tracy admitted with a laugh.

"Mercedes always knows that I still look up to her as that big sister. So she'll continue to use that angle whenever she needs to. But she'll protect me, too. And she'll fight for this movie whether she's concerned about her role in it or not. Because if it's a bad role, she knows she can squeeze me even more for it."

"What do you think about Bruce as a grown man?"

I was intrigued by what my cousin thought of people, so I just kept it rolling.

Tracy said, "He seems bitter. He's a loser. But that doesn't mean he's not right in what he says. He has a lot of valid points, but when you're a loser you tend to have less optimism. You just don't believe in good things happening. So he didn't believe in Kiwana."

"Do you believe in her?"

"Of course I do. She's my girl. I have to."

"Did you call her back again and ask her about the movie yet?"

"Not yet, but I will."

We arrived at Germantown Avenue near Victor's store, and I became nervous again.

"Are you nervous around him?" I asked my cousin.

Tracy smiled at me. "I get nervous right before I see him, but that's only because I still want him to look good. I mean, I'm not nervous to talk to him or anything like that. I'm too grown for that, and I've known him for too long. But I do get nervous when I think about whether he'll still be attractive to me or not."

"How do you think he feels about seeing you? How do you even know he's gonna be here today? Did you call and tell him you were coming?"

She said, "I have people who check in at his store for me to make sure he still works in and out of the store. So I know he's going to be here. And no, he doesn't know we're coming. That's a part of the nervousness for me. What if I catch him on a bad day?"

I smiled and shook my head. She seemed to be very superficial about him.

"I know you don't only think about his looks," I stated rhetorically.

She said, "Oh, of course not. I was just answering your question about nervousness. Victor's a brilliant man, no question about it. He's really grown into his role as a grassroots-type leader, and he can speak on every issue through experience."

I said, "It seems like he could run for politics or something. He has a lot of likability."

Tracy agreed with me. "Yeah, he does."

Our black limo pulled up to the curb of the commercial storefront property of Germantown Avenue near Chelten, and we both took a breath before we climbed out to approach Victor's store.

"Well, here we go," Tracy commented.

As soon as I stepped out of the limo and walked toward the store, I didn't feel nervous anymore. My nervousness was wiped away as we approached our goal.

It was an everyday store with a plate glass window, health foods on counters to the right, drinks inside of freezers to the left, and a tall order counter toward the back center where you ordered hot and prepared foods from their menu.

An attractive honey brown woman was behind the counter in a white headdress. All we could see were her face and hands behind her clothes, but her skin, eyes, nose, and lips were as perfect as you could get. I was nearly staring at her.

"May I help you sisters?" she asked us. She looked to be in her late teens or early twenties. I was guessing early twenties. I believed she only looked like a teenager because she was so naturally attractive. No makeup or additives were needed.

Tracy said, "Actually, we were wondering if the owner Qadeer Muhammad was available this morning." It was after eleven o'clock by the time we had arrived. The plan was to arrive closer to ten when the store first opened. The fight at the hotel with my girls ruined that plan.

The sister nodded to us and said, "You're Tracy Ellison Grant, aren't you?"

Tracy nodded back to her. "And you are?"

"I'm Felicia," she answered. She extended her hand to Tracy over the counter. That's when I noticed that she was pregnant.

"Pleased to meet you," Tracy told her.

She nodded and smiled. She said, "I'll go back and get him for you."

As soon as she left the counter area to slip into the back, I looked at Tracy.

"Who do you think she is?" I whispered.

Tracy said, "I don't even want to think about it. But I know she's not his wife. Victor has two sons that are nearly ten years old by now, and I know she's not old enough for that."

I said, "You saw that she was pregnant though, right?"

"Of course I did."

I had some ideas, and I'm sure that my cousin had hers, but before either of us could get out another word, Victor "Qadeer Muhammad" Hinson walked out from the back to greet us.

He grinned and said, "I figured it was only a matter of time before you made your way back over here. I heard all about the film you're about to shoot."

Tracy smiled at him and said, "Not yet. We're just in the pre-production stage."

Victor was clean-shaven and a healthy dark brown, wearing a basic gray sweat suit with white sneakers. He was still wearing his white apron from the back kitchen area and plastic gloves.

He nodded and said, "It'll happen. It's only a matter of time. But let me finish up what I'm doing back here and I'll be right back out."

"Okay," Tracy told him with a nod.

Felicia, the sister behind the counter, continued to smile at us.

She said, "You have a lot of courage, my big sister. And your writing is phenomenal."

Tracy grinned and said, "Thank you."

Felicia nodded. She said, "I would love to read more of your poetry. Your poems in *For the Love of Money* were so uplifting and usable for a young woman. Are you going to publish a whole book of your poetry by itself? I would be the first in line to support it."

Tracy said, "I'm flattered, but I would really need more time to sit down and think about that. I mean, I just have so much going on right now. But the poetry book is always on my mind."

Felicia maintained a look of understanding and peace as she continued to nod.

She said, "I don't believe enough of your fans pay attention to how well you write. And your spirit is just . . ." she shook her head and said, "so strong. I really admire you," she told my cousin.

I don't think Tracy was ready for that. She looked stunned by it.

She said, "Okay. Well, I admire sisters who really work within the community to make it a better place for us to live. I admire what you do. We all have to be supportive of the higher cause."

My cousin was just running off at the mouth. Not to say that she didn't mean what she said, but she was just trying to flatter Felicia back for balance. I understood. I understood it perfectly.

Victor walked back out from the kitchen area with no apron or plastic gloves on and led us to the front door.

"Let's talk out front."

"Nice to meet you," I told Felicia. Tracy told her as well.

"Nice to meet you," she responded.

We followed Victor out the door. By then, our limo driver had found enough room to park right out in front of the store.

Victor noticed it and joked, "Now where are my customers supposed to park?"

Tracy told him, "We're not going to stay long. I just wanted my little cousin to meet you. She's my personal assistant for the film process, and I wanted her to actually meet most of the real people that will be a major part of turning *Flyy Girl* into a successful film for the community to enjoy and learn from."

Tracy was still attempting to patronize them.

Victor only grinned at us. He said, "That's a strong film you're about to make. I had to sit up and read the book again once I heard what you were about to do with it. And it's about time, too."

Tracy asked him, "You're not concerned about your portrayal in the film?"

He said, "Hey, the truth is the truth. I was a wild man back then. It'll make me proud to have these younger brothers see how far I've come, and how far we still have to go. That movie'll be good for all of us."

Wow! I had no idea how cool and down-to-earth he would be. I had no reason to be nervous around him at all.

"Hey, Mr. Muhammad," a young boy riding a bike in a Sixers baseball cap greeted him.

"Hey, family, you watch them cars when you hit them corners now."

"I know," the boy responded.

"Hey, Q," a man hollered from a moving car in the middle of the street.

"Hey now," Qadeer hollered back.

I didn't know if I should refer to him as Victor or Qadeer, but his community had definitely accepted him as Mr. Muhammad, so I figured that "Q" for Qadeer was right.

He smiled and said, "You know you had a hot can of beans cooking for me on that sequel book you wrote."

Tracy grinned and looked away. I'm sure it was embarrassing for both of them.

She said, "Hey, the truth is the truth. But most people still say that you played me."

He said, "Yeah, I know. But I did what had to be done that night. A lesser man would have run from it, or bent his own will to serve your personal lust. And I just wasn't that man for you."

Tracy nodded to him and looked back into the store at Felicia. I knew it was coming. I was waiting for it. Tracy was thinking the same way I was thinking.

"Who is Felicia married to?" she asked him. She was assuming that a pregnant Muslim woman would be married. I was assuming the same thing. Muslims believed very strongly in family bonding and responsibility. Or at least we all believed that they did.

Qadeer said, "If you're taking the time to ask me that question, then I do believe that you already know."

"So you divorced Malika?" she asked him.

"I don't believe in divorce," he answered plainly.

We all paused for a moment.

And I ended up asking the obvious question, "Felicia's your second wife?"

Qadeer answered, "She read your sequel book while she was still a student at Temple University, and she came after me. You know I own a lot of properties around Temple now," he commented to Tracy. "So she caught up to me at one of my properties and said, 'I'll be your second wife.' And I explained to her that I wasn't necessarily looking for a second wife. That was only my proper response to your advances to me. But Felicia went on to tell me that she was thinking about becoming a Muslim woman, and that she wanted me to be her husband."

He said, "She explained to me how mature she was for her age, and how she wanted to be linked to someone who was more spiritually involved in the community. I told her that I was flattered, but it doesn't quite work that way. I told her she would have to come into the mosque on her own, and go through a proper courting process that I may not be a part of.

"Well, she stayed in touch with me, kept doing what she needed to do in school, joined the mosque on her own, and she actually approached Malika," he told us. "Now, I still have plenty of women who find themselves attracted to me. And it makes me feel good just to know that I still have those attractions, but I don't pursue them. Nevertheless, we all have our moments of weakness, and before I went there and fell a victim to that, Malika told me she thought marrying Felicia would be a good idea. We were adding a lot to what we were already doing, and Felicia was a skilled and educated young woman who was dedicated to helping us in the task."

Tracy was still stunned. I could see it in her eyes.

She said, "So this girl actually approached you after reading that chapter in my book?"

It seemed unreal, but I could imagine it. Qadeer still lived in Philadelphia, and he was still very handsome. Why wouldn't a girl read the book and wonder about him?

He said, "You still have no idea how much power you have in the pen, do you? Women still approach me about that letter from jail that I wrote you in the first book. People read, Tracy. And after they read it, it becomes the facts."

My cousin was speechless. She stood there dumbfounded.

I broke the silence and asked him, "Does it wear you out to have two wives?"

What the hell, the question was on my mind, so I asked it.

He looked at me and chuckled. He said, "Busy married folks may not have as much sex as some of us believe. And that goes for one wife or three."

I said, "Well, somebody is pregnant."

Tracy looked at me and frowned. "Show some respect, Vanessa," she told me.

But Qadeer didn't sweat it at all. I felt like I could talk to that man about anything.

He smiled and said, "It only takes one good time to impregnate a fertile woman."

Tracy looked and stared at him. She said, "So you went ahead and actually did that. Isn't that against the law?"

"Whose law?" he asked her.

Tracy stood there in a daze. The man still had that power over her.

I nodded my head to him and said, "Well, congratulations." There was no reason for me to be upset about anything. Felicia sure seemed happy. Tracy, on the other hand . . .

She asked him, "Well, what does Malika think about this pregnancy?"

"We're all looking forward to the new family member," he answered calmly. "Felicia will have an experienced mother around to help her."

Tracy said, "And everybody knows about this?"

Qadeer nodded his head and grinned.

He said, "Your pen is also a double-edged sword. You have the power to make everything known through publication. So I guess now that I've told you, everybody will know. But we don't hide it. We understand that not everyone will agree, but it is what it is. The black community has lived with these kind of extended families without them being organized for years. So we consider it a plus to be able to organize our union into something that will benefit us all."

Tracy was still amazed by it. He had actually gotten away with having two wives, and they were getting along with it.

My cousin finally broke her silence. She said, "Okay."

She didn't know what else to say to him.

"Well, we have a busy day ahead of us," she commented. "Like I said, I just wanted to stop by and introduce my cousin to you."

I reached out my hand to him and said, "You're a very interesting man, Mr. Muhammad."

Tracy eyed me sternly again. But she declined to speak on it.

Then she told him, "Let me go back in and say good-bye to your second wife before we leave."

Qadeer nodded to her.

When Tracy walked back inside the store, he looked at me and said, "It looks like I'll be a heavy reference in her book for the rest of her life, and she'll be a heavy reference in mine."

I told him, "You'll also be a heavy lead in this movie that we're about to make. There's just no getting around that."

"I know that already," he agreed. "I already know."

When Tracy walked back out from the store, she was suddenly in a big hurry to get away.

"All right, well, we'll be in touch if we need you to help out with our cast. You know, we want everything to be as authentic as we can make it."

Qadeer nodded to us one last time while opening the door to his store to walk back in.

"You always know where to find me," he said.

"Okay," Tracy told him. And we climbed back into the limo.

Family Affairs

Tracy stared at me inside the limo and asked me, "Do you believe that? I don't believe that just happened. Tell me I'm dreaming, Vanessa. Tell me I'm dreaming."

I smiled and said, "If you are, then we must be in the same dream together."

"And that girl is just as happy as she can be, talking about how she admires me," she said of Qadeer's second wife.

"What did you say to her when you walked back in?" I asked my cousin. You know I had to ask her.

"I asked her if it was true."

"You thought he would lie about something like that?"

"Maybe. Just to get a rise out of me," she answered.

I shook my head at the idea. "He doesn't seem like that kind of man. But what did she say to you?"

"She said it was true, she is his second wife, and then she said she loves his behind with all of her heart and soul. I didn't believe they made women like her anymore," Tracy commented.

"Women like what?"

"Women who will be that damn happy to have a *piece* of a man, and the *leftovers* at that."

I said, "Well, what if Qadeer had divorced his first wife, Malika, to marry Felicia? Would that make it any better for you?"

"No. He still would be married to some other damn chick."

I chuckled at my cousin's obvious envy of the situation. "So, you wouldn't be happy unless he married you somehow, and as his first wife."

"He should have come to me years ago when he first got out of jail," she told me. "That would have solved everything. But no, he gets out of jail and marries the first Muslim chick he gets his hands on."

194

I said, "I doubt that. He doesn't strike me as the kind of man who would make that hasty a decision."

"Vanessa, please. Cut the shit. You just met the man all of two minutes ago, and you're in here giving me advice about him. 'Cause see, I knew him when he would hop from one girl's bed to the next and wouldn't even take a bath in between. Now that's just plain nasty."

"But you liked him," I reminded her. And she still did.

She took a breath and said, "Yeah, I just needed to outgrow that whole situation."

I thought about it and said, "Which one?" My cousin had had plenty of situations with Victor/Qadeer.

She snapped, "All of them."

She was talking out of sheer frustration at that point. Then she calmed down and shook her head.

She said, "I could never be that kind of woman. She doesn't look like she would try and challenge him at all. Why would a man pick a woman like that?" she pondered.

I answered, "He didn't. Remember, he said that she chose him."

"I bet she did. Off of my damn book at that."

"Does that bother you?"

"Of course it bothers me. That's like somebody stealing your best dress out of your closet or something."

I said, "But you put it in a book. It was no longer in the closet. And you said in the book that you would never agree to being a second wife. You called him crazy for even bringing up the subject to you. Don't you remember?"

Tracy looked me in the eyes and said, "Don't play with my patience, Vanessa. Now is not the time for that. And I'm not Maddy. I fight now with a whole different urgency."

I didn't doubt it, but I wouldn't go there with my cousin anyway.

"So, outside of the second-wife issue, what do you think about Qadeer's life?" I asked her.

"Oh, hell, with two wives, store property, and campus real estate, he's doing good for himself," my cousin answered. "And you can see that he's not bitter like Bruce is, because he's not a loser. He knows I can do it."

"Bruce didn't say you couldn't do it. He was only giving you pointers on who and what to look out for."

"Yeah, whatever," my cousin huffed. She said, "Bruce would love to do what Victor is getting away with, but he lacks the game. So he's miserable because of it, and now he's trying to make everyone else feel miserable. You see now how the pieces are beginning to come together?"

I said, "Well, what about you? Would you rather be Felicia or Malika, and be satisfied with your position as the supportive wife of a handsome and brilliant man, or be the free-to-roam, rich and famous, but never satisfied Tracy Ellison Grant that you are now?"

My cousin stared at me again and began to chuckle.

She said, "So you got it all broken down, hunh, little cousin?"

"That's what you brought me here to do, right? You want me to analyze things so you're not just looking at them from your own perspective. Well, when you go back to the past, you have to confront these issues."

"Well, let me read you for a minute," she commented.

I said, "Go ahead. Be my guest."

"Okay, well, you really think that you're smarter than all of us. And you're sitting back gathering your information to write your own book. In the meantime, you're not trying to get caught up in anything, but you can't help that, because life won't allow you to be a simple spectator."

I grinned. She was about right, but I couldn't admit to it. I said, "But without you allowing me in, I'm just a nobody with nothing to say and no one to listen to me."

Tracy said, "Oh, they're gonna listen to you all right. You'll be holding the keys to the castle before it's over with. I just wonder what young man is gonna get your nose wide open."

I hated to admit it, but after hanging out with Tracy and her older friends, I doubted if I would ever fall for a young man. I was really feeling the straight logic of older men. I could clearly see their goals in life. They no longer wore the mask of bullshit. Older men told you exactly what they wanted or didn't want, and it was up to you to accept it or not.

I said, "Do you think Felicia is wrong for making the choice she made?" I was asking my cousin for myself as well. Not that I would choose to be with Qadeer or Bruce, but just with an older man in general, who may have already had someone, and who had lived a fuller life with more to give than to take from me.

As we approached my house in North Philadelphia in our limo ride, Tracy nodded to me with her answer.

She said, "You know when the girl said she admired me?"

"Felicia," I reminded her.

"Yeah, well, you girls are really figuring things out. And what she was really saying is that she admires herself for trusting in him. She went ahead and threw up her hands for that man, just like I threw up my hands for my career. And she's being courageous enough to let the pieces fall where they may, just like I was with my career in Hollywood. And here I am again, jumping full-fledged into the fire with my ideas. But will I do the same for a man? No. Not even for Victor. So she admires me for having the courage to be who I'm going to be, and herself for being who she's gonna be.

"I mean, we all are different," Tracy concluded. "And we all have to live with who we are and accept ourselves."

She said, "I'm a single woman, Vanessa. I'm a free woman. And I may not like it all the time, but this is who I am . . . until further notice."

I wondered how long a woman could remain single with no children. My cousin was still getting her groove on whenever she needed to, but how badly did she miss real love, marriage, and kids? I also wondered how long I could remain a virgin. Nineteen wasn't that old to start. I was still officially a teenager until my twentieth birthday, so I still had time to ponder. Nevertheless, some people were already beginning to look at me funny for not having a man. Especially since I was considered attractive. I walked up the front steps to my family's North Philadelphia home with that thought in mind and rang the doorbell.

I heard Veronica approach the door. My mother was not home from work yet, and Tiffany would have approached it with more energy—and my guess was right.

Veronica looked through the peephole and said, "Speak of the devil."

I shook my head. It seemed as if everybody was saying that. Were we all devils in our own ways?

Anyway, my sister opened the door and let me in, wearing some extra-tight low-rider jeans that showed off her assets from behind.

"Jesus Christ, can you even breathe in those things?" I asked her.

"Can you breathe in your head?" she asked me back.

I faked dizziness just to humor her.

"Oh, I need brain oxygen. It's not enough room left in my head."

Veronica stopped and stared at me. "Stupid."

She was about my height, but at least twenty pounds thicker, browner, and a lot more jaded in her attitude.

I said, "So let me see a picture of this guy Mommy caught you with."

I walked over to sit down on the sofa that had been in our living room for years. Not much had changed in the house, it was just a lot cleaner and more organized when I was still there. Now they had magazines and throw pillows all over the floors and tables, with dust over all of the shelves and pictures, and half-swept dirt on the floors. My sisters just couldn't see dirt like I could, I guess. They needed to have their eyes checked.

Veronica said, "I don't have any pictures of him."

"Does he have pictures of you?" I asked her.

"For what, he knows what I look like?"

Tiffany bounced down the steps carrying all of her balls of energy before I could respond.

"Vanessa, is that you?" she called before she set her eyes on me.

"No, it's the Easter Bunny," I joked.

"Yeah, that sounds like your corny ass," she told me.

I didn't care if they felt I was corny. I was just happy to be there with them. And I was still their big sister . . . no matter what.

Tiffany had already grown taller than all of us, and she was still gangly. But even she had some tight jeans on.

"I guess ass-hugging jeans are in now," I commented.

She asked me, "What they wearing in California? Because low-riders have been in."

I pulled out Flyy Girl Ltd. shirts and hats that I had saved just for my sisters.

"Well, I got the new hookup," I told them.

Tiffany grabbed the gear and gave it a better look.

"Oh, snap, I'm wearing this tomorrow. That's Tracy on the logo?"

"Yeah."

She grinned and said, "Now that's flyy." Then she put on the rust-colored hat and pulled her ponytail out of the hole in the back.

"Oh, shit, it's a perfect fit."

I was pleased that my sister liked it. So far so good. Flyy Girl Ltd. was passing the urban-girl cool test.

Veronica held hers up. I had saved the blue for her.

She said, "So now she's gonna have everybody wearing her flyy girl stuff? For what?"

"Because it's flyy, bitch," Tiffany snapped at her.

Veronica rushed over to her in the room and said, "Tiffany, you're gonna call me one more bitch and I'm gonna pull that damn ponytail out your head."

Tiffany scrambled out of the way and to the other side of the room.

"You just mad because you can't grow one. Not a real one, anyway. So blame it on your nappy-headed daddy."

Veronica said, "Fuck you and your skinny-ass father. At least mine ain't on life support from a crack addiction."

Tiffany said, "Your father can't afford crack. Now you know that's messed up. You ain't even got a pair of clean socks to sell. Damn, all you gotta do is steal some from Kmart."

Nothing had changed at home. That was the kind of stuff I used to ignore to finish my homework. But now I was only visiting.

I said, "What's wrong with having our own Flyy Girl line of clothing? You wear Rocawear and Baby Phat, don't you?"

"Ecko design," Tiffany stated.

Veronica said, "What do you mean, 'our own line of Flyy Girl clothes'? Are you part owner?"

I thought about it and answered, "Yes." Tracy did tell me to name my cut, and I planned to hold her to it, too.

"So, she put you down with her own clothing line? And all of those girls my friends saw you with on South Street are her models?" Veronica asked me.

I had to be careful with that. I needed to see where she was going with the information. Maybe I had put my foot in my mouth already.

Tiffany said, "Can I be a model?" She wanted to be everything.

I was more concerned with Veronica at the moment.

"So, she hooked you up, hunh?" Veronica stated. "She don't even talk to us. It's like we don't even exist. But she hooked you up, though."

There it was. Finally. Veronica was letting me in on my assumptions. She was envious of me.

I looked at Tiffany and asked her, "Do you feel the same way?"

She said, "What, like you gettin' all the breaks? I keep telling you, man, in a couple more years, I'ma punch Mom in her face, too, and get me some breaks."

Veronica said, "Yeah, a broken foot up in your ass. You better stop talking that crazy shit."

I said, "So, you really do talk about this all the time then."

Tiffany said, "I told you that."

I took a minute to clear my thoughts. I said, "Both of you actually think that fighting Mom is what allows me to do what I'm doing now? I mean, I would have always been doing something. I always had ideas. I always finished what I started. And I always tried to get y'all to do more. And you guys always looked at me like I was crazy."

Tiffany said, "You are crazy. But that's not a bad thing. It's a good thing. I'm try'na be more crazy like you."

I shook my head and said, "Trust me, Tiffany, you're a lot crazier than me. All you need is a damn stage and a microphone."

"Well, find me one then. Tracy got connections, right?"

I had put my foot in my mouth again.

I flipped things around and said, "So, you guys both want to work for me, is that it?"

My sisters both looked confused, like I thought they would.

"Work for you?" Veronica asked me. "What can you do?"

I said, "I can manage your careers and find you work. Now what are you talented in? I know Tiffany can do jokes. Would you like to perform at the Marriott tonight?" I asked my baby sister.

She laughed it off and didn't respond to me.

Veronica said, "Wait a minute. If you manage our careers, then you work for us."

I shook my head and said, "No I don't. I only work for you if you hire me, and that's after you've built up some value in your talent. Because if I have all the value in my contacts, then you work for me. And that's the same way it goes for all supermodels and comedians until they build their own names."

Veronica looked at me and grunted. She said, "You ain't no damn hustler. Who you think you are, a female Damon Dash or somebody? Tracy has the power, not you."

"Well, why are you mad at me then, Veronica? I don't have the power."

I had her where I wanted her. We had to get down to the facts before we could understand each other.

My sister smiled at me. She knew I had backed her behind into a corner.

She said, "But you can get to her though. I can't."

I said, "So, what do you want me to tell her?"

"You shouldn't have to tell her anything about us," Tiffany stated. "We're family, too."

"Okay, so what do you want her to do?" I asked them.

Tiffany said, "I want to move out to California. And I want to be in a movie. And Veronica wants her big ass in some Flyy Girl Ltd. jeans."

"I didn't say all that," Veronica spoke up. "But it would be nice if she noticed us, and not just because you told her to either."

They had me in a bind. Tracy couldn't concentrate on everyone. She was just one woman.

Veronica added, "And then you come home and say you're gonna take me out to dinner, and you haven't even done it yet 'cause you're too busy hanging out with your model friends."

I said, "We're going out to eat tonight."

"I have other plans tonight."

"I don't have any plans. You can take me out," Tiffany commented.

I said, "I'm only in town for two more nights until we come back to film, Veronica. Why don't you give me this opportunity to take you out like sisters. And yeah, you can come, too, Tiffany," I told her.

"Oh, I can come, too, like I'm some kind of Cabbage Patch kid in a backpack."

"Yeah," I told her. "And I have a giant backpack just for you."

She shook her head and shut her mouth for a minute.

Veronica said, "It just don't seem right. How come you get to do everything now?"

"Because she's Vanessa Tracy Smith, that's why," Tiffany stated.

"No, because I busted my ass to prepare myself for opportunities," I told them. "I could just be sitting out there in L.A. at the beach doing nothing. But no, I did all my research on things, and I pushed Tracy into doing this movie. I pushed her into doing this clothing line, too. And I got my girls to model her clothes. And I'm the one who she trusts now to take around with her when she's handling her business. Why? Because I'm prepared for it."

I said, "Tracy's not just hooking me up. I'm paying off for her because she knows I'm using what I have, my intelligence, to make things happen for all of us."

Veronica began to shake her head.

"There you go, thinking you're so much smarter than everybody again."

I was growing tired of the guilt trip Veronica would always try to pull about my intelligence. So I let her have it.

I said, "So what? So what if I think I'm smarter than people? What do you want me to do, apologize for using my damn brains? You use what you have to use, and that's what I happen to have."

"Yeah, but you don't have to throw it in people's faces."

"I don't."

"Yes you do," Tiffany butted in. "You always made us feel like we were dumb."

I said, "Because you were my little sisters and you were always getting into shit. But that didn't mean that you weren't intelligent. You just have to learn how to use your brains more."

"Well, maybe we just couldn't see things like you," Veronica stated. "And maybe we couldn't get into Engineering and Science. And maybe our cousin didn't get to meet us and take us out to California. That's all we're saying."

They had a point, but that was life. Everybody couldn't do the same things, and everybody wouldn't get the same breaks. There was nothing I could do about that.

I finally said, "Look, we are all still teenagers. That means we still have a lot of life left to live. So nobody's putting a limit on what we can do. And you shouldn't put a limit on yourselves. That's what Tracy told me, and that's what I'm passing on to you as my sisters. So yeah, you may not get the breaks I'm getting now, but who's to say that you won't get even bigger breaks than me later.

"But you still have to be *prepared* for when it happens," I told them. "There's no getting around that. And there's nothing I can do to help you if you're not prepared. All you would end up doing is wasting an opportunity."

I had said a mouthful, and I didn't know what else I could say to them. They still had to finish high school, and Tracy and I didn't have time for babysitting out in L.A. We would be working. So my sisters would just have to wait their damn turns.

Tiffany broke the silence and asked, "Anybody want a Snickers bar?"

We all laughed together at her perfect timing of humor. She was definitely talented, but so were many other girls who never pushed their talents further. So that became my new mission. If my sisters wanted to complain about and envy my position with Tracy, then once I came across a break for them, I planned to push them until they would either beg for mercy or take control of the situation and shine.

I hung out and kicked it with my sisters all day, laughing, joking, watching movies on DVD, and just relaxing until my cousin Jason called me on my cell phone.

"What happened this morning?" he asked me. It was nearly five o'clock by then.

"We just got into it, Jason. What do you want me to say?" It was obvious that someone had told him. I was assuming it was Alexandria.

"Who started it?"

"Actually, your girl started it by having a shitty attitude this morning. Did you promise her something that she didn't get last night?" I questioned him. He still didn't know what I knew about them.

"She started it? How?" he asked me.

I said, "They were talking about me and your sister in their room and beefing with us because of last night apparently. And when we all met up in the hallway to leave this morning, it all came out."

"So, you started fighting Alexandria?"

"No, she told Jasmine to mind her business, shut her damn mouth, and some more stuff, so Jasmine surprised us all and went to town on her. Then Maddy jumped in it. So I tried to break Maddy away from the fight, and that's when she turned on me."

"So y'all were all fighting this morning?" he asked me.

"Everyone but Sasha. She was still trying to figure out why we were fighting in the first place."

Jason said, "That's crazy, man. I thought y'all were friends."

I said, "I thought so, too. But you know how crazy things can get when the opposite sex gets involved."

"Yeah, I see," Jason told me. "So where are you now?"

"I'm at my mom's house. She should be back home from work soon, then we're all going out to eat together."

"Tracy's supposed to do that with us tonight, too."

"Yeah, we've all been busy at work all week."

"So umm . . . what do you think about Alexandria? You think I should just leave her alone?" he asked me.

"Is that what you want to do? I mean, do you have any real feelings toward her? You just met her and you hardly even know her, right?"

He said, "Yeah, but . . . I mean, she *bad*. And she likes me."

I asked him, "Were you really just walking her to the elevators last night?"

"Naw, I was just trying to keep her out of trouble with Tracy," he admitted. "That's why I didn't say that you introduced us. I didn't want Tracy pointing her fingers at you either."

"Yeah, I noticed that," I told him. I said, "But if you really like Alexandria, then Tracy's gonna find out eventually. I mean, what's the big secret about?"

I wasn't planning on getting in their way whether we were all fighting or not. If Alexandria wanted the boy, and Jason wanted her, then they should be together.

Jason seemed hesitant. He said, "Yeah, I just gotta figure out . . . I mean, y'all flying back to L.A. Sunday anyway."

"Yes we are," I told him. "But what does that mean? You have money to fly out west, and Alexandria has money to fly back east."

"Yeah, but she's still in college, I'm ready to get out of college. I'm in Philly, she's all the way in L.A.—"

I cut him off and said, "Well, just leave it the way it is then, Jason. If you don't want to push it any further, then don't."

He didn't respond to me. Alexandria had his mind twisted. I guess it felt too good to him. Puppy love must be nice.

Veronica looked over at me from the sofa and said, "It sounds like somebody got somebody's nose open."

I smiled at her and nodded my head.

Jason said, "You should see how people look at her when I'm out with her."

I shook my head and smiled wider.

I said, "I know how they look at the girl, Jason. But is that all you think about? I mean, do you like her personality?"

"I don't know. She seems a little bossy sometimes," he answered.

"Don't we all," I told him. "So you want a pretty little mouse girl?"

"I'm not saying that, but I'm not trying to spend a lot of time arguing with a girl either."

I said, "Well, do whatever you plan to do then. I have nothing else to say about it. Every decision you make is between you and her now."

"I know."

"I'm glad you do."

When I hung the phone up with Jason, Veronica asked me, "Jason fell for one of your model girls?" Tiffany was off in the house doing something else.

I nodded to my sister and said, "That's what it looks like."

"And he doesn't want Tracy to know about it?"

"Not yet."

Veronica studied me for a second. She said, "Is Tracy intimidating all like that? I mean, I read a little bit of her sequel book, *For the Love of Money*, but I couldn't follow it. She kept confusing me with the dates and stuff."

I said, "She can be very intimidating if you don't come correct with her. But I get along with her because I always come correct. At least so far," I added with a smile.

Who knows when Tracy would fire off at me for some reason. I could be just holding on by a string with her myself.

"Is she ever getting married soon?" my sister asked me.

I grinned and said, "We were just talking about that this morning. Why is marriage so important for her? I mean, is Mom ever gonna get married? Nobody sweats her about marriage."

Veronica frowned at me and said, "They're totally different, Vanessa. Mom is overweight and just making it, with three kids. But Tracy is a Hollywood star with her own money and no kids. They are so different it's a shame."

"So nobody would want to marry Mom, but everybody would want to marry Tracy? Is that your logic?"

She said, "I hate to admit it for Mom, but yeah."

I had a lot of comments about that, but I decided to take it one step at a time.

I said, "Do you think Mom would marry anyone who asked her?"

Veronica paused. "No, not anyone," she answered. "But she can't be too choosy either."

"What about Tracy?"

"Oh, now, she can choose who she wants to."

"What if the person she chooses is already taken?"

Veronica eyed me with confusion. She said, "Well, choose somebody else. It's a million guys out here who would want to marry Tracy."

"But does that mean she wants to marry them?"

"Why not?"

"Because it may not be the right fit for her."

"Well, what kind of man does she want? I'm sure she can get him. All she has to do is put her mind to it like she does with everything else."

"So it's that easy to you, hunh?"

"For her, yeah."

I had lost my train of thought. Was it that simple? Could it be that simple? You just walk down the street and say, "Hey, you, let's get married."

I gathered my response and said, "You have to find a man who wants what you want, basically. And Tracy wants her freedom. But can you be free and be married at the same time?"

I was asking myself the question just as much as I was asking Veronica.

She said, "Well, this may sound crazy to you, Vanessa, but everybody wants to belong to somebody. That freedom stuff"—she shook her head—"it may sound good, but all I can see is an old, lonely woman with a bunch of pets and plants in her house, walking around talking to herself with no man and no kids."

I started laughing. I said, "Well, what about a man who never gets married or has kids?"

She said, "Either he just don't have no game, or he's a con man and a criminal who doesn't want any ties that can be used as his weakness. Like in that movie *The Usual Suspects* when that guy kills his own family to let his enemies know how ruthless he was. That was insane. So I don't trust guys who don't have kids or families either."

My sister had me forgetting everything I wanted to say. It was cut and dry to her; either you marry and have kids, or you were crazy.

She said, "There's a reason why marriage has been around for so long, Vanessa. And I don't care what you say, everybody wants to be with somebody."

I said, "Okay, I can agree with that. But let's just say this about Tracy; her career aspirations may conflict with marriage and kids right now, but once she decides where she wants to go and what she wants to do with herself in the future, then she can decide on her own about a man and having kids and stuff.

"Is that fair enough?" I asked my sister.

Veronica was hesitant to agree with me. She smiled and said, "I know I would have me a gorgeous husband right now if I was her."

I was able to respond to that. I said, "Well, that was not Tracy's goal when she went to Hollywood. And if it was her goal, she probably wouldn't be who she is right now."

I said, "You still have to be focused on doing you, and if you find someone who you enjoy on the way, then so be it. But there's a lot of women who are trapped right now because they didn't get an opportunity to do things before they ended up married with kids. Like that scene in *Waiting to Exhale*, when Angela Bassett burns all of her husband's clothes in his car after she found out he was cheating on her and hiding his money."

I said, "It was like she had to start her life all over again."

Veronica grinned and nodded. I guess she had finally gotten my point.

Out of the blue, she said, "I would have shot his ass if he wasted my life like that."

Wow! I was stuck again. How could Veronica go from one extreme to the other? On the one hand, she begs for the husband, and on the other, she shoots him when he fucks up. It didn't make any sense.

I shook my head and said, "Okay, I give up. Because I can see that this discussion will never end between us."

Veronica laughed and said, "I was just joking. I wouldn't shoot him. Besides, she had all that money after that. Shit, I would have gone out and gotten me a new man."

That was it for me. There was no sense in even talking about it anymore. I wanted to leave the subject alone with my sister. But out of curiosity, I asked her, "What about me? When do you think I should settle down with a man?"

Veronica looked at me and said, "Oh, I already know, you're gonna be one of those women I talked about, with the cats and plants and no man. I mean, Tracy had like *ten* boyfriends by now. You've had about what, *two*? And you treated both of them like they were on punishment. 'You can't call me at this time. You can't call me at that time.

You can't come over to my house. I can't come over to your house.' I mean, what the hell was the point?"

I screamed out laughing. My sister had been eavesdropping on my conversations.

She said, "So I don't even worry about you. But I thought Tracy liked guys."

I said, "Well, there was a time when dating had rules, you know. But now I guess anything goes, like your tight-ass jeans."

Veronica said, "Not anything, but a lot more than what you had going."

We heard the key turning in the lock at the front door and knew that our mother had arrived.

Veronica looked at me, and I looked back at her.

"Here she comes," my sister told me.

I stood up to greet my mother when she walked in. I was a little nervous again, so I wanted to get the greeting over with as quickly as possible. And since my sister had already assumed my mother's lack of prospects on a workable marriage, I felt sorry for her.

My mother walked through the door bent over with brown shopping bags in both her hands and arms, and I immediately grabbed them from her to help her out.

She looked up at me and said, "Thank you, Vanessa. I miss having somebody around here to help me out when I walk through that door. I'm gettin' to be an old lady already, and I'm not even forty yet."

Veronica heard her but didn't respond to it. Then Tiffany scrambled down the stairs.

"Hey, Mom, what you got to eat?"

My mother just looked at me. I could feel her pain already. It was everyday use for her. She was a mule. No wonder she was so mad all the time. Sometimes being away from it all gives you a chance to see things more clearly. So I stepped up and hugged my mother at the door for love's sake.

She leaned back from me and said, "What's this for?" She looked skeptical. That's how a lot of people react when they're not used to good things happening to them.

I said, "It's just because I love you, Mom."

Tiffany said, "Does that mean you're coming back home?"

She had me on the spot.

My mother answered her before I could. She said, "No, Vanessa has things to do now . . ." Then she paused. "And I'm proud of her for it."

My mother had no idea how good it felt for me to hear her say that. We had fought about everything for so long, and she was finally allowing me to spread my wings and fly.

I said "Thanks, Mom" and buried my head into her neck and shoulders. "I didn't mean to hit you," I mumbled to her. "I didn't mean it."

Tiffany said, "Aw, don't start that Sunday-afternoon-special crying stuff."

My mother told her, "Shut your mouth, girl."

Sure enough, I was crying into my mother's shoulder, and I didn't want to let go because I didn't want my sisters to see me cry.

"It's okay, Vanessa, I know you didn't mean it," my mother told me.

"I didn't," I mumbled again. "I just can't let nobody stop me, Mom. Nobody."

"I know, girl. You have to do what you have to do," she told me. "I understand."

"Thank you," I told her again.

I wiped my face before I let go of my mother because I knew my sisters were still watching me. I had a lot of pride, I guess. And when I turned to face them, they both had a lost look on their faces. They didn't know how to feel. They didn't know what it was like to go all out and experience the full emotions of life. So I had to get them to feel it. It was my job as the big sister to do that for them.

"Come here," I told them.

They were both still hesitant.

"Come here," I said more forcefully.

"You hear your sister talking to you?" my mother told them.

When they walked over to me, I grabbed both of them into a bear hug and pushed our heads together. I said, "I love you guys. I love all of you. And if you let me do what I need to do, I'm gonna hook all of us up. I promise you that. So just let me do my shit."

Tiffany said, "As long as it don't stink too bad."

We started laughing again, like sisters who love each other.

My mother shook her head and said, "That damn girl . . ."

I said, "It's all right, Mom. That's just who she is. But no cooking for you tonight. We're all going out to eat. Wherever you guys want. And I'm paying for everything, including the taxi ride."

My mother looked at me and said, "Okay, you're the boss. Let me go and freshen up, and I'll be right back down."

Focused

When I got back to the hotel after dinner with my family, I felt like nothing could get in my way. Everything had to be successful. It was like I had a fresh pack of batteries in my brains, and I was just pulling them out of the pack.

So I walked right over to Maddy and Alexandria's room to clear the stale air between us.

Maddy answered the door with her face still bruised from our fight that morning. She had nothing to say to me.

I told her, "First of all, I want to apologize for our fight this morning. Second, I wasn't trying to get involved with Shamor, he was after me. And third, I had nothing to do with last night. You guys just happened to walk in at the wrong time."

She said "Whatever" and began to close the door on me.

I said, "Just hear me out for a minute. I just want to talk to you."

"Talk about what?"

"About life, Maddy. Life and aspirations."

"What about it?"

"Can I come in?"

Maddy still wanted to get her revenge. I could see it in her eyes.

I said, "You can kick my ass if you want to, but I'm not here for that. I want to talk to you. Both of you," I told her.

She said, "Alexandria's not here. You know where she is."

"Well, let me talk to you alone then."

Maddy continued to stare at me. Then she slowly opened the door wide enough to let me in. She was watching a movie and eating room service, a Caesar salad with grilled chicken, at the small desk. She had vanilla ice cream on the side for dessert.

I sat down on Alexandria's bed and took a breath. Maddy went back to eating her food and ignored me.

I said, "There are so many trivial things that get in the way of real progress in life. Small stuff, and we're not supposed to sweat it, but we do."

Maddy paid me no mind. So I kept talking.

"I don't know what everybody else wants out of this, but I'm going for everything."

Maddy still didn't say anything. She was busy eating and watching her movie on the television.

"Girls, in particular, will bicker about stuff that means nothing half the time. But I've never had the chance to hang around a lot of guys because they always want to get me. Even the smart guys get it confused. I try to do study sessions with them, and all they can think about is what my perfume smells like, even when I'm only wearing cocoa butter."

"Look, if you came over here to talk about yourself, then you can go back to your own room and talk to your walls, because I don't want to hear that shit," Maddy finally spoke up.

I asked her, "Well, what do you want to do with your life, Madison?"

I had just finished talking about life aspirations with my sisters. I guess I was on a roll with the subject.

Maddy spat, "I wanna eat my fuckin' food in peace. Is that all right with you?"

I sat quiet for a minute. Then I said, "We have plenty of time to eat food, but the real work gets done when we're hungry. You notice how they call it a lunch *break*, or *break fast*? Even dinner is supposed to cap off your long day of hungry work."

Maddy took a deep breath and kept her silence.

I was rambling a bit, but I still had a point to make. There was so much that people could get accomplished in life, but they didn't because too much bullshit took up too much of their time.

She said, "If you don't eat, you die."

That was what I wanted from her. I wanted a mental debate. I wanted to make sure that Maddy didn't stop thinking just because of our fight that morning. Sometimes conflicts served to shut you down, but you could use those same conflicts to get yourself started.

I said, "But if you don't work, you don't eat. So what comes first?"

"You don't have to work to eat. I know plenty of people who don't do a damn thing, and they get to eat every day," she argued.

"Where are they getting their food from?"

"From other people."

"Do those other people work?"

Maddy stopped talking again.

Then she said, "The point is, everybody doesn't have to work to eat."

I said, "Well, why would anybody give a person food who doesn't work?"

She said, "You got babies, teenagers, old people, crippled people, crazy people, even bums, who don't work, but they all eat, don't they?"

"Okay, but none of those people are independent either," I argued.

Maddy said, "Who said anything about independence? You were talking about eating."

"I was talking about how eating relates to work, and when you do your own work you have independence. And when you have independence, you can eat whenever you want to, and as much as you want to, but not while you're working. It's better to be hungry while you're working so that you look forward to the food that caps off your day. That's what I was talking about," I told her.

Maddy looked at me like I was crazy. And maybe I was. But somewhere in all of that, I still had a point to make.

I clarified my point and said, "We all have an opportunity to turn this work into our own independence, but instead we're fighting each other over some dumb stuff."

Maddy looked at me and said, "How is this creating independence for us? We're out here working for your cousin. She's the only one benefiting from this. We're not even getting paid. We're getting to spend a week in Philadelphia while we bust our ass all day on some film we won't even star in. Well whoopty-fuckin'-do. I'm so excited."

I said, "You took plenty of pictures that you can use for your own purposes. You're in contact with professionals you didn't know before. People are getting a chance to see you on stage and think of you in ways of importance. And it's up to you to work your opportunities to your own advantage."

I told her, "J. Lo was only a dancer once, and so was P. Diddy."

"So fuckin' what?" she snapped at me.

"So they wanted to be more than that, and they worked hard to get there."

"Well, maybe everybody doesn't want that, Vanessa. Maybe you're the only one who's all gung-ho about this shit. And maybe I just want to eat my fuckin' food, like I said."

"That's why I asked you what you wanted," I told her. "But if all you want out of life is to eat your food, then I guess you're no different from the crippled bums, babies, old people, and teenagers you talked about who eat but don't work."

"I do work," Maddy insisted.

I said, "Well, make it worth something then. And you can be mad at me all night, but the reality is, you're here, and you still have an opportunity to make something out of whatever you do. And beefing with me and Tracy has nothing to do with that. So don't blame us for your wasted opportunity."

Maddy said, "Who do you think you are, Oprah Winfrey or somebody? You're a nobody without your cousin. Everything you're doing right now is through Tracy. You take Tracy away and you don't mean shit. So you need to stop your fuckin' frontin'."

I said, "Yeah, but you take me away and you don't mean shit either."

"So what do you think, that I owe you something because of this? Well, you know what, as soon as we get back to L.A., you don't have to worry about doing anything for me again, 'cause I see how you work now. In fact, you're worse than your cousin. At least she's not trying to paint some bullshit picture to us. I mean, you talk about sisterhood and all of that, but this is all about you. Well, you can have it all without me. And if you don't mind, I'd like to eat my food now, because I don't like being hungry."

So much for talking to Madison. I started off good and ended up sounding very selfish. I probably made the situation worse. Then she would tell Alexandria.

I stood up from the bed where I sat. I told her, "I'll leave you alone then." I thought about apologizing again for my slipup, but I don't believe she wanted to hear it. I had said enough for one night.

Instead, I came up with a simple and overused cliché, "Life is what you make it, Madison. That's all I can say."

Before I could walk to the door to let myself out, Maddy said, "Thank you, Vanessa. I never knew that before. Now I know that I can do anything I want to do in life. And I owe it all to you."

I walked out the door and closed it behind me. I felt small and insignificant again. Madison had shot me down with her sarcasm. Did Sasha and Jasmine feel the same way about me? Was my head that damn big? I walked over and knocked on their door to find out.

Jasmine opened the door and said, "Hey."

She wasn't bouncing with energy like she normally was.

I walked in behind her and took a seat at the desk chair.

"Hey, Vanessa? How'd the rest of your day go?" Sasha asked me.

"Actually, good," I told her. "I got a lot of things squared away with my family."

Sasha nodded to me. "That's good."

They were both watching a movie from their beds. They had already finished their room service dinners. Their trays were on the desk and the floor.

"No South Street tonight, hunh?" I joked.

"I mean, how many times are we gonna see it?" Jasmine stated.

"I know what you mean. So how did you like seeing the rest of Philadelphia today?"

"I mean, we really couldn't concentrate on everything because of what went on this morning," Sasha admitted.

I shook my head. They were letting the conflicts get in their way as well.

I said, "We can't allow something that happened in the morning to ruin our whole day."

"That's easy for you to say, you got to get away from them. But we had to keep looking at their sour faces all day," Jasmine told me. She had a point.

I said, "So, what happens for tomorrow? Do we keep this thing going, or do we move on?"

"I'm ready to move on," Jasmine said, "but you can't make everybody feel that way. You need to talk to them about that."

"I already did. And I think I only made the situation worse," I admitted. "Maddy didn't want to hear anything I had to say, so we started arguing about the whole idea of this trip, the clothing line, the movie, and our sisters' support club. And she's ready to wipe her hands with all of it now, just because of me."

"Well, what did you say to her?" Sasha asked me.

I answered, "Her main point is that she thinks I'm big-headed, and that I look at this whole trip as something that I put together."

"You did put it together," Jasmine told me.

"No," Sasha countered. "You were a major part of it, but we all instigated it. Because at first, you started talking about starting something without Tracy. You didn't even want to use the Flyy Girl name. You were talking about an urban ladies club."

She was right.

I said, "So Maddy felt like she wasn't getting anything out of this trip, and that it was all about me and Tracy, and that's part of the reason why we were fighting this morning?"

Sasha said, "Well, I feel they both need to be appreciative, but obviously they're not. They're trying to use this whole trip for their own purposes, and that's not right."

I said, "But I don't mind that. Use this trip the way you want to. That's my whole point. Tracy's not stopping any of us from making our own contacts and things while we're here. She only asked for us to be safe and to stick together when we can. But they turned that into some kind of control thing."

"Maddy always thinks somebody's trying to control her. That's just how she is. Like she always has to break the rules or something," Jasmine stated.

I said, "But let's all look at it. Maybe you do irk people by talking too much, Jasmine. Tracy had to tell you that several times."

"But that's no reason to want to fight me."

"If anything, I should be the one beefing with Alexandria about your cousin," Sasha reminded me. "But I'm not even like that. I only like him as a friend. But you know they've been sneaking around together."

"Everybody knew that but me, hunh?" I asked them.

"Because you kept going out with Tracy every night," Jasmine told me. "And that made us feel like we had babysitters or something after hanging out with Robin."

I smiled. "What, she wasn't cool?"

"Yeah, she was cool, but we wanted to meet some of the people you were getting to meet with Tracy," Sasha told me. "We wanted to meet some of the people in the book, too."

"So, you all felt like I was getting special privileges then?"

"I didn't sweat it, myself. I mean, you're her cousin. What do you expect?" Jasmine reasoned.

"But do you think I act extra because of that?"

"I think you would be that way regardless," Sasha answered. "That's just your personality. You like for things to be in order. And I don't see anything wrong with that. But when you're dealing with people who don't like order, you're bound to have a problem."

She said, "So, if we would have had Petula and Tonya out here with us instead of Maddy and Alexandria, everything would have been fine."

I nodded to myself and thought about it.

She said, "Every team has to be organized for a specific task. But we all came together for this because we were friends. And sometimes friends are not the best people to go into business with."

Well said. I agreed with her.

"So, no matter what you say or do, some people are just not going to see your point," Sasha summed up.

"That's life, man," Jasmine agreed. "I have sisters and cousins, too, and they don't see anything that I'm trying to do. I mean, they get it, but they don't get it, you know. They all feel like things are supposed to come to you instead of you going to get them."

I nodded to her. I said, "You're exactly right. Some people just don't get the work that you have to put in, so they look at you as if you're crazy, until they can see the end result."

"Yeah, and then they all want to share in the results," Sasha added.

"So, if you had a bad apple like that, then you can't change them, you just have to weed them out?" I philosophized.

"Yeah," Jasmine agreed. "That's always."

Sasha was more analytical about it. She said, "I wouldn't look at it as all apples. Sometimes you have oranges, bananas, peaches, pears, and you just have to figure out the best way to use each fruit. Because all people are not alike."

"Yeah, that's a good way to put it," Jasmine said.

I felt better about myself after talking to Jasmine and Sasha. So I retired to my room to call Petula and Tonya out in California. I hadn't talked to them at all that week. It was close to eleven o'clock in Philly, which meant that it was close to eight o'clock in L.A.

Petula answered her cell phone on the first ring. "Hey, Vanessa. How's everything going?" she asked me. "You're the only one I haven't talked to this week."

I said, "Have you talked to anyone today?"

I was wondering if anyone had told her about our catfight in the hallway that morning.

She said, "Last night, but not today. Not until you called."

"Well, let me ask you something, Petula. What do you think about the professional skills and personalities of each one of us?"

"You mean our girl clique?"

"Yeah."

"Oh, okay. In all honesty?"

"Yeah, in all honesty," I told her, "starting with me."

"Okay, well, you're definitely the leader. You always come up with new ideas. You have plans of execution. And you definitely know how to push your point to make sure things get done. But that doesn't leave you much room for a personality. So you get talked about in the positive and negative all the time, with not much balance in between."

I said, "Okay. All good points. But do you think that I'm big-headed?"

Petula chuckled at it. She answered, "Well, I'm sorry, but that comes with the territory of being a leader. Big-headedness is the reality for ninety percent of the leaders around the world, some of them just know how to hide it a little better than others. And you're not one who hides it well."

"And do you think I use my cousin to boost myself up?"

"Hmm, that's a hard one. I would say that you would be the way you are anyway, but the famous cousin factor will blur the line between how much is really you, and how much can be attributed to being Tracy's cousin."

She said, "But knowing you like I do, and being bluntly honest about it, I would say that if you didn't have a famous cousin, you would probably create one."

"I would create one?"

"Most leaders need a focus point for their vision. And Tracy is yours. So, until you're able to move past her, which won't be anytime soon with all of us working on *Flyy Girl*, she'll be what everybody thinks about when they mention your name."

She said, "It's kind of like Snoop Dogg and Dr. Dre. Snoop Dogg is finally getting recognition on his own now, but for a long time, whenever someone said Snoop Dogg, you thought about Dr. Dre, too. But not the other way around. You could say Dr. Dre by itself, because he already had his name. I used to talk about that with my brothers all the time, because they were big rap fans, and my parents would hate it."

Petula could go on a tangent if you let her, so I had to reel her back to the subject.

"Okay, now, what about the rest of us?"

"Ah, Sasha's a good, around-the-way girl who wants to be down. She's a lot like me. We just like being there and a part of the clique. So she'll help out and be unselfish, just like I will.

"Man, I wanted to go to Philadelphia with you guys," she stopped and told me. "But I'll play my part and stay out here with Charmaine and Tonya, and do what we have to do until you guys get back.

"Sasha would have done the same thing," she stated. "But she does like to be included. And sometimes I think she holds back her true feelings a lot more than the rest of us because she's Asian, and either that's part of her culture, or she just doesn't want to jump out and be too noticeable while she's trying so hard to be down.

"You know what I mean?"

I knew exactly what she meant. Had Sasha been black, or even mixed, she would have fought for my cousin, at least in principle, instead of just giving him up to Alexandria without a fight. Then again, Sasha had held out on Jason where Alexandria obviously did not.

"Yeah," I agreed with Petula. "What about Maddy?" I asked her.

"Oh, now, Maddy has whatever social disease is plaguing a lot of black American girls who live in the inner city. She trusts nobody. She has a foul mouth. She's cynical about everything. She rarely applies herself. But at the same time, she's a stabilizing factor for the group. And she'll be the first one to tell you that your head is getting too big. She'll also be the first one to fight you. Fighting for her is a way of life. It says that she's alive, and that she has feelings. And it says that she has something to say that won't be ignored anymore."

Wow! Petula was downright scary with her accuracy. Was it because she was African? Anyway, she really needed to be a psych major, because she was the queen of analyzation.

"Okay, and Jasmine?"

"I like Jasmine a lot," Petula admitted. "She has a different part of me, the part that says 'express yourself.' Jasmine can embarrass all of us because we try so hard to suppress that excited little girl in us that I talked about before. But Jasmine doesn't suppress it. She lets it be. But as silly as she may seem sometimes, she's really not. She knows as much as we all know, and maybe more, but she hates being bored, so she'll say something just to get a rise out of you. And sometimes that can get on people's nerves. But I don't mind that, because I have a big family and I understand it. It's just her way of getting attention."

I said, "Yeah, I have a baby sister who's the same way. She just makes jokes all the time. Now what about Alexandria?"

Petula said it dramatically, "Alexandria is the exact opposite of Jasmine, and you should never leave the two of them in the same room alone."

I broke up laughing. I said, "Wow, you are really good at this. I mean *really* good. You get another A from me."

Petula laughed with me. She said, "Thank you. You want me to finish?"

Petula was more of a show-off than I was with her smarts. I used my intelligence mostly for plotting and planning, but Petula used more of hers in general conversation.

I said, "Of course I want you to finish. I know how you are once you get started. You want to complete the whole term paper."

She said, "Thank you, my sister. You know me well. So . . . where were we?" she asked me with a laugh. "I lost my train of thought."

I said, "Alexandria."

"Oh, yeah. Alexandria hides herself like nobody's business. She doesn't want anybody to know what she's up to. Why? Because she hates the fact that she's not perfect.

"She's typical of a privileged daughter," Petula added. "She's been told since she was young not to act in certain ways because she's supposed to be better than everyone else. And she'll get most of the attention, and still want more. In the meantime, she'll do what she wants to behind closed doors."

She said, "Every culture has these privileged daughters. And they're always talked about as closet sluts. So the first time I looked at Alex, and she didn't speak, I knew what kind of girl she was. Her type feel that they don't have to speak to you unless they have a reason. And most of those reasons have to do with their own personal gain."

She said, "So, Alexandria would be the one who would do everything with us as a group, just so she could find something extra to break off and hide for herself. And then she wouldn't have anything else to do with us."

Like she was doing with my cousin Jason, I thought to myself. Alexandria had broken him off in secret, while claiming to be sick.

I told Petula, "You're downright spooky, man."

She laughed and said, "But these are just my opinions. Africans can be very opinionated, you know."

"You don't say," I joked to her. "Well, let me do you."

"Oh, no, don't do me. I don't want to be a part of this," she whined.

I read her anyway, because she wanted me to.

I said, "You're the outside leader. You'll let me lead from the inside, and all the while, you're just taking things in so you can redirect us later. You're like the off-the-field coach, while you allow me to be the team captain on the field."

Petula laughed hard at it. She said, "You got me. I wait for you to make your mistakes, then I speak. Like now, you're calling me because something happened, right? Now you want to know about all of us. So, you call me to explain."

I laughed hard with her. I said, "Girl, we got into a big fight this morning because of everything you just said." I stopped and told her in lowered tones, "And this is between me and you."

"You know I'll never tell," she promised. And she wouldn't. Petula loved having inside information. She would share only pieces of it when she wanted to. I had already witnessed her in action.

I said, "Well, here it is: Alexandria is doing my cousin Jason, and they think I don't know about it."

"Oh, no, she really went there," Petula squealed. She had never met Jason, but she heard about him, read about him, and knew about him.

I said, "Yes she did. And then Madison got upset with me over this camera guy from New York that she liked, when he liked me, and I didn't pay the boy no mind. And then she got upset with me and Tracy for busting her groove with my cousin's friend when they were on their way up to their room with them last night. So me and Maddy got into a fight this morning."

"No-o-o."

"Yes. But that was after Alexandria told Jasmine to shut her mouth, and they got into a fight."

"Oh my God! And all of this happened this morning?"

"That's what I'm telling you. So I'm calling you to stop myself from going crazy."

"Yeah, don't do it. Keep your sanity. I need you in the game to make everything happen," Petula told me. "Then I can be proud of playing my part in it.

"So what did Tracy say about all of this?" she asked me.

"Oh, Tracy called us all fools and went back to work. She just put us in separate orbits until we all cooled off."

Petula screamed laughing. She said, "She's the queen, she's the queen! Tracy has no time for that nonsense. Let's fix the broken wheel and get the show back on the road."

I loved Petula's little notes of wisdom.

I said, "That's what she did, too."

"But let me tell you something else," Petula told me.

I was all ears. I said, "Spit it out."

"All right, here we go. You know who I think is going to play the most important part in this whole *Flyy Girl* thing?"

I paused for a minute. Petula was dropping the African wisdom on me. I hate to stereotype, but that's what I was thinking.

"Who?" I asked her. I honestly had no one in mind. I was a baby waiting to be fed. Then I would determine whether I liked the food or not.

Petula said, "The most important person in this whole thing is you."

My heart stopped and started up again.

I backed away from it and I said, "No, we all know that Tracy is the key to everything. You just called her the queen yourself."

"Yes, she is the queen. And I meant that. But that is why she can no longer do the work that needs to be done."

I began to see Petula's point. I was hungrier than Tracy. She was eating too well now to finish the job as handily as I would. But she was still in the queen position.

Petula continued before I could respond to her.

She said, "Tracy has already completed her journey. But you have just begun yours. And the only way she can be a bigger queen is for her helpers to push her there and keep her there. That is the basic law of nature. And her biggest helper is you."

She said, "It was not by accident that you fought your mother to get here. You were supposed to be here. And eventually your story will be as important as Tracy's. And she knows it. That's why she invited you to live here. And now it's your time to push her where she needs to go.

"It's already started," Petula told me. "And as we get closer to everything happening, Tracy's going to hand the keys over to you. And I'm not just telling you this because I'm your friend and I want to see this *Flyy Girl* movie and legacy happen. I'm telling you this because it can be true. It can be true if you make it true."

She said, "Because if Tracy had the ability to do it on her own, it would have been done already. But it has not been done, because she needed you to help her finish the job."

I was speechless. Petula wasn't telling me anything that I didn't know. Tracy had already admitted it to me herself. But imagine being told that you held the key to a multimillion-dollar industry, and you were still only a teenager? It was scary, but that's where I was. I was another urban American phenom; Serena Williams behind the big sister Venus, and it was nearing my turn to shine.

"Well, I don't know what to say to all of that," I told Petula.

She said, "It doesn't matter. You're just gonna do what you're gonna do, Vanessa. And I'm gonna watch you do it. And when it all happens, I'm gonna be the first one to say, 'I told you so.' "

The hotel phone rang while I was still on my cell phone with Petula. I wouldn't dare use the hotel phone to call long distance. Tracy told us all that long-distance phone calls was a sure way for a hotel chain to stay in business.

"Hold on, Petula."

She said, "It's Tracy."

I smiled and said, "We'll see."

"Hello," I answered on the room phone.

"You're not in bed yet, are you?"

It was Tracy. I started smiling.

"No, I'm still up," I told her.

"Good, I need to talk to you up in my room."

"Okay."

I hung up the hotel phone and returned to the cell phone with Petula.

"Was it Tracy?" she asked me.

I chuckled. "Yeah."

Petula laughed and said, "I told you so."

"Whatever," I told her. "I'll call you back later."

"Yeah, you make sure you do. I want to hear all about it."

Smoke Screens

As soon as I walked into my cousin's hotel suite, she said, "That damn Alexandria. I told you I didn't trust that girl."

"What did she do?" I asked her.

"She got Jason to bring her to dinner with us, and he introduced her to my parents, like he's about to marry this girl or something. Now how in the hell did she get him to do that in one week? She got his damn nose wide open."

She was pacing the room like a woman ready to overdose on coffee.

I tried to stop myself from smiling and couldn't. Alexandria was working her thing. I had to give it to her. But it was no longer my concern. If Jason liked her, then so be it.

Tracy read my smile and said, "I don't think it's funny, Vanessa. Did he ask you anything about this girl?"

She was acting as if she didn't know Alexandria from a can of paint.

I said, "Tracy, she's been in your house plenty of times. You've been around her for at least a year now."

"Yeah, but I've never known her like that. She's your friend. Miss 'I'm-So-Sick,'" my cousin snapped. "Yeah, I know what she was sick doing now. I thought Jason was talking to Sasha anyway."

I shook my head. "He knew he wasn't getting her years ago when he was still out in L.A. with us."

"But he can get Alexandria, hunh?"

"Evidently," I told her. "But why is that such a problem for you?"

"Because it seems like she's scheming. How is she gonna go out to dinner with a boy's parents when she just met him. And with *my* family at that. She's rubbing her shit all up in my face. Got me sitting there looking like a fool."

I said, "Well, what did you say to Jason about it? He was the one who invited her. All he had to do was not call her or not pick her up."

"Yeah, I talked to his silly ass," my cousin told me. "And he sat up there and told me that he was just trying to come clean."

She said, "So we had a new argument about him using me to get some. That's what he did when he was at my house for the summer. He would invite girls over to the house, knowing that they would ask him about me. And he thinks he's so fucking slick about it."

I smiled again. I couldn't help it.

"It's not funny, Vanessa. Nobody seems to be learning anything from my book. I mean, you really need to talk to that girl."

I said, "Why didn't you talk to her? She was right there with you."

Tracy looked at me and said, "Oh, she doesn't want me to talk to her. Because if I do it, she's not gonna like me at all. I already had to restrain myself and act cordial to her while my parents were around."

"You could have asked to speak to her in private," I suggested.

Tracy said, "No, you're not getting me. I didn't *trust* myself to talk to that girl tonight. I need *you* to talk to her. She's *your* friend."

"Well, where are they now?" I asked.

"Call her and find out."

I said, "You think she's left Jason yet?"

"I doubt it, but call her ass anyway. Bust up her cell phone."

I hesitated, while waiting for the punch line. I just knew that she couldn't be serious.

Tracy stopped pacing the room and told me, "Vanessa, I am not playing. Call that girl up right now."

I took out my cell phone and called her. The cell phone line rang, and rang, and rang again with no answer.

Tracy said, "Okay, call Jason then."

I stopped the call to Alexandria and called Jason with the same result. No answer.

As soon as I hung up the line again, my cousin said, "They're fuckin'."

She was embarrassing me. I had to hide my face in my hands to stop from grinning.

She said, "Look, when I was doing my thing at your age, you at least had to talk to me for a while and buy me some stuff. You had to visit me a few times, call me up for hours on the phone, sit out and get to know me. But this damn girl, here. She can't know Jason. And he surely doesn't know her ass."

She said, "I wasn't that damn fast. This girl is as fast as Carmen and Carmen got four kids now."

I said, "My mother has three."

Tracy looked at me and said, "Exactly. And your mother made the news in our family papers, too."

I smiled and shook my head. Tracy was only telling me the truth, and I had to stand there and take it.

I said, "Alexandria is twenty years old, and Jason is what, twenty-three, twenty-four now?"

"And he's still not out of school yet," Tracy reminded me. "I was doing my graduate studies by then."

"Well, Jason is not you," I told her.

I could see my sisters' point of view now. I couldn't judge them on what I was able to do, nor could Tracy judge Jason based on her life. At least he was finishing college. It was just taking him a little longer.

Finally, Tracy took a seat at the desk chair in her office suite. She took a deep breath and raised her hands to her temples.

"This has just been a long-ass day," she told herself. "You guys start off by fighting in the damn hallway, Victor has two damn wives now, and has *me* to thank for it, and now my damn brother went ahead and got pussy-whipped by some too cute for everybody . . ."

She couldn't even finish her sentence. I walked over to my cousin and put my hand on her shoulder. She was really working herself up.

She took another breath and asked me, "You think I should have been his second wife, Vanessa?"

She knew better than to ask me that. But I think I shook my head a little too soon. Was I being selfish about it? I wanted Tracy to stay out in Hollywood so I could do what I planned to do. I didn't want her to become a loyal and obedient housewife. But it was obvious that she continued to fight with the idea.

I told her, "Most likely you're older than both of his wives. So that doesn't even add up right. You would be the first one, or none. He even knows that."

I hated to be that real about it, but that's what it was. You don't become second to a younger woman. I don't even believe Qadeer would have allowed that. He would have been asking for trouble, especially from a woman as hyper as Tracy could be.

She said, "There's a million fine-ass men out here to choose from, and I'm still sittin' around here sweatin' this motherfucka'."

Tracy was breaking her language down into straight ghetto talk. I was smiling at it, but she was beginning to worry me. Selfishly, I didn't like the husband talk. It would get in the way of business, just like her friend Dalvin was already trying to do by giving Tracy ultimatums and such. So unless she found a Russell Simmons or a Sean Combs type, who would help her push her career forward, I didn't want it, and I was ready to cock-block if I had to. Tracy had to be ready to just get up and go, and I was ready to go right with her. I didn't need her to have to get permission from somebody, and that's what having a husband would mean to me.

So I was ready to remind her about the difficulties she was already having with her friend out in L.A. when my cell phone rang. I pulled it out and answered it while my cousin watched me.

"Who is it?" she asked me.

I looked and read the number.

"It's Jason."

She got her spunk back and said, "Okay, find out where they are."

I answered, "Hey, Jason. You got my call?"

Tracy was already pointing at me to make sure I asked him where he was, and if Alexandria was with him.

"Yeah, I had to get my phone out," he told me.

"What, you were driving?"

"Naw, I'm just chillin'."

"At the house in Germantown?"

He said, "Naw, at my apartment. You know I don't stay home anymore."

"Okay, so, what, there's nothing to do on a Friday night?" I asked him. "You're not trying to hang out with Alexandria?"

I was asking him a line of questions that he wouldn't suspect anything from. Tracy watched and listened in silence.

Jason answered, "I am hanging out with her."

"What, she's over at your apartment?"

He said, "Yeah. She went to dinner with us and everything. Tracy ain't tell you?"

Instead of answering his question, I asked, "She's over at your apartment, right now?"

"Yeah."

"Let me talk to her."

Tracy smiled. "That's how you work it," she whispered to me. "She shouldn't even be over there."

I smiled back at her.

Alexandria came on the line and said, "Hey, Vanessa. Make sure you tell Jasmine no hard feelings."

Why, Jasmine got the best of it, I thought to myself.

I said, "Okay. I'll do that."

She said, "Yeah, we need to squash that. For real."

I guess Alexandria was feeling much better now that she had her man.

I said, "But what are you doing at my cousin's apartment, that's what I want to know."

She said, "He told you already, we're just chillin'."

"And you went to dinner with him, and Tracy, and their parents. What is wrong with you, you don't know them like that?"

"He invited me."

"Well, you should have turned him down. I mean, you just met my cousin."

Tracy was nodding her head to me in full agreement, while I did her dirty work.

Alexandria said, "And what does that mean? Sometimes you just know."

"You just know what?" I asked her. At first I was speaking more for Tracy, but now I was curious myself. What was on Alexandria's mind?

"Jason said he never really wanted to introduce a girl to his parents before. I mean, sometimes, it's just that right time."

Her answer was deep, if I allowed myself to believe it. But I know Tracy didn't.

I decided to continue playing devil's advocate, going to the extreme.

"So, you would actually have babies for my cousin?" I asked her.

Dating was dating, but having a guy's baby was totally something else. I wanted to get straight to the point to see if Alexandria was bullshitting.

However, Tracy looked at me as if I had lost my mind.

"What are you saying?" she whispered to me. "I don't want any nieces or nephews from that girl."

I ignored my cousin and listened for Alexandria's answer.

She said, "If he wants me to."

That's when I lost my own cool. I said, "Are you crazy? What are you talking about? You just met him on Monday."

She said, "Yeah, but we just clicked so well. It's like, we can talk about anything."

Yeah, but he called your behind bossy, I thought to myself. *He thinks he's going to be arguing with you all the time.*

Tracy asked me, "What did she say to that? What did she say?"

Too much was going on at once. Alexandria was talking, Tracy was talking, and I was thinking a mile a minute.

I said, "I don't believe this." I was talking to myself while still holding the phone.

Tracy just stopped and stared at me.

Then I thought, *I don't even care.* That was Alexandria and Jason's life. I figured they'd get over each other in a month when their long-distance phone bills started to rack up anyway.

Out of the blue, I asked Alexandria, "And how do you think my cousin Tracy is gonna feel about this?"

Tracy paid strict attention to me.

"I mean, she doesn't like me?" Alexandria questioned.

I didn't know how to take her question. It sounded to me like she wanted sympathy, and that she knew Tracy didn't like her.

I said, "What if she doesn't?"

Alexandria paused. "I don't know why. What did I do to her?"

You snuck up on her kid brother and whipped him, I thought to myself. But Jason wasn't a kid anymore, and he had been with enough girls by then to know better than to let his guard down that easy. So it was all on him.

I said, "Let me speak to Jason again." I didn't even want to answer her question.

Alexandria hesitated before she said, "Okay."

Jason came back on the line. "What's up?"

"Do you realize what you're doing with this girl?" I asked him. "We are flying back to L.A. Sunday afternoon. Then what?"

I was beginning to sound like Tracy.

"You think I don't know that?" Jason asked me back. "I know how to get back out there. And she knows how to get here."

I looked over at Tracy again. She began to shake her head. I guess she could tell that it was a lost cause for her brother. Jason would need his nose repaired back to its normal size.

I wanted to ask him the same question I had asked his love slave. They were slaves to each other. Or at least for that night, because I still had my doubts about how long their hold on each other would last.

"How do you think Tracy is gonna feel about this?" I asked him anyway.

He said, "Vanessa, let me ask you a question. If Tracy has someone she likes and wants to kick it with, you think she's gonna ask me for my opinion?"

He had an excellent point. How long would the eldest child rule apply to the younger siblings? Alexandria had an older sister herself. So they were both rebelling.

I nodded my head and said, "All right. I see your point."

He said, "I know you do. And as long as you stay out there under her roof, Vanessa, she'll try to control as much as you let her. But eventually, you gon' have to do you. And that's with everybody."

When I disconnected the phone call with Jason and Alexandria, Tracy was awaiting the results.

"So what happened?" she said in a monotone.

She sounded as if she already knew.

I took a breath before I answered.

"To make a long story short, they said that they have their own lives to live and to make mistakes with, just like you have yours and I have mine."

Tracy exhaled and nodded to herself.

"He's making a mistake," she stated.

"How can you be so sure?" I asked her. "At least give them a chance."

"A chance to do what?"

It appeared to me at that moment that Tracy might have been blocking Jason. Did she prefer he remain unattached to alleviate the pressure of having to link up with someone herself? You never know what people are thinking, even when you believe you know them.

I asked, "What would be so wrong with the two of them being together if it's sincere? They look good together. I can't even lie."

I said, "They remind me of your parents, actually. The only difference is that Alexandria has the light eyes instead of Jason."

Tracy said, "Yeah, and my parents spent eight or nine years separated because they got married too young."

"But they're together now. And they came together when it counted," I reminded her. I could only dream of having a father come back home to stay at my house like hers did.

Tracy settled down. "Leave it alone," she told herself. "Even though I know it's a mistake."

I thought about it and said, "Tracy, remember when you first decided to go out to Hollywood, and your mother was skeptical, but your father supported it?"

She began a slow working smile.

She said, "I already see where you're going with that, Vanessa. Okay. I'll leave Jason alone. But I still don't have to like your friend."

I grinned at her and said, "That's on you. But we'll see how long they last anyway."

"So, is she even coming back to the hotel tonight?"

"Why should she? She has what she wants over at Jason's crib."

Tracy said, "Because she's still on my clock until this trip is over with, and if she ends up coming back home with a biscuit in the oven from my damn brother, then I'll be held responsible for it, whether they *think* they're both grown or not.

"So let me call these damn kids back over here," she told herself. She jumped right on her cell phone to make the call. But they didn't answer.

"Okay, so they're gonna answer your call and not mine. I should just drive on over there and get her myself. And see how she likes that," my cousin stated in her insanity.

I had heard enough for the night, and I was starting to yawn. It was after midnight again, and I was bone tired myself. It had been an extra long day for all of us.

"Well, I've said all I can say," I told Tracy. "I'm going to bed now. I'll see you in the morning."

When I started to walk to the door, she said, "All right, I'll call you up and tell you what happened."

Hell, I was thinking about turning my cell phone off and taking the hotel phone off the hook, because I didn't want to hear it. The horse of Alexandria and Jason was officially dead, and I was putting my whip away. Tracy needed to think about doing the same.

Locations

I *grew up a while back / and took off my tight jeans / and those other little, skimpy things / to liberate my body.*

I put away my / old love letters / from long-gone boyfriends / to liberate my heart.

I discarded my false notions of / how young ladies should act / in male-dominated societies / to liberate my mind.

I dared to picture myself a heaven / so that I could reach / for a better tomorrow / to liberate my soul.

And then I flew / far away / like a bird / in no cage.

"A Woman's Liberation," by Tracy Ellison.

I remembered my cousin's poem, published in her sequel book *For the Love of Money*, and I thought about all of the distractions that seemed to get in our way and cripple us from progress. And I didn't believe that liberation was a onetime event. A person could be liberated several times in life. And each liberation should create a new direction.

It was obvious that Tracy needed a new liberation and direction. And I didn't believe that the grind of a new film would satisfy her needs. My sister Veronica had said that everybody wants to belong to somebody. Well, Tracy seemed to belong to us, the urban, inner-city brown girls who read her truth in the book and believed in it. We gave our imaginations to it and let it feed us social nourishment. We just needed her to finish the job now and let us see it on the big screen. We needed that final validation to see ourselves larger than life, and in full color. I just didn't know if Tracy was fully up to the task.

Petula was right. If my cousin was ready to spend so much of her energy on small stuff, then I would surely need to take over with more plotting to do. So I was up bright and early that Saturday morning after falling asleep late. I had notes of ideas all over my hotel bed. It may sound crazy, but I was able to think better by using individual pieces of paper instead of using a joined notepad. The notepad represented the box of ideas that became one, but the individual pieces of paper represented freedom, and the ability to collect ideas from various sources.

Tracy told me once that the best filmmaking was all about collecting visions, words, sounds, events, colors, emotions, angles, responses, confusion, illusion, and excitement. I believe her comment to me about it was a poem that she hadn't written yet. Tracy could be so creatively vibrant when she wanted to be. Nevertheless, like everything else, creation took a lot of energy out of her.

I was up early and full of energy, but no more ideas came out of me. I had a case of writer's block, or thinker's block, I should say. So instead of beating myself over the head with nothing more to explore, I turned the television on and started watching Saturday-morning cartoons. Imagine what the creators of cartoons have to come up with? Some of those cartoons had been on the air for more than thirty years, and new cartoons were always popping up. But what made one cartoon stick and other cartoons fall to the floor?

That was the question of the century. What made some things hot and other things not? What would make *Flyy Girl* hot?

I stopped and thought about that question.

I nodded my head and told myself, "I should ask other people that question. I should even post the question on Tracy's website."

We had started a new website for the clothing line, and instead of us racking our brains about all the new ideas, we could ask our supporters their opinions on clothes as well. We could post a poll on the website of "Hot" or "Not," and a list of ten reasons why Hollywood should make *Flyy Girl* into a movie.

Once my ideas started to flow again, I grabbed my pen and wrote them down on separate pieces of paper. I just had to make sure that I collected them all. It would be a disaster not to be able to find the hottest of my ideas, lost in the room somewhere.

Before long, someone was knocking at my door. I looked over at the clock, and it was a quarter after eight in the morning. Obviously, someone else was up early.

I walked over to the door and looked through the peephole to find

Maddy standing out in the hallway in her pajamas. I opened the door and waited for her to speak.

"Are you gonna invite me in?" she asked.

"Oh, yeah."

I was startled. I didn't think Madison wanted anything else to do with me.

She walked into my room and turned to face me.

She said, "I still don't like the fact that you think you know so much. But I just wanted to tell you that I'm not here because I don't want to do anything with myself. I'm here because I do. I got plans and ideas for myself, too."

She said, "And sometimes I may not have the best patience with things, but I'm trying. I also don't have a famous cousin like you to look up to, so I just do what I can do."

I didn't know what to say to her. I just stood there and waited. Madison had really surprised me with her visit. I didn't even think she was a morning person.

I finally asked her, "Were you up all last night like I was?"

She said, "I kept waiting for Alexandria."

"She never came back?"

Maddy shook her head.

She smiled and said, "Your cousin made me call her three times last night."

I said, "She made me call her, too."

"That's all I came to say," Maddy told me. She began to walk back toward me at the door. Then she said, "And by the way, I owe you one. So don't ever think I forgot. And I'm gon' win the next round."

She was eye to eye with me and talking about fighting again. She actually scared me with it, too. Not that I was afraid of fighting her, but that she could calculate another round and let me know about it in advance. That was kind of clever. I already knew that Maddy would be thinking about our fight, because that's the kind of person she is. She wanted the first and last punch. But letting me know that she thought about it would force me to respect her at all times, knowing that we could fight again at any minute.

I nodded to her. I said, "I hear you. And hopefully we won't have another round."

Maddy said, "We'll see," and she walked out the door.

When I closed the door, I smiled to myself. Maddy was showing me that she could get along to accomplish what she wanted to do. We all realized how big *Flyy Girl* was, and Madison was in no way trying to lose her position. I had to respect her for that as well.

Alexandria arrived just in time to shower, change her clothes, get herself together, and rush out to meet us inside the limo that was parked in front of the hotel. It was 10:15 AM, and Tracy had wanted to leave by 9:45. She was already hot at Alexandria about Jason, and then she didn't return to the hotel at all Friday night, so she was flying over an active volcano in a parachute.

"We were two seconds from leaving your ass here," Tracy snapped at her.

I don't believe Alexandria would have cared. All she had to do was call Jason back over and finish spending time with him. Everyone inside the limousine knew the deal between her and Jason by then. It was no longer a secret, and it hadn't really been one. Everyone already assumed correctly about them.

Tracy had a copy of the *Philadelphia Daily News* in her hand. She had it folded back to a page that she was reading that morning and brought it to our attention.

"I want everybody in here to read this," she told us before she passed it off to Jasmine. Jasmine was sitting the closest to her.

Jasmine read the article with wide eyes and began to comment on it. But Tracy silenced her immediately with an index finger to her lips.

She said, "Not a word. I want everyone in here to read it first."

I received the article third after Maddy had read it.

The caption read: "Flyy Girl Catfight Breaks Out at the Marriott." They had a picture of my cousin walking away from the hotel looking pissed at us and everything. The article didn't have our names or a lot of the details, but it surely named Tracy Ellison Grant and what she was trying to do with the Philadelphia-based movie. I was so embarrassed.

When we all finished reading the article, Tracy said, "Needless to say, I am very disappointed with all of you right about now. You have to understand that I'm no longer a private person, and anything that goes on around me gets reported, especially in my hometown. Now I was pissed as hell when my mother called me this morning to bring this shit to my attention. But then I stopped and thought about how this would be a lesson for you. Because you all need to understand what you're dealing with when we actually start shooting this movie."

She said, "This kind of shit will not stop. And they always do this to black films. They try and report any damn thing they can just to make us look bad. But I decided that I'm not going to let them ruin my day because I still have things to get done, and I do plan to finish them."

We were all soundly checked that morning, and none of us said a word. What could anyone say? Our catfight at the Marriott could have derailed the entire movie, and we hadn't even finished casting yet.

We pulled up to a playground on Germantown Avenue in Mt. Airy, with Robin and her New York casting crew in cars and equipment vans behind us.

Tracy stepped out of the limo and immediately started directing the camera guys on the scene before they even got a chance to pull out the cameras and size things up.

"This is the basketball court where we shoot the first scene," she told them. She said, "But no one will be playing basketball. We're going to turn this into a playground party, nineteen-eighties style. So I want you to shoot tight on the DJ spinning the records, and then angle out at the people—fashion, dances, and activity going on around the court."

Shamor and the camera guys all nodded to her and began to take pictures and general measures of the surrounding area.

Robin said, "This is a good location for the scene, but what about the sounds coming from this major street out here?"

Her sound guy turned and listened for all the street noise and cars driving by on Germantown Avenue.

"We may have to block off the street for a couple of days," he stated.

"How many scenes are you trying to shoot here?" they asked Tracy.

She said, "Well, on the first scenes, we can just let the DJ's music play while we shoot over and through the crowd. That way we don't have to worry about the street noise so much."

She then looked at us. "Can you guys do some of the latest dances?"

Everyone looked at each other. We were not exactly the partying type. I mean, we went to parties, but actually dancing was not a top priority for us.

Tracy snapped, "Do you all know how to dance or what? We need some movement for the cameras here."

Some of the New York crew started to dance, then we followed suit with a whole lot of laughing and goofing around.

Jasmine started singing the summer party anthem from 50 Cent, *"We gon' party like it's your birthday."*

Shamor sized us up and moved through us with a make-believe lens.

He nodded and said, "You could do several moving shots from different angles."

"Then I want you to gradually move toward those steps over there," Tracy told them.

Behind the basketball court was a flight of steps on the left and on the right that led up to another part of the playground.

Tracy said, "I want a group of guys gambling right here against this wall as the camera works its way up the stairs."

Jasmine jumped into place and said, "Ay yo, put the money back down, man. Put your money where your mouth is, yo."

We all started laughing. That girl was crazy.

Tracy corrected her and said, "The word is 'cuz.' 'Yo, cuz, put your money back down.' "

"Yeah, cuz, put them ends up," Sasha spoke. She was right on it, but she had family still in Delaware, so she was more familiar with Philadelphia lingo.

"What do they say now?" Maddy asked us.

"Fam' or family," I told her.

"So they all think of each other as family and cousins here?"

I laughed again. "I guess you can say that," I told her. "But the guys generally use more slang than the girls."

"That's in every city," Alexandria commented.

Tracy said, "Now let's move up the steps."

We all followed her up the steps to a higher level of the playground where they had the football field.

"Now up here we shoot the football game," she told everyone.

The camera guys looked around at the wide field of grass.

"So, you actually want a football game going on up here with parents and fans?" one of the crew asked.

"And cheerleaders," Tracy told him. "You didn't get a chance to read the script yet? This is where you get to meet the lead character in her cheerleading uniform and pompoms."

Tracy looked at the older guy with graying hairs as if she was disgusted. How could he miss that in the first couple pages of the script? I was confused by his comment myself.

He said, "Okay, but from the basketball court to the football field, you're looking at shooting an entire week on this one opening scene."

Tracy said, "And? If I'm going to do this movie, then I'm going to do it right! It's been ten years now since the book first came out, and if it takes a year to shoot it right, then so be it."

"That's right," Robin agreed. "There's no sense in waiting this long just to fuck it up."

Tracy and Robin both told him what time it was, so he shut his mouth and finished listening. Most likely, a lot of those people wouldn't be on the real shoot anyway. Tracy was just scouting everything to take back to the money players at the Hollywood studios.

"So, we introduce Tracy in her cheerleading pose . . . ," Robin stated.

Jasmine jumped into position again with imaginary pompoms, and started chanting with her hips swinging left and right.

"Go team go / That's the way you take 'em down / Go team go / That's the way you shake 'em."

Tracy said, "What the hell kind of cheers were you doing?"

We all started laughing again.

Jasmine said, "Oh, I just made that up."

"Don't lie," Maddy told her. "You know that was your high school cheer."

"I didn't cheer in high school."

"Anyway," Tracy told the camera guys. "We want to follow the running back on a long touchdown run to win the game from the perspective of our cheerleader."

"You want to shoot from the cheerleader's view of the field. That would be a shallow angle," the camera guy stated. He seemed cynical about the whole process.

Tracy said, "No, we don't have to shoot from her angle of the field. We just do cut backs to keep her viewpoint with the audience. That's in the script as well," she told him.

He smiled it off. "Looks like I'm gonna have to reread the script."

Tracy said, "No, I just thought we'd make all of this up as we went along."

She was really letting him have it, but he deserved it. If he didn't read the script right the first time, then he needed to shut his trap and just listen.

She said, "We end the scene with everyone happy with the win, and our lead cheerleader eyeing the running back while moving closer to him."

My girls and I were all excited. We could see Tracy's vision of the film with clear movement and activity. It was the correct way to shoot an eighties film. You give it the pulsating energy of hip-hop.

We moved along from the playground and took a walk down the street that cut across Germantown Avenue.

"We don't have a pair of homes to shoot from yet, but we want to follow our lead and the running back down one of these nice streets. And that sets us up for the entrance of Raheema and Mercedes."

We all walked down the clean Mt. Airy street like a herd of sheep following the shepherd. But none of us minded. It was Tracy's show. I was just glad she was back to business and moving past the distractions.

After Tracy showed us a good amount of the neighborhood scenes where she wanted to shoot, we drove over to Cheltenham Mall.

"Are we going shopping now?" Sasha joked.

Tracy smiled and said, "This is where we did clothing *and* boy shopping."

Jasmine asked, "How do you shoot a mall scene, with a whole lot of security?"

The lead camera guy answered, "No, you would have to shoot early before the mall actually opens."

"Before the mall opens? But what about the stores?" Alexandria asked him.

"You talk to a few of the store managers to open up early for you," Tracy told her. At least she was still willing to talk to the girl.

Alexandria nodded. "Is that what they do with all movies?"

Shamor grinned at her. He said, "You'd really be surprised how a film crew is able to create the illusion that a location is full of people. It takes a lot of extras sometimes, but the locations are usually secured. You have noise issues, lighting issues, and countless setup hours to make sure everything is shot just right. Some of those scenes can take a week to shoot."

"Like our opening playground scene," I commented.

He nodded to me. "Yeah."

I was sure glad he wasn't chasing after me anymore. I guess he finally got the point that I wasn't interested in his advances.

I listened to all the filming details and took mental notes to add to what I already knew about the film game from Tracy's acting roles. But I hadn't actually spent that much time on the production and direction side before. So it was still a fresh perspective for me, as it was for Tracy.

"So, you're just going to film one store, half of the mall, or what?" Maddy asked.

"We'll probably do an exterior walk-in, one of the hallways, and then a store or two, yes," Tracy answered.

Robin said, "You'll probably need to talk to at least a hallway of stores to open for you to create coverage for the walk-in."

"We'll work it out," Tracy told her.

"And you're still thinking about directing, right?" Robin quizzed her.

I looked at Tracy for her answer. I still didn't think of taking her seriously on the direction end. She had her hands full as a producer.

Directing would be even more work. I had nearly forgotten that Tracy had asked me about directing.

She looked at me before she answered Robin. "We'll have to see."

She was being careful and diplomatic about it.

I exhaled after I heard her answer. Then again, if Tracy did decide to direct, then I would be assured that she would be right in the middle of things to make sure that the film was executed correctly.

We all walked through the Cheltenham Mall, sizing things up, with Philadelphians doing their normal shopping and walking, and the guys started looking and hollering at every last one of us.

"What are y'all, models?" a guy asked us. He had a full beard, growing long. A lot of guys in Philly were wearing their beards long, particularly the young Muslim guys.

"Yeah," Maddy told him. "What's it to you?"

He grinned and said, "You just looking good, sis'."

"Thank you."

"All of y'all looking good," his taller, smooth-faced friend added.

"We know," Jasmine bragged to them.

I had to laugh it off as we walked away.

Then I warned Jasmine, "You better stop talking that conceited stuff in my city."

"People like when you're confident," she argued.

"But not when you throw it all up in their faces," Sasha told her.

"I didn't throw it in his face. He already said we looked good."

"Then all you need to say is 'Thank you,' " I advised her.

Tracy turned to address us all. "Look, you got exactly one hour to look around the mall and shop or whatever, and then we're meeting back in the first hallway where we entered."

"What if we get lost?" Jasmine joked.

"Don't," Tracy told her. "And that goes for all of you."

We had a good time at the mall before we left and drove around the streets of Mt. Airy, West Oak Lane, and Germantown. By the time it was dark, we were all falling asleep inside the limo.

"What do you think?" Tracy asked me before we arrived back at the hotel. We had stopped for ice cream on Ridge Avenue in Roxborough. It had been a very full day.

"Hunh? What do I think?" I asked my cousin. I was barely conscious.

"About the locations?" she asked me.

I sat up straight and nodded my head to her. "They're all good. You made a lot of good choices," I told her.

We had even visited a YMCA building off Chelten Avenue where Tracy wanted to shoot one of the hip-hop parties in the film. She told us that DJ Jazzy Jeff was once the talk of the city, and much more popular than the Fresh Prince, a.k.a. Will Smith. She said that the Philadelphia DJs were more popular than the New York DJs, who started it all. She was really giving us a history lesson in the roots of hip-hop.

"I'm just presenting the real places that were spectacular at one time," she told me. She was very excited about it all. She said, "Germantown Field was where we played the annual Thanksgiving Day game against Martin Luther King High School. You couldn't get any bigger than that. We had one of the strongest football rivalries in the city.

"And downtown on Market Street, there used to be blocks of jewelry stores, clothing stores, record stores, penny arcades, movie theaters. Going downtown was a real adventure back then."

Just talking about it was bringing back great memories for her.

I said, "So, you think the eighties was way better than it is now?"

She said, "Of course it was. And in my day, we didn't hang on the coattails of New York, like so many rappers do in Philly now. We had our own sound and identity. We had a whole posse of Philadelphia rappers: Cool C, Steady B, Schoolly D, EST, Larry Love."

I started laughing.

"What's so funny?" she asked me.

It was funny to hear her talking so enthusiastically about hip-hop. Once you reached a certain age, it seemed that hip-hop music was no longer viable.

"That's all old school," I told her.

She said, "What, I know about Fifty Cent, Eminem, and Ludacris. And I know about Beanie Siegel, Freeway, and The Roots in Philly. I'm hip."

That only made me laugh more. Even some of my girls began to laugh as they listened to our conversation.

I said, "Of course you know about them. They're all over the radio, the clubs, and the news. How could you not know?"

Tracy said, "But I'm gonna tell you who's gonna be the next big star. That Beyoncé girl from Destiny's Child. I can tell she's waiting to break out. I can see it in her every time I see those girls perform. And I know her daddy's gonna push her to make sure it happens, too. So they're all doing solo albums now. Well, watch when her album comes out."

"I like her," Jasmine stated.

"What about Ashanti?" Sasha asked. "Is she yesterday's news already?"

"It depends on where she takes it," Tracy answered. "Because that Irv Gotti camp is falling down just like Suge Knight's did with Death Row. So she might want to find a new label to deal with. That criminalistic stuff doesn't pay off in the long run. It eventually catches up to you."

"Yeah, especially after those Fifty Cent songs attacking Ja Rule," Maddy added to the discussion. "Their camp may not be able to recover from that. Fifty was going at 'em hard."

It seemed that everyone was joining the discussion about the latest in hip-hop.

"So, who do you want on the soundtrack, Tracy?" Jasmine asked out of the blue.

I hadn't even thought of that yet.

Tracy said, "Missy, of course. She still has that old-school flavor. She still knows how to have fun with the music. Then I'd invite my girls MC Lyte and Queen Latifah."

"All on a song together? That would be hot," Sasha commented.

"Yeah, we can call them the Flyy Girl Crew," I joked.

Tracy shook her head and said, "We're gonna have to stop using that name for everything. We don't want to wear it out."

Sasha looked at her and said, "I disagree. If you look at the most successful products, they say their names all of the time: McDonald's, Pepsi, Nike, Sprite, Def Jam."

"Yeah, they got Def Jam everything now," Jasmine agreed.

"It's a strong name," I told them, "just like Flyy Girl is."

"At first, you didn't want us to use it," Alexandria reminded me.

"That's because I didn't want her to," Tracy responded. "Those companies still control how, when, and where their names are used, just like I will with Flyy Girl."

I put in my two cents. "Well, once you have it trademarked, it's nothing but free advertising for you when people use it."

I still didn't get why Tracy didn't want to push the Flyy Girl brand more, like we all wanted her to. Was she plain scared of heights or what?

She said, "There is such a thing as overkill. And sometimes less is more. Like Polo. They are always in the cut with what they do."

"But they advertise all the time in men's magazines," Alexandria noted. "They just know where their audience is."

"Yeah, if you chose like *Essence* magazine or something, and did a consistent ad, it would connect to a loyal audience," I suggested.

Maddy frowned at me. She said, "*Essence*? What kind of audience are you after? They're not really into designer clothes. Them people look like they make their *own* clothes."

"It was just an example," I told her.

"The wrong example," she argued.

"Yeah, you would try something more like *Vibe*. It's not too street like *XXL*, but it's not all stuffy like *Essence* either," Alexandria explained.

Tracy looked at her and said, "You look like an *Essence* reader yourself, talking about stuffy."

We started laughing again. Alexandria did seem like an *Essence* magazine woman.

She said, "I do read it, but not like I do with *Vibe*. I flip through a lot of *Essence* to see what they're talking about first. But with *Vibe*, I think a lot more about what they're wearing, their makeup, their hair, and what they're listening to because it's closer to my age. But my older sister will do the opposite. She reads her *Essence*, and then she'll flip through my *Vibe*."

"Well, the Flyy Girl brand is definitely for a younger audience, because a lot of older readers try to act like they read it a long time ago, so I know they don't want to wear the clothes," Jasmine assumed.

"Not necessarily," Tracy told her. "We do plan to have a more elegant line to balance out the commercial line."

"Yeah, but with the word *Girl* in the name, a lot of mature women just won't go there," Alexandria argued. "Like my sister, she called it 'cute.' And when she uses the word *cute*, what she's really saying is that it's below her."

"Oh, you don't say. Sounds like somebody else we know," Maddy mocked her.

"But I'm not all that bad," Alexandria said with a grin.

"I'm learning a lot listening to you girls," Tracy commented to us.

"Anytime," Jasmine told her.

"So, what do you guys all think about the locations we visited today?" she asked all of us.

"All thumbs up to me," Jasmine spoke up first. "I mean, once you have the people there with the music, and color, and action, it looks like a movie that hasn't been done in a while."

"It's just real. Like when I watch *Boyz n the Hood* and *Menace II Society*," Maddy commented. "It's just real. I mean, you really feel it."

Sasha said, "I like street movies because they feel more like actual life. With Hollywood movies, you know you're just watching a movie. But with street movies, you don't know if you're really watching someone's life or not."

"I know. They do seem that way," Jasmine agreed.

"That's exactly how *Flyy Girl* will feel," I told her.

Tracy took it all in. She said, "Well, the first trip to Philly is just about done. Next time we go into more detail with the budget, licenses, schedules, and the works. Tomorrow it's back to L.A."

No one said anything.

Then Jasmine said, "It seems like we just got here. I mean, I know we did a lot of work here, but . . ."

She sounded like she was sad to leave.

"Aw, don't cry, girl. If you make it as a production assistant, you'll be back," Maddy told her.

"Not if you guys plan on fighting in the damn hallway again," Tracy warned all of us.

Just like that, she shut us all up inside the limo. We were all as quiet as a whisper and at my cousin's mercy. And as much influence as I thought I could have on her, the reality was, Tracy was still the boss lady.

Withdraw

I sat up on the bed in Sasha and Jasmine's room while they packed up their clothes. We were all glum, realizing that our excursion to Philly was coming to an end.

Jasmine shook her head and said, "I can't believe we're leaving. I mean, it's like I'm ready to do this movie right now, and I'm not even in it. I just want to be around it."

Sasha nodded to her while folding a pair of her jeans. "We all feel that way."

"Are you sure?" I asked her. I was thinking about Maddy and Alexandria. But I already knew they were both full tilt for the film. I just wanted to hear someone else say it.

Sasha never wavered. She said, "Yeah, I'm sure. It's not every day where you get this close to a dream being turned into a reality."

I asked her, "But do you think this movie will feel the same for all girls? White girls don't seem to watch our movies. It's like we're all outsiders to them."

"They watched *Mulan*," Sasha joked.

"And they watch the cartoon *Dora*, and the Disney show *Taina*," Jasmine added.

"Yeah, but not like they watch Hillary Duff in *Lizzie McGuire*," I told them. "I mean, this is a black-girl movie. Will they watch a black girl from inner-city Philadelphia?"

"We have to make it and find out," Sasha concluded.

Someone knocked on the door and we all looked around at each other. It was close to eleven at night.

"Okay, who's gonna go get that?" Sasha asked.

Jasmine said, "Vanessa, you're the guest, you go get it."

"But it's your room. You should be the one to greet a visitor, not me," I argued.

250

Jasmine sighed and went to see who was at the door. When she opened it she said, "Look what the catfight brought in?"

I leaned my head toward the door to see who she was talking about. Alexandria and Maddy walked into the room wearing their pajamas.

"Okay, where is everybody's pajamas?" Alexandria asked us. "We're ready to do the pajama party thing and order some more pizza for room service on our last night here."

"You didn't tell us that earlier," I stated. I guess Alexandria and Maddy were both willing to let the fight end and move forward with our friendships.

"Yeah, give us an announcement or something," Jasmine added.

Maddy said, "You want us to come back in twenty minutes? It shouldn't take you that long to change."

"What, we're all girls in here. You don't have to leave the room for that," Sasha told them.

"Well, you're all acting like we caught you off guard with it," Maddy responded.

I said, "You did. We didn't know if you guys were still beefing with us or not."

Maddy said, "After we done spent an entire day together, if we still had a beef, you would definitely know about it."

"For real," Alexandria agreed with her. She said, "We thought about it, and we didn't want to end this trip on a bad note like that, especially after it was reported in the newspaper. It really made us feel silly."

Sasha said, "Wasn't that crazy? I don't think I want to be a celebrity if it's all like that."

"No joke," Jasmine agreed.

Alexandria then looked at me. She said, "So we went ahead and called up Tracy to apologize to her before we walked over here."

I nodded to them. "That's good to hear."

Maddy spoke up and said, "We wanna apologize to you and Jasmine, too."

"Apology accepted," Jasmine told them. "I fight and make up with my sisters and cousins all the time. It's no biggie."

Sasha said, "So that means we're all family again?"

Alexandria grinned and said, "Yup, that's what it looks like."

"Well . . . I guess we can order pizza then," I commented.

Sasha said, "The works."

"But no onions," Alexandria told her.

"Why not?" Jasmine asked.

"Because you both talk too much with onions all on your breath, that's why," Maddy told them.

Jasmine opened her mouth wide and exhaled like a dragon.

Alexandria shook her head. "She's crazy. We need to check her in somewhere."

I jumped on the phone and began to order the pizzas.

"Yes, we would like room service."

The pizza had just arrived when Tracy called me on my cell phone.

"Hello," I answered.

"What are you all doing?" she asked me. "I guess you're not in your room."

I answered, "I'm in Sasha and Jasmine's room. We're all eating pizza and watching a movie."

"All of you are together?"

"Yeah."

"Even Alexandria?"

I guess Tracy was surprised by our last-minute unity as well.

I said, "Yup."

"And Jason didn't show up at all tonight?"

"Not that I know of."

"Did he call her?"

"You want me to ask her?"

Tracy paused. "No, just leave it alone. But I do need to talk to you a few minutes just to wrap things up."

"I thought you were hanging out with Raheema and Mercedes again tonight."

She yawned noticeably over the phone. She said, "I thought so, too, but I've been pushing it all this week, and I really couldn't hang tonight. I'm exhausted. They said they might swing past late."

"Are you sure you're still gonna be up?" I asked her. It was already late.

"No, but they can try me anyway," she joked.

I chuckled and chomped on a slice of my pizza.

"Hey, stop being greedy, Jasmine. You always have to show off," I snapped.

The girl had grabbed three slices at once.

She said, "Look, I'm hungry. Don't let this great body fool you. I have to feed it to keep it this way."

"Whatever," Sasha told her. "You got nothing on me."

Sasha stuck her nicely rounded ass out and smacked it.

We all started laughing.

"Well, what are you, the amazing Asian?" Jasmine joked. "You just got lucky, that's all."

"She got some black in her somewhere," Maddy stated.

Sasha said, "We all come from Africa in our genealogical roots."

Maddy shook her head. She said, "Now you know she's Asian when she starts talking that scientific shit. Genealogical roots."

We were having a ball in there, laughing it up like old times.

Over my cell phone line, Tracy said, "It sounds like you guys are back to being the best of friends."

"I wouldn't say all of that," I told her.

She said, "Well, I don't want to take you from your girls. You go on back to having your fun."

"Are you sure?" She sounded lonesome.

"Yeah, I'll be all right. I got a lot of stuff to organize up here tonight."

Once she said that, I came up with an idea. "You need help with it?"

"Well, I could use some help, but . . ."

It sounded like she didn't want to ask me.

"We'll help you with that," I volunteered.

She said, "I don't know if I want all of them up in my room like that."

I walked toward the door to have more privacy. "Hold on," I told her. It was still pretty loud in the room, so I had a good reason to step out into the hallway to finish our conversation.

"Where are you going, Vanessa?" Jasmine asked me.

"Just out in the hallway. You all are too loud in here."

"Well, at least we have three rooms in a row so no neighbors can complain," Sasha commented.

"Only Sasha would think about something like that. You know how quiet Asians like to be," Maddy kept at her.

"Would you stop it with all of the Asian jokes," Sasha complained.

"Yeah, you're about to start another fight up in here," Alexandria told her. "And Tracy'll end up in the newspapers again."

Maddy opened her mouth, then she caught herself and changed her mind.

"Nope, I'm not even gonna say it."

I looked at Maddy and nodded to her with a smile. She had to accept that every argument was not a fight. Then I walked out into the hallway.

As soon as I was out of the room and closed the door, I walked away from it and said, "Tracy, they've been feeling like you've been alienating them this whole week. Especially with all of the extra meetings you've taken me to with your old friends. That also created some of the tension that built up into the hallway fight. So if you let them help you organize your things tonight it would be a good move to massage their egos.

"I mean, let them feel close to you for the night," I told her. "It's our last night here."

Tracy sighed and said, "My room is not in the best shape right now. But I don't hold that fight against them. I told them that."

I said, "Okay, but at least let us help you clean up or something."

"What, and have those girls complaining about me making them do more work on their last night here? They've already been working for free. That would just add more drama to the next ridiculous newspaper article."

"They're not gonna think that," I told her. Nevertheless, I think I spoke too soon. Tracy was probably right. My girls were ready to play for the night, not work for the night.

I said, "So, you just want me to come up by myself then."

"No, I told you to go ahead and stay there. I'm okay."

I wasn't convinced of it. I said, "Oh, did you ever catch up with Kiwana to ask her what she thought of the movie?"

"Yeah, I called her, but we didn't get a chance to go into detail about the movie. She was with her daughter again. I didn't want to push it."

I was wondering again if Bruce was right in calling Kiwana a fence-jumper. The issue of our film project was still being avoided.

"But like I said, Raheema and Mercedes are supposed to swing by tonight anyway."

As soon as she finished her sentence, there was a slight stutter over Tracy's line connection. That usually meant someone was calling in.

"That's them right now," she told me. "So I'll just get them to help me tonight."

I was still hesitant.

"Oh, okay. You sure?"

"Go on back to your friends, girl. I'll see you in the morning."

I said, "Well, how come Robin and her crew are not helping you tonight?"

"They're out partying, too. But I get harassed too much when I go out. And I don't want to have to punch a cameraperson out tonight for catching me out on the town just enjoying myself. That's why I like Zanzibar Blue. Folks usually know how to act in there."

Finally, she said, "Look, let me call back my friends and you go on back to your friends. Okay?"

She was the boss, so I said, "Okay. I'll see you tomorrow morning then."

When I walked back inside the room, Alexandria was on her cell phone. She walked toward the door for more privacy herself. I assumed it was Jason calling.

I still felt bad for Sasha about my cousin jumping ship on her. But you win some, you lose some. She wasn't taking it bad.

"We're just chilling," Alexandria said over the phone. "Okay. It's whatever . . . It means, whatever," she repeated with a grin.

It sounded like Jason was giving her a hard time about her plans for the night.

"Tell him to just come on down," Maddy suggested for all of us. "Because you're not going anywhere tonight. A girl's gotta do what a girl's gotta do when she gotta do it."

Alexandria shook her head and didn't respond to Maddy.

"Okay," she repeated over the phone line. Then she hung up.

"So is he on his way down or what?" I asked her.

Alexandria didn't want to answer. But it was pretty obvious to all of us. So she went ahead and said it. "Yeah."

"So much for our girls' night," Maddy concluded.

We were all rested and fattened up with breakfast food in the morning. Our flight back to L.A. was not until three o'clock in the afternoon. Since the Marriott was only a twenty-minute drive from the airport, we had all morning to be lazy. Sasha and Jasmine's room seemed to be our headquarters, so we were all holed up in there again.

"Well, this is it," Jasmine commented.

We had our luggage stacked by our doors ready to take down to the limo. We had all said our good-byes to everyone, including my phone call to my family in North Philly, and it was nearing our time to check out.

"We'll be back," Sasha stated. "We have a movie to make, remember? This was just phase one."

It wasn't that we doubted it, we were just in shock that phase one had come to an end.

I sighed and said, "You're right. Now we have to head back home and get these Hollywood studios to see what we see."

"Maybe we need to bring them out here on location," Maddy suggested. She said, "A lot of those people are just sitting up in their offices somewhere with a Hollywood window."

"I know that's right," Alexandria agreed.

There was a knock on the door.

"Well, here goes our luggage," Jasmine assumed.

She went to open the door, and Tracy surprised us all with Raheema and Mercedes. They all walked into the room on us.

Tracy said, "Well, you guys met Mercedes briefly at the casting call, but you didn't meet her sister Raheema."

My girls were all speechless for a minute. It was a very pleasant surprise for them.

Jasmine spoke up first with her hand over her heart.

"Okay, let me calm down. I'm gonna stay calm," she told herself.

We all started laughing nervously. It wasn't every day that you get to meet the real characters of a famous book. Of course, I had already met them, but I became excited and nervous all over again for my girls.

"It's good to finally meet the real thing," Alexandria said with her hand extended to Raheema.

The rest of my girls began to speak and shake Mercedes's hand as well.

"I just thought I'd make sure to introduce you all to my girls before we all left," Tracy told us.

"So, you're the flyy girl of this crew, hunh?" Mercedes asked Alexandria.

"We're all flyy," Alexandria responded. That shocked me. She was usually out for herself.

"Okay, I can respect that," Mercedes told her. It didn't seem like she believed her, but she was willing to move on.

"So, everybody's excited about the movie?" Raheema asked all of us.

Jasmine said, "You know it. Of course, there's no part in it for a Hispanic girl, but that's all right."

My girl was punching her little two cents in.

Mercedes said, "Are you kidding me? Lisa Lisa and the Cult Jam were big time in the eighties. And Puerto Rican dance girls, hanging out with the graffiti artists. You never saw the movies *Wild Style* or *Breakin'*? You better recognize. Tracy could pop you right in."

"She was just saying that to get a rise out of me. She knows I'm gonna put all of them in the movie," Tracy commented.

Maddy spoke up and said, "We all heard that." And we did. Tracy had just promised us our cameo roles with Mercedes and Raheema as our witnesses, and none of us would allow her to back down from it.

On the plane back to L.A., we were all thinking about meeting Raheema and Mercedes, and all the fun we had in Philadelphia. However, all of our patience had been tried in different ways. I believe we were all returning a little more mature about life. We had learned something more about ourselves. And we all understood the humility and stamina we would have to have, not only with the *Flyy Girl* film, legacy, and franchise, but with anything that we tried to achieve individually.

From her window seat next to me, Tracy asked me, "So, outside of the fight you guys had in the hotel the other day, how do you think this trip went?"

I smiled and nodded to her. I said, "It's been great. We all learned a lot from this. And I really mean that."

Tracy nodded back to me and said, "Me too."

Then I asked her, "But why are you flying coach with us? I just don't get that."

I felt for sure that stars were used to getting the star treatment. But Tracy had a simple answer for me.

She said, "I just want to know what it feels like to be normal again sometimes. This trip for me was like returning to my roots as a little girl. You guys won't understand that until you reach my age yourself."

I smiled. But I thought I did understand. I had only been living in L.A. with Tracy for three years, but I was returning home that week as well. So I reminded her of that.

I said, "I understand. I was returning home to my roots, too." And I thought again about the promise that I had made to my mom and my sisters. I was out in L.A. with a serious job to do.

Back to Hollywood

When we arrived back out in L.A. after the *Flyy Girl* casting and location scouts in Philly, it was like, "Okay, now what?" Everything seemed to be moving in slow motion. We got our three hours back, and they seemed useless. In fact, the time difference seemed like a reason to procrastinate. The East Coast hustle and bustle forced you to move a heck of a lot faster in everyday transactions. But I seemed to be the only one missing that hustle.

I created a things-to-do list as soon as the plane touched down, but it took everyone three days to move on anything. It was like my friends had gone into hibernation. Even Petula disappeared on me for a minute.

I guess they all needed time to rest from the moviemaking process.

My cousin Tracy, the boss lady, went right back to seeing her friend Dalvin, as if they had had no arguments about the film. Not much was going on at the Flyy Girl Ltd. office in Inglewood either. Did we fly out to Philly to begin casting a movie and set up a clothing line office just for the hell of it? I really had to ask myself how serious we all were. I know I was serious, but I couldn't speak for everyone else.

Charmaine, however, had remained busy on the clothing designs. So I was over at the Flyy Girl Ltd. office looking at hot new designs she had come up with for jeans, wraparound skirts, and tops. We seemed to be the only ones working. Charmaine was also from the East Coast, out of Orlando, Florida.

She said, "So, product sales went pretty good in Philadelphia?"

"Yes they did. I think we have a hit on our hands," I told her.

She asked me, "But was it Tracy they were buying into or the clothes themselves?"

I thought about it. "That's a good question. I believe it was a little bit of both. I mean, they liked the designs, but surely they were buying into the Flyy Girl franchise, and Tracy's popularity is a major part of that franchise. It's nearly impossible to separate the two. I mean, she is *Flyy Girl*."

Charmaine nodded and said, "That's what I'm afraid of. Because if they are buying the clothes more because of its novelty and the connection to Tracy, I don't know how long it will last past Tracy's interest in it."

She said, "As a designer, I would rather the clothes be able to stand on their own."

"But doesn't she present a good launchpad for the clothes?"

"Yes, she does, but it's a blessing and a curse," Charmaine commented. "A launchpad is all that we'll get if the clothes don't catch on on their own. That's why I'm working overtime on the ideas to make sure the clothes stand up. Otherwise, this opportunity for me goes down the drain."

She had a good point. I had always like Charmaine's coolheaded logic anyway.

She said, "I hate to admit it to you, Vanessa, but I would rather your cousin be more of a celebrity guest to events that I do for the Flyy Girl Ltd. line than a true business owner. I mean, she'll still be the owner, but I'll need her to back away from everyday business and just let me run things the way I know how to. So I'm kind of glad she's not here much. It gives me the space I need to do what I need to do."

Charmaine was being bluntly honest about using my cousin's popularity as a figurehead for the company, while declining Tracy's attempts to be a true businesswoman. I didn't know how I felt about that. I still respected my cousin as a businesswoman. She had the stuff of an owner. There was no question about it. Tracy got things popping.

I said, "So, you don't think it's good for Tracy to be too involved. You make it seem like she's going to be in the way."

Charmaine looked at me a minute and collected her thoughts before she spoke.

She said, "Vanessa, you have to understand that your cousin is more of an artist than anything. Her whole life has been about getting things started. She jumps into things with both feet on fire. And fortunately, a lot of things have gone her way. So she has been able to make a lot of things happen seemingly overnight. But that's not the way most businesses are run. Real business is about an everyday grind. Does Tracy have an everyday grind mentality for business? Honestly? No. But that doesn't mean she can't learn it. I just don't know if she's ready or willing to do that right now."

She said, "Even now, if you notice, Tracy's decision to finally do this clothing line was all of a sudden. I mean, she just called me up out of the blue and set up this office, after I had been asking her to do this for two and a half years. And I believe that had more to do with you than anything else. So it's ironic that you and I are the only ones still at work over here. And I was just waiting for this conversation to happen."

I just listened to her and heard her out.

She looked me in the eyes and said, "Now, do I consider Vanessa Tracy Smith an everyday grind kind of businessperson? Yes I do. And you have what it takes to run a company. Will you ever be as popular as your cousin? Probably not. People love Tracy's passionate flair. But not everyone can run a business like Donald Trump or P. Diddy, where they're out in front of the band blowing their horns. And that's actually not a good thing for most strong companies, because that lead horn becomes the focal point of the business and not the business itself.

"Like Sean John," she mentioned. "It's a good, long-lasting clothing line because it's not called P. Diddy or Bad Boy. So it gets a chance to breathe away from the man's antics and public personality. That's what Flyy Girl Ltd. will need to do to survive from Tracy. So we have to remain strong whether she's successful with a new film or not. The clothing line will then become a real source of income, power, and stature by her allowing it to do what it needs to do away from her."

I said, "So you're telling me that my cousin will benefit more by not being involved in the company?"

Charmaine said, "All we need is her launchpad and her capital, and we can run the business the way we need to on our own. And it will be better for all of us."

I understood what she was saying, and it all made sense. But at the same time, I was loyal to and respectful of my cousin, so I decided not to say any more about it until I had a chance to talk to Tracy about her own plans.

A few days after my conversation with Charmaine, I finally caught up with my cousin long enough to talk to her about everything. Tracy seemed to be running around and staying away from me on purpose for the majority of that first week back. But I caught her in the living room watching one of the reality shows on network TV. She was in some kick-around clothes with her feet up, eating ice cream, so I knew it was a good time to talk to her.

I sat beside her on the sofa and asked her how she was doing.

She nodded to me. "I'm good. I'm good."

She sounded like she was trying hard to convince herself.

I hated to bug her about the progress on everything, but I needed to know that all of our excitement and hard work on the *Flyy Girl* projects were not meaningless.

"So, have any meetings been set up for you and Susan to talk to the studios about *Flyy Girl*?"

She nodded her head but didn't face me.

"Yeah, we, ah, have a few meetings set up for next week."

She sounded too nonchalant for my liking.

I asked her, "Are they strong meetings, or just meetings?"

"There's no such thing as a strong meeting until you have them," she answered me. "You could go from hot to cold from one meeting to the next. That's just how things go out here."

"Well, you had a lot of hot meetings when you first moved out here," I reminded her. It was all documented in her sequel book *For the Love of Money*.

Tracy finally looked me in the eyes. She said, "No, I had hot and cold meetings then, too, but no one remembers the cold ones after you accomplish your goals. They only remember the winning meetings. But I had plenty of losses as well."

"Are you trying to tell me something?"

She took a breath and answered, "I'm not *trying* to tell you,

Vanessa, I *am* telling you. Getting a movie made is all a process, and a very tedious one at that."

I changed the subject and asked her, "What about the clothing line?"

She said, "It's a good idea. But I have to find more time to make it work. The movie would really launch it though. So I'm trying to tie the two of them together."

"What about before we do the movie?"

"We keep the clothing line small and move forward."

"You're not trying to have the clothing lead into the movie? That could be an idea that could get the movie deal done faster," I told her.

Tracy said, "Vanessa, you don't sell merchandise before you shoot a movie, you sell it after the movie is in the tank. Your favorite guy, Spike Lee, is the king of that. He'll promote whatever other product he's selling while he's getting attention for his films, or whatever other artistic controversy he's involved in."

"So, what, we shut down Flyy Girl Ltd. until the movie happens? We just sold a bunch of stuff at the casting call with no movie," I reminded her.

"And that was a very successful test run of what will happen if the movie deal gets done," she responded. She looked at me a little harder and said, "So I'm gonna say it again, we'll keep the clothing line growing small until we have the movie as a true launchpad for it. That's the way all smart businesspeople do things. It's just like staying away from the media until you have a new project you're pushing. That way you maximize all of your goals."

She said, "You don't just throw money into marketing and promoting a product that you haven't properly maximized your attention on. That's good business 101. You kill two or three birds with one stone. You don't use three stones to kill one bird. Because before you know it, those three stones will become twenty. And that damn bird will still be sitting there."

She continued, "That's how so many athletes and entertainers end up going broke. Everybody wants to use your damn money for their own pipe dreams. So you need to take a few business classes while you're over there at UCLA to really study how business works."

"Good idea," I responded with a half grin.

I was really getting confused. Charmaine made a lot of sense, but so did Tracy. In the end, I understood that I was going to have to be patient to see how things played out. I had no choice.

I watched a little bit of the reality TV show with Tracy in silence before I stood up to retire to my room.

Tracy studied my sullen mood and said, "You have a lot of great ideas and enthusiasm, Vanessa, but you're gonna have to learn to have patience and poise, too. I've already gone through that phase where I'm running around like a madwoman out here, and that can make you old real fast. So learn to relax a minute and enjoy your fun while you can. Because once you step into this business for real, you won't get a lot of time to drop your guard down. You're always protecting yourself while looking out for your next meal."

She said, "My book and first film royalties gave me the chance to do what a lot of Hollywood types don't get a chance to do: relax," she told me. And she looked like she meant it.

Hot, creative / lava / boils in my brain / searching for an orifice / to erupt on nature / violently / burning the old soil / and terrifying the settled creatures / who have gotten used to things / as they were / so they run, shriek, and squeal / as my lava rolls / quickly down on them / from up high.

But when it is over / I cool off in fresh ashes / raising those old things / to higher levels / so that the creatures can return / enlightened / and start again / while the earth awaits / my next / eruption.

"Volcano," by Tracy Ellison.

My cousin still had a few tricks up her sleeve, and a lot left for me to learn from her. A lot of people still underestimated her, but I didn't. And each time I confronted Tracy about something, she always had a logical and reasonable response to my concerns. But that didn't mean there weren't more tests to come.

My girls had fallen back into the fold of things, and were in and out of our Inglewood office as we continued to move small units of Flyy Girl Ltd. clothing around the retail stores of L.A. and Philadelphia. Then my girls began to ask me what progress had been made on the film. It had been a month since we'd returned home from

Philadelphia, Tracy had bought me a new car to get around in, and I was maintaining my poise like she had advised me to do. But then I went to another one of those Hollywood party functions with Tracy, and that changed everything.

Evidently, Susan Raskin had some connection to the Marriott Hotel chain, and she was having a party inside their ballroom at the airport location. We were all dressed to impress, with Susan and her man, Kendra and her husband, Tracy and her friend, and Yolanda Felix and me, when Susan's long-term boyfriend popped the question in front of the crowd.

He held her hand and pulled out the diamond to put on her finger. Then he sank down on one knee and asked, "Susan, will you marry me?"

The crowd gushed and waited for her answer.

But first she teased him. "What if I said no?"

Yolanda screamed through the crowd, "You better not tell that man no."

We all laughed as Susan prepared herself for her answer.

"Of course I will, honey. I love you," she told him. He rose to his feet and kissed her on the lips, while the crowd went crazy.

I looked over at Tracy to see how she was taking it. She was smiling and clapping next to Dalvin, who was following her lead. I couldn't read her response through a look. She was doing what was expected of her. But it didn't look good for the *Flyy Girl* film from my perspective. I understood that most of the studio deals would most likely run through Susan and Yolanda, and if Susan was busy getting married, while Tracy and Yolanda were running out of time on their own biological clocks, then our *Flyy Girl* movie could very likely be pushed off the immediate to-do list.

The crowd dispersed after the big announcement, and I found myself coupled up with Yolanda Felix again.

"So, how did you like your big Philadelphia excursion? I heard you guys had a blast," she commented.

I nodded to her with a spiked drink in hand. It was red fruit juice with some kind of alcohol added.

I said, "We did what we had to do out there, now we have to do what we have to do out here."

Yolanda looked at me curiously. She had already had a few strong drinks. I could smell them on her breath.

She said, "And what is it that you're supposed to get done out here?" she asked me.

I answered her frankly, "Find the studio that will green-light the *Flyy Girl* film."

"You mean find the right players who will want to combine in an effort to get the film made," she corrected me.

I shrugged my shoulders and said, "Whatever."

I really didn't feel up to having a discussion with Yolanda about getting films made. I already realized how jaded she was about the whole film process. Her philosophy was to get in where you fit in and leave everything else alone. However, that philosophy didn't leave much room for any out-of-the-box creativity. And most of our urban ideas were definitely out of Hollywood's cute little, whitewashed box.

"It's gonna take you guys a lot of work and time to get this film placed at a studio. You do know that, don't you?" Yolanda asked me.

I was already looking around the room for Tracy, Kendra, or even Susan to bail me out of another conversation with Yolanda. I didn't feel like being bit by her poisonous teeth that night. I had already decided to ignore her.

Then she said, "Tracy wrote a damn good script though," and that got my attention.

I turned and faced her. "You think so?" I asked.

Getting anything positive from Yolanda Felix was a godsend. I wondered how she and Mercedes would get along, two serpents from separate sides of the street.

Yolanda said, "In fact, her script is a little too good for its own good. Had she written something trite and ghetto, she could have done a straight-to-DVD movie and made a killing off of it. But Tracy wrote a thirty-million-dollar script, with no stars in it. That all but kills the project unless you get some major players to back it."

She said, "Black, urban American films is not where the major players' heads are at right now, unless it's a comedy. And *Flyy Girl* is nowhere near a comedy."

I cut through the bullshit and asked her straight out, "Do you think *Flyy Girl* would be a good movie?"

She surprised me when she nodded. "I would love to see Tracy's story told on the big screen. And yes, it would be a good movie if cast correctly. Nevertheless, unless you can get white girls your age to be interested in it, the audience just won't be big enough to make it. At least not for the theaters."

I said, "Yeah, but a lot of women your age have read and loved the book: your age and older. That was the initial audience, people who grew up in the eighties."

Yolanda looked at me and began to chuckle.

She said, "Honey, women my age and older are not gonna be caught dead in a teenage movie. And they can tell you all the lies they want to about that. Reading the book ten years ago, and going to see the movie now, are two totally different things. And I don't even count because I would see it for free."

"But what about mothers and daughters going to see it together?"

I was reaching for anything at that point to keep my dream alive.

Yolanda said, "That sounds like a made-for-television special. And I'm sure you do understand that the material of your cousin's book is about four times too raw for the average TV rating. However, HBO might like it if packaged to them correctly. Now that's an idea."

"But beyond HBO, we just can't get it done?" I questioned.

"Some things are just gonna be better left as books. I mean, look at this *Lord of the Rings* trilogy," she told me. "It took many years for them to figure out how those books could be made into a successful film series. And there are no black people to even dream about in that thing."

She said, "We are just not in a position for making meaningful black films, honey. Nobody wants to see them. Even black people show up late and uninterested in films that try to do more than entertain us. John Singleton realizes that now. He's not wasting any more of his career dealing with black films. With *2 Fast 2 Furious*, he's now reaching out to get some of that white money. Gary F. Gray. Antoine Fuqua. The Hughes brothers. They're all grabbing after that white money now."

I said, "What if Tracy directs the movie herself?" I don't even know why I asked her that. I guess I just wanted to see what Yolanda had to say about everything, since she was running her mouth so much.

She looked at me and said, "Child, please. Tracy's begging to get her next movie to act in, let alone try and direct something. She didn't tell you that she was trying to direct *Flyy Girl*, did she? Her best idea would be to start a letter-writing campaign to Steven Spielberg to see if he'd try and do the movie to get another award out of it or something. He did Alice Walker's book *The Color Purple* twenty years ago."

Yolanda was really draining me. She had me thinking now about the whole Philadelphia casting call. Was it all an illusion to make me and my friends feel that something was getting done when it really wasn't? Tracy had paid for everything through Susan's hookup with the Marriott Hotel chain, and the Flyy Girl clothing line sales. So she really didn't even spend anything. She had all of her bases covered.

Did my cousin mastermind the whole trip with Susan before she agreed to it? Maybe that was why it was all of a sudden. They had to work out the details first. And now Tracy was back home in Hollywood bullshitting me, while she and Susan looked for her next film job. Only Yolanda was willing to tell me the truth.

I said, "What about the film crew we had with us from New York? If we just got the money . . ." I was more or less speaking out loud to myself, trying to justify the energy, ideas, and hope I had spent on the project, but Yolanda took that information and ran with it as well.

She said, "Those New York people can't touch this film. Tracy knows that. They were just out there playing with the cameras and having a good time in Philadelphia. Susan and I didn't go anywhere near Philadelphia with you guys—did you once stop to think about that?"

I was only thinking about whether Yolanda was supposed to tell me so much information at that point. If it had all been mapped out, and they all knew about it, then they were all in on it, and Yolanda was now spilling the beans to me. Maybe she had had too much alcohol in her system already.

I said, "Why would she do that to me?" I was speaking out loud again when I didn't mean to. Maybe my spiked drink was getting to me as well. I wasn't much of a drinker.

Yolanda said, "From what I understand, you came out here ready to take on the world. But you're gonna need a little more education before you get your feet wet in Hollywood, honey. You can't just come out here, walk up to a door, and expect it to open for you."

I said, "Well, how did Tracy get in?"

"Science-fucking-fiction," Yolanda said, spraying me with some of her drink. "I told her where to go, and who to talk to, and she got in with science fiction, just like I said she would. Then she tried the little black television show thing, and that didn't work. She tried the freelance script writing thing for the major networks, and wasn't paying any consistent bills. And then she lucked up with *Led Astray* because it was a raw emotion project that struck with the right people at the right time."

She said, "But now your cousin's luck has run the hell out with those two last films she tried to do, and what are we discussing now to get her back in, a science fiction movie. All she has to do is look good, and let those computer graphics people do what they have to do. Because, see, when white folks watch science fiction movies, as long as there are enough special effects going on, they can finally get past our damn color."

I had heard enough from Yolanda, I really had. She made me not want to fuck with Hollywood at all. Was it that damned racist out there? Black people still seemed to be in movies. But how the hell were they getting in them if it was that difficult to pitch anything black?

"Excuse me, I have to use the restroom," I said, just to get away from Yolanda.

She said, "Well, when you come back, I can tell you more of what you need to know."

"I'm not fucking coming back," I mumbled under my breath. I was using bitter language and everything. That was not even my style. Yolanda had really gotten under my skin. So I romped on my way to the bathroom, feeling shitty about my big cousin duping me with the *Flyy Girl* project, and somebody reached out and grabbed my arm.

I looked, and was ready to let whoever have a piece of my sour mind at the moment, and spotted Anthony Coolidge, who had taken a couple of media courses with me at UCLA. He was a slightly older guy who had returned to school to finish what he started years ago, after dropping out to get involved in straight-to-video movies. Once that stopped paying off for him, he was right back in school to finish his education.

He said, "I see you're here mixing with the in-crowd."

Anthony was mixed with Indian or something. He had the prettiest brown skin and thick curly hair that he managed to keep cut just right.

I was startled by him. He was over six feet tall and dressed in a charcoal gray suit, with white shirt, and an eye-popping tie.

"Where are you on your way to?" he asked me.

"The restroom," I told him.

He said, "To rest, or to do something else?"

It was a corny joke, but he still held my attention with it somehow. He was hinting at being fresh.

"What do you think I'm about to do?" I asked him. I wanted to see where he was going with it.

He smiled with perfect white teeth and said, "To relieve yourself. We all have to do that at some point or another."

He was being fresh and tactful at the same time.

So, fuck it, I decided to play his game. I had nothing better to do. My damn cousin was bullshitting me about my dream, and she had dragged me to another one of her bullshit-ass Hollywood parties. I was all dressed up in electric blue silk like a damn grown-up, black Barbie doll, so I decided to act grown.

"And what do you know about it?" I asked Anthony.

He stopped and searched my face to see if I was willing to go there.

He said, "I know plenty about release. Sometimes it just jumps up and grabs you without warning. You know what I mean?"

I asked him, "What if I don't? What if I never been jumped up and grabbed before?"

He read my face to see if I was serious again.

"Well, there's always a first time, too."

"Is it?"

"Yeah, it is."

"And how do you know when it's gonna be first?"

He looked deep into my eyes and said, "You just let it happen and be natural with it. And I don't mean like, natural without protection.

I mean natural emotions. When you feel it strong enough, you just let it go."

I nodded to him. I said, "I'll think about it while I'm in here . . . relieving myself," I added with a grin.

He smiled back at me and said, "Yeah, you do that."

I walked into the restroom and felt tingles all over. I had never gone there with a guy before, but I had imagined it. Every girl had her fantasies whether she allowed them to happen or not. But I was ready to allow them to happen now. Like Anthony said, when you feel it, you just let it go. And I was feeling it.

I did what I had to do in the bathroom, and made sure that everything was up to par with me, just in case I let somebody explore something that night. Like I said, I did have my fantasies.

When I walked back out from the restroom, I spotted my cousin Tracy. She had appeared just in the nick of time to cock-block my flow.

"It figures," I mumbled to myself. Fortunately, I had driven myself to the event that night in my brand new Volkswagen Bug. I never said that Tracy didn't take care of me. But that was besides the point. She had pulled the rug over my eyes regarding the real business of Hollywood, and I wasn't feeling too happy about that.

Once she spotted me, I walked in her direction and away from Anthony on purpose. I would deal with him later.

When I reached her, Tracy asked me, "Are you okay?" She was just checking up on me, I guess.

I said, "Tracy, I really don't feel like hanging out here all night. So I think I'm about ready to drive on home and see what my girls are up to."

It was closing in on eleven o'clock on Saturday night, so the night was still young.

Tracy looked me over. "Are you sure?"

"Actually, if I had my own car before, I would have left a lot of these parties earlier. I mean, it's just not my thing to hang around and talk if things are not getting accomplished by it," I hinted to her.

She nodded to me. I'm sure she understood.

She said, "Well, drive safe tonight, and stay out of trouble."

I looked over at her friend Dalvin and asked her, "And what kind of trouble are you gonna get into tonight?"

She smiled at me and declined to answer.

"Go on out of here, girl. I'll see you when I see you. You're responsible enough to know what to do."

She was telling me in her way that she might not be coming home that night, and that was music to my ears. I was mapping out my own plans for the night.

So I kissed my cousin on the cheek, and walked back in Anthony's direction on my way out.

As soon as I approached him, I asked him boldly, "Do you have a room here?" I didn't have any time to ruin my plans with too much small talk out in the open. I didn't want too many people to see me talking to him for too long. I would talk to him more in private later.

"I do," he answered.

"Are you sharing it with anyone?"

"Not if I don't have to."

"I would prefer that you didn't," I told him.

"Well, then, I won't."

I said, "What room are you in?"

"Twelve-eleven."

"I'll meet you there in ten minutes," I told him.

He hesitated. I guess I had caught him off guard with my urgency and forwardness, but I had no time to waste.

I smiled at him as I spoke and shook his hand to make my fake exit. I said, "If you're not there, or if it's too complicated, then I'm leaving. Now let me make my exit and then sneak up to see you."

He smiled real calmly and said, "I like your style."

I told him, "You make sure you make a clean exit, too."

"I will."

I let his hand go and waved good-bye. He waved back to me as I made my final rounds.

When I reached Yolanda again, she had her eyes wide open for Anthony.

"Who is that?"

"He goes to UCLA with me, but I don't really know him like that," I told her.

She said, "Well, you need to get to know him."

I grinned and shook my head. I said, "I'm just letting you know that I'm cutting out of here. I want to go catch up with my girls. You know, Tracy told me to enjoy myself while I'm still young so that's what I'm gonna do."

Yolanda said, "Are you trying to call us old in here?"

I grinned. "No, but you know."

"No, I don't know," she responded to me. "Because I'm not old yet." She was still staring over at Anthony when she said it.

"Well, let me get out of here," I told her.

I walked away from her and found Kendra and Susan to say my good-byes to them, and to congratulate Susan on her engagement. Then I headed out of the ballroom toward the lobby area and managed to slide right onto a just arriving elevator. Since Tracy had taken a limo to the event, I didn't worry about her spotting my car in the parking garage. My black Volkswagen didn't really stand out in a parking lot anyway. Unless you were right next to it, you barely noticed it.

I rode the elevator up to the twelfth floor with no other guests onboard. It was a perfect setup.

I arrived on the twelfth floor and walked past Anthony's room on purpose. I wanted to act lost, just in case someone spotted me there in the hallway. So I walked all the way down to the opposite end of the hall, slowly looking at the room numbers. By the time I turned around and began to make my way back up the hall toward his room, he walked out from the elevator ahead of me.

He turned immediately toward his room and didn't even see me behind him.

"Looking for somebody?" I teased him.

He turned and spotted me. He grinned and said, "Yeah, I'm looking for this stunning UCLA college girl out here from Philadelphia."

"Is she supposed to be coming to your room or something?"

"She said she was. I guess I'll just have to wait and see if she was serious," he told me.

As we said all this he opened his room door and motioned for me to walk in. There were two double beds in the room. I sat on the bed closest to the bathroom and the front door. He sat on the dresser and faced me.

"So, who are you rooming with?" I asked him.

"This buddy of mine I've shot a few movies with."

I nodded. I said, "He doesn't mind you kicking him out?"

He smiled. "I would do the same for him. We already have that policy."

"Oh, so you do this a lot then." Maybe I was talking too much. I didn't need all of that information. But I did ask him. Maybe I was asking too much.

He said, "Well, it's just a policy based on a what-if. That's not to say it's going to happen every time."

"So why are you here?"

There I was asking too many questions again. I guess I couldn't help myself.

He said, "We're trying to get in with the in-crowd. It's a work situation thing. We don't all have famous cousins to walk us in like you have," he stated.

I didn't even want to talk about Hollywood business anymore. I was feeling daring and sexual, so I changed the subject.

I said, "So, why did you feel the need to flirt with me?"

He smiled again and chuckled at me. "Actually, I didn't think of it consciously. It just came out how it came out," he said. "But I always noticed you at school. I just haven't seen you away from school and looking like this."

"What, like a debutante?"

He said, "Yeah. So I guess it turned me on a little bit. I mean, I've always been attracted to you, but you seemed like you were all about your work. Either that or you had a man already, so I didn't really bother you."

I nodded. I didn't know if it was all game or not, but I didn't really care. My girlish fantasies were on my mind, and I just didn't know how to start them. Nevertheless, I still could have waited. But in my frustrations with Tracy and the whole *Flyy Girl* movie development, I was just becoming tired of waiting around for shit. I wanted something to happen. And this was it.

"So, here we are," I hinted, and I uncrossed my legs.

Anthony chuckled and said, "Yeah, here we are," but he still didn't make any moves.

I grew impatient with him and said, "So, what do you want to do with me?" I didn't have all night to play guessing games. I mean, he had started talking fresh to me, now he was getting all hesitant. Did he want my goodies or not?

"What do you want me to do?" he asked me back.

That was the right question to ask me.

I said, "You'll do it?"

"Try me."

I said, "Okay. I want to know what it feels like if you put your tongue on me."

He said, "It'll feel good."

"Well . . . I wanna feel good then."

He sunk to his knees on the floor right in front of me.

He said, "You do?"

He smelled good, too.

I looked into his dark eyes and said, "Yeah."

Then he reached out with both hands and caressed my breasts. He started to scratch my nipples straight through my silk with his pinkie fingers, and they hardened instantly.

"Go on and lean back and close your eyes," he told me.

I leaned back and closed my eyes with my legs still hanging off the bed.

Anthony slid his hands under my dress and found my panty and stocking lines to pull them off.

I relaxed, inhaling and exhaling. It was only sex. And I refused to allow myself to be freaked out about it like Raheema had been in *Flyy Girl*. I was just going to relax and let it happen.

Anthony pulled off my stockings, panties, and shoes, and spread my legs, while placing them over his shoulders. Then he sunk his head between my legs and inside of my dress.

Oh my God, I thought to myself. *This is it. He's about to do it.*

I felt his cold, wet, licking tongue on my good spot and began to shiver. Then he reached up with his hands and started to softly scratch my nipples with his pinkie fingers again.

I moaned and reached down to grab his head through my dress. *"Unnnhhh."*

Talk about feeling good. *Damn!* What did I wait all that long for?

I began to work my hips into his mouth as he continued licking me.

"*Uuuuewww, yeaaahhh,*" I moaned to him.

He kept working my nipples with his fingers and my good part with his tongue until I was vibrating on the bed with pulsations running through my body.

I felt all wet down below and nasty, but I wasn't going to tell him to stop. It felt good nasty. I'm not even gonna try and be discreet and lie about it. The truth was the truth, and that man was eating me out like some kind of addictive tropical fruit.

When he finally stopped, my body, mind, and soul were all exhausted. I was all limp on that bed like a peeled banana skin.

Anthony stood up from his position on the floor between my legs and asked me if he could put his thing inside of me.

He said, "I have protection."

I couldn't even talk. I just nodded to him weakly. There was no sense in stopping him. While I was already wet and nasty up between my legs, I figured I might as well let him finish the job. I didn't feel like moving from the bed anyway. And he didn't even bother to take the rest of my clothes off.

I said, "I'm still in my dress." I figured he would want to take it off.

He said, "Leave it on. I like that. It's kinky."

Who was I to argue? I could barely move to take it off myself, so I left it on.

I happened to look down at Anthony's thing while he slid the condom on, and I was scared to death. I don't know what the average size was supposed to be, but it looked like he needed both hands to hold it. So I just closed my eyes and got ready to hold in the pain or scream from it.

As soon as it pushed up inside of me, I tried to pull back from him.

"Oh my God. Wait, wait," I told him.

He said, "I got it. Just relax."

I could feel a single tear roll down the side of my face as he entered me. I mean, there was no room left inside of me to move. But he found a way to position his body just right, so that he could slide his big thing in and out of me extra slow. And I made sure to hold on to his hips with both my hands to stop him from hurting me with any sudden movements.

"I got it," he continued to whisper to me. "It's nice and tight."

"Is that good?" I whimpered to him.

"Oh, yesss," he hissed to me. And he started moving faster.

But it didn't hurt anymore. It was starting to feel warm. My whole insides felt warm. It felt like a giant, slippery worm was moving inside my body. So I moved with it. And moved with it. And moved with it.

"*Oooh, shit,*" Anthony moaned into my face. His body began to lose its steady rhythm until we became one. I couldn't tell where his body ended and my body began. So I used all of the strength in my arms to pull him down to me and make us a human sandwich.

And it got hot. So hot that I lost control of my mouth and started squealing.

"*Nnnnnhhh,*" I moaned to him.

And "*Uuuuuuhhhh,*" he moaned back to me.

Our bodies became a mess of hot wetness as we shook like crazy in each other's arms, burning up and sweating, with my damn silk dress still on between us.

I had to regain my breath for nearly five minutes before I had enough energy to speak again.

I said, "I feel so nasty right now."

Anthony was still on top of me with all of his weight. When he laughed, he felt even heavier. But somehow it didn't bother me. It just felt warm and comfortable. I guess that's how a man was supposed to feel to a woman. No wonder we fell in love. He could lie on me like that forever, and I wouldn't even care.

He said, "Girl, that felt like . . . it was tailor-made."

I smiled. I said, "I didn't know that big thing could fit inside of me. That's amazing," I told him.

He said, "Yeah . . . but it's all about how you work it."

I said, "So . . . now what happens?"

We both had to breathe in between our words like sprinters at a track meet. I didn't have the faintest idea of how it all worked next. All I knew was that plenty of girls had gotten strung out afterward, while guys only seemed to beat their chests like some kind of *King Kong* movie.

Anthony said, "Well . . . we rest for a while . . . and then if you want . . . we can do it again."

That wasn't exactly the answer I was looking for, but I definitely wanted to try it again, if just to see if it would feel the same way it did the first time.

I said, "Okay . . . but this time, we have to take my dress off first."

He chuckled and said, "All right . . . I'm sorry. I guess I have to pay to take it to the cleaners now."

That was the other thing I had heard. Guys start making promises that they rarely keep, and then they complain about it when you remind them that they made it. And I didn't even ask for him to take my dress to the cleaners.

Exhausted

I slept all the way into the afternoon that Sunday, and I had to hide my dress in the trunk of my car until I could take it to the cleaners sometime that week. I was also sore around my private parts, walking carefully and gingerly so as not to bring any attention to myself around Tracy.

I met up with her at the kitchen table after lunch, where I ate Frosted Flakes with milk, and she drank a cup of coffee. She had just gotten in herself.

After a few minutes of silence around each other, she asked me, "What club did you all go to last night?" She was just starting a conversation. She wasn't probing or anything.

I said, "I didn't go to a club." I didn't feel like making up anything. However, I didn't plan on telling her the truth either. I still wanted to talk to her about all the things Yolanda hipped me to at the party.

I told her, "I didn't feel like clubbing it up last night. All I could think about was the *Flyy Girl* project."

Tracy pulled the cup of coffee away from her lips and shook her head.

She said, "Girl, you have to learn to let the pieces fall where they fall. You thinking about this movie all of the time is not going to make it happen any sooner."

I said, "Well, when is it gonna happen? My friends all want to know the same thing. I mean, we went to Philly and did all of that to do what?"

"To start our preproduction," she told me.

"Well, how long is the preproduction stage?"

"Sometimes producers can build a film for years."

"This is not that kind of film," I argued. "All we need is the money and the right people in place. I mean, what happened at the meetings you've already had? If you really even had them," I hinted. Was it all a facade?

Tracy asked me, "What are you trying to say, that I've been making things up for you?" She said, "I'll tell you what happens at these meetings. They hee and haw about other projects that they really can't even compare *Flyy Girl* to. And then they talk about what stars would work, or who wouldn't work, and who is available to attach, and who is not available. And then we shake hands and smile at each other, only so the next set of assholes can come in with their movie ideas and do the exact same thing."

I said, "Well, if you knew that already, Tracy, then why take us to Philly and pretend like we were doing something important, when you already knew what we were up against?"

Tracy stopped cold for a minute. She gathered her thoughts and looked me hard in the eyes. She said, "First of all, I've been telling you the same thing about this movie process for years now, and you still won't get it through your thick skull. So I'm gonna call up Susan and get you in on a meeting with us. Then you can see exactly how things flow out here for yourself. Okay?"

I nodded to her. "Okay." I surely wasn't going to back down from the challenge. A Hollywood meeting was what I had been asking for.

She said, "Now, second, I wanted to go to Philly for myself just to see if *Flyy Girl* is still a viable film to get excited about. I mean, I haven't done a book signing or whatever for *Flyy Girl* in years, so I needed to see if people were still even interested in it."

She said, "There's been a ton of new books about urban girls that have come out since *Flyy Girl* was first published ten years ago, including Sister Souljah's *Coldest Winter*. So going back to Philadelphia for a casting call was a litmus test for me.

"And third, I wanted to see what all of the people who were a part of my life story would think about bringing it back to life. Maybe some of them wouldn't want to relive the past. I still haven't talked to Kiwana about it. So yeah, maybe she doesn't think it's a great idea because of the wayward sexuality of my youth. I would have to deal with that all over again myself."

She said, "So I am not going to allow you to sit here and tell me that I'm not interested in making my story into a feature film, because

I am. I just happen to know that it's a lot more complicated than you think it is. And I also understand all of Hollywood's shortcomings when it comes to black America films, so I'm pacing myself for the long haul."

I heard everything she said, and I was sympathetic to her points, but at the same time, I didn't feel the need to pace myself. I was still young enough to be gung-ho and reckless. And I'm sorry, but sex was a part of life, and a major reason why so many girls connected to the book. It was all the stuff of reality.

I said, "Well, I'm just ready to do these meetings so I can find out for myself what you already know. So you and Susan set them up, and I'll be there with my notes ready."

I mean, I was really crazy about getting this movie done no matter what my cousin had to say.

Tracy just stared at me. But I was still determined. I had no choice. I had to make something work for the sake of my family. I had promised it to them, and I owed them. But not only was I pushing for my family, I was pushing for myself and for thousands of urban girls who had a story to tell about their lives in America. We existed! And we wanted everyone to know that we had something to say.

Tracy suddenly smiled and shook her head again.

I said, "It's not a laughing matter to me. It's more like life or death."

She said, "Whose life or death, Vanessa? Because you're surely not going to die if this movie doesn't get made tomorrow. So who are we talking about?"

"I'm talking more about the life or death of our ideas, loves, struggles, and our existence, Tracy. How come everyone else gets a chance to show they exist but us?"

"Who's everyone else? There are plenty of people who haven't had their individual stories told. And movies are not the vehicle to correct history or to show that people exist. They're movies to entertain people. If they do more, then great. But don't count on it, because people will surely disappoint you. They don't want these movies to do much more than entertain them. And those who complain the most about them are the same people who rarely even go to the damn movies to support a good one."

I stared back at Tracy and couldn't believe that she had gone there. She sounded closer to Yolanda Felix than to the go-for-it cousin I used to know. Maybe she was only out to protect her assets now like Yolanda said.

I said, "So the struggle to do the right thing for art's sake, and for the people's sake, is all over with now. Is that it?"

Tracy took another breath. "Vanessa," she said, "I am so tired of going through this same shit with you. There is no movement going on here, okay? This is not the Black Power era where we're making movies for this or that purpose. I'm sorry, but we missed the boat on that. And the people just don't care about that anymore."

She said, "Now you're gonna have your chance to tell your story one of these days, and I hope they care about what you have to say. Because I already told mine, and just maybe, it will be better off told in a book, where everyone can still read it and know that yes, black girls do exist, and think, and feel. So let's just agree to disagree on this. Okay?"

Yeah, my cousin was done all right. She had run out of gas. So I decided to put the *Flyy Girl* film on my own shoulders to take it as far as I could take it. Nevertheless, it was still her story.

I said, "So once we have this studio meeting next week sometime, and I start to get things going with the film myself, will you back me on it?"

Tracy looked into my eyes again and read how staunch I was in my determination.

She said, "Okay. If you can get things rolling on your own, then you can count on my full support."

I said, "So, in essence, if I get this film moving forward, then I would become a producer and you would be more or less working for me?"

I was attempting to throw all of the realities of the situation together.

Tracy read my logic and began to smile. She said, "I can see where you're going with this. But yeah, if you become a producer on this project, then we all end up working with you: the writer, director, camera crew, PAs, everybody. Is that what you want?" she asked me.

I answered, "I just want to get things done. And if that's what it takes, then so be it."

And I went back to eating my cereal in silence.

Tracy eyed me a few seconds longer and chuckled again. I guess she thought it was all cute and humorous, but I was taking things a lot more seriously than that.

I was jotting down new and improved ideas in my notepad, while sending and returning emails from the computer station in Tracy's home office when my cell phone rang. It was late that Sunday, and I was already on the job, taking over as the producer of *Flyy Girl* the movie. It was now obvious that my cousin was not really up for the task, and she had been blowing smoke in my face the whole time.

"Hello," I answered my cell phone.

"Hey, Vanessa, what's up?"

It was Alexandria.

"Hey, Alex. I'm just sitting here going through some stuff, and emailing *Flyy Girl* fans with our movie questionnaire on who they would like to see in the roles and why. You know, just trying to keep it going."

I had a list of a couple hundred responses already, and I was pumped with energy to collect a few hundred more before the big studio meeting.

Alexandria said, "Oh." She didn't seem too interested in what I was doing. But that was okay. I already understood that I would be doing most of the work. That was just my legacy. I wasn't even going to complain about it anymore.

I said, "So, what's up with you?"

I had three things going on at once: my notes, the emails, and now Alexandria on the phone.

I said, "You know what, let me call you back on the office phone instead of using my cell phone, because I'm sitting right here next to it, and there's no sense in me using this cell phone for no reason."

Alexandria grunted and said, "Okay. Whatever suits you."

She sounded glum for some reason. I immediately suspected that something had gone wrong with my cousin Jason. We just left them alone and allowed them to be a couple, because their attraction was not going away overnight. Even Tracy understood that after a while.

I said, "Okay, I'll call you right back," and hung up to use the office phone.

As soon as I got Alexandria back on the line, I asked her, "Did you get into a fight and break up with Jason over something petty?"

I was assuming things. I knew she had flown back out to Philadelphia by herself to see him a few weeks ago. And Jason was scheduled to stay with us for a week right before the fall semester of school in late August. It would be his final nine credits at Temple University, for a degree in business, after changing his major three times. Alexandria was going into her senior year at USC in fashion and design, after changing her major twice. Although she seemed to wear more fashion and design than create it, with Charmaine around to run the Flyy Girl Ltd. office, Alexandria figured she was set to learn on the job.

She answered, "No, we didn't have a fight. But something else happened, and I needed someone to talk to about it."

I hesitated a minute. I needed to gauge how serious it was.

I prepared myself and said, "Okay, shoot."

She said, "This is between me and you until I figure out what to do. Okay?"

That made me even more skeptical, but I had to hear her out first.

"Okay, just tell me what it is." I was a little short with her because I was busy at the moment.

She said, "Well, when we were in Philadelphia the first time and, you know, we got into things or whatever, on one time, you know, the condom broke."

I heard her, and I thought about a condom breaking, and I needed to hear the rest.

"Okay . . . and?"

"At first, we didn't really sweat it, but when I didn't get my period last month . . ."

"So, you're . . ." I didn't even want to say it out loud. Tracy was still at the house and could have heard me through the walls or something. I don't know. I just wanted to be careful.

Alexandria said, "I found out this morning when I took one of those home pregnancy tests."

"Are you sure it was accurate? I mean, are those things really fool-proof?"

She said, "I took it twice today to make sure."

"And both times . . ."

"Yup. It's positive," she confirmed.

I didn't know what to say. All of a sudden, I stopped everything else that I was doing.

Then I started to whisper to her, "Does he know?"

"Not yet. I wanted to talk to you first."

"So nobody knows but us."

She said, "Madison knows, too."

"Well, what did she say?"

"She was the one who guessed it when I missed my period. But I had missed it before so I wasn't sure. I mean, I didn't want to jump to any conclusions, but Maddy had an abortion before, so she recognized the changes that I was having this month."

I don't know if I was supposed to know that, but since Alexandria had told me, I had to go with the information.

"Is that what you're thinking about doing?"

She said, "Well, I thought about when you had asked me in Philadelphia if I would have babies for your cousin, and I had said I would. So . . . I mean, unless he doesn't want me to."

Shit! Shit! Shit! I panicked to myself. My question to Alexandria up in Philly was now backfiring on me. And Tracy was sitting there right next to me when I asked her that craziness. What the hell was I thinking? I guess I thought Alexandria wouldn't want babies so soon. But maybe that was my own thinking and I had incorrectly assumed that it was hers as well.

"Well, what do you think he's going to say?" I asked her.

"I don't know. What do you think? You know your cousin, don't you?"

I said, "Not like that. Jason was always playful and immature to me. I mean, I don't see him the way you see him. And that's a major part of this problem. I still feel like you guys hooked up a little too fast."

As soon as I said that, I thought about my own hookup with Anthony the night before. But at least I knew him from school first.

Then again, we had only been on speaking terms before. It wasn't like I really knew him. He could have been a male gigolo waiting to take women up to his room for pay for all I knew, because he damn sure knew what he was doing in bed. Yolanda would pay him for it. And I began to wonder what kind of videos he had been doing with such a large dick.

Alexandria told me, "Like I said, I just clicked with Jason. I mean, he does have a serious side to him. He's not all fun and games all the time. He gets mad when he needs to, and I like that. I like a lot of things about him."

Obviously, I thought to myself.

I said, "Okay, so now you need to talk to him. But before you do, I just wanna know, how do you feel about . . . you know?"

I still didn't want to say the word *pregnancy* while Tracy was still somewhere in the house.

Alexandria caught on to my question. She said, "I mean, I would have it."

"And then what?" I asked her.

"I mean, I could move to Philadelphia or he could move out here. We're already doing that."

"And then what?" I asked her again. She really needed to think the whole thing through.

"And we get married, I guess."

"You *guess*? Do you know if *he* wants to do that."

"We talked about it."

I said, "Yeah, but were you playing make-believe house, or were you talking about it for real?"

We all played those little house games with guys, where you assume the roles of a married couple, but that didn't make it real. And Alexandria needed to understand that.

She said, "I thought about a lot of things with Jason. I mean, I know that we're gonna have very healthy and attractive children. They'll have a sense of humor. Good families surrounding them."

I said, "But what about you? How do you really feel about this? How do you really feel about him?"

I didn't want to hear all of that talk about family. Alexandria was doing exactly what I thought she was doing, playing house. But she needed to think about how she would feel in an everyday relationship as a wife, a mother, and a woman. It wasn't some overnight decision to make.

She said, "I love being around Jason. And I feel connected when I'm with him."

"Connected?" What was she talking about? "Connected like how?" I asked her for clarity.

She paused to gather her thoughts. She said, "Well, I can't even lie to you about it, Vanessa. When I first met Jason, I was like, 'Wow, he really looks good.' And I liked his personality and everything, but he was also family to you guys. So that's what made me feel even closer to him. I mean, I don't just jump for guys like that. You know me better than that. But with Jason, it was, like, he was family. And he just came on to me in that way, like, we're already supposed to know each other or something.

"So I liked that idea of being connected to you guys through Jason," she explained to me. "And I know that Tracy wasn't feeling me or whatever, but she could get past that because Jason really does like me. I mean, it's real. I can tell by how he looks at me. I can tell by how he makes love to me. I mean, we're just what we are."

I said, "Alexandria, every guy looks at you like that. And they would all love to make love to you, I'm sure."

"Well, I don't choose every guy. I chose Jason," she told me. "And I really feel like I'm a part of something when I'm with him. I never really had that in my family. We all do our own thing. We don't even really talk to each other like that. We're all like cookie cutters or something. But when I'm around Jason, and with you guys, it's all real. We even got into a fight and made up. And I love that."

Alexandria was really explaining her position. And you know what, it made sense. However, just because it made sense for her to desire the essence of family, that didn't mean that it would make sense for Jason. Maybe he was still too immature to get what she needed, or to continue to provide it.

I nodded my head with the phone to my ear and calmed down. I was at peace with it now. I could handle it.

I said, "Okay, I understand. I understand everything. But you still have to talk to Jason about this. And after that, everything may change if he doesn't feel the same way."

I was just explaining the reality of life to her. Other people had to agree to dance with you.

Alexandria was eager to say, "I know. I'll talk to him about it."

Then I thought about what Jason told me concerning her being bossy, and I decided to warn her.

I said, "But Alexandria, you can't push him into this. Because if you do, and you get away with it for now, we're all going to regret it later."

She said, "I know. It has to be his decision."

But for some reason, I didn't trust Alexandria to keep it his decision. I knew how she was, so I would need to talk to both of them separately to get the balanced story.

When I hung up the phone with Alexandria, I was thrown totally off track from what I was doing. I couldn't concentrate on my work anymore.

On cue, Tracy popped her head into the room. She was eating a bowl of microwave popcorn.

She asked me, "How long are you planning on being up in here?"

I looked up at her and said, "Why, you need to use the computer?"

"In a minute, yeah. Susan and I are setting up a meeting to include you in on for Tuesday afternoon."

Tuesday afternoon, I thought to myself. That was really soon. That left me with only a day to prepare.

I said, "I thought it would be next week or something." I didn't say it in alarm, I just said it casually. I didn't want Tracy to think I was nervous about it, but I was. I didn't want everything to go down the drain because I didn't know how to act in a meeting. But from what they had all been telling me, one meeting wouldn't determine much of anything anyway.

Tracy said, "Well, they had some time this week over at Wide Vision Films to go over our updates on *Flyy Girl*, and to read over my script. But I don't expect them to tell us anything that we don't already know. The only difference is that you'll get a chance to be there and see how the process works."

I nodded to her. There was nothing left that I could do but get myself prepared for the meeting. But since it would only be a test run for me, maybe I didn't need to sweat the preparation so much.

I said, "Okay. I'll be off in a minute."

As soon as Tracy left the room, my mind was locked again. It was like I was mentally constipated with too many things going on. So I finished sending out the rest of the emails and I decided to shut down and let Tracy get on the computer to do what she needed to do with it.

Tracy walked into the room as soon as I stood up to leave.

"She's all yours," I told her.

"Thank you."

Then the office phone rang. I looked down and saw Jason's Philadelphia cell number on the Caller-ID screen. I immediately thought about his response to Alexandria's pregnancy, and I snatched up the phone before Tracy could.

"Hey, Jason," I answered. "I figured you would be calling me," I told him as I walked out of the office with the cordless phone in hand. I wanted to get that conversation away from Tracy with haste.

She said, "Bring that phone back in here when you're finished, Vanessa."

"I know," I told her. "What did you fix to eat?" I asked her as I walked away. I wanted everything to appear perfectly normal. I was hungry by then anyway.

"There's some Caesar salad with grilled chicken in the fridge," Tracy yelled after me.

"Okay," I hollered back as I approached the stairs.

As soon as I was safely away from Tracy, Jason asked me over the line, "So I guess you know the news already."

I played the innocent. "What news?"

"You know what I'm talking about. Alexandria told me that she talked to you about it already."

I was busted. I said, "Okay, and what do you think about it?"

I reached the kitchen to put together my chow.

Jason said, "Man, I'm just now ready to get out of school. And this girl is expensive. She always has to have shit."

I said, "But she uses her own money." I had been around Alexandria, so I knew. She was quick to hook us up if we needed it, too.

Jason said, "Yeah, but those habits are gonna extend to me. Then she's gonna want all kinds of fancy shit for the baby. I can see it now."

Jason was on his cell phone in his Ford Explorer. I could hear the traffic noise in the background.

I smiled at his response. He was thinking about the small stuff, or I guess it could be big stuff for a man who would have to find a much better job soon.

I said, "But how do you feel about it, Jason?"

I continued to steer clear from using that word *pregnancy*.

Jason said, "We talked about it, man. And my mom already likes her. My dad said she's a neck-breaker. And Tracy . . . she just gotta get over it. I don't know why she don't like Alexandria anyway. They already look related. And Tracy didn't even think about casting her for the movie."

"Well, that's because Alexandria can't act. She doesn't express enough emotions," I told him.

He said, "She does around me."

"So, it sounds like you're accepting it," I commented. I didn't want to assume things, but that's how it sounded. If Jason had been dead set against having a baby with Alexandria, he would have come right out and said so, but he didn't.

He said, "Well, it wasn't expected, but it would be worse if it was with some girl I didn't like. But I mean, I know what I got with Alexandria. She bad. People be tripping over their feet trying to look at her. I just gotta do what I gotta do now."

I laughed out loud. That boy was crazy. But I was proud to hear Jason speak of his responsibility. Maybe he was growing up.

I said, "Okay, what if she wasn't so attractive?"

"Well then, we wouldn't even be having this conversation," he joked. Or maybe he wasn't joking.

I grinned and said, "You are a mess, you know that, right? You better hope and pray that Alexandria doesn't blow up and turn into a nightmare on you."

He said, "Naw, never that. I saw pictures of her whole family. They keep it tight over there."

"So, you don't have a problem with marrying her?"

I felt so relieved about the whole situation to hear that Jason was okay with things.

He said, "Well, that's what's next, right? I gotta put my seal on her and make her an Ellison."

He kept me laughing, but I needed to get serious about it, too.

I said, "Okay, all jokes aside. Do you really think you're ready for this? I mean, your mom and dad went through their own struggles because they got married so young. And I know they're back together now, but it was a long, trying separation, too."

"Yeah, but you gon' have to do it sooner or later, Vanessa," he argued. "I mean, I'm not planning on being out there as long as Tracy. And I kind of feel like she's blocking me because she's uncomfortable with hooking up like that herself, but I'm not."

He said, "And like I told Alexandria, it's all about us having fun with each other. She likes me for that. I mean, I look good and lay a mean pipe, too, but she really likes how I make her feel when we're just hanging out and talking trash. So I told her, as long as she don't stop liking that, and she keep looking good like she do, we gon' be aw'ight. It's all good money."

I just shook my head with a sustained grin. Jason was making things sound seriously simple, but I liked the simple more than the complicated from him. I knew Jason enough to know that he likes having fun, and if he had to explain too much about his relationship with Alexandria, then it would seem forced and I would be skeptical. But to hear him tell it as all fun and games, I really liked their chances together.

"Well, we may as well start looking at those baby-shower presents for my girl then," I joked to him. "And wedding presents, too."

I stuffed my mouth with my Caesar salad and grilled chicken, and Tracy strolled right into the kitchen on me. I was so excited that Jason was taking things in good spirits that I was no longer whispering, and there was no doubt in my mind that Tracy had heard me.

I nearly choked on my food being busted like that. She really shocked me. My eyes got big, and I almost dropped the phone and everything.

Jason said something, but I wasn't even listening to him anymore. I was eye to eye with his big sister.

She looked me dead in the face and asked me, "A baby shower and wedding presents for who?"

She had her full attention on me. There was no blowing it off or lying about it. But what the hell, it was what it was. So I went ahead and told her.

"For Alexandria."

Tracy continued to stare at me.

"She's pregnant?"

"Yup."

Tracy nodded. She said, "I knew it."

I asked her, "You knew it?"

I had to ignore Jason on the phone to get things straight with Tracy in the kitchen.

"I knew this was gonna happen," she said. "And now they're talking about getting married, hunh? And only known each other for two months."

Tracy sounded more like a mother to me every day. And she was right, but it didn't matter.

I shrugged my shoulders and repeated the mantra to her, "It is what it is."

"And that's what it's gonna be," she added. She walked over to the refrigerator, took out a canned Pepsi, grabbed some snacks from out of the pantry closet, and walked back out of the kitchen without another word.

Jason said, "That was Tracy?" I guess he had caught on to it. "What she say?"

I told him, "Nothing, yet. But the night's not over. So I'll tell you about it tomorrow, if she doesn't call you back first."

He chuckled and repeated me, "Yeah, if she doesn't call me back first."

"So, what's Alexandria doing?" I asked him. "I thought she would have called me back by now."

He said, "She's telling her parents about it. And then I'ma talk to mine. It ain't like they can stop us, but at the same time, they could help us out. So we gotta go ahead and be frank with them."

I thought about it and said, "Yeah." Both of them were college students who could use the help on the income until they could establish themselves in their careers. That was just one of the many complications of getting married and having kids early instead of late. But like Jason said, no matter when you would decide to do it, adjustments would always need to be made.

I was in my room reading a new sex novel from the author Zane. Now I understood what all the fuss with sex was about. In the meantime, I was waiting on two things to happen that night: a talk with Tracy about Alexandria and Jason, and a call from Alexandria about what her parents had to say regarding her pregnancy.

Tracy's talk came first. She knocked on my door after she had finished in the computer room for the night.

"Come in," I told her.

She walked in and was noticeably exhausted. She didn't have bags under her eyes or appear to be falling down or anything, but her energy level and spirit were practically hanging on by a string that night.

She said, "All I want to say about this is that I hope they're not looking for a savior when they get into trouble, because I am not the bail-out woman. They got themselves into this, and they'll be the ones who'll have to figure out where they're trying to go with it, and how they get there, on their own. And that's not to say that I won't lend a hand or a dollar when needed, but I'm going to make it perfectly clear that this is not my situation, it's theirs."

I just let my cousin talk without interrupting her. I understood her. She had worked extremely hard to get where she was, and was a success, which had become a blessing and a curse for her. On the one end, she could live well, travel abroad, and really enjoy the spoils of her life. But on the other end, her success made people push her to do more than she believed she could do, or felt like doing. Tracy had become a target for people to attach themselves to, including me. Her success was also my target. And she was understandably tired of being hit by other people's dreams.

So when I thought again about my promise to my mother and sisters through my own aspirations of success back home in Philadelphia, I understood that I had made myself a target. And as my cousin Tracy had become exhausted with all of the attachments draining her of her everyday energy, I realized that I would have that same problem if and when I ever became the powerful woman I desired to be.

New Flavor

When my girl Alexandria broke down her situation to her family, the first thing her parents and sister did was call my cousin Tracy for an explanation. So Tracy dealt with the Greene family civilly, and explained to them that Jason and Alexandria had started a courtship that she had no control over, and that they all would be much better off helping the young couple rather than ostracizing them and harming them. They went back and forth over the phone about it for a good hour, with Alexandria's family threatening to keep her under wraps and some more craziness, before my girl threatened to move to Philadelphia with Jason and disown her family.

On the other side of the country in Philadelphia, Tracy's family was ready to accept Alexandria with open arms. They understood that Jason and Alexandria were both adults. They were young, but still adults.

Tracy hung up the phone with Alexandria's family and was pissed all over again.

She looked at me and said, "You see what the hell I'm talking about, Vanessa. I knew this shit was gonna happen when they first started sneaking around and seeing each other at the hotel. And them people are acting like something is wrong with my damn family, like they're all fuckin' perfect. And I met her sister, too, as fake as she wants to be."

She said, "Shit, I think I like Alexandria after dealing with the rest of them. At least she went ahead and fought for what she wants. But I can see it already, it's gonna be us against them all the time now. And you know who the kids are gonna like more?" my cousin asked me.

I smiled and said, "Us."

"Exactly. Even when her fake-ass sister gets married and has kids, they're gonna want to be around our family. Fake-ass assholes."

I sat up and smiled in my bed.

Tracy took a breath to calm herself down. She was all hyper again.

She said, "All right, girl, I'm going to bed. You do whatever you think you need to do for this meeting on Tuesday, but I'm just letting you know that these meetings happen every day. So learn what you can from it, and get ready to set up for the next one."

I was anxious for the next thirty-eight hours, at the end of which, I would have my first face-to-face meeting with a Hollywood studio executive. I would finally get to see, up close and personal, how it all worked. The meeting was set for 2:00 PM Tuesday, at the Wide Vision Films studio lot in Culver City.

I got phone calls from all of my girls before Tuesday, and I let them know that I would be in on things and taking good notes. So I arranged for us all to meet at the Flyy Girl Ltd. office on Wednesday for my meeting report and strategy. Attendance was mandatory.

I even got a call from Anthony about seeing him again. I told him that I was still sore and rather busy, but to stay on standby for the end of the week. He laughed and said he liked my style again.

I told him "Of course you do" and went back to work.

When it was showtime on Tuesday, I was dressed in my full Flyy Girl Ltd. gear: my lime green pants, the lime green baby-tee, and the lime green hat and high-heeled shoes. I wanted to really stand out in an office space without having to say anything. I would let Tracy and Susan do all the talking so I could study the responses. Then I would make my counterpoints or speak when asked.

I flipped through *The 48 Laws of Power* again for more information on how to execute in this first meeting. I was ready to attack with several of the first laws that fit: Law 3, Conceal Your Intentions; Law 4, Always Say Less Than Necessary; Law 6, Court Attention at All Costs; Law 8, Make Other People Come to You—Use Bait If Necessary; and several other laws.

I walked out of my bathroom to meet Tracy downstairs for the ride over to Culver City in her black Mercedes, and she looked me over and smiled.

"You're taking a page out of my book, hunh?" she asked me. "You're showing up ready."

I said, "Well, if they won't pay attention to what comes out of my mouth, then maybe they'll pay attention to what they see."

"But then they'll only want to see you and never hear you," my cousin warned me. She was dressed in a gray business suit and looking more executive.

I said, "If it gets the deal done, it gets the deal done. I just want to make this movie. I'm not gonna be in it anyway."

Tracy smiled and said, "That's what I first thought when I started shopping scripts out here."

I said, "But you still have more personality than me for an actress. Most of my moves are made mentally, not physically, so I wouldn't translate well in film."

"Not if you come dressed like you are now. You'd definitely translate on-screen," she teased me.

I smiled back at her and said, "We'll see."

We stepped into the car; Tracy put the top down so the wind could jet through our hair on the way over to Culver City. It wasn't a long drive from Marina Del Rey. They were both on the west side of Los Angeles.

While she drove, I felt cocky enough to slap my right arm up on the door. You should have seen all the male drivers who usually paid me no mind, starting to look my way. Other women were checking me out, too, admiring my colorful spunk, I guess. Even Tracy noticed it.

She said, "There's something different about you now. Did you get some recently?" she joked.

I grinned and shook my head. "I've been reading those Zane books," I told her. I didn't know yet if sex could change your outlook or not, but I wasn't willing to admit to my cousin that I had gotten laid. Especially on account of being angry at her for stringing me along on the *Flyy Girl* project.

She said, "Oh, yeah. Those things," and turned up her nose.

Tracy was ultra discreet nowadays after having so much of her racy teen years documented. Even Zane was a mystery. So she wrote the books and remained detached from them, while making a fortune from the hidden, freaky secrets of women's sexual fantasies that included my own.

We arrived at the low-key studio lot at Culver City where Susan was already waiting for us in the parking lot.

I stepped out of the black Mercedes in my high heels and lime green getup, and immediately caught everyone's attention.

Susan spotted me and nodded her approval. "Great idea. I like that."

She was wearing a dark green business suit herself.

"I see we're both thinking about money," I joked to her.

She said, "Yeah, your bright, new money, and my dark, ugly, old money."

"They all spend the same," I told her.

"They sure do," Tracy added.

As we walked toward the front doors of this ordinary-looking light blue building for my first Hollywood meeting, Susan said, "You know, your outfit reminds me of when Tracy first started taking these meetings with me years ago."

"I told her that at the house as soon as I saw what she was wearing," Tracy commented.

"But I'm not trying to be an actress," I told them both.

"Nor was Tracy," Susan reminded me. "Everyone forgets now that she was a writer."

Susan opened the heavy glass door and held it for us to walk through. And as soon as I walked in past the office cubicles inside the building, it seemed that all eyes were on me.

"Looking good," one white man said.

"Thank you," I told him.

Tracy looked at me, smiled, and nodded. Then we strutted into this tiny room in the far corner of the building.

"Hey, Louis, good seeing you again," Susan greeted a short, balding white man in a light blue tennis shirt. He looked very casual and nerdish.

He was all enthusiastic about seeing Susan. He walked out from behind his desk to shake her hand.

"Hey, yeah, it's been a minute," he told her. Then he focused on my cousin Tracy. "And there's our girl." He blushed. "*Led Astray* is still doing well for us in DVD."

"When is it gonna buy you a new building?" she joked with him.

"Hah, soon, soon," he told her with a laugh. He even hugged Tracy. That was love and much respect.

There were only two chairs in front of his desk, so I had nowhere to sit. Behind his desk to the left was a tall bookshelf of stacked movie scripts and a few books. On the bookshelf wall behind us was the same. There were various picture clips and film posters covering the walls around the room. One of them stood out, a poster for a film called *Wanted*. It looked like a dark-edged love story. A *Fatal Attraction* reversal with the man chasing the woman.

"And, ah, who's this, our *Flyy Girl?*" Louis asked in reference to me. He was already jumping to conclusions. I considered that a good thing.

"She could be a lot of things," Tracy spoke up for me. "Her name is Vanessa Smith, another Philadelphian."

Louis nodded and asked me, "You're not related to Will Smith are you?"

"Could be," Susan filled in. "You never know. A lot of cousins don't find out they're related until they have those big family reunions sometimes."

"But you're not related to him from what you know of?" he asked me specifically. I guess he wanted to see if I could talk without Tracy and Susan speaking for me.

I said, "Would it get me more opportunities if he was my first cousin, or no? I'm still trying to decide on where I want to go with that," I told him.

I was taking Tracy and Susan's lead on bullshitting the man.

He laughed again and said, "Good answer. You guys have coached her well. So, you're still not telling me if you are or aren't Will Smith's cousin."

I had no idea they would spend that much time on me after just walking in the door. So the pressure was on for me to keep the bullshit going.

"Let's just say I have a job to do first, then we can talk about who

I'm related to," I told him. "And if I do well, I'm related, but if I don't, then I don't want to bring anyone's name down. I mean, I know how important a person's name is in Hollywood. Names are everything out here."

"Yes, indeed they are, especially when you start talking about the big bucks people," he told me. "Will Smith is big bucks people."

"So, her name is a good thing?" Tracy asked him.

He frowned and took a seat back behind his desk. Tracy and Susan followed suit and took their seats, leaving me the only one standing.

He said, "Actually, there have to be plenty of Vanessa Smiths, it's a very common name. I was just making the connection to the Philadelphia Smiths."

"I would be Vanessa T. Smith," I commented. "They didn't get a chance to say that."

He nodded. "Vanessa T. Smith?" He was running it through his mind.

"Or maybe just Vanessa T.," Susan added to him.

He nodded again and raised his index finger. "I like that even more. So, the big question is, is she our 'Tracy' from *Flyy Girl*?" He looked specifically at my cousin when he asked it. He said, "By the way, I read the script and it's fabulous. You did another fabulous job."

"Thank you," she told him. "But can you see Vanessa T. in the lead role, or do we need a *Biker Boyz* Meagan Good in the lead, and then move Vanessa T. over to a 'Raheema' role? And with Vanessa T. being from Philadelphia, she can coach any- and everyone on the roles."

He nodded and said, "Yeah, the girl in *Biker Boyz*. Meagan Good, is it? And she was the main girlfriend."

"Exactly," Susan told him.

It sounded like Louis was bullshitting himself. I bet if I showed him some pictures, he wouldn't know Meagan Good from Shaniqua Jackson. And if he didn't really know who Meagan Good was, then how would it matter?

He finally cut the bullshit and said, "Well, that's a casting issue anyway. We'll get to those decisions when we need to. But the problem I'm having right now is with the script. I mean, it's a great script, no doubt about it, but what kind of budget are we talking here?"

He looked at Susan for that question.

"Can we do a coproduction deal with another studio possibly?" Susan asked him.

"Well, sure, we can get in bed with someone on this if we can work out all the right terms. But who's really shooting urban-girl movies right now? I mean, not for theater. And not for this budget. You're talking a ballpark figure of twenty-five million dollars here. So even if we did a split deal down the middle, you're talking twelve-point-five that we won't see a dime back from until we double it."

He searched for an explanation from Susan or Tracy.

But I did the math myself and could no longer hold my tongue.

I said, "This movie will do far more than twenty-five million. John Singleton did fifty-four million with *Boyz n the Hood* with no cult following. This book has thirty years of cult following."

"Yeah, but John Singleton had Ice Cube, Laurence Fishburne, Cuba Gooding Jr., the popularity of West Coast hip-hop, big guns, and Columbia Pictures behind him."

"Well, we can build our own group of stars, too," I argued. "A lot of those people were not big names yet. They became big names after the movie."

"Yeah, but they had a big studio behind them and a mega marketing campaign," he countered.

I said, "Well, anytime you make a movie from a book, you're going to have an added campaign coming from the book industry. Simon and Schuster would definitely back your marketing of this movie, because they're going to sell more books behind it."

Louis looked away from me and at my cousin Tracy. She and Susan had not intervened yet to stop my arguments. It all happened so fast that I don't believe they could have stopped it if they wanted to.

He asked Tracy, "How many copies of the book have you sold? Can you get me the numbers?"

Tracy nodded and said, "That's as easy as a phone call."

Louis looked back at me and nodded with a slight grin. He said, "You remind me of a lot of young fiery starlets. They come in with their hearts afire, and they usually stick to it long enough to win. Tracy was that way herself," he commented.

"You have to be that way in this industry," Tracy stated.

"In every industry," Susan added.

Louis continued to nod. He said, "Now that doesn't mean that you'll be able to get *Flyy Girl* done here. It's just too expensive. But we'll see what we can do. Maybe we can get, ah . . . Lil' Kim or Queen Latifah involved," he commented. "They're both hip-hoppers."

Susan agreed with him and said, "Yeah, we have a lot of different names and ideas to run through."

I decided to hold my tongue at that point. I was forgetting the laws of power that I had studied. Arguing with the man was not going to secure us a film deal. And he was right. We needed a bigger studio. He was already trying to think of marketing gimmicks to make the film happen. And shooting *Flyy Girl* with gimmicks would make it cheap, cheesy, and disappointing for all of the girls who believed in the book and would die to see the movie.

I had nothing against them, but Lil' Kim and Queen Latifah did not fit the *Flyy Girl* script. Period. End of story. The man was only trying to name-drop with them because they were both popular at the moment.

Suddenly, I couldn't wait to get the hell out of there. I had nothing else to say about it.

When we got ready to walk out of his office, after another thirty-five minutes of worthless chatter about other film projects, everyone was peachy and cordial.

"Well, call around and see how many people you can get involved," Louis advised Susan.

"Oh, we'll stay busy on it," she promised him.

Louis smiled in my direction and said, "Oh, with Vanessa T. involved in the project, I'm sure you will. I'm sure she'll find a way to get it done."

I was cordial myself, so I smiled back at him and nodded with no comment.

Then he looked over at my cousin.

He said, "With all three of you on the job, there's no way in the world that it won't get done."

It just won't get done here, I thought to myself.

* * *

We walked out of the studio building toward our cars in the parking lot, and Tracy and Susan were all over me with praise.

"You did good in there," Tracy told me.

"Yeah, you'll have no problem holding your own out here," Susan added.

I was surprised by it. I figured my little temper tantrum was unprofessional. But they were both cheesing away.

"You don't think he took offense to me getting in his face like I did?" I asked them.

Tracy said, "Not at all. You see what he said about it. He was impressed by you. And you stayed with the facts."

"Yeah, that's the most important part. If you're going to make a stand, then make sure you make a stand with the facts, and you leave the other opinions at home," Susan told me.

I nodded and assessed the meeting for myself.

I asked, "So is that the typical Hollywood meeting? You go in and exchange niceties, talk a little about your project, and then talk a lot about everything else that they're doing?"

The rest of the meeting was all about what Wide Vision Films was up to.

Susan spoke up first. She said, "You have to understand that every studio we take a meeting with will have their own projects on the table and other projects they're thinking about doing before we even reach their door. And every executive understands that buzz is buzz, so they'll talk you up about their projects, and their stars, and the things they would like to do because word of mouth always leads to more business."

Tracy looked at me and nodded in agreement.

She said, "I usually don't allow them to stray too far from what I want to talk about. But after two failed films at the box office, I have no choice but to listen to them. I still have to find new projects of my own."

I was beginning to understand things perfectly. When you're hot, the focus is all on you. But when you're not, you have to take whatever conversation you can get. And the only way to be hot was to have something that was out and selling.

As we approached our cars, I asked my cousin, "So what are the sales figures on *Flyy Girl* by now?"

She said, "We're getting close to a million sold now. But the problem is, I still have more girls who like to share the book than buy it. So whenever I bring those numbers to a Hollywood meeting, they're really looking at a *fourth* of the reading audience. However, we all know that plenty more people would be interested in seeing the movie who have never read the book."

Susan said, "Not only that, but as you've stated yourself, Vanessa, *Flyy Girl* has more of a cult following than a target audience. Tracy has an audience that she hasn't really marketed to. And the difference is that a successful and specific marketing program would create a concentrated platform where the Hollywood execs would be forced to deal with us. But with *Flyy Girl*, you're not dealing with any recent marketing attention, you're dealing with the business as usual of a steadily selling book, and those books generally take much longer to pitch."

Tracy added, "It's like all of these comic-book movies that Hollywood is so fascinated with now. Comic books have been selling steadily for years, but all of a sudden, *X-Men* works, and now they want to make everything."

"But you had a specific marketing program with the sequel, *For the Love of Money*," I reminded my cousin. "And it worked. The book hit the *New York Times* bestseller list, and won an NAACP Image Award."

"But that was three years ago," Susan commented.

"Well, maybe we should write another one," I responded.

Tracy just shook her head as I reached the passenger-side door of her Mercedes.

Susan smiled and said, "That's a thought."

As Tracy and I returned home in the car, I was in my own world. I was already thinking about the meeting with my crew of girls at the Flyy Girl Ltd. offices in Inglewood. What could we all do to make *Flyy Girl* a hot property within the Hollywood circles? That was all that was on my mind. I didn't have much to say about anything else. I still had a lot of work to do and talk meant nothing.

Tracy looked over at me from the driver's seat. She asked me, "So, how do you think this first meeting went?"

I didn't feel like discussing it. My mind was already in a hundred other places. So I shrugged my shoulders and answered, "It is what it is. I just have to learn how to work it like you did."

Tracy smirked and grunted, "Hmmph." She said, "To tell you the truth, I stop and wonder myself sometimes how I made it in Hollywood. It still seems like a dream to me as well."

I took another look at us cruising in her black convertible Mercedes-Benz out in sunny Los Angeles, California, and I said, "But it's not a dream. This is really your life. You've made it. So I know it can happen."

Tracy was still unsure. She hesitated a minute. I could see her thinking about telling me something, but she didn't want to. But then she let me have it anyway.

"Everybody's not gonna make it, Vanessa," she told me. "That's just the reality. And every film is not gonna get made."

I didn't respond to my cousin. I couldn't. What was I going to say? I had to prove that I would get the film done. There was no other way around it. But I couldn't help myself. I had to respond to her. So I shook my head and eyed Tracy with spiteful intent.

I said, "You've really changed since you've been out here. I never would have thought I'd see the day where you would give up on anything. I always looked up to you because you went for it against the odds, and you came out a winner. But now . . ." I shook my head and looked away from her.

To my surprise, Tracy held her tongue. I felt for sure she would give me a piece of her mind, but she didn't. Or at least not immediately. So after a few minutes of silence, I looked into her face again while she drove. I wanted to see if she really had nothing to say to me.

That's when Tracy smiled. She didn't even look at me when she did it. She kept her eyes glued to the road.

"What's so funny?" I asked her.

She had me just where she wanted me. But I had to pick her brains regardless. I knew she was thinking something. Tracy Ellison Grant was always thinking something.

She shook her head back to me and answered, "Everybody thinks it's that easy. And you know what? It is. Because when you're going through whatever it takes in life for you to be successful, you just get in a zone. And you feel the burn, but then you don't, because you're too busy doing it.

"Well, I'm not in that zone right now, Vanessa. And everything I do is a lot more painful now," she told me. "It takes a lot more out of me to fail. So yeah, I'm taking a rest. And I need it."

She looked me in the eye and said, "But that doesn't mean that you have to take a rest. You're just getting started. So you find that zone for yourself, and whatever you need, I'll help you with it. But for me . . . I think I've challenged myself in enough ways already. And I'll challenge myself again. I know I will. But not today. That's all I'm saying.

"Maybe it's your turn now, Vanessa," she commented. "So you show the world what you got. And you stop hiding behind me."

I listened to her with no comment.

She nodded her head and continued. "So yeah, I give you permission to outshine the master now. Break law number one. I'm just curious to see how far you can go with it."

"So you're putting me in charge now?" I asked her to make sure.

Tracy shook her head. "No. Not hardly. You're putting yourself in charge. And that was the way it was supposed to happen," she said. "You're following the script, Vanessa. This is your movie now. And your book. I'm just a character in it."

I heard her, but I didn't believe her. So I started smiling and shaking it off. My cousin was trying to patronize me. It was reverse psychology.

I said, "I haven't done anything to deserve a book. And I surely don't have a movie. I'm just out here trying to get your movie made."

My cousin smiled at me and said, "We'll see. You need Omar Tyree's number?"

I started laughing. Tracy had turned what could have been a tense moment between us into ridiculous sarcasm.

I said, "Nobody would want to read a book about me. What have I done?"

Tracy said, "No, the real question is, 'What *could* you do if given the opportunity?' That's what all people want to know. How far will we push ourselves to get what we say we want? And that's what you're doing, Vanessa. You're pushing yourself, you're pushing me, you're pushing everyone around you. And that's interesting. Because I believe that eventually you're gonna get what you want. And I think people need to see that, from the bottom up."

I thought about it, and I finally saw my cousin's point. There I was, a little lost black girl from North Philadelphia out there in Hollywood trying to push white folks' buttons into making a film about another little lost black girl from Philadelphia, who just happened to be my big cousin.

Tracy asked me, "You ever heard of Elaine Brown from the Black Panther Party?"

I shook my head. "No. I've heard of Assata Shakur after you told me about her and her book. And Tupac's mother, Afeni Shakur, was a Black Panther. And then Angela Davis."

Tracy said, "Everybody's heard of Angela Davis."

"Not everybody," I argued. There were plenty of people my age who knew nothing about the Black Panther Party.

"Anyway," Tracy said, "Elaine Brown was from North Philadelphia, too. And she wrote a book called *A Taste of Power* around the same time that my book first came out, in the early nineties. You need to get that and read it. Then you'll see what I'm talking about. It's time for urban black girls to have their stories told on film. You're right about that. And I want to see it happen as much as you do. So I'll give you all of the support you need to make it happen."

I listened to my cousin and accepted the challenge. It was all up to me now. And that made me a little nervous. Did I really have what it took to get things done? I wasn't even out of school yet.

Once we arrived back home, I got to thinking to myself and brainstorming for the rest of the day. Then I came up with my own poem. Not to say that I could compete with Tracy or anything, but we all had to start somewhere. So I wrote it out in my notepad while stretched out on the bed:

I was driven out of poverty / I was driven out of desire / I was driven out of purpose / I was driven off of need / I was driven by my girls / I was driven by my sisters and mother / And I was driven for the love of the girls in the hood / to make magic shine on us for a change / and then my cousin gave me the key to the car / and told me to take us all to the drive-in / so that we could watch our movie / with popcorn / and soda / and cherry Twizzlers.

I called it "Driven." I had written better poems before, but like I said, I couldn't compete with Tracy in the writing department. At least not yet. But "Driven" was what I was feeling at the time, so it was relevant.

Then I got another phone call from Anthony.

I smiled as soon as I heard his voice. I thought guys were supposed to act up once they got some from a girl. Maybe he just needed seconds before he would act up. But his phone calls were flattering while they lasted.

"You can't wait until the end of the week to get at me again, hunh?" I teased him.

He laughed. He said, "Naw, I was just calling to see how things were going with the *Flyy Girl* movie."

I had forgotten I had even told him about it. I guess I was thinking about having sex with him more than he was.

I said, "Yeah, I can see now that it's gonna take a while to happen, but I'm up for it. We just have to find the right people to attach to it to make it attractive enough for a studio to shoot."

"Well, good luck on that," he told me. "Hollywood finds ways to shoot as many silly films as they can for black folks. But when it comes to films that actually mean something . . . This *Flyy Girl* movie would mean something."

I was surprised he was so interested in it all of a sudden.

I said, "How do you know?"

I was assuming that he was just talking me up and hadn't even read the book.

He said, "I just finished reading it. It was a good fast read with lots of action in it. I think guys would like the movie, too. It had enough edge to it. And all of those girls were going through a lot. I mean, *serious* shit. It's not like a happy-go-lucky white girl movie. *Flyy Girl* is real. And you had a whole lot of criminals in there for guys to play."

I started laughing. He had no idea how good it made me feel to have him support the idea. I could just kiss him through the phone.

I said, "Well, thank you. So I can count on your ticket at the box office when the movie comes out?" I joked to him. But I was serious.

He said, "Wait a minute, I'm supposed to be at the premiere, right. I'm an insider."

I asked him, "So what does that mean, you get all freebies?"

He said, "Look, I'll pay for my whole family to see it when it comes out, I just want to be at the premiere."

"Oh, so you think you're special or something?" I teased him again.

He said, "I better be. Or are you just using me for my moves?"

He had me laughing. I said, "We'll see how long you behave. We'll see."

"Behave?"

He made it sound like a foreign word.

I said, "Yeah, treat me right. We'll see how long you last."

He said, "You make it sound like you expect the worst."

I didn't want to respond to that right away. I mean, honestly, I just did Anthony out of frustration. I didn't expect him to follow up with me like he was. Nevertheless, it wasn't a bad thing. It was just unexpected.

Finally, I said, "No comment. I don't have anything to judge, so I won't. Is that fair enough for you?" I asked him.

"Yeah, don't judge me until I give you something to judge," he agreed.

"Okay, that's a deal then."

When I hung up the phone with him, I smiled my behind off. He was surely sweating me hard to get on my good side. I wasn't used to that with guys. Or maybe I had chosen too many egomaniacs who thought too much about themselves to sweat a girl the right way.

My cousin Tracy walked into the room on me and caught me cheesing.

She said, "That didn't sound like a girlfriend call." She looked into my face and added, "And it don't look like it, either."

I tried to contain my smile and couldn't.

Tracy asked me, "So, who is he?"

It was the moment of truth between us. But why did I need to put my business on the table?

"I mean . . ."

How exactly could I tell my cousin to butt out of my private affairs? Now that I had something going, I didn't feel so open about telling her any more.

She said, "You promised you would tell me," right on cue.

I looked away and couldn't believe it. I had put my foot in my mouth, not knowing how hard it would be to spill the beans on my love life. It was like making love out in the hallway. But I was unable to realize that until I had done it.

Tracy shook her head and grinned at me. She said, "I knew you would regret your tough talk. Your silence only proves that you're ready now. So it's time for us to get together and work out our system to keep you safe and sound. I won't worry you about it tonight. We'll talk later in the week, after you've warmed up to the idea."

I sighed and said, "Thank you." I had other things on my mind to think about and to prepare for.

"So, what's this big meeting about at the office tomorrow?" my cousin asked me on point again.

I guess she had heard about it from Charmaine or one of my girls.

I answered, "Building the *Flyy Girl* franchise," and that's all I had to say about it. Tracy knew what I planned to do. I was going to go for it all.

She nodded and smiled at me.

"Does anyone else know about Alexandria's pregnancy?"

I shook my head. "That's for her to reveal when she's ready to. But she's gonna have to eventually. So I'll just wait it out and respect her privacy."

Tracy nodded and said, "Good idea." Then she headed back out the door. "I'll talk to you tomorrow," she told me.

I got right back to my brainstorming. I would have a power meeting at the Flyy Girl offices in Inglewood, where I planned to shock my girls into submission with candor, organization, and my solid plan of execution. And I couldn't wait.

My Turn

I showed up at the Flyy Girl Ltd. office for our meeting bright and early that Wednesday morning. I wore the rust-colored Flyy Girl tee with blue jeans and high heels, and I was ready to be all business. The meeting was set for ten o'clock sharp, before any of my girls had classes or work that day. But I was there before nine, and so was Charmaine.

As soon as Charmaine saw me walk into the office, she began to smile. She nodded her head and said, "I'm proud of you, Vanessa."

I was confused by it. I hadn't even said anything yet.

"You're proud of me? I haven't even done anything," I told her. She had me puzzled.

She said, "You're about to. I can already see it. This is your graduation party."

She said, "You have so much maturity at your age. It's amazing."

I smiled back at her. I said, "That's what you get when you have to run a household of two younger sisters with a mother who expects you to handle them like you're an adult. I've been in leadership training for years. So this is nothing but the next level for me. I'm already used to it."

Charmaine nodded again and showed me the new designs that she had been working on. Instead of the Flyy Girl logo running along the ribs, she had it running across the shoulders and down the arms now. I had told Charmaine that we needed to continue making our brand name visible, and she had listened to me.

I smiled and said, "No one can miss that. And I like how you tapered the sides to make it fit tighter."

She said, "I got that idea from Hooters. Tapering the sides makes the breasts stick out a little more."

She also had samples of Flyy Girl Ltd. business cards. My girls were all listed on the cards as sales agents. Tracy was the CEO, Charmaine was the president, and I was the vice president.

Imagine having a business card that listed you as the vice president of an explosive, up-and-coming company before turning twenty. And I had no doubts in my mind, we were definitely ready to explode. Tracy was allowing us to use the Flyy Girl name, and with Charmaine's talent, and my die-hard energy to make it all happen, we were sure to take the country by storm.

I looked at the card samples and pondered out loud. "I wonder how my girls will take this."

Charmaine grimaced and said, "What, you being the vice president? Look here, today will also be your official leap into authority. Because if they're too close to you to follow orders, then we have plenty of other pretty girls in California who will. Hell, we could do our own Flyy Girl fashion shows."

Charmaine had jumped on one of my many ideas before I had a chance to reveal them to my girls an hour later.

I said, "Oh, trust me. Now that Tracy is allowing me to run the show, there are going to be plenty of things that we're going to do to create attention for ourselves."

Charmaine continued to smile at me. She said, "Well, let's go get 'em, girl," and made me laugh.

Petula was the first to arrive at the office at half-past nine, followed by Jasmine and Sasha at quarter to ten. Alexandria walked in at five of ten, and Maddy hustled into the office at seven after ten. By then, we were all engaged in small talk about the new designs and our business cards. But as soon as Maddy took her seat, late, I went into my planned speech.

I stood in front of everyone in our meeting room while they were all seated and listening.

I said, "As we all know by now, our trip to Philadelphia was a mere taste of what could happen. We were able to see up close and personal just how popular the franchise of Flyy Girl is, and we were able to sell every piece of clothing we had. Now we have enough orders for our initial designs to pay for themselves. But that's not enough."

I told them, "I learned in my first Hollywood meeting yesterday that sex gets you attention, and everything revolves around money."

"Well, who didn't know that?" Maddy spoke up.

I ignored her and kept going.

I said, "So our goal is to be sexy and to make noise at every event in L.A. that means something in fashion, hip-hop, and film. At least one of us has to be there, and while we're there, we have to find out who are the power people and movers and shakers in the room, and we get their business cards, cell phone numbers, hobbies, pet peeves, you name it. Then we bring that information back here to the office to file in our Rolodex of contacts and add it to our email lists."

I said, "Now while we're out there, we *always* have to be dressed in something from the Flyy Girl Ltd. line, and we make sure that we don't get personal with these people. So do plan to keep your panties on," I told them.

They all began to laugh, but I was dead serious.

Maddy said, "That means you, Jasmine. If you even have any panties on." She was all jokes and sarcasm even after walking in late to the meeting. But I didn't sweat her antics that morning, because I realized that whoever could not get the job done could be replaced.

Maddy would be her own bad medicine. I had no more time for games—with her or with anyone else. I was on a mission. Period!

"After a while, we want to begin hosting our own parties, fashion shows, sponsored events, et cetera, to continue pushing our brand name and products while gathering more contacts," I told them.

"Our goal is to always be seen and heard, and when we're seen and heard, people will continue to talk about us and whatever we're pushing. And eventually, we want to be able to award Flyy Girl scholarships to colleges, have a Flyy Girl of the Year pageant. Everything."

Maddy said, "It sounds like you're trying to sell us like Pepsi."

They all laughed again, but I figured why not.

I said, "The original meaning of a flyy girl is someone who rises above the mundane, who is bold enough to stand out. And in a world where so many young urban girls are afraid to express themselves in positive ways, I figure that being flyy should be looked at as a good thing. And I want us to be able to stand up and express ourselves in every way that's good for us."

Tonya raised her hand.

I nodded to her and gave her the okay to ask her question.

"I hate to bring this up while you're on a roll and everything, but will we be paid for all of this? Because I have bills and things to be paid."

It was a legitimate question, and one that I was prepared for.

I told her, "Yes, you will be paid. And important names and phone numbers of new contacts are extra commission. But again, I don't want any of us sleeping around with people just to get those contacts. So keep your one man or whatever, and keep everything else business, because I don't want any of us getting the wrong reputation and poisoning the brand."

Sasha nodded and said, "You're right about that. Otherwise, they'll start to call us the flyy hoes."

"Speak for yourself," Petula commented. "I know how to stay professional."

"And you're saying that I don't?" Sasha argued with her.

"You made the comment. I'm just defending my honor."

Charmaine looked at me and shook her head.

I told my girls, "We're all going to have to use our young ages to our advantage, and be mature about everything we do, while allowing people to know that we're young and doing it. I've noticed that powerful people like to use and identify with the youth, so we want to use that. However, we never want to *act* young, so keep the bickering to a minimum. We really don't have time for that."

Charmaine nodded and smiled at me again. I was working it.

Alexandria was all ears and hadn't said a word. I didn't know how long she would be with us anyway. She was preoccupied with her life and her new pregnancy.

I said, "All of the details concerning our pay will be worked out as we continue to meet orders for Flyy Girl Ltd. But I want none of us to expect to get rich at this stage. We'll make enough for us to do what we need to do as college students, and by the time we're all finished with school or whatever, the company shall have grown into a real force for all of us, with the hope of our film hitting the silver screens. So if we all play our cards right, and meet the people we need to meet to make all of the right connections, we'll be on our way to getting the green light that we need to make our movie. And once our movie gets made . . ." I paused for effect. "The sky is the limit," I told them. "Everything we do turns to gold from then on."

I said, "Now, I didn't want to hold us for too long, because I know we all have things to do. But we'll be starting with our program this weekend. Everyone will be contacted by cell phone and by email, and each event will be added to the schedule at the office. So if anyone is ever confused about what event you agreed to attend, all you have to do is stop by or call the office, and whoever is here can tell you what's on the schedule. We'll also place the schedule on our website, FlyyGirlLtd.com, which is still under construction.

"So are there any more questions at this point?" I asked them.

Jasmine said, "So this is really it then. We're about to become the coolest girls in L.A."

I smiled at her and said, "The coolest girls in the country. Because remember, we're still starting a club membership on a national level. And once we have enough members in one city, we'll visit the city and throw a party. Philadelphia is ready for us now. But we just left there, so we'll wait for a while before we return."

Maddy looked at Alexandria and said, "Oh, I know Alex can't wait for that to happen."

"Shut up," Alexandria told her. She said, "For all you know, I may be moving to Philadelphia soon."

She dropped the bomb that fast on everyone.

Jasmine looked at her and said, "Are you serious? You and Jason have gotten like that?"

"Maybe we have," she admitted.

There was a dead silence in the room for a minute, but I had to keep the focus on our task.

I said, "We all have to understand as well that although we may be the initial members of the Flyy Girl crew, some of us will move on to other things, and I expect that to happen, but we'll always be a part of the family no matter what."

"But you won't ever leave the family," Petula commented to me.

I agreed with her on that. I said, "Flyy Girl *is* my family, and I've been connected to it for my entire life. So yeah, there's no quitting for me. I'm in it for life, like P. Diddy and Bad Boy."

My girls chuckled at it, but they all understood how serious I was, and that I would allow no one to get in my way. It was Flyy Girl or bust for me, and not just on a national level, but worldwide. Tracy had emails coming from London, Canada, Africa, the Caribbean islands, and Australia. And once we spread the clothing line and membership through our website, parties, functions, media events, mass marketing, and ultimately the *Flyy Girl* film, I saw no reason why we couldn't brand Flyy Girl International. All it took was the intelligence, stamina, and drive to do it. And as everyone had already noticed, I might have been young, but I had exactly what it took to make it all happen.

About the Author

Omar Tyree is a *New York Times* bestselling author and winner of the 2001 NAACP Image Award for Outstanding Literary Work—Fiction. His books include *Diary of a Groupie, Leslie, Just Say No!, For the Love of Money, Sweet St. Louis, Single Mom, A Do Right Man*, and *Flyy Girl*. He lives in Charlotte, North Carolina.

To learn more about Omar Tyree, visit his website at www.omartyree.com.

More powerful fiction available
bestselling author

Diary of a Groupie
0-7432-2871-5

A suspenseful thriller of what happens when a young woman threatens the famous and powerful.

Just Say No!
0-684-87294-3

The *New York Times* bestselling story about two childhood friends lured into the sex, drugs, money, and madness of R&B stardom.

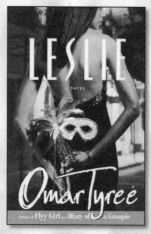

Leslie
0-7432-2870-7

The *New York Times* bestselling novel about a beautiful young woman with a dangerous secret.

from *New York Times* Omar Tyree